W9-ALK-661

SCHEME

Also by Jennifer Sommersby

Sleight

BOOK TWO of the AVRAKEDAVRA

SCHEME

JENNIFER SOMMERSBY

Sky Pony Press
New York

Sky Pony Press books may be purchased in bulk at special discounts for sales promotion, corporate gifts, fund-raising, or educational purposes. Special editions can also be created to specifications. For details, contact the Special Sales Department, Sky Pony Press, 307 West 36th Street, 11th Floor, New York, NY 10018 or info@skyhorsepublishing.com.

10 9 8 7 6 5 4 3 2 1

Library of Congress Cataloging-in-Publication Data available on file.

Jacket illustration © Sarah J. Coleman
Jacket design by Kate Gartner

Hardcover ISBN: 978-1-5107-3209-4
EBook ISBN: 978-1-5107-3213-1

Printed in the United States of America

To my movie-star muses:
Mark Strong
Jessica Chastain
Saoirse Ronan
Dwayne "The Rock" Johnson
Oscar Isaac

I wanted to be a movie star
but turns out I'm a terrible actor.
You are not. Thank you for living
in my head all these years
and breathing life into my beloved characters.

When I despair, I remember that all through history the way of truth and love has always won. There have been tyrants and murderers and for a time they seem invincible, but in the end, they always fall — think of it, always.

~ Mahatma Gandhi

My drops of tears I'll turn to sparks of fire.

~ Henry VIII, Act 2, Scene 4

DRAMATIS PERSONAE

Genevieve Flannery (**Life**), a seventeen-year-old, very magical girl

Henry Dmitri (**Memory; Death**), an eighteen-year-old, very magical boy

Baby (Bamidele Duncan), Genevieve's talisman, legal guardian, surrogate dad

Delia Flannery (**Life**), Genevieve's late mother, founder of *La Vérité,* Baby's life partner

Nutesh (**Memory**), a.k.a., Thibault Delacroix, Original Creator of the *AVRAKEDAVRA,* Henry's maternal grandfather

Hélène Delacroix, Thibault's wife, Henry's maternal grandmother

Alicia Delacroix (**Memory**), Henry's late mother, daughter of Nutesh and Hélène

Lucian Dagan Dmitri (**Death**), Henry's father, owner of Triad Partners Group, son of Belshunu

Aveline Darrow/Mara Dunn (**Life**; trained with **Death** text), related to Genevieve

Belshunu (**Death**), Lucian's/Dagan's late father, Original Creator of the *AVRAKEDAVRA*

Udish (**Life**), Genevieve's late fifth-great-grandfather, Original Creator of the *AVRAKEDAVRA*

Etemmu, a Mesopotamian demon

Montague, caretaker, trusted friend, soldier for Nutesh and *La Vérité*
Thierry, soldier for Nutesh and *La Vérité*
Lucas, soldier for Nutesh and *La Vérité*

Xavier, *La Vérité* Guardian, soldier, lifelong friend of Nutesh
Sevda, soldier, acquaintance of Xavier, *La Vérité* member

Violet (Vi) Jónás, trapeze artist, Genevieve's childhood best friend
Ash Jónás, trapeze artist, twin brother to Violet, Genevieve's childhood best friend
Aleks and Katia Jónás, trapeze artists, the twins' parents

Ted and Cecelia (Cece) Cinzio, owners of the Cinzio Traveling Players Company, Gen's "uncle" and "aunt"
Dr. Philips, the circus veterinarian

Gertrude, Gen's elephant, matriarch of the circus
Houdini, Gertrude's baby boy
Othello, a very friendly lion

SCHEME

I

Calling Andronicus a mean lion would be like calling a tsunami a big wave.

He tore off our wrangler Montague's face. He didn't mean to. Lions are wild animals, even if they live with a circus—*especially* if they live with a circus—and the show Andronicus came from used bullwhips and cattle prods to train him. That cat had some stuff.

But I saved Montague. I was young—six? Seven, maybe? I heard the screams coming from the menagerie, and if you spend any time at a circus, you get to know the good sounds from the bad ones. Montague's hollers for help, the yowl and roar of an enraged big cat—definitely not good sounds. Naturally, all the important players went running: Ted Cinzio, my "adopted" uncle and owner of the Cinzio Traveling Players Company and the man who rescued Andronicus and his girl Hera (and Gertrude and countless other beasts) from their terrible situations; Baby, the show's tentmaster and Ted's right-hand man in all things, and the other half of my mother's heart; crew leads and roustabouts and Aunt Cece, Ted's wife; Aleks Jónás of the Jónás Family Flyers, Ash and Violet's dad; my mother, Delia.

And me.

She didn't want me to see it, but out of all of them, I was really the only one who could do anything for Montague. Baby and my mother warned me, but I loved Montague, just as I loved all of my circus family. I couldn't just let him die there in the lion's pen, hay and dirt matting to his hair and neck from the incredible blood loss.

I saved a bird once. It flew into the side of our Airstream trailer. I picked it up and my head exploded in a firework of pain and light. I squeezed that little bird gently and mended its wing and it went from almost dead to alive and flying away in less than a minute. Then I threw up and my mom told me that we have secrets. It was the first time I really listened to the story—the one she told over and over again—about the little girl whose mother told her of a secret family treasure. I knew from then on that we were different.

Which is how I knew I was the only one who could save Montague.

While Ted and the wranglers tranquilized the lion, I sneaked in under their legs and laid my hands on Montague's face. I pushed the skin back where it should be. I stopped the bleeding and saved his eye.

I was just a kid, so I wasn't strong enough to restore him completely. I might have been able to if Baby hadn't scooped me up and run out of the menagerie tent. Too many people were watching. But this was before everyone recorded everything on their phones. No one thought to record the little girl with the magic hands.

No matter. It has all caught up to me now.

And as I watch Montague in his predawn jog across the massive lawns of the Delacroixs' French estate, his heavily scarred face a reminder of that day at the circus, I think about how I'd give anything to go back to that life, to those people, to that day, when I saved someone I loved.

When I believed I still could.

2

The door opens behind me, quiet except for that tiny squeak when it catches on the plush carpet.

"I come bearing gifts. Hélène made us hot chocolate." Henry enters, holding a tray with two mugs.

"With whipped cream?" I ask.

"So much whipped cream," he says, setting down the tray. "Did you sleep in the chair?"

"I wanted to watch the sunrise."

Henry hands me a cup, pulls the ottoman closer, and then sits next to me in front of the window that overlooks the rolling green hills of the massive estate belonging to Thibault and Hélène Delacroix—his grandparents. This place is a fortress, hospital, and five-star hotel all in one, in the middle of the French countryside. Henry leans in and pushes the springy curls back from my forehead.

"I hate how short it is. And how dark," I say. The weirdest part—when I look in the mirror, I don't see my mother's face staring back at me anymore. Our shared red hair, mine wilder and frizzier than hers, but still—it's all gone. Not even long enough to make a ponytail anymore. It's like being naked.

But it's necessary, to keep us hidden, and alive.

"It makes your green eyes pop." His smile fades when he runs a hand over his own head. It's been cut so close I can see his scalp, his messy curls shorn and dyed from his usual blond to dark like mine. His cheeks are pink again, his eyes less purple this morning. He lost so much blood—it wasn't just the car accident near Boeing Field when Lucian Dmitri and his witchy minion, Mara Dunn, ran us off the road and flipped us like a diner pancake. Mara Dunn, the talented aerialist brought to our circus after my mother, Delia, died, now known by her true identity of Aveline Darrow, my half sister, stabbed him. They wanted the magical *AVRAKEDAVRA* texts so much—my mother's and the one Henry stole from his father's study—they were willing to kill for them.

During the circus's New Year's Eve fundraising gala, my mother was pushed from her lyra to the circus floor thirty feet below, murdered by an Etemmu, a vicious Mesopotamian demon made of swirling arms laced with hate and pain, controlled by Lucian Dmitri and his *Death* text. I tried to save her, but as her life drained into the fine soil, she took with her too many secrets. About the daughter she had long before I was born, about the world's most powerful magical books, about how, in the wrong hands, they could rewrite everything.

About how all this secrecy and torture by the Etemmu would land firmly upon my shoulders in her absence.

I miss her, fiercely. I see her in every flower stretching out of its vase, in every tree that whispers in the breeze, in every tiny sprout pushing out of the dirt. Mirrors trick me when I pass by, thinking I'm seeing her face when it's only my own.

But I'm so angry. I'm so angry, I could burn a hole through a granite wall with my bare hands.

I run my hand through what's left of my hair. "We're still ourselves," I say. "Right?"

Henry leans in and kisses the whipped cream off my lip. "Still ourselves."

"For now."

"For always."

"How do you feel? Since . . ." Since last night, when Thibault Delacroix—aka Nutesh, Henry's grandfather, one of the three Original Creators of the *AVRAKEDAVRA*, and our host and chief strategist—sealed his grandson to his book. For something so important, it is such a brief, quiet undertaking. Like he did with me on the plane hurtling away from the carnage left at Boeing Field with Lucian and Mara Dunn, Nutesh pulled on his leather gloves, placed a hand flat on the *Memory* text, and voilà! Henry was a sealed heir, all ready to be assailed by whatever new magical endowments the text might decide to share.

Henry is in line for two books, though—*Memory*, through his mother's family, and *Death*, the text he stole from his father's study back in Oregon. Why Henry has only been sealed to one family's book remains a mystery, but it's probably better that way, for now. I love Henry—I know this in my heart—but my head tells me that one person sealed to two books? Unwise. It's only a short walk across the house for him to take the third, and this whole mess starts over again.

"I'm fine. Nothing new or weird yet."

"The day is young," I say, wishing I felt as light as my words suggest.

Henry moves to the coffee table, retrieving the TV remote. "So, you might want to see this. New developments . . ." He clicks on the flat screen hugged on either side by whitewashed bookshelves stacked to their limits.

Lucian Dagan Dmitri—Henry's father and the man now hunting us—fills my room, microphones at his chin. He's talking to the press.

The red-and-white news banner at the bottom of the screen reads: "Teens kidnapped, on the run after art heist." Lucian's at the fairgrounds, the Cinzio Traveling Players Company big top billowing in the background. He's standing with police, and my heart jumps into my throat when the camera pans left to show a very worried Ted and Cecelia Cinzio.

"It took him thirty-six hours to come up with this?" I ask. We've been in Croix-Mare, France, just long enough to have our significant injuries healed, put restorative food in our bellies, and change our appearances for the mission yet to come.

"He's smart," Baby says, standing in the doorway, eyes on the TV, ceramic mug dwarfed in his hand. He's healed—we're all mostly physically healed from the car accident and subsequent attack by the Etemmu in Washington just a few days ago—but Baby's color still isn't right. His black skin lacks its normal vigor and warmth.

"Lucian's pacing himself. Timing it for maximum impact. He knows we won't linger here long," Baby says. He walks into the room and sits on the long, cushioned bench that abuts the end of my bed.

A picture of Bamidele "Baby" Duncan flashes on the screen and includes his full name, height, weight, ethnicity, eye color, and tattoo descriptions. The man who has been my father and guardian my whole life, who kept my mother and me safe from harm, is being danced about on international news like some hardened criminal.

"How . . . how could he say this? How could he lie to everyone?" I ask.

Henry's face is sad. His father stands as buttoned-up and in control as ever, not a shred of physical damage after our electrical dance the other day, his bald head protected from the elements by an umbrella held aloft by an unfamiliar individual wearing one of the standard-issue black Triad Partners jackets. "We have reason to suspect that my son Henry and his new female friend have gone to Europe in the company of Mr. Duncan. It is our belief that these two young people were coerced into committing the theft, as certainly Henry would have access to my collection. Mr. Duncan was very recently a guest in my home, at which time he would've had the opportunity to survey the target of his plot. Given his relationship with young Genevieve Flannery's late mother, it is presumed that he manipulated his surrogate fatherhood over the girl to convince her to play a part in his scheme. Genevieve, in turn, recognized a soft target in my son and engaged him in a romantic ruse to win his trust and thus gain access to our home's private collection."

Henry looks at me for a long moment before turning back to the TV. I don't have a read on his emotions—his jaw flexes and he's blinking a little faster than usual.

That's his *dad* on the television, lying to the entire world about his own child.

Lucian is still talking. "We will be working with international law enforcement and private agents who specialize in these sorts of cases so we can bring Henry and Genevieve home safely. That is our number one priority."

"God, the smug, lying bastard. International law enforcement? What, like, Interpol? Scotland Yard?" I ask, moving to the bench to sit nearer to Baby. I take his coffee cup, sipping, shuddering.

"French coffee is strong, *a leannan*," he says, his smile tired.

"Baby, Ted and Cece couldn't possibly think you kidnapped us. Come *on*. You can't *kidnap* someone you're legally responsible for. And Henry is eighteen. He's an adult."

"I'll find a way to get in touch with the Cinzios. This is all bluster. Dagan wants the world to think he's the hero, that he's the wronged party, so now everyone will have eyes out for you two. It's his way of maximizing visibility."

"Nothing he's said is the truth."

"Welcome to the post-truth age," Baby says. "The people who count—the people who know how Dagan works and what he's really talking about—this is like the Bat Signal to them. He's going to make sure this gets maximum airplay. He's got eyes everywhere."

This does not feel good at all. Eyes everywhere?

I scrutinize the screen—Aveline is nowhere in sight.

My stomach drops. Where *is* she?

And what about Violet and Ash? I can't even imagine what the twins—my *siblings,* for all intents and purposes—must think of what's happening. Violet and Ash Jónás and I have grown up together, done everything together. Baby and I just gone—vanished into thin air—the police involved. A stolen car, a robbery from the esteemed Dmitri estate, a rich philanthropist's son missing too. It sounds bad. And it is bad—it's just a different kind of bad than what they're probably thinking. They don't know anything about ancient books or heirs or the threat of our lives being erased if Lucian gets his hands on the *AVRAKEDAVRA*.

And my poor elephants . . . thinking of Gert and Houdini and sweet Othello the lion—actual physical pain forces me to clench the fabric over my chest. God, I hope they're safe.

I send a quiet plea to Alicia, Henry's mother—she's a ghost, one of my mother's long-time companions only she could see. Delia's gift of communing with the dead was hers alone—until Alicia showed up in that post office in Cannon Beach, floating and weightless above the sandy floor. It was the first time I'd ever seen a ghost, and since that day, I've needed her help more than I ever thought possible.

And I need her now.

Alicia, show me the elephants. Show me they're okay. Please tell Gertrude I am so, so sorry.

I hold my breath, willing her ethereal shape to appear. Of course, it doesn't.

I have to find a cell phone. I need to get a message to Vi and Ash that what Lucian is saying is a lie—and that I need them to keep the elephants safe.

"What the hell are we going to do?" I ask.

"We're going to be leaving a little sooner, *ma chère.*" Nutesh glides into the room. "Dress, eat, and meet me in the hall in thirty minutes, *s'il vous plaît.* We have work to do."

3

Henry's arm is wrapped tightly around my shoulders, for which I'm grateful—it does double duty of calming my nerves and keeping me warm. We follow Nutesh, Thierry—his lead soldier and bodyguard—and Montague into the lush gardens. It's such a relief to see Montague here with us, learning that he was never just a member of the Cinzio Traveling Players Company but one of Nutesh's soldiers, put in place to watch over my mother and me. It's one lie I don't mind.

"Shouldn't Baby be a part of this?" I ask Nutesh.

"He is helping Hélène in the kitchen and will join us shortly," he says. But I'm anxious without Baby here, without him hearing whatever is to come.

We approach a huge greenhouse. The men walk with purpose, Thierry and Montague constantly scanning, their hands never far from the scary firearms on their belts. Thierry holds a card in front of a card reader above the wide wooden-and-steel door handle. The reader light flashes green, and the thick opaque glass door clicks outward. Inside the greenhouse, we follow Nutesh through the rows of lush plants, the warm air heavy with the smell of compost and dirt and flowers, such a contrast to the biting winter outside.

At the back, we stop before a wall covered in flowering vines. Nutesh pulls up his sleeve, revealing a tattoo of the symbol that has been haunting me: the inverted triangle overlying a circle. Holding it in front of a square of climbing flowers, the wall kicks out a door-shaped rectangle. Sure enough, it's an entrance to another hidden room.

This place is loaded with secrets.

"After you, *mes enfants*," he says. Henry takes my hand, and we step inside.

The overhead lights are almost too bright, and the six TV monitors lining the room's western wall are all tuned in to news channels. We are again assaulted with Lucian's face on the muted screens, every network offering a different angle based on their camera's position in the crowd.

Montague moves to a digital whiteboard at the north end and touches it on, pulling up a map spanning from Iceland to Kazakhstan. Nutesh offers Henry and me seats at the wide black wood-and-glass conference table that takes up the majority of the densely packed war room. At the table head, a long, embroidered red-and-purple cloth with golden-fringed edges is draped over three rectangular mounds.

Henry and I exchange a nervous glance. Under that cloth is the power to destroy everything we hold dear. All three *AVRAKEDAVRA* texts: *Life, Death, Memory*. In one place, at the same time.

A shiver of low-grade electricity hums through me. I've never been so close to so much raw power.

"You're a rare beast, you know. The descendant of two *AVRAKEDAVRA* families." I nudge Henry; he pulls my wheeled chair closer and whispers against my ear.

"That means you should be extra nice to me."

"Just remember who has the electric hands," I say, elbowing him. He kisses the side of my head.

Once the tech is queued, Thierry and Montague sit; Nutesh stands, shoulders back, at the front of the table. "We have much to say, and little time to say it." He clicks off the TV monitors. Henry straightens slightly in his chair, as if turning off his father takes a weight off his shoulders, and a twinge of guilt bites at me—while I'm glad to be rid of Lucian's face, Henry's emotions with regard to his father's betrayal are something I can't even begin to understand.

Nutesh then launches into a different version of the history Lucian—Dagan—gave me in the big top just a few nights ago. Nutesh recounts that Dagan's family died of a terrible illness, which is where Dagan's bloodlust for the *AVRAKEDAVRA* texts comes from, but where Dagan blamed Nutesh and Udish for not coming to his family's aid, Nutesh explains that it was simply a matter of an insurmountable lack of communication.

"We were all on the move, all facing the same persecutions and risks to our lives. Communication was extremely difficult. Parts of the world hadn't even been colonized yet, if you can imagine that. Even if Dagan's couriers had found us, we would not have been able to get to Belshunu and his wife, his sons and daughters-in-law and grandchildren. Even if we had been able to *fly*, we would not have been strong enough to save them. Our magic was too new, and the pathogen that took them down was too strong. Thousands of people in the Fertile Crescent died of this same epidemic, though you won't find anything about it in history books. This was still a time when man didn't understand disease or germs.

"I have mourned for Dagan's father, Belshunu. I still mourn him, and his family who perished. He was my dearest friend, alongside Udish. The three of us were boys together. We were three sides of the perfect triangle.

"With the *AVRAKEDAVRA*, we set out to do good in this world, and I have done everything in my power to stay alive, to protect the missing two sides of my brotherly triangle. That is why we are surrounded by this compound, by these very strong, very brave people." Nutesh nods toward Montague and Thierry. "But now we have come to a crossroads. We have, for the first time in over two thousand years, possession of all three texts in one place." He places a hand on top of the middle covered text. "The time has come to make a decision about what we are to do with the future—with *your* futures, Henry and Geneviève."

That uncomfortable, low-level burn kindles behind my sternum.

As Nutesh talks, I quietly pull my hand from Henry's and scoot my chair a few inches away. Just in case.

"If the decision is made that we are to destroy the books, the only way to do that is to deliver them to where they were created. There, a ritual must be performed that will seal the magic away forever, bringing to an end the *AVRAKEDAVRA* as we know it."

The room is quiet.

"But it is very important that you understand what destroying these books will mean, for you, for all of us," Nutesh says.

"If the books are eliminated, the Etemmu will leave me alone. No more attacks, no more swarms of spiders or stench of death sending me into a spiral that has almost killed me more than once. *That* is what you promised," I say.

"I promised that while you are in my care, I will do everything to keep you free from its harm," Nutesh says.

"But that's not a guarantee it can't find me again." My chest is on fire. "Could it still find me?"

He doesn't respond.

"Tell us the truth!" I'm on my feet. My hands zinging, if anyone gets near me, I can't be responsible for what happens—mostly because I don't know what might happen. *Where is Baby? He's the only one who can keep me safe from the Etemmu. What if it finds me here and he's nowhere to be found?*

Nutesh takes a deep breath. "The books were born in Mesopotamia. For us, Babylon still exists; for the rest of the world, it is a pile of ruins in the middle of Iraq, on the shores of the Euphrates River. The books must therefore be taken back to this once-fertile land. Destroying the magic means we will lose our magical gifts, the long-life component will be severed and we will all proceed to age toward death, and connections we have with those who have gone on before us"—Nutesh looks at Henry—"will cease."

"You're leaving out the most important part," I say, my voice hard. "Lucian Dagan Dmitri and my half sister, Aveline Darrow, will no longer be chasing us—*all* of us—to get their hands on a tool that they could use to turn back time, erasing all of us anyway." I swallow and shake my hands vigorously, turning to face the entire group. "We have no other choice."

"There is always a choice, *ma chère,*" Nutesh says.

"To stay here? To be a hostage to my own destiny? I don't want my mother's life! I don't want to be on the run for six hundred years. I want to go home—I want to go back to my elephants and go to college and have a normal life like a normal human. I didn't ask for any of this."

"And for that, I am truly sorry," Nutesh says.

"If we go to Iraq—if we destroy the books—does that mean I lose my connection to my mother?" Henry asks quietly.

I can't look at him; I don't want to see the pain in his eyes as he contemplates standing in the way of what absolutely must be done.

"*Oui.*"

"So, no more memories from her," Henry continues.

"That is correct." Nutesh's eyes are watery as he looks at his grandson. "But as Geneviève said, it also means a normal life. No more pursuits. Your father's all-consuming desire for these books will end because they will no longer exist."

"You truly believe that?" Henry asks. "You don't think he'll come after us—that he won't kill us as revenge for destroying the books?" Henry leans forward, elbows on the table, his eyes far away as he stares blankly at the map on the digital screen.

"I don't know the answer to that, Henry. One would hope Dagan would see reason. But his actions over a vast expanse of time would point otherwise," Nutesh says. "Of course, you will have my full protection." When he nods at Montague and Thierry, I'm assuming he means the protection of hired muscle; once the books are destroyed, the magic will be gone.

My arms shake, desperate for release. "If we go to Babylon, does this mean you will die?" Henry asks his grandfather.

"This is not about me, or Hélène, or even Dagan. This is about the two of you." Nutesh nods at Henry, and then me. "You must do what you think is best as you are the rightful heirs to the *AVRAKEDAVRA*. We have lived long, beautiful lives. And we will support you in your decision, whatever it may be."

"Henry, please . . . I can't live this life. Neither can you. You saw your father on the news. He will stop at nothing. Are we just supposed to run for the next god-knows-how-many centuries? Like Delia? Like everyone else who's gotten in his way?" I take a breath and lower my voice. "*Please*. We can never go home again if we don't end this."

He laughs under his breath, but it's sad. "Seems I have no home to go back to anyway."

Nutesh flattens his hands on the tabletop. "You will always have a home here, in Croix-Mare. *Always*."

Henry sniffs and looks down. Then he clears his throat and his blue-green eyes shine brighter than I've seen them in days.

"Well, then . . . when do we leave?"

Nutesh folds his hands reverently before him, his eyes first on Henry, and then on me before he answers. "Tonight."

4

Nutesh provides answers no one else has been able to give us. The *AVRAKEDAVRA*'s Original Creators—Belshunu, Dagan's father and Henry's paternal grandfather; Udish, my own fifth-great-grandfather; and Nutesh himself, father to Alicia, Henry's mother—made a pact that would keep the three books apart, "never to be brought together by a solitary man, or woman." Specially chosen Guardians have been tasked with keeping the *AVRAKEDAVRA* separate and secret, protecting the information that would enable the Undoing—the destruction of the books—once and for all, should the need arise.

It appears that need has arisen.

"These Guardians have been afforded certain privileges and protections in exchange for their loyalty and service. With the right words and medicinals, the *AVRAKEDAVRA* can extend the life of a person deemed worthy of such a gift—and such a burden," Nutesh says.

"This magic—this is what you used for Baby?" I ask.

"Yes. And my Hélène," he says. "It is how we are able to maintain the continuity of protecting our sacred way of life. However, immortality is not something even I am capable of granting, so from time to time, a Guardian dies and must be replaced." Nutesh pauses for a moment to remove the cloth covering the three magical texts. It's as if an invisible force is trying to pull me toward the front of the table.

"To accomplish the Undoing, you must find the Guardians who hold the pieces required to complete the ritual." Nutesh then moves to the first book—the *Life* text. My text, the one Delia hid for me to find. The one she never told me a thing about before she died. Before Lucian murdered her that night in the big top.

As Nutesh touches it, it's as if his hands are on my upper arms, squeezing. It's warm, not painful, but when he flips the book open, my nerves sing painfully. I'm short of breath.

"This feeling will lessen with time," he says. Good to know.

He repeats the action with the *Memory* and *Death* texts. Henry shivers in his chair, but he seems to manage better than I am. Where I can heal broken bodies with a single touch—and now leave third-degree electrical burns, it seems—Henry's unique gift is all about memory. It's why his mother Alicia Delacroix, even in death, can plant memories in her son's head while he sleeps. It's why Henry can touch someone and dig through their thoughts and how he's able to transmit memories, like those shared by his mother.

It's also why when we kiss, I have to be careful to not let him too far into my mind, for fear he will see something I'd rather keep hidden.

I can only imagine what new gifts will pop up now that he's properly sealed.

I'm trying to focus on Nutesh's history lesson, but the presence of the open *Life* text is almost too much to bear. Finally, one at a time, Nutesh closes the books and re-covers them with the cloth.

"Thank you," I say on an exhale. Henry leans back in his chair heavily enough to almost unbalance himself.

"It will get better, with practice," Nutesh says. "The Guardians I spoke of—you will meet with one specifically, and he in turn will lead you to the three who possess the items you need for the Undoing."

"What items?" I ask.

"Did you ever wonder where your mother's fondness for keys came from?" Nutesh asks. I flatten my hand against my sternum. The *vérité* key still hangs from its chain, warm against my skin.

"The only way to complete the Undoing is to go to the temple where the *AVRAKEDAVRA* was born."

"In Iraq," I say, "in the middle of a warzone." The line from my mother's story echoes in my head: *Take the treasure . . . Follow the river to where the bones of kings lie.*

Nutesh crosses his arms over his chest. "Yes, though, officially, the war is over."

I lock eyes with Henry, wishing his face would register that he feels as outraged as I do that we have to be the ones to fix this. Instead, he looks scared.

"You are sending us on a mission that could cost us our lives," I say. "You *have* to let me get a message to my family back in the US. My aunt and uncle—my circus siblings, Violet and Ash—is there *any way* we can tell them where I am? That I'm safe so they don't worry? Can I at least tell them goodbye?"

Thierry shakes his head softly, and I notice that he's wearing an earpiece, a clear plastic coil extending down the side of his head and disappearing under his collar. "I'm sorry, Geneviève. We will let you know when it's safe for us to make contact."

Nutesh nods and continues. "To access the temple's magic, we must possess the key to open its 'lock.' To create one key, you must find its three components: one for *Life,* one for *Memory,* and one for *Death*—one piece for each book. These components are unique in that, once together, they form the symbol you have both come to know. That is the key to reawaken the sacred temple so we can do our work." The inverted triangle overlying the circle flashes on the screen behind him. "The Guardians protecting these components are members of an extended network of trusted *AVRAKEDAVRA* followers. A singular Guardian is the only person who knows of the other Guardians' whereabouts at any given time."

"Won't Dagan be looking for these Guardians? He has to know about the key thing—he has this symbol as a tiepin, for Pete's sake," I say.

"We have worked very hard to keep this secret protected," Nutesh says, sighing, "but with his expanded network, it won't take him long to figure it out."

My head pounds with anxiety at the thought of Lucian and Aveline always on our heels.

"The Guardian's identity, like all of us who've lived protracted lives, is difficult to pin down. It's like chasing ghosts. Regardless, the mission objective is to find the Guardians and secure the pieces before Dagan does." Nutesh pauses, looking at me, and then Henry. In that moment, the sadness in his eyes speaks volumes about the ghosts in his life. "In the most general terms, based on our intelligence reports, you will be visiting Spain, Italy, and Turkey before we rendezvous in Iraq."

"Any more specific than that?" I ask.

Nutesh shakes his head. "That will come later."

"So Henry and Baby and I hop on a plane, fly to wherever the Guardian is, get what we need, and get to Babylon," I say.

"It would be beautiful if it were so simple," Nutesh says. "Covert arrangements must be made to ensure the Guardian's safety, as well as your own. In fact, the rendezvous point may change while you are en route; that will be for your handler to manage."

I laugh involuntarily. "You're kidding, right? Not even you know? Who is this mystery handler?"

Nutesh uncaps his metal water bottle and takes a drink. When he answers, his eyes are on the bottle, not on me. "His name is Xavier Darrow," he finally says.

Darrow. Like Aveline Darrow?

I'm about to ask, but Nutesh beats me to the punch. "Yes, Darrow is his name. Aveline Darrow's father. And yours as well."

5

"I'M SORRY—WHAT?"

"Xavier Darrow is your biological father," Nutesh repeats.

I stare at him like he's sprouted a second head. Because that would be more logical than the information he's just dropped on the table. The burn renews itself behind bone, but I don't know what emotion I'm supposed to feel first. I don't know who I should grab onto and cook until their teeth chatter out of their duplicitous skulls.

Shock, because I *do* have a father, and he's still alive, somewhere on the planet?

Fury, because these people have withheld so much of the truth from me?

Resentment, because Baby has presumably known my biological father's identity this whole time and he and Delia kept it a secret?

Hurt, because if this mystery man is my father, why hasn't he ever come for me?

And then I cycle back to rage.

"Aveline Darrow . . . that means she's not just my half sister," I say, throwing my head up. "How is that even possible? We're hundreds of years apart! I'm only seventeen. I *am* only seventeen, right?" I yell at Nutesh. "Where is Baby? How could they do this? How could they *know* and not tell me?" I pop up, shoving my chair back so hard it topples. The slightest whiff of metallic smoke and burning hair wafts from my skin.

"Genevieve," Henry says, standing, a gentle hand on my upper arm.

"*Don't* touch me." I yank away. "Let me out of here. I have to go find Baby."

"Miss Geneviève, I know this must come as a terrible shock. But time is of the essence. We will answer your questions, I promise—if you will allow us to proceed," Nutesh says, gesturing at my chair. Henry has picked it back up, but I can't just sit down and pretend like I give a shit about anything he's going to say next.

I have a real father, and he's alive.

I move toward the door and lean against the wall, hands flexing and contracting, my fingers and elbows and shoulders aching like I've just done an intense workout on the silks. What I would give to go back to the simplicity of days that revolved around aerial rehearsals and scooping elephant poop and violin practice. My eyes sting with angry tears.

When he can see that I'm not going to sit and behave, Nutesh picks up where he left off, as though he didn't just drop a bombshell that craters everything I thought I knew about my identity. "Xavier Darrow is our longest-surviving Guardian. He is responsible for the oversight and safekeeping of the Guardian network. It will be your mission to work with Xavier and fold yourself into his protection."

I interrupt. I can't help it. "I'm supposed to find this man who is my biological father, who, in almost eighteen years hasn't lifted a finger to get in touch with me, and then travel to some foreign desert with him to save humanity—are you even *listening* to what you're saying?"

"Once you secure the necessary pieces to the temple key, I will meet you at our final destination with the third text for the Undoing."

"That's *if* we survive long enough to get there. *If* Xavier doesn't hand us over to Dagan as soon as we have the pieces."

Nutesh shakes his head. "You have no cause for concern."

"I have *every* cause for concern."

"Geneviève, I've known Xavier for the better part of five hundred years, and he has never once given me cause to question his loyalty. He has never let me down," Nutesh says.

Well, I haven't met him at all and already he's let me down.

While Nutesh speaks of logistics, I flatten my hands against the wall behind me. The power in the room dips briefly; the overhead lights and whiteboard screen flickers, warping the maps. Everyone looks at me. Nutesh again moves from the head of the table.

"Child," he says. Handprint-shaped burn marks smoke from the wall.

"I . . . sorry," I say.

He inspects my flaming-red palms. "We're going to have to work this out for you, aren't we?"

"I can't help it."

He offers his hands, palms up, and then nods pointedly at my own hands, stretched before me. "If I touch you, I'll hurt you," I repeat. "Ask Henry."

Nutesh doesn't move. *Fine. If you don't believe me . . .*

I lower my flattened hands over his, and then make solid contact. As expected, the energy rushes out of me and into him. "Control it, Geneviève," he says, his voice vibrating with the electrical exchange. "*Control it.* Imagine it slowing down as it leaves you. You will burn yourself if you do not slow it down."

Eyes closed and teeth gritted, I try to pull back the electricity as it gallops out of my skin. The smell of ozone fills my nose.

"Slowly . . . ," Nutesh sings.

And then all at once, the charge dissipates. My hands are beet red but not scalded or sooty, and the bodily pain and urgency there just moments ago is gone.

Nutesh is still standing before me, seemingly unscathed.

"Thank you," I say. He pats my cheek before turning back to resume his prior position, picking up where he left off.

"Now, the most crucial aspect of the operation—I cannot emphasize this enough—no one can know who you are. *No one* can know what you're doing." Nutesh explains that we'll be outfitted with appropriate clothing and provided with an out plan so we can make our way back to Croix-Mare should the mission go sideways, and on and on.

I zone out, rubbing my throbbing fingertips as I watch Nutesh's pointer bounce around the map. *Aveline Darrow is my sister, and my mother and Baby kept this truth from me.*

How in the hell is it even possible that we have the same father, hundreds of years apart?

There's never been any question that Baby isn't my biological father—one look at his African-French physique compared to my red frizzy hair and see-through skin is enough to answer that question. Regardless, he's been my father from day one. He's the father who has fixed my boo-boos and kicked my butt when I tried to get away with stuff and held my hand as we walked into one of many hospital psych wards to visit my mother, mistakenly locked in and doped up because the world didn't understand her.

Baby is my dad. Baby will *always* be my dad.

And no new guy with keys to the magic kingdom is going to change that.

Thierry and Montague pull two sizable backpacks from a cupboard along the wall and commence unloading the supplies onto the conference table. "These are designed to hold everything you need to keep yourselves alive. When you get closer to entering Iraq, you will be provided with the necessary tactical gear. However, for now . . ." Thierry talks as he pulls item after item from the backpacks—both of which have been made to look like they'd belong to teenagers trekking across the continent on vacation. Henry's has soccer patches sewn on it, much like the pack he was carrying the first time I saw him in the mess tent back in rainy Eaglefern. Mine has an elephant keychain dangling from the zipper and a Canadian flag patch stitched onto the front zippered pocket.

"I'm Canadian now?" I ask, running my finger over the embroidered red maple leaf at the flag's center.

"Canada is lovely," Nutesh says. "Safer than being American where you're going."

"Won't they know the minute I open my mouth?" I ask. Henry should be fine with his posh British accent.

Thierry smiles. "Maybe mention your pet moose."

The slice-proof backpacks hold everything from fake passports to hemostatic gauze and injectables to plastic envelopes with cash to scary-looking automatic knives. If it's necessary for a secret mission, it's probably in here.

"What about clothes?" I ask.

"You will take two complete sets of travel clothes each. Xavier will provide you with whatever else you'll need once you're in position," Nutesh says.

"Is it safe for us to carry the texts with us?" I ask. "What if people find out?"

"The packs have been designed to conceal as much of the bulk as possible," Thierry says. Though neither pack yet holds a true *AVRAKEDAVRA*, he again demonstrates where the books will fit.

"You will need proof of who you are," Nutesh says, "which is why the books—the *Life* text for Geneviève and *Memory* for Henry—will travel with you. The Guardians will have to see the texts to know you are the true heirs. Xavier's word is not enough."

Xavier Darrow. My stomach lurches every time I hear his name. My *father's* name.

How is this even going to work? How is Baby going to travel alongside the man who was somehow responsible for my conception? And what am I supposed to say to him? *Oh hey, Xavier, nice to meet you, I hear you're my dad, where the hell have you been?*

"When we reunite on the shores of Babylon, I will deliver the final text," Nutesh's words snap me back to the moment. At least we won't have all three books in one place for Dagan to swoop in and steal.

"Do either of you have any questions about the gear?" Thierry asks as he and Montague repack the bags. Henry and I exchange a glance and shake our heads. It's one thing to hand two teenagers backpacks full of gear; it's wholly another to expect they'll know how to use any of it when the time comes.

But time is not on our side. Henry and I will have to make do and hope that the special tricks we both have hiding up our sleeves will be enough.

Nutesh resumes his position at the whiteboard. "Xavier Darrow will usher you undercover. You will join our ultrasecret network of followers of the *AVRAKEDAVRA* and its teachings, called *La Vérité*. One branch of *La Vérité* works in traveling shows globally. It's a perfect way to hide under a wider umbrella and still do our very important work."

I nearly choke on my cooling coffee. "Wait—you're saying we're joining a circus?"

"Yes. Several. Though some are performing troupes without the flair of a tent and arena. *La Vérité* members travel with circuses and shows around the globe and offer philanthropic services as necessary. As I said, this will be your cover—they will offer you haven while you seek out the Guardians. Be aware that all bona fide *La Vérité* members will possess a key."

Nutesh pulls at a necklace concealed by his shirt. Hanging from it is a burnished, ancient gold key; along its shaft is a faded engraving that reads *La Vérité*. Montague and Thierry follow suit—they all have old keys.

And then I hear Baby's words in my head from that day in the field when he told me about all this madness: *This is the perfect life—the greatest thing about a circus is a person's ability to hide in plain sight.*

How many people in circuses around the world wear *La Vérité* keys? How many of us are there protecting the *AVRAKEDAVRA* and one another from the bad guys?

"You will rendezvous with Xavier in Paris, and then you will travel to the first performance venue nearest the first Guardian. The Guardians have been alerted that the time has come, and when Xavier deems it safe, your meetings will be coordinated."

Nutesh continues, explaining that knowledge of *La Vérité* and an understanding of its operations are two very separate things. As far as Lucian is concerned, its activities were retired centuries ago when such organizations were considered heresy and therefore outlawed. Until very recently, Lucian believed Xavier Darrow to be dead.

Huh. So Lucian and I *do* have something in common after all.

"Word was put out via our extended network to test where leaks are—and while it wasn't my first preference to reveal that Xavier is very much alive, we had to sacrifice one piece of actionable intelligence to maintain credibility. If everything we'd fed the network was false, Dagan would sniff us out."

I can't wait to hear Henry's take on all this. Asking him to join a circus would be like asking me to enroll in his private school and join the cheerleading squad.

"The most important thing is to place your trust in Xavier. He will do what is best for you. The people of *La Vérité* trust him implicitly—he has been there for them for centuries. Udish started the network, and then Delia nurtured it. *La Vérité* was their brainchild. Xavier and I took over when Delia left Europe for good."

I sit back in my chair.

Another revelation. Another secret. Another lie by omission.

Nutesh moves to the head of the table and rests on splayed fingertips. "Now, as far as the performers are concerned, you are friends of Xavier's in need of shelter. He's a formidable ally to these folks. Think of *La Vérité* as an umbrella impenetrable to radar. Under its protection, the outside world cannot see you."

Apparently, Baby, Thierry, Henry, and I will drive to our first location to keep public exposure to a minimum. "Dagan's current efforts with international law enforcement will make air travel precarious. When flight is absolutely the only way for you to get where you need to be, we will arrange private transport."

"I'm sorry—you may have grand faith in Henry and me to kick ass across the European continent and save us all from the end of the world, but this is totally ridiculous," I say. "And where is Baby? Isn't he supposed to be bringing us food? He needs to hear all this. I can't take a step outside this compound without him—he's my talisman. Baby is the only thing that keeps the Etemmu from tearing my beating heart out of my chest."

"The topic of your parentage is a sensitive one, Geneviève," Nutesh says, his tone soft. "I was trying to deliver the news without Baby present, out of respect for his relationship with you, and your mother."

"Baby has only ever wanted what's best for you, and now for Henry," Montague adds.

"Even though he lied. Everyone lied," I bite back.

"To protect you, Geneviève. And no one is lying to you now," Nutesh says.

"Baby and I will get you all to Paris, to Xavier," Thierry says. "I will serve as your personal guard. Please rest easy that I won't let anything happen to you. On my own life." He places his hand over his heart, as if swearing an oath.

"Don't make that deal. You've never seen an Etemmu," I say. I turn toward Nutesh. "So, we go do all your dirty work, collect the pieces, you meet us on the shore of the great magical river in the middle of the desert, then you say a few magic words, and *boom*, we're done?"

"Gen . . ." Henry turns in his chair. I give him a hard look. I don't want to hear anything rational right now. I just want to be pissed off.

"No. I didn't ask for this. I can't believe you adults managed to screw this up so badly, and now you're leaving it to us to clean up."

"*Ma chère*, you and Henry are the heirs. You must take these books yourselves, collect the components, and finish the Undoing. No one else can undertake this task except for the two of you. You know what the alternative is—you can preserve the books. Spend your lives making sure they are safe. This choice is yours, but it is yours alone."

I want to scream at him to give my book to Aveline, but even before the thought finishes forming in my head, I know how absurd it is. Aveline seeks only to serve herself. Wonder how long before Dagan figures that out.

I yank my coat off the back of my chair and move toward the door. I don't know where the concealed handle is, though, so I stand there for a beat, waiting for someone to let me out.

The lock clicks free and the thick, vault-like door springs open a few inches, allowing the humid greenhouse light to wash over me. I don't want anyone to catch up—I need a moment of outdoors, alone with nothing but the oppressive cloud cover over head and the storm of thoughts in my brain.

The exterior door is heavy—too heavy. It's supposed to open out, right? I tug inward but it doesn't budge. I throw all my weight against it; it's not locked as it does move a tiny bit.

Something is in the way.

I step back and squint through the opaque glass, pulse thudding in my ears, my paranoid mind conjuring pictures of Lucian and Aveline waiting on the other side, the door blocked with their own soldiers—

But there's a shape, slumped against the outside of the thick, frosted-glass. The shape is human, big, and dark.

"Oh my god, *Baby*!" I scream.

6

Thierry and Montague push hard against the door, giving me enough room to squeeze through and find my surrogate father, my guardian, my *talisman,* unconscious on the ground, our lunch tray scattered and broken around him. My healing hands are on his face, begging him to wake up as Thierry issues urgent commands through the walkie on his wrist. Within seconds, more men sprint toward us from the main house.

"What's happened? What's wrong with him?" I yell. Thierry and Montague and two of the other soldiers lift Baby's limp body from the ground; Nutesh has his fingers at the pulse point on Baby's neck. "He's still alive, right? Is he alive? Nutesh!" Blood has soaked into the walkway pebbles, but I have no idea where it's from. I can't see. Too many people in the way.

"Inside. Now!" Two extra guards, guns drawn, skirt our awkward run toward the house, helping to open the door as we push through. I have hold of Baby's left hand, refusing to let go even as we get inside and Baby is flopped onto a gurney in the medical suite and Montague sets to cutting off his heavy weatherproof jacket.

"What can I do?" Henry says above the din.

"Keep Geneviève back," Nutesh says.

"Like hell! Don't touch me! I can help him! Please, Nutesh, I can heal him—"

Hélène materializes behind me, the shock registering on her face. "Geneviève, let Nutesh find what is wrong. Stand with Henry and me. You can help Baby in one moment."

"What happened? I don't understand what's happening—"

Hélène wraps her slim arm around my shoulders, though she's smart to keep her hands from mine. I can't guarantee I won't hurt her if she touches me. I push back my sleeves. My chest is a lit incinerator.

"I sent him with a tray, knowing he planned on joining you for the briefing," Hélène says. "That was near on forty-five minutes ago now."

"Everyone except Geneviève and Montague needs to leave the room immediately," Nutesh exclaims. Baby is sprawled on the table, legs and arms lax, mouth slightly ajar.

"I knew his color was off," I say to myself as the main door whooshes closed. "I knew something was wrong."

Before Nutesh can answer, Baby's body is overtaken by spasms. "Seizure! Montague, hold his head," Nutesh says.

"What can I do?" I yell. I stand uselessly—I can't touch Baby yet or else I might make his seizure worse. I'm short of breath, damp with sweat, terrified I won't be able to help.

"Please, Baby, please . . . please . . ." I chant under my

breath, burning fingers steepled in front of my nose. "Don't leave me. Don't you dare leave me."

As soon as the worst of the jerking subsides, Nutesh injects something into Baby's thick upper left arm. Then his body really goes lax. "Geneviève, cold compresses from the supply cabinet. Hurry!" I do as instructed, rushing back to hand over the armload of white-and-blue packages. One at a time, he cracks and shakes them to activate the cold inside. He nods at the pile and I follow what he's doing.

"Pack them around his neck and under his armpits, behind his knees." Montague finishes slicing through the front of Baby's blue flannel shirt and the black T-shirt underneath, lying his chest open to the world. His severe chest bruising from the car accident is gone, but his torso is scorching hot.

"There was blood—on the walkway. Where is it coming from? Is he infected?"

"It appears so."

"From what? We HEALED him!"

"I do not know, *ma chère,*" Nutesh says. "More ice. We have to bring down his temperature."

"Should I put my hands on him? See if I can slow the progression?"

"I fear there is something else going on here that may be beyond our ability to remedy."

"Don't say that!" I clasp my hands in front of me, eyes closed, pushing the electricity aside so I can use whatever healing power I have. The back of my head sings with pain as the star within ignites.

Eyes open, I step to Baby and put both hands on his upper chest, just below his neck. The heat radiating off him frightens me.

Baby, please come back to me. I'm going to heal you. Work with me. Calm your heart. Listen to my voice. Let's work together. Let my hands fix you.

I shove as much energy into his body as my own body will allow, until the twinkling lights close in along the periphery and my legs threaten to give out. Gently, I ease myself to the floor next to the bed, eyes closed as I try to control the pain in my skull and the short, terrified breaths in my chest; Montague tucks a bottle of juice into my palm.

"Thank you," I whisper. I drink, and within a minute, I'm strong enough to stand and try again.

"Geneviève, we must cool him down. That is the only way to help him now," Nutesh says. "We must get his temperature, and the infection, under control." He hands me a pair of surgical scissors. "Cut the rest of his shirt off."

Nutesh quickly moves to the head of the bed and speaks to Montague. I again chide myself for resisting the French lessons Baby and my school tutors tried to foist on me.

As if they've done it a thousand times before, Nutesh and Montague work in harmony. They intubate Baby and connect him to a machine that breathes for him. "The medicine I gave him will induce a coma. It's the only way we can prevent seizures and manage his body temperature. He needs to fight this infection, whatever it is."

"Don't you know?" I ask, the lump in my throat straining my voice as I slice through the fabric covering his left arm, to the shoulder, trying to pull the two layers of shirt from his skin. "Don't you know where it's coming from? Does he have any open wounds? How can he be so *sick* when Henry and I are fully recovered?"

Nutesh does not answer as he tapes the breathing tube in place. I've moved to the right side, and as I cut through the fabric overlying Baby's forearm, my heart thumps hard in my chest as I tear the sleeve away.

"Oh my god," I say, stepping back, the scissors hitting the floor with a muted *tink*. "Nutesh . . . his arm."

In the untattooed skin of Baby's right forearm, a bloodied message has been sliced:

Aveline sends her love.

7

"WHO DID THIS . . . WHAT THE HELL DOES THAT MEAN?"

"Geneviève, I am as stunned as you," Nutesh says. "It is impossible. Baby is too strong. No one would be able to get near to him to do this."

Someone here wants to hurt us.

Without asking permission, I move my hands over Baby's arm, again pulling from the star in my head, hovering over the viciously scored flesh. Upon opening my eyes, it's as if I've done nothing at all. In fact, it almost looks worse, angry purple veins spidering away from the slices.

"He has streaking," I say. "His blood is infected."

Nutesh steps beside me and cradles Baby's limp arm in his hands. "This is not what it looks like," he says.

"To me it looks like someone in the building—someone on your *staff*—wants to send a message. *Someone here* hurt him!" I yell.

"Geneviève, please, if that were the case, the wounds would have healed when you laid hands on him just now.

Instead, the cuts are still as fresh and angry as they were upon discovery."

"I've seen this before . . . with Udish," I say. "Alicia showed me his death—he had a terrible infection. The *AVRAKEDAVRA* symbol had been carved into his chest—the inverted triangle overlying the circle. It killed him—he died in Delia's arms."

I turn to Henry's grandfather, gripping the fabric of his shirtsleeves. "I am begging you to fix this."

Nutesh's eyes soften as he nods and pulls off his exam gloves. *"S'il vous plaît,* do not leave. I will be right back." He nods to Montague, standing near the wall of vital-signs monitors to the left of the bed where he adjusts Baby's head and neck and packs more cold compresses around his forehead and shoulders.

I finish removing Baby's shirt, but I leave it to Montague to cut free his black military-style cargo pants and cover him with a light sheet. The breathing machine is the only sound in the room for a moment—*whirr, click, whirr, click*. In, out, in, out. Though Baby's head is packed with ice, I move to the bedside and kiss his glistening forehead, trying to keep my eyes away from the festering message on his forearm.

Aveline sends her love.

I'll kill her myself if anything happens to this man.

The door swishes open again, and Nutesh hurries in, a thick bundle in his arms—he has one of the *AVRAKEDAVRA* texts. He nods at Montague, who rolls over a stainless steel cart. Gently, Nutesh places the book on the square surface and pulls back the cloth.

A slight tingle shivers through me, but right away I know that is not my text. The leather is too dark.

It's *Death.*

When Nutesh opens it, a chill blows through the room. On instinct, I sniff, hoping the stench of the Etemmu won't seep out of the pages and find me.

"What are you doing?" I ask, watching Nutesh finger through the crackled pages. He doesn't answer but continues turning, scanning text I can't read, his fingers hovering over haunting, millennia-old illustrations.

He pauses, looks up though his eyes are far away, and then flips forward through the book. When it is splayed open, he takes a step back.

I step closer.

The image on the pages are of scored flesh. Ancient renderings of sketched body parts, words carved into the skin, but despite the lack of color in the images, the angry infection is obvious. Blistered and festering, darkened veins streaking away from the injured areas.

Just like Baby's arm.

"I can't read this. What does it say?"

Nutesh's silence layers the medical suite in ice.

"Nutesh! What does this say?" I stab a finger at the open *Death* text. "Is—is this a curse? Has Aveline cursed him?"

Before Nutesh can answer, the medical suite door slams open. Henry stands in the doorway, eyes wide, jaw set in a mixture of anger and fear, gloved hands fisted at his sides. One of the guards steps in directly behind him—he's standing too close, his bulky body partially obscured by Henry's height. The guard looks away just long enough to close—and lock—the medical suite door. That's when I see his sidearm is no longer holstered but pointed squarely at the back of Henry's head.

"If I shoot him, not even the power of the two of you can fix him again," he says, nodding at us, jabbing Henry in the shoulder with the gun's barrel. He steps forward.

"Mathieu, what has come over you?" Nutesh asks, holding up his hands and then flat in front of him, as if he's welcoming the guard in for tea. Out of the corner of my eye, I see Montague move ever so slowly. Mathieu raises his gun arm at him, but Montague doesn't freeze. I steal a glance as he positions himself at the bedside, his body now protecting Baby's head and upper chest.

Mathieu jabs Henry forward another step, but the key hanging around Mathieu's neck—it turns a hellish, sooty black against the desert-brown of his shirt.

"Have you gone mad?" Nutesh says.

"*Moi?* Your possession of the three texts will make you mad with power, Thibault. We cannot allow this to happen," Mathieu says. "The *AVRAKEDAVRA* can remake this world. We can do better."

I've heard these words before, that night in the big top.

Mathieu is a mole.

"Geneviève, your *soeur chérie* Aveline wishes for me to send you her sincerest greetings," Mathieu says.

"Did you do that to Baby? Did you cut him?"

Mathieu laughs. "No. That love letter is from America. Though, they won't be in America for long. But I see the realization dawning on your face, Geneviève. Dagan and Aveline will find you, even after I deliver the books to them. Before Dagan finishes what he should have started millennia ago, he will make sure you pay for the sins of your dead mother."

My insides burn. "Don't you dare speak of Delia, you bastard."

"Oh, Americans and their love of foul language. So unbecoming," Mathieu says. "If you were my daughter, I'd wash your mouth out with soap. Though, by the looks of things, you won't be anyone's daughter for long."

I jerk forward with every intention of putting my hands on him, like I did with Lucian and Aveline at the airfield in Washington, but Nutesh grabs me hard above the elbow just as Mathieu shoves his weapon harder into the back of Henry's head.

"Oh, no, no, no, you keep your hands to yourself, *mon chou*."

Mathieu moves Henry two more steps forward but, unexpectedly, Henry looks left toward the wall of stainless steel cabinets and raises his arms out to his sides. "Your timing is impeccable."

"Henry?" I ask, but he doesn't look away from whatever he sees. He smiles, light from the wide upper windows reflecting the tears rimmed along the bottoms of his eyes.

Henry losing his shit right now does not bode well. Is he possessed?

Mathieu scans the area Henry is glued to. "It looks like it is your grandson who is mad, Thibault. I think you may have bigger problems than—"

His sentence hangs unfinished in the charged air as three things happen all at once: Mathieu stumbles backward, the gun fires, and Henry drops flat to the floor.

And then, quiet.

Just the *whirrrr-click* of Baby's ventilator and the adrenalized collective inhale-exhale of the people in the room.

Montague rushes to kick the handgun out of Mathieu's reach as Nutesh leans over to check the pulse at his wrist. I scurry to Henry—"Are you hurt? Did the bullet hit you?"—frantically surveying the button-down shirt covering his newly patched torso, looking for the blossom of blood.

He smiles again. "I'm fine. It didn't hit me. I'm okay." I help him to his feet, though I'm careful to only touch his gloved hands, my own extremities charged with electricity in search of release. He pulls me against his chest as soon as we're both upright again, burying his face in my hair, the warmth of his relieved exhale whooshing through me.

I unbury my face and look at the scene to my left. "Is he . . ."

"No. Unconscious only," Nutesh says angrily. Loud bangs echo from against the locked main door—Nutesh stands and opens it to Thierry and two other scary-looking soldiers, each with weapons drawn. I hold my breath, waiting to see if they're going to finish Mathieu's turncoat takedown.

Nutesh quickly explains what has happened as Montague rolls Mathieu onto his side and secures his hands with a pair of silver cuffs. I don't realize how hard I'm shaking until Henry whispers "We're okay it's okay we're safe," against my ear. The armed men holster their weapons, and the tension in the room deflates like a week-old balloon.

I move to Mathieu's still form, kneeling to touch the key around his neck. With a single swipe, I yank it off him and hold it in my palm. The black dissipates, the key again a tarnished silver.

It turned black before my eyes—when it was touching a traitor—and now it's silver again. I glance around me—did anyone else see that?

Hurriedly, I tuck the key and chain into my pocket. Mathieu doesn't deserve what this key stands for.

Montague then empties Mathieu's pockets and Thierry helps lift him onto another gurney along the wall, securing his feet to the metal and vinyl bed with leather belt straps. The four soldiers speak in hushed tones for a moment before the decision is made that the compound will go into full lockdown. Thierry instructs the soldier whose nametag reads *Lucas* to gather a team and tear apart Mathieu's quarters. "Bring everything you find to me. We will need to run a full scan on whatever tech he has. We must see who he's been in contact with on the outside."

On the outside? Dagan and Aveline—who else could we be at risk from? Are there other people who want these books, who want us dead?

The two other bearded soldiers leave, but my confidence in their loyalty has evaporated. What's to say they're not in on it too?

Can anyone be trusted here?

Panic prickles through me. Again.

The sadness in Nutesh's eyes as he looks at Mathieu . . . it hurts in my chest to witness the disappointment so heavy in his features. And just as quickly, he resumes the role of commander, speaking to Thierry and Montague in a low but fierce voice.

I move to check Baby, the back of my fingers pressed to his still-scorching forehead. I'm so grateful Mathieu's errant bullet didn't hit him. The carving on his arm is unchanged, and the small digital heart on the monitor flashes in time with his pulse—faster than it should be. His temp and blood pressure are still too high, all secondary evidence of severe infection.

"Everything will be okay, Baby," I whisper into his ear. "I will fix you. I promise."

A gentle hand rests on my back. "Genevieve," Henry says softly.

I turn and face him. "What was that? Who were you talking to?" I ask.

Henry pivots and again looks at something I can't see, watching movement of a figure that isn't there, his smile wide. He nods at nothing, and then turns back to me.

"Give me your hand, Gen," he says, his gloves now removed. I don't comply. "Please. Trust me."

Tentatively, I fold my hand into Henry's, and Alicia's ethereal form takes shape, her dark-blond hair floating as it always does, her green eyes bright, her smile soft and warm.

"Genevieve, I believe you know my mother," Henry says proudly.

8

"You . . . you can see her?"

"And I can talk to her. Isn't it incredible?" Henry's face is like a little kid who's just met Santa and the Easter Bunny on the same day. Alicia's lips move, but just as before when she showed herself to me in Oregon, I can't hear her.

"What's she saying?"

"She wants you to know she's proud of you for being so brave. For saving us in Washington," Henry translates, looking between me and his mother's ghostly shape. Alicia places the hand not connected to Henry over her heart and dips her head reverently.

"Your son is brave too," I say. She smiles and looks up at him with so much love. "Wait—Henry—can you see other people?" I want to know if he can see Delia.

"I'm sorry. So far, no. My mother is the only one who's presented herself to me." He turns his head and listens to words only he can hear. "She says it's because of the *Memory* text. That's how we're connected."

"But I haven't seen her since we left America. And I couldn't see her in here—not until you touched me," I say. "Usually I can see her without her making contact."

Nutesh, finished with his other conversation, steps alongside me. He looks lovingly at his grandson.

"*Grand-père*," Henry says, "your daughter says hello." Nutesh bows at the waist.

"Can you not see her?" I ask. Nutesh shakes his head. "How are you unable to see your own daughter?"

"I do not know, Geneviève. It has been this way since her death, despite my every effort to access her through our family's text. Given that she has passed into another realm beyond ours, she is under the purview of Dagan, of his ownership and control of the *Death* text."

"But *you* are *Memory*. And you have Dagan's book now," I say. "Can't you use it?"

"I am not schooled in the intricacies of the *Death* text as Dagan is. He has had many more years with his father's volume than I. These books grow and evolve under the ownership of the possessor. Once Belshunu died and Dagan assumed control, my connection was greatly diminished."

"Then how could I see Alicia before I was sealed to my book? How was I able to see my mother in the mausoleum?"

"That is your unique gift, one I sadly do not myself possess." Nutesh takes a deep breath. "Some magic is even beyond my skills, Geneviève." He touches Henry's arm. "But if my beautiful grandson can at last have a moment with his mother, my precious Alicia, I have no complaints."

Henry releases my hand, and Alicia again disappears—at

least from my sight. "This is so weird," I mutter. While seeing Alicia's ghost was a terrifying new development that happened three weeks after Delia's death, I learned to appreciate her presence. I'm happy for Henry that he finally has a real connection to his mom, but I'm selfishly sad I won't be able to see her now myself, without Henry connecting us.

A pained growl issues from across the room. Mathieu is coming around, which brings our attention back to what has just happened and around to the very real danger we are now in.

It doesn't take a genius to connect the dots—even though he wasn't in the greenhouse with us earlier, if Mathieu's a mole, there's little doubt that every word from Nutesh's lips has been delivered into the ears of Lucian Dagan Dmitri and Aveline Darrow.

They're going to find us, and they're going to kill us.

Mathieu is removed from the medical suite, though his deafening threats necessitate use of a cloth gag. Thierry seemed to take a strange pleasure in tying it around his head. Perhaps knowing time was running short, Mathieu made his move, though if his plan was to collect the three books and skedaddle out of Dodge, it was a terrific failure. Did he really think he'd make it out of this compound with little more than a handgun as protection?

No. No one could be that dumb. No one with military training.

Which means there is a bigger plan in action. Mathieu is merely the distraction.

Nutesh calls Hélène into the operating suite; she agrees to sit with Baby, monitor his vitals, and change his ice packs for the next hour. Without saying a word, Nutesh nods at Lucas, now returned from depositing Mathieu downstairs. In his hand, Lucas holds a menacing, club-shaped wand. As soon as he turns the switch on the wand's black handle, the device beeps. Lucas begins scanning the room, moving slowly and carefully around every cart, cabinet, and fixture.

He's scanning for bugs.

I've stepped into a Jason Bourne film.

Baby's discarded, cut clothing is heaped on a cart near his bed. While Nutesh is busy with Lucas, Henry talks to his mother, and Montague and Hélène replace cold packs around Baby's body, I quietly move to the pile of shredded cloth.

His cell phone is in one of these pockets. He's never without it.

And I need it.

I find it and tuck it into my pocket, covering the bulge with the bulk of the Irish sweater I'm grateful to have on, even if it's too warm for inside.

I'll have to sneak in later to get Baby's thumbprint and then reprogram the phone to recognize mine.

If Mathieu has put word out to people who want us dead, I have to put word out to my own people that I am doing everything I can to stay alive.

9

THIERRY'S MEN SCOUR THE COMPOUND FOR ANY EVIDENCE OF INTRUSION, electronic or otherwise. Everyone is tight-lipped about the results of their search; however, even Nutesh seems a bit tenser than usual as the afternoon progresses. If they found something, I'm guessing it wasn't good.

While I'm curious about what will become of Mathieu, his betrayal likely has a direct connection to what's happening to Baby. It's a good idea to keep him away from me in my emotional, electrically charged state.

Alone in the medical suite with my talisman, I try not to look at the monitors. I don't want to see the evidence that he's slipping away from me. Instead, I'll do what I can to anchor him to my side, even if he's a million miles away. His soulful brown eyes are closed, his body covered by one of Hélène's beautiful quilts, motionless save the up-and-down of his barrel chest under the influence of the machine helping him breathe.

In the brief interim that we're alone, I pull his hand free

and unlock his phone with his thick thumbprint—careful to shield what I'm doing with my body, as I'm sure Nutesh has cameras in here. I then quickly adjust the security settings so the phone will respond to me. I don't know what GPS-blocking technology he has installed, but for safety, I'll turn the phone off before hiding it in my backpack tonight. I'm also going to need to find his charger.

Before powering down, though, checking over my shoulder and listening for footsteps outside the suite, I hunch over to hide the phone between my body and Baby's bed and start a new text:

> *Vi, it's Gen. I'm safe. Please don't listen to the news. It's all BS. I'll explain everything as soon as I can. PLEASE watch over the elephants and lion. Everything Mara told you was a lie. STAY SAFE.*

My heart races—this is a ridiculous risk, but I cannot let Violet believe the terrible things Lucian is saying in the press conferences. And I need her to take care of Gertrude, Houdini, and Othello. She and Ash are my family; I know they'll do what's right to protect our beasts.

And I'll deal with the fallout later when Baby wakes up and realizes his phone is gone. I look forward to that punishment, in fact—because it means he's made it through this.

The door whooshes open. I shove the phone into my front pocket and again cover it with my bulky sweater.

Montague pulls up one of the white leather-and-chrome chairs and sits beside me, taking my hand in his.

"Don't worry," he says as I try to pull away. "I know what these hands can do." He smiles. I slide one hand free and run a finger over the scarring the lion's claws left behind. "I healed. I survived, because of you."

I nod. He's right.

"You were so brave, even as a little girl. Always ready to help those who needed it most."

"Except now. I can't save him. How can I *leave* while he's so sick? What if he dies when I'm gone?"

"What choice do we have?" he asks. "You can save him, though." Montague kisses the back of my hand before returning it to me.

"How? My attempts at healing are useless on whatever Aveline has done to him."

Montague nods. "Nutesh said they are using a very dark magic. To save him, that magic must be undone at the source."

At the source. In *Babylon*.

"I have to tell all of you—Aveline's gifts? Her hands? Where mine can heal, hers can take a person apart. She is very, very dangerous. Together, she and Dagan are . . ." *Lethal.* I can't say the word out loud. "I can't go, Montague. I *cannot leave here* without Baby. He's my talisman. He's the only thing that keeps the Etemmu from destroying me. They used the Etemmu to murder Delia—you know that, right?" While I'm so grateful to have had a reprieve from the demon's terror while safe inside the compound, I'm vibrating with fear over what's going to happen once we leave.

Montague's head bobs once as he looks down at the floor. "Your mother was so beautiful and kind."

"She was . . . and they took her from me." My clenched knuckles bleed of color and I wipe away an angry tear.

"But this is about more than revenge, Geneviève. If you don't go, if you don't fight this evil, Baby will not survive, and Dagan will chase you and Henry until he has the books. This will never be over for you. You said yourself that you wish to be rid of this curse, that you wish for a normal life. There is only one way to do that."

"It wasn't supposed to happen like this," I whisper, leaning forward to rest my forehead on Baby's burning-hot wrist. "It wasn't supposed to happen like this. Come back to me, Horatio. Come back to me."

Sobs rack through me as Montague rubs my back. When a hand brushes my neck, glove-free, the exchange of energy tells me it's Henry. He takes Montague's place, standing over me as he wraps an arm around my shaking shoulders, hugging me to him. He holds on, bending with me when I howl my fear, sadness, and frustration into Baby's quilt.

Montague leaves quietly, allowing us a few moments with Baby. Henry offers tissue and whispers that everything will be okay, that we will do what's necessary to save everyone we love.

I straighten and fold myself against him.

"Come. Hélène has set up food for us in your room," he finally says.

I wipe my nose and eyes and kiss Baby's forehead, whispering a promise I'll come sit with him before we leave. I then let Henry lead me out of the medical suite and down the hall toward our rooms.

Inside mine, Hélène has performed her own magic—in the sitting area near a roaring fireplace, the wooden square coffee table is covered in food, wine, and a cluster of stout, white candles, their lit wicks dancing shadows against the bookshelves.

"She thought it might be nice for us to have some quiet time before . . ."

"Before the end?" I finish.

Henry clicks the door closed. "It's not the end of anything, Gen. Not when we have each other to get through it." He clasps his pinkie finger around mine and pulls me to one of the two facing love seats and then sits opposite.

"This seems awfully romantic for a grandmother to prepare," I say, picking up a ripe strawberry from a bowl of vibrant fruit.

"She's a rather modern grandmother, I think," he says. "I may have made a special request. Or two."

"Maybe she sees this mission could kill us, so why not enjoy a few precious last moments?"

"Ahh, there's my cynical Genevieve. I was worried I'd lost her," Henry says.

I toss the strawberry stem onto the plate. "I can't do this without Baby. What if the Etemmu comes for me again?"

"Then we'll handle it the best we can. My mother's presence can't be for nothing—if seeing her is my newest gift, then surely it must be useful. Maybe she can help us."

"Maybe."

"I asked my grandfather to make me your talisman. To repeat whatever ritual he performed with Baby that made him your mother's protector, and now yours. He said it isn't possible because I'm an heir too."

"Thank you . . . for asking. Seriously."

Henry pours wine for us. We are in France, after all. "And I'm sorry you had to learn about Xavier like that—in front of all of us. That couldn't have been easy."

I accept a glass and take a drink. I'm not used to wine—it makes me shudder. "I don't get it, though. How could he be my dad? Why wouldn't Delia mention him?" I run my finger along the glass's rim. "Then again, Delia didn't mention a lot of things."

"And we can't ask Baby. At least not right now."

I nod, sipping to wash away the lump in my throat. *Baby* . . .

"If Nutesh trusts Xavier, then we must too. My grandfather wouldn't steer us wrong. He has everything to lose, just like we do."

"And isn't that what makes a story so compelling? When everyone has everything to lose?"

When Henry looks at me, firelight dances in his blue-green eyes, and even with the loss of his deliciously mussed curls, he's still that handsome kid all the girls want to impress. I stand and turn away, pulling the heavy sweater over my head—and tucking Baby's phone into its folds so Henry doesn't see it.

I then move across to his couch and slide next to him, hardly a breath between us. His eyes linger on my hair—he reaches up to pull at a short dark coil.

"Beautiful." He kisses me, hard, his ungloved hand cupping the back of my head, the other gripping my shoulder. I wrap my arms around him, pulling him close, kissing him back with all the fear and worry and trepidation and longing we share. We should be talking about mission objectives and meeting Xavier and how the hell we're going to pull this off, but instead images of our prior encounter at the shitty motel back in SeaTac flow from his head into mine—him kissing me, what he really wanted to do that night, his hands on me, my hands on him, the heat between us when I zapped him—

We chuckle against one another's mouths. "It was really hot until you electrocuted me," he whispers.

I push him back a few inches. "Um, Alicia . . . she's not in here, right? Because that would be creepy."

"She's not here," he says, his lips brushing mine, his bisected eyebrow lifting. "And yes, that would be really creepy." He presses his lips to mine again, pausing only to pull me onto his lap so I'm straddling him, my hands on his lightly bristled face, in the fuzz of his tightly trimmed hair, on his neck.

He pulls me as close as two people can be while fully clothed, and while our bodies and mouths are pressed together, I send my own images into his head, of us first meeting, of us with the elephants, of our first kiss . . .

Shirts are untucked and skin is explored, and while the burn beneath my sternum steadily increases, I'm able to control it. Well, mostly.

"You're like kissing static electricity," Henry says into my ear as he kisses my neck. "And do stop thinking such impure thoughts. I'm afraid of my grip on my self-control, and in my grandparents' house, no less." His eyes bore into mine, his chronically ink-stained left thumb caressing my cheekbone.

"You're the one who plied me with wine and a romantic meal."

"A romantic meal we have yet to eat." He kisses me again, biting at my lower lip. With my hands on his neck, searching his collarbone, I come across a new addition to his ensemble.

A necklace. With a key.

"From Hélène," he says, allowing the *La Vérité* key to dangle over his fingers. "She said we all get one, in the tradition your mother started."

I reach down and kiss the key.

"Did you notice earlier, with Mathieu in the medical suite—I watched his key go from old silver to pitch black." I dig into my pocket and pull it out. "I took it—it's silver again."

"Honestly, Genevieve, I didn't notice much about Mathieu except his pistol pushed against the back of my skull."

"Right. Sorry," I say, tucking Mathieu's key away again. "Are you all right? After that, I mean."

"It wasn't the highlight of the trip so far," he says, his bravado slipping a little. "I'm just glad it stopped where it did."

I push my forehead against his and kiss him. "Me too," I say against his lips. "Henry . . . what if we don't survive this?"

"We *will*. We will," Henry says, kissing the tip of my nose, his hands on my shoulders. "And when it's over, I promise to kiss you like this every day until we're old and withered."

"Promise?"

"Cross my heart and hope to—"

"Don't say it." One more lingering kiss, and then I lean back, pluck a strawberry from the bowl, and feed it to Henry. "We should eat." I pull back slightly. "We're going to need our strength so we can save the world."

IO

When Henry and I deliver our tray of emptied plates to the kitchen, Hélène offers more hugs and squeezes, some quiet words of advice, followed by the instruction that we retire for a few hours of rest. We're to leave the compound at 0300, "under cover of a moonless sky," she says. Five hours from now.

The travel clothing Nutesh mentioned earlier hangs in my closet. I change into one set—black cargo pants and black turtleneck—rather than pajamas, so I can spend every remaining moment with Baby. Maybe my presence will help him find his way back, since Nutesh is out of medical, or magical, options to bring him around. More than anything, I want to crawl under the duvet of this amazing bed, to hide away in this incredible estate for the rest of my life, wrapped in Henry's arms, safe and secure from whatever awaits us outside the compound walls.

But I live in the real world, and for me, for Henry, right now, the real world isn't made of dreams or fantasies. It's made of danger and deceit and a fortitude I don't think I have.

Once Henry is tucked away in his own room, I grab Baby's phone and turn it back on, nervous about what I might find. While I desperately want to make contact with Violet—with home—I'm scared what she might say, or worse, that someone else intercepted the message.

Gen! OMG! WHERE R U? Everyone here is freaking out! Lucian said Baby kidnapped you guys and you stole some crazy expensive art? Can I call you? Plz text me back ASAP.

I smile and release the breath trapped in my chest.

Can't talk much. PLEASE tell Cece and Ted I'm OK. We're with Baby. We're safe.

I pause—we're not safe. But how much do I tell her? She can't possibly wrap her head around any of this. No reasonable person could.

I'll explain as soon as I can. Don't tell anyone else. Could be very dangerous. Please, Vi. I love you & miss you so much.

I love you too. I'm so worried. The circus is shutting down. Everything is falling apart. Police everywhere. They think you're in danger & it's Baby's fault?

All lies, Vi. I SWEAR. One day soon I'll explain.

OK. I miss you. When R U coming home?

Dunno yet. Please take care of the elephants for me. Promise? Keep them safe. Tell Dr. P & Ted to watch them closely. Mara Dunn is not who she says she is & she might hurt them.

Mara left—an aunt in Quebec died so she had to leave? She seemed very sad when she went. Gert & the baby miss you so much. And Othello won't stop pacing—he roars at everyone who walks by him.

I choke on a sob.

Please give them a kiss & hug for me. Be careful, Vi. Love you.

Love you too, sister. Come home. We're all so worried.

GTG. I'll check in as soon as I can.

XOXOXOXOX

I turn off the phone. I've lingered too long, and now I listen, frozen in the doorway of my bathroom, straining to hear the plod of boots in the hall to tell me I've compromised the whole mission with my selfishness.

The faucet drips.

Water rushes through a pipe in the wall from an adjacent bathroom.

An owl hoots outside the window.

No human bursts into my room.

Relief washes over me in a cold sweat. I hide the phone up my sleeve, just in case, and move to the closet where my new backpack awaits. As I unzip, the familiar shiver runs through me—the *AVRAKEDAVRA* is tucked in its pouch, ready for its final journey.

I grab my mom's hand-painted playing cards from my nightstand—the one thing I managed to bring with me from home, a little piece of Delia that tells the story of our people—and then I bury the cards and Baby's phone in the mess of supplies in the pack's bottom half. I pull my second set of travel clothes from their hangers. Once rolled and stuffed into the bag, the phone is totally concealed.

I have nothing left to do except say goodbye to my talisman.

Goodbye for now.

At 0230, Hélène taps me on the shoulder—I dozed off sitting

in the chair, holding Baby's fevered hand, my head resting on his bed. "It is time to prepare, *ma chère,*" she says.

I'm chilled with fear. But looking down one last time at Baby's shuttered face . . . if destroying the books is the only thing that will break this curse and bring my real dad back to me, then that is what I will do.

I kiss his forehead and then follow Hélène back to my room.

At 0300 on the dot, there's a knock at my door. I open it to Thierry standing in the hall, outfitted in head-to-toe black. He hands me a black stocking cap; I fit it over my short hair. Hélène then steps close and hugs me, wiping away the single leaked tear.

"We believe in you. Everything will be as it should be. Be strong, be brave, and above all else, *be safe.*" She hugs me again, tighter this time, and I'm grateful for my new gloves so I can't hurt her with my unrestrained current.

"I wish we'd had more time," I squeak. Hélène nods at me once and squeezes my fisted hands.

"Everything you need is in here. The key to good is found in truth," she whispers as she flattens her hand against my chest, over the top of Delia's concealed *vérité* key. It takes me by surprise—I thought this was something only Delia said. Hélène's eyes sparkle in the dimly lit room, but there is strength within.

"Take care of Baby for me," I say.

She bows her head. "I promise you."

Thierry situates my pack onto my shoulders. The

vibration coming from the bag, connected to the Tesla coil inside my chest, reminds me that the *Life* text is tucked inside.

And then Henry is at the door with Montague, signaling that the time for goodbyes is over. In solemn procession, we follow Nutesh to the elevators. As soon as the doors close, I'm clammy and shaking; Henry's eyes are wide and fearful. He grabs my hand and we interlace our gloved fingers.

I'm so grateful I'm not doing this alone.

I'm so scared that Baby isn't coming with us.

In the fortified underground garage that brought us into the Croix-Mare compound just a couple days ago, the soldiers stand at attention in two lines facing one another. Every single one nods as we walk past: Nutesh, Montague, me, Henry, and Thierry at the rear. Ahead sits a slick black sedan with darkly tinted windows. Lucas opens the back door and then steps aside, waiting for us to climb in.

Nutesh stops before Henry and me. "Thierry will keep you safe. I trust him with my own life, and I trust him with yours," he says. He then places a hand on Henry's shoulder, and one on mine, closes his eyes, and speaks under his breath in a language I don't recognize.

Warmth shivers through me; a glance at Henry indicates that he is experiencing the same unnerving feeling.

Eyes open and head up, Nutesh offers his hand to each of us. "Remember your mission objective. Remember why you are doing it. I will see you in Babylon," he says, and after a solemn look to his grandson, Nutesh steps aside to allow us access to the car.

With a final glance around, I pull my backpack off and

climb in, wedging my precious goods between my legs on the floorboard. Henry follows suit, and the door closes solidly behind him. Nutesh and Thierry exchange a few unheard words, a quick manly hug, and then Thierry climbs behind the wheel.

When the vehicle hums to life and eases forward, I close my eyes and send Baby one last missive he will never hear: *I will come back for you.*

II

The outside world is black, though the stars twinkle like holes punched in a circus tent. The weather's been blustery over the past twenty-four hours, but the rain has cleared.

"The trip to Paris will take approximately two and a half hours. There is a quicker route, but I want to avoid construction so we are not slowed down," Thierry explains. "The windows are tinted so no one can see in, but I will ask that you keep your gear at the ready in case we have need to exit the vehicle quickly."

"Will there be a need for that?" I ask, my paranoia spiking.

"*Non,*" Thierry says, smiling at me in the rearview mirror. "You should sleep now. When we get to Paris, we will leave the car and meet Xavier."

"And then what?"

"It will be okay, Geneviève. Please, get some rest. I will wake you when we arrive."

Henry scoots as close as his seat belt will allow and drapes an arm around my shoulders, pulling me into his side. I want to close my eyes—I want to rest—but I'm two and a half hours from meeting my father, a man I didn't know existed until yesterday.

What I would give for another five minutes in the mausoleum with Delia. But I have so many questions, I would need hours.

However, if we fail, I will be meeting her again before too long anyway.

There's no way I can sleep right now. When I look up and find Henry scanning the passing landscape, it's safe to guess he's feeling the same way.

So instead of sitting in the back of this car and letting my anxieties get the best of me, I want questions answered: Where are we going first? How long will this mission take? Have you met Xavier before? What's he like? How will Nutesh know it's time to go to Babylon? How in the world will we get into Iraq in the first place? Isn't Iraq still unstable since the American invasion? All we ever see on the news are bombed-out buildings. I can't believe they're sending us there . . .

Thierry does his best to stem my inquisition by giving me the very basics, though whether that's because he doesn't know the answers or whether Nutesh has told him that less is more, I can't tell.

"Paris first. Monsieur Darrow will coordinate your next stop. *Oui,* Xavier and I are friends. He's a good man. Quiet, but very smart. Nutesh will know when it's time because he will communicate with you and Xavier. Don't you fret about Iraq now. Yes, it is dangerous, and especially for Americans. The northern part of the country, in the Kurdish autonomous zone—those people are more welcoming of US citizens. The invasion effectively curtailed the genocide of the Kurdish people by Saddam Hussein and his administration, so they are grateful. However, the rest of Iraq—it's mixed. You are neither Catholic nor Jewish, so as long as you maintain the ruse that you aren't American either, it should be fine."

"Are there followers of the *AVRAKEDAVRA* in Iraq?" I ask.

"Of course. *La Vérité*. But they live in secret. Religion and spirituality are dangerous subjects in a country that has been torn apart by many centuries of conflict. Even the Muslims are torn in two—the Shiites versus the Sunnis—and add to that the instability of Daesh, plus whatever is going on with Iran, who very much wants Iraq under its thumb after their terribly bloody eight-year conflict . . . *Mon dieu,* it's a mess."

"Wow. Sounds great. We should totally visit there," I say.

"You are not visiting as a tourist. We will find shelter at the University of Babylon. Students are still young enough to believe there is hope for Americans to do the right thing. Baghdad is a functioning city. Schools are open and roads are passable. People live their lives. I'm more concerned about Dagan's people finding you there than I am about the locals discovering you're American."

"Dagan's people?" You'd think I'd be used to the nausea that swarms me every time Dagan's name is mentioned. But, I'm not. So this is fun.

"Just as Nutesh has followers and people who believe in his cause, so does Dagan."

"Except Dagan's cause is very different from what Nutesh

is doing. Nutesh believes the *AVRAKEDAVRA* does good, that it helps people. Dagan just wants to take everything for his own selfish purposes. He's thrown his own son away in the pursuit of these stupid books," I say.

Henry moves his arm from my shoulders, his head turned toward the window again.

Shit. "Sorry, Henry," I whisper. He nods. Barely. Like he needed my big mouth to remind him what Lucian has done. "But what Dagan is doing is wrong. He wants to go back in time and undo everything. How can anyone believe in that? How can anyone be so misled to think this is a good thing?"

"Tell me, Geneviève, that anger in your voice—where does it come from?" Thierry asks.

"Are you serious?"

"Humor me."

"Well, let's see—I had to move to a small town in the middle of nowhere because my mother was murdered by a man who wants possession of a *book*; I'm being tortured and taunted by an ancient demon because of a *book*; my whole life has been turned on its ear because of a *book*; the only person who is really my family is now lying comatose in a jacked-up farmhouse in the middle of France, under some invisible spell likely issued by a bloodthirsty sister I had no idea existed until very recently, a spell I have no power to reverse, and *POOF*! I have a daddy who is actually alive and well and hiding out—guess what! Because of a *book*. Does that about cover it?"

"So, family. You're angry because the *AVRAKEDAVRA* has taken your family from you."

"Yes!"

Thierry again looks at me in the mirror. "*Ma chère,* you have answered your own questions."

The car gets very quiet. The storm in my head does not. I feel like a dick now. Henry's body language tells me I've hurt him. If Baby were here, he'd scold me.

I'm not the only person suffering in all this. I'm not the only person who has experienced loss, or who has to face this very scary journey.

I take off my seat belt and scoot to Henry, wrapping my arm around his.

"I'm sorry," I say. "I'm just freaking out a little." His eyes still scan the passing terrain, which doesn't look so different from Interstate 5 going through Washington. Narrow shoulders bordered by overgrown shrubbery and clumps of evergreen trees interspersed with wide open fields still dormant in the wintry air; power lines like giants straddling the fields; the small farms wrapped protectively around their sleeping farmhouses.

It's obvious we're getting closer to a metropolis when fields give way to industrial parks and cargo trucks and six-story apartment buildings. The graffiti-covered retaining walls and nonstop greenery . . . if I'd woken up here, I'd think we were driving through Seattle. Except for some of the houses, maybe. And every once in a while, we get a view of the Seine outside the left side of the car before it disappears to snake away in a different direction.

The freeway is busy here, even in the predawn hour, spiking my anxiety.

"We are getting closer to the city limits," Thierry says. "We're skirting the city, taking *le Boulevard Périphérique* around the edge to the 20th *arrondissement*. Maybe you have heard of it? It is home to *Cimetière Père Lachaise* where many very famous people are buried." Like a tour guide, he talks about Paris. And I listen because I'm so scared, I'm grateful for the momentary diversion.

"We will be meeting Monsieur Darrow in the 20th," Thierry says. "It is a very busy district with nearly 200,000 residents. It is easy to blend in." That's a little reassuring, I suppose. "But this is a rough part of the city. Pickpockets, beggars, people who will harass you for money. You would be wise to stick close."

My nerves burn a little hotter thinking that there are more threats than just the people after the *AVRAKEDAVRA*. There are those flashes when I consider that Lucian's plan to undo the world and remake it might not be such a terrible thing. Then again, humans being what they are, it only takes five minutes to glance through a history textbook to know that the streets of Paris have seen a lot of blood in her two thousand years.

The sky has pulled back the nighttime cloak over the city. I'm shocked to see how big it is! It's like driving through Los Angeles. *Boulevard Peripherique* is as busy as any LA freeway—residential and business buildings flank both east- and westbound lanes, construction cranes tower over high-rises under construction, overpasses with trains, so many tunnels, skeletal trees still winter bare, streetlamps, and seriously, the most brazen motorcyclists I've ever seen.

"Our exit is coming soon. Prepare for arrival," Thierry says. As if that were possible.

Shops are already open. Vendors organize their wares and holler back and forth in languages other than French or English. Buses swallow people, humans of every size and shape and color and age. When Thierry cracks his window, the dry air is bitingly cold. I'm taken aback at the amount of graffiti, and while we're stopped at a light, I watch as a woman lets her bulldog crap right on the sidewalk—and doesn't clean it up.

Thierry sees it too. "Always watch your step in Paris," he says.

Usually a good judge of north and south, I'm completely turned around. The streets are hardly wide enough for two cars to fit down, especially with all the parked vehicles along the right edge. Six-story buildings, a mix of the architecture I've often seen in Google Earth images of Paris and then newer designs, are so close that you could play Frisbee with the people across the street.

After another few rights and lefts, Thierry pulls off and parks as close as he can behind another car. "We're here." Before he unlocks the doors, though, he pulls a gun belt from under the passenger seat, straps it around his waist, and checks the black handgun, chambering a round. He looks in the rear- and side-view mirrors again. "Please, stay close. Follow me, do not fall behind, backpacks on your bodies at all times. Do not stop if you are approached."

The doors unlock.

We're out, quickly. Thierry moves like a meerkat, tall and stretched above the crowd. He nods, and we're off down the block, past quiet doors and around corners occupied by shops and produce stands. One door opens to release the aroma of baked goods; the next door, strong coffee. My stomach growls.

But the romance wears a little thin when we pass overflowing garbage bins and sad-looking homeless people sitting next to ATMs and near café doors, faces etched with their pasts.

"Keep near to me," Thierry says under his breath. Just before the end of the next block, he takes an abrupt right into a cobblestone laneway with separate houses on each side, their outer walls mere inches from each other. And each house is fronted by a garden wall covered in ivy, the only parts bare being the numbers that provide the house its identity.

Thierry stops in front of #17, looks around us, and then presses a silent doorbell. He turns to look up at an ivy-hidden camera I wouldn't have otherwise noticed, and the gate buzzes open.

My heart thuds in my ears, my body overcome with the jitters I get before a performance. Despite the gloves, my fingers ache from stress-induced cold. Where is that electricity when I need it?

The walkway inside the gate is old red brick; the inner yard has no grass, just mortared-in flower beds with dirt and dead leaves. Thick shrubbery hides what I now see are two huge windows along the front of the house, the glass obscured by shutters on the inside. The white stucco exterior walls have been repaired with gray compound, and a round brick chimney protrudes from the tile roof, white smoke puffing lazily from its mouth.

Not at all a house one would take notice of if passing by.

Which is perfect.

Thierry climbs the three brick porch steps and places a hand flat against a biometric scanner just above waist level, at first concealed by a white panel matching the house. It reads his handprint in blue, and then glows a muted green. The front door clicks open.

Henry wraps his arm around my shoulders and whispers close to my head. "Grandfather wouldn't have sent us here if it weren't safe." He sounds like he's reassuring himself at the same time.

And of course, I know this. But it's about more than the *AVRAKEDAVRA* for the next little while. I'm about to meet my biological father. I'm allowed to look like a deer in the headlights.

We step inside, at once greeted by competing smells of burning wood, fresh coffee, and something equal parts sweet and yeasty. Henry pushes the front door closed behind us, but my focus is on the man coming down the creaky wooden staircase ahead.

His face cracks into a pleasant smile as he nears the last stair, his hand extended toward Thierry. I watch as the two men exchange a hug that tells me they've been friends for a while. As soon as he looks at me, I know exactly who he is.

No mistaking he is Aveline's father.

His eyes, a blue like the heart of an iceberg, are made that much more striking against his olive complexion and onyx-colored curls, his face shadowed by whiskers.

Thierry and Xavier speak to each other in quick French before letting go of the other's elbow. When Thierry turns to Henry and me, I almost faint.

"Xavier Darrow, this is Henry Dmitri." Xavier shakes Henry's hand, though the warm smile is replaced by a stoic set to his lips. Xavier knows Henry is Lucian's son—will he suspect him of betrayal even before we take our first step out the door?

After a tense beat where he examines Henry's face, Xavier's expression softens. "You are the mirror of your mother," he says. He then releases Henry's hand and turns to me.

"And this, of course, is Geneviève," Thierry says.

My fingers, still freezing, prickle with energy. When Xavier clasps my hand in greeting, I'm grateful for the gloves. Otherwise he'd be on the old hardwood floor gasping for breath.

"Nice to meet you, sir," I say, my voice not as strong as I want it to be.

"I was very sad to hear about Delia," Xavier says. "I'm sorry for your loss." I detect a flash of pain in his eyes as he looks me over, and I wait to hear him repeat his sentiments offered to Henry, how I too am a mirror of my mother.

But then he doesn't.

"Thank you, Monsieur Darrow," I say quietly, my earlier bravado dampened. I will have to find it again if I'm going to get answers to the million questions pinging around my head.

His lips part again, but then he nods once, looks down at his feet, a subtle but sad smile on his lips as he lets go of the handshake.

He then shifts toward Thierry, and as if not registering that this is one of the biggest moments of my life, he gestures toward the back of the house.

"You should eat. We have a lot of work to do."

12

We follow Xavier down a narrow hallway and into a spacious kitchen—a braid of bread rests on the black iron stove. In the back corner in front of a door rendered useless by the boards nailed over it, a purple-hued grow lamp hovers over a vibrant collection of herbs and smaller plants. How many of those were Delia's . . . ?

The kitchen is practically devoid of decoration except for the flowers painted in swooping vines above thresholds and on the plaster wall above the sink. Pendulum lamps hang from the ceiling. All sources of natural light have been blocked out with the heavy shutters.

It's good, I guess—no one can see in. But that I have to be paranoid about being spied on . . . will I ever feel normal?

Xavier gestures for us to sit at a long rectangular table tucked into an eating nook, bench seating on each side of the table. Henry slides in first; I follow.

"Leave your packs near you. Use the strap to loop around your leg. This will become your new routine. When the packs aren't on your body or locked up, they must be tethered to you," Xavier says from the center tiled island, pouring coffee into small cups from a French press. "When you sleep, the pack is your pillow. You will take turns with toileting and personal hygiene so that one of you has his or her eyes on the packs at all times. When you are working, the packs must be in a secure location. We have no room for error in these rules."

Nope. I will not be feeling normal for a very long time.

In the table's center, Thierry places a cutting board covered in meats, cheeses, small round crackers, cherry tomatoes, and chunked melon, and then slides onto the bench across from us. Xavier brings the bread and cutlery.

"Hold your questions until the end. This house is protected by sound masking, so no one outside can hear us. You may relax," he says, his voice gruff but his accent less pronounced than Thierry's. "You eat, I talk."

And talk he does. We will be leaving to join our first circus, *Circ de l'Anell d'Or* ("Circus of the Golden Ring" in Catalan) located in Barcelona, tonight. It is one of the shows that provides sanctuary and cover for *La Vérité,* who also owns this safe house. For now, it's our staging area until the sun goes down. Today will be spent strategizing and double-checking pack supplies. We will be provided with appropriate work wear once we are arrive at the circus, and both Henry and I will be assigned jobs taking care of whatever is needed.

"I don't know what Nutesh has told you, so . . . *La Vérité* is a group dedicated to helping others. They travel globally throughout the network. They work the shows, some even perform, and while they're there, the members conduct the business of *La Vérité*. Because of our stealth, no one outside the network knows what we do."

"What if someone figures it out? What if someone defects and tells the secret?"

Xavier's hard stare feels like I've asked a forbidden question; he then looks to Thierry, but the glance shared between them tells me everything I need to know.

People don't defect. And if they do . . .

I swallow hard.

"That is why involvement is sacred, and secure. Few are willing to risk their lives to keep these secrets, and those who are willing are fiercely protective of the network, of *La Vérité,* and of the teachings of the *AVRAKEDAVRA*."

"Because the beautiful thing about a circus is a person's ability to hide in plain sight," I mutter.

"It's the perfect cover. And for you two especially. No one will be the wiser of who you truly are. I often bring orphans into the fray."

"We are *not* orphans."

"You may be before this is over," he says, smacking his lips.

I am anything but, and neither is Henry. He still has a father, and I've not given up hope that before this is over, Lucian Dagan Dmitri will remember that he loves his son.

Xavier shoves a bite of thinly sliced meat into his mouth and follows it with a chunk of cantaloupe. He loudly licks the juice off his fingers. He's noisier than Othello. "We will leave Paris tonight for *Circ de l'Anell d'Or*. One of the Guardians who possesses the treasure you seek will meet us in an as-yet-undetermined location. Once we reach the secure rendezvous point, the two of you will present your texts as proof of identity; the Guardian will then relinquish the item, and off we go to the next location."

I find it odd that he isn't using the word *key* to describe what we're after. Perhaps even with the sound masking activated, Xavier is still nervous?

"Now, the *Circ* people will welcome you in, because you're with me, but everyone who joins up is expected to work. No free rides."

"I'm not afraid of hard work," I say.

"It's not you I'm worried about." Xavier nods at Henry; his cheeks pink up.

"I'm sure Henry can hold his own. I'm more worried about being attacked by Lucian and Aveline. You know her, right?" I instantly regret my big mouth.

Xavier sits ramrod straight and sets his coffee cup down with the slightest *tink* against its saucer. Fire consumes the blue of his eyes.

Yeah, maybe that was a step too far.

Henry grabs my knee under the table. The room suddenly feels twenty degrees colder, as quiet as a tomb.

"Genevieve, I'm going to say this once to you now. We have a singular mission to accomplish. I don't need to remind you what's at stake, or what's already been lost in the pursuit of all this madness. So you will knock that chip off your shoulder, work with *Circ* to help the people who are putting their lives on the line for the betterment of humanity, and save your questions till the end—and by the end, I literally mean until we are en route back to civilization. Then maybe you and I can have the conversation I can see you gnashing in your gritted teeth. *Bien*?"

I don't answer. Not because I'm being a smart-ass but because I have no spit left in my mouth.

Thierry offers an appeasing smile when Xavier resumes shoving food into his mouth, but I don't think I can eat another bite.

"I'm glad to see Hélène took measures to change what you look like," he says, gruffly wiping his mouth with a cloth napkin. "Dagan has your faces all over the news. Everyone will be looking for you. But not like this." He looks at Henry, and then at me; he lingers on my face for a beat longer, and something flashes in his expression. Pain? Regret? Anger?

Maybe it's nothing. But I want him to feel all of it.

"Thierry, are you coming with us? Tonight?"

His coffee cup looks small in his hand, and when he shakes his head no, I can see the "I'm sorry" written on his face. "You will be in excellent hands with Xavier, I promise."

I nod, willing the emotion swirling in my head to stay put. "Promise me you'll look after Baby." *What I would give for him to be here.*

"*Oui*. I promise."

There is much more to be said—questions piled like the crackers on the cutting board—and yet few words make their way into the air that deceptively smells like home and safety and warmth.

This place is anything but home.

The smoke coils off Xavier's cigarette. He's trying to hold it near the barely opened shutters that cover the cracked window as he and Thierry talk in hushed tones, but instead the bluish haze dances in the scant sunlight peeking through split curtains, like an aerialist on silks in her very own spotlight.

"You doing all right?" Henry asks, his sketchbook resting on his lap. We've repacked our supplies—after we ate and cleaned up the kitchen, Xavier made us empty everything onto the living room floor so he could double-check. I had to be very careful to keep Baby's phone concealed in my pack, trying to maintain my cool when Xavier moved the canvas bags to the side so he could look through our stuff.

"I'm fine." I'm not, but this is hardly the place.

"I wish we could take a walk. Get a little fresh air," he says, throwing a look at Xavier and his cigarette. I laugh under my breath. My uncle Ted's a smoker—I'm used to it. It's terrible to breathe, but it makes me miss my family even more.

I stuff the other pair of rolled-up black pants into my bag and stand up, about to ask where the bathroom is, when Xavier and Thierry startle and reach for their phones. Their expressions change; my stomach drops into my feet.

Xavier douses his cigarette in his coffee cup and puts a finger to his lips. He and Thierry communicate with hand signals I don't understand, but I've seen enough movies to know that talking with one's hands, eyes wide, lips pursed—that usually means the bad guys are here.

13

Confirmation arrives in the form of that unmistakable smell.

And then the floor is eclipsed by spiders.

I'm backing up, trying to climb onto the furniture, the scream building in my throat—

As soon as Henry's eyes meet mine, he knows. He knows because he's seen this happen before, during movie night at the circus when he had to drive Baby and me to the ER because I split my head open running from the Etemmu.

And just like I told Nutesh it would, it has found me.

Baby isn't here.

I have no talisman, no one to stop the Etemmu's onslaught.

The electricity burning behind my sternum, firing into my hands, it can do little to help me against a wraithlike demon. I can't electrocute air.

And if the Etemmu is here, then Aveline and Lucian can't be far behind.

Henry jumps behind me, clamps a hand over my mouth so I can't scream, even though I do anyway, his wide hand muffling the sound as Xavier turns abruptly and hisses for me to keep quiet.

But he can't see it. No one else can see it.

Henry murmurs into my ear: "It's not real it's not real it's okay everything is all right I'm right here fight it don't let the demon take you please, Gen, you're safe it's not real."

But it *is* real, and the swarming arms are reaching for me, the sickeningly long, black, skeletal fingers brushing against my cheek, burning my skin with every stroke, and then there's a voice in my head:

"Once upon a time, there lived a young girl with hair like the sun's fire, feet like the wind, and hands that enchanted even the lowliest sufferer . . ."

I scream so loud that not even Henry can muffle it. Xavier is on me quick as fire, and with a swift move to the back of my neck and a rip of pain into my head, everything goes black.

I'm jostled awake, the pack heavy on my back, someone's shoulder ramming into my gut with every step. An intense flashlight illuminates our surroundings: close walls on each side—concrete, but free of graffiti and only wide enough that a man could touch both sides and need to have his elbows bent—concrete underfoot, footfalls splashing in murky puddles. The damp smell of earth and stagnant water and stale cigarettes. Are we underground? God, my head hurts; my chest aches like I've coughed too hard.

"Put me down," I say, pushing against the back of the person carrying me.

We stop, and Xavier deposits me onto my feet. "If I let you walk, can you not scream again?"

I glare at him. He doesn't know anything about why I was screaming.

"Are they here? Are they following us?"

Xavier starts walking again. Henry steps in beside me and hands me gloves pulled from a pocket in his cargo pants. Once they're on, he laces his fingers through mine.

I'm so relieved not to be surrounded by supernatural spiders or the stinging arms of the Etemmu, but the relief is temporary. And the back of my head hurts. "Where are we? Where are we going?"

"We have a long walk. Conserve your energy with silence," Xavier snaps.

When the light swings toward us, I notice Henry is limping badly. His right pant leg is soaked with red, a strip of cloth wrapped around and tied in a haphazard bow just above his knee. Is that more blood on his jacket? Splattered, like it doesn't belong to him.

I stop. "Wait—where's Thierry?"

It's here I notice in the dim light that Henry's eyes are wide and red-rimmed; he looks shell-shocked. Henry's hurt, he's covered in blood, and Thierry is gone.

"I am not taking another step until someone tells me what has happened—"

Xavier turns and closes the gap between us in three long strides, his face so close, I can see the pores on his nose. "You will walk, and you will remain as quiet as a mouse. Your lack of self-control has already cost us dearly."

And then he turns and stomps off, taking the brilliant LED light with him.

Henry wraps his arm around my shoulders and pulls me forward, our steps mismatched because of whatever is going on with his right leg. I look down at it and then meet his eyes.

"It's okay. You can fix it when we stop," he whispers.

We walk for what seems like forever. On and on through this bizarre underground network. I'd never be able to find our way out.

And then Xavier stops at an iron gate blocking our way. He unlocks it with his thumbprint, inviting us through and clicking it closed behind us. He then drops his own pack and unzips it, pulling out three small metal canteens. "Drink," he says, taking a long pull himself. "This tunnel joins with *les Catacombes*. Stay very close. Cataphiles—people who trek the tunnels illegally—lurk about, and we are strangers. Talk to no one. Just follow me. We will emerge and proceed to our next safe house. Hats on."

Henry and I unharness our backpacks and retrieve our knitted hats from earlier. Packs back on, and Xavier again picks up the pace. At once, the quality of the tunnel degrades; these stones are old, many covered in tags and graffiti; the ceiling is lower, the smell ancient and musty but mixed with the harsh tang of smoked substances other than cigarettes.

Fear flutters in my chest, sparking through me. I tuck my canteen in my jacket pocket and release Henry's hand, flexing my fingers into fists, afraid I'll burn through these gloves.

We reach what looks like a dead end, until Xavier braces himself against the wall and, using his legs, pushes a huge round stone out of the way. "Crawl through," he says, gesturing with the flashlight. All I can think about is what might be on the other side, and what creepy crawlies are waiting to get lost under the collar of my jacket.

"Genevieve, you first," Xavier says, flooding the hole with light. The look on his face leaves little room to say no.

"Henry's hurt—I don't know if he can crawl through."

"Right behind you, Gen."

I drop to my knees, the ground littered with broken stone and dust and cigarette butts, trying not to panic about the tightness of the space or the cobwebs that brush my face as I crawl through. The hole barely fits me and the backpack, but ahead is the hint of daylight. I shimmy faster.

There's no way Baby would've fit through here.

I climb out the opposite end, and down the way, daylight slices between the seams of two closed doors. I want to run ahead and burst through into the fresh air.

Henry drags his injured leg behind him through the pipe. I offer him a hand as he reaches the end; he grimaces and pushes to standing, his face red and sweaty. Xavier comes quick behind, the light from his torch bouncing off the walls with every move forward.

Then the hole births him, and he's off toward the doors, which I'm alarmed to see are bolted closed with chain and a padlock. However, the padlock has another biometric reader, and with the press of Xavier's thumb, it unlatches, releasing its hold on the impossibly thick chain.

"A black cargo van waits for us down the block. Eyes forward and follow me. Do not stop for any reason."

With a heavy-shouldered shove, the door opens. Xavier is out first, pausing long enough to re-bolt the door. He takes off again, us close behind. We've exited in another area busy with life. We blend right in—or at least we would if Henry's right leg and his army-issue coat weren't soaked in blood.

Just as promised, a boxy black cargo van sits idling at the curb. As we approach, the side door opens and Xavier practically launches me into the dark interior, though he's gentler with Henry. Xavier hops in behind and before the door is even latched, the van takes off.

No rear windows, and the only cabin illumination is from dim, yellowish light strips attached to the ceiling. It smells like dust, mixed with body odor and tobacco smoke. Under us, the floor is textured black rubber, but the only proper seats are the front two, and a wall of thick plexiglass separates the driver and passenger compartments; a two-by-two-square panel slides open to allow conversation between forward and rear. Xavier speaks quickly to the driver in a language other than French.

"Xavier, what is happening? *Who is chasing us*? I thought you said it was a safe house! Was that Lucian? *Please*!" Panic prickles my nerve endings and squeezes my throat.

But Xavier ignores me, carrying on his hurried conversation with the driver, his ice-blue eyes wide and olive skin flushed, as we maneuver through Paris traffic. He even pulls out his weapon and double-checks the magazine.

Henry.

I yank my pack free and dig inside for the hemostatic gauze I never thought I'd have to use. I hook my ankle through a looped nylon cargo strap anchored to the floor to keep from falling over every time we turn a corner.

"Genevieve . . . ," Henry whispers. I slide closer to him propped against the van's side, the sickly look on his face something I've seen too often lately. This boy may not survive our journey if terrible things keep happening to him.

"Let me see your leg. I need to fix you." I swallow hard. "Whose blood is on your coat, Henry?"

Without a word, he takes off his glove and nods toward my hand.

He's going to show me what happened.

"Please . . . don't electrocute me," he asks.

Reluctantly, I remove my own glove, squeeze my hand into a fist for a count of five, and then slide my palm across his, hoping the current will stay under control. *Breathe, like Nutesh showed you.*

Though I know something horrific is coming, the initial flush of warmth sends a calming shiver through me and puts a slight smile on my face.

The smile dies quickly.

We're in the room, Henry watching me as I watch Xavier and Thierry. This memory drips with tension. Henry is scared. And he's worried, about me. My queries to Xavier go unanswered and then both men, startled, grab at their phones. Their faces change. The cigarette is abandoned. Hand signals, wide eyes. More fear.

And then the moment when I see the spiders—no one else can see them. It's bizarre to watch me freaking out when nothing is there. I scream; Henry clamps his hand over my mouth, his face close to my ear as he whispers assurances. He's frightened, but he's begging me to come back to him. He cannot see the Etemmu; he cannot see what I know was there at that very moment, its acidic touch burning my skin, the whispering in my head. He can't see any of it.

I scream louder. Xavier scrambles toward us and does something against the back of my neck, and I go limp onto Henry. "Get her out of here!" he hisses. Henry, his pack still on, grabs under my shoulders; Thierry runs over and picks up my legs to help drag me out of the room—as he stands, the first bullet blasts through the shutters and shatters the window and hits him in the back of the head, blood spraying as if from a misdirected garden hose. Its warmth on Henry's face brings a swell of panic; he struggles to hang on to my weight.

Thierry drops like a stone.

A second shot—this one hits Henry. Just above the right knee.

Jesus, that burns.

He sucks in through his teeth and grabs at his leg, dropping me against the floor, though my landing is awkward because of my enormous backpack strapped to my body. Xavier pulls a firearm and shoots back; a shadow falls over the room and there are feet on the roof. Heavy, plodding. They're coming for us. I can feel Henry's heart pounding in my own chest as he hoists me under the arms again and drags me into the long hallway.

*Xavier shoots at the windows—*bang bang bang bang*—and then he rejoins Henry where he opens a hatch in the floor. We drop two floors' distance onto a pile of mattresses; Henry's leg is absolutely on fire. Xavier pulls a lever that seals the hatch above us;*

he then rushes to the end of a dank, dark basement and opens yet another door, this one camouflaged by cluttered shelves of various tools and garden implements. He races back to throw me over his shoulder, gestures for Henry to run ahead, and we're moving.

Xavier pauses only to slide closed the door behind us, struggling to balance the weight of me and both of our packs. Henry skip-hops down a long wooden corridor lit only by the occasional yellow-caged work lamps strung between draped cords, the kind we use in the big top when we're setting up. A plump rat runs ahead of us. Henry's leg is leaving a blood trail like Hansel and Gretel's crumbs in the woods. Xavier sets me down on the floor against the plywood wall and inspects Henry's leg through his pants. Henry winces and bites down so he doesn't yell—I can feel the jolt of searing pain as Xavier's finger finds the wound.

"Lucky. It's through and through. You wouldn't be walking if the bone had been hit. Can you make it?" Henry nods. He's never been so afraid in his whole life.

Xavier extracts a length of cloth from his pack and ties it around Henry's leg. He pats him hard on the face, and then scoops me off the floor, throwing me over his shoulder again. We race down the corridor until the wood becomes concrete. Every step is fire.

Henry pulls his hand from mine, the flush gone, reality flooding back in. "And then you woke up," he says. He sniffs against his own emotion.

"Thierry . . . I'm so sorry," I whisper. No one was supposed to die. This isn't how it was supposed to go. I'm at once consumed by sadness and rage and guilt. If I'd just shut my mouth—if I could just figure out how to deal with this demon—Thierry would still be alive. If I hadn't screamed; if Baby were here, the Etemmu couldn't touch me; if Aveline were dead . . .

If these fucking books had never been created.

I stuff the heels of my hands against my eyes. I'm so angry—but Henry is still bleeding. He needs me.

I sniff hard and wipe my face. I cannot melt down right now. "I need to see your leg."

"Don't cut his pants. We'll have to wash those and mend the hole," Xavier says.

"Thierry's dead, Henry's been shot, and you're worried about some stupid pants?" I say as I help Henry out of his pack.

"Thierry is dead because you screamed. That should give you something to think about. Your *actions* have repercussions," he says.

"You have no idea what I'm dealing with."

"Do you have more to say?" Xavier asks.

I turn toward him. "*You* have *no idea* what I'm fighting against because *you can't see it.* The demon that killed my mother? It's after me now. It's Aveline and Lucian running the demon show. Baby is my only defense against it. *And he's not here because they are torturing him to death.*"

Henry rests his hand on my shoulder, but it does little to calm the shudders and tears. So much for not melting down.

"This whole situation is not our fault. And I don't care that you're my long-lost daddy. Any illusions that you give a shit about me were destroyed within the first minute of meeting you," I say, wiping my snotty nose against the arm of my coat, "but you will honor my mother by keeping me, and Henry, safe. You will tell us what is going on. And you will know that I am fighting as hard as I can against a demon whose master wants to kill us. You said it yourself—we have a singular mission—so maybe start acting like it."

There is flame in Xavier's eyes as I holler at him, but also the hint of understanding, especially when I mention my mother and the Etemmu.

"Nutesh told me the Etemmu had found you," he says as he looks right through me. And then he snaps back to focus and nods at Henry. "Do what you need to do to fix his leg. And settle in. It's going to be a long night."

14

The wound on Henry's leg is meaty, but Xavier was right—the bullet went right through, impacting just above the kneecap, narrowly missing his femur. I'm able to keep my current under control long enough to access the nuclear reactor in the back of my head, the star I pull from that allows me to heal. I feel Xavier's eyes on me while I put my hands on Henry's wounds.

When I'm done, Henry exhales what sounds like relief, leans forward, and with his hand on the back of my neck, he pulls me in for a kiss.

"Thank you. Again. You are truly magical."

"Feels better?" I'm shaky and light-headed, and no juice to be had.

"Like new. That is the most incredible trick." He digs into the front of his pack and finds an energy bar, and then kisses me again lightly.

I take a bite of the foul bar. "You need pants," I say, looking at his now-healed leg. "You're hairier than I expected."

Henry's quick laugh is a pleasant diversion from the tension in the van. "Well, according to one of my new passports, I am French." He pulls his other pair of pants from his pack and shimmies into them.

"But are you? What are we, really? And are Frenchmen hairy?" I ask.

"I've not seen a lot of naked Frenchmen, thankfully."

"And technically, you're not French."

"Not even on my mother's side?"

"Where was Alicia born? We don't even know how old she is," I say. "Even if she was born in France, she's Mesopotamian, from both of her parents. So are we."

Henry looks over my shoulder at Xavier resting awkwardly against the plexiglass wall, his eyes shut. "Where is he from?"

I lower my voice. "Somewhere mean." Henry smirks.

I rearrange the packs so we can use them as pillows against the van wall, and then stretch out facing Henry, my back to Xavier. Healing makes me so tired, even more so because I don't have a fast-acting sugar source to replenish the energy lost and this bar is almost too gross to choke down. I'll need to find some juice boxes or soda.

Henry slides off his wool cap, and then reaches over and pulls mine off too, the back of his fingers lingering against my face, his thumb stroking my cheekbone.

My eyes burn with tears. "Thierry . . ."

Henry scoots closer and pulls me into his chest. He's not wearing the coat that holds the last moments of Thierry's life in its fibers, yet the smell of blood lingers.

I don't want to get used to the smell of blood. Something tells me I will.

Henry rubs my back, his lips pressed softly against my forehead as he whispers quiet words of condolence and strength and promises that we will be okay and Baby will be okay and we will finish this together . . .

I need to find a way to keep the Etemmu from destroying me before our mission is ended.

Before I kill anyone else.

We've stopped—it's dark, and we're on the side of the road. The van jostles as other cars fly past.

"We are nearing the Barcelona border. Need to gas up. Sit tight." Another truck has pulled close to us. We're gassing up with a mobile tank? Makes sense—keeps us off surveillance cameras at gas stations.

Once the gas truck has finished, the side door opens and Xavier scoots a cooler toward us. A new face climbs in behind the wheel, a dark-haired woman. Her long brown braid drapes over her shoulder, her eyes big and round and the color of soil, skin smooth except for the few crinkles around her eyes. Her black ensemble makes her teeth look very white in the dim round overhead cabin light.

"This is Charlene. She is with *Circ de l'Anell d'Or*. She will take us into the city. Charlene, these are my latest orphans."

I flinch at being called an orphan again.

"Bonjour, orphans. Do you have names?" She smiles. She can't be older than thirty.

I stare at Xavier—we didn't discuss this. And I didn't think to memorize whatever name my fake passport has on it. Are we supposed to give our real names? How much does she know?

Without missing a beat, Henry speaks. "I'm Jack, and this is Diana." His British accent has melted away. He sounds more American than I do.

Henry saves the day.

"Well, orphans Diana and Jack, I hope you know what kind of trouble this one causes." Charlene hikes her thumb toward Xavier.

"I am innocent of all charges," Xavier says, his hand over his heart. It's weird to hear him be nice.

He then points to the cooler, his gruff tone back in place. "Food in there. When we arrive, it's straight to work."

Charlene starts the van.

With one last look at us, Xavier turns in his seat to face front.

This is all so confusing.

Henry and I dig into the cooler, glad to find sandwiches and more canteens. I consider offering food to Xavier, but he doesn't ever look back toward us, so whatever. He can figure out his own meal.

"I wish this van had windows so we could at least see Spain," I say quietly. Henry nods as we dig in.

His last bite finished, Henry leans over to whisper in my ear. "Alicia wants me to show you something."

"She's here? Right now?" Man, I really miss being able to see her.

"I woke up with a new memory. It might provide . . . context."

I pointedly bounce my head toward Xavier and Charlene to ask *what about them?*

"Pretend you're asleep. I can show you. It might help you understand your fa—, I mean Xavier, a little better."

"Do I really want to?"

Henry hikes his sliced eyebrow. "We're going to be spending a lot of time with him for the foreseeable future. It would be . . . less tense, if you guys didn't hate each other."

"Fine." I crumple my food wrapper and stuff it back in the cooler. "Also—Diana? Where is that from?"

Henry is so close to my ear, it tickles when he speaks. "Princess Diana of Themyscira, aka, Diana Prince, aka, Wonder Woman. I, Jack Kirby, one of the fathers of the modern comic arts."

I smile. "I should've known."

"Sit back. Close your eyes. This won't hurt a bit," he says. I kiss his cheek, trusting that whatever he's going to show me isn't going to send me screaming and clawing to escape the confines of this lightless, four-wheeled box.

Delia dismounts and ties up a huge brown horse she's eased along a waist-height stone wall. Heavy tree branches hang low overhead, their leaves dripping and the heady smell of recent rain underfoot.

Her long red braid ropes down her back. The horse whinnies behind her; she offers a green apple from her pocket and rubs the white patch on his forehead, her hands soiled, nails dirty and broken. Torn foliage has snagged on the lengths of the weighty cloak over her shoulders. Underneath, she's again in pants and boots, like at the marketplace where Udish died, only this time, there's no elaborate half dress. These are clothes for movement.

A leather messenger-style bag hangs crosswise over her front. It's the same bag from Udish—the saddlebag that was empty that terrible day in the field.

"It is yours now, my Delia. You . . . must find it. I will . . . come back to you," *he'd said.*

She rushes the wooden front door of a small stone cabin, trees and overgrowth dense around the outside, only a scant light from a square window along the cabin's front. She enters.

A fire crackles in a modest stone hearth as Delia moves to pull a carpetbag from a rustic wooden wardrobe. As she kneels, the messenger bag thumps onto her thighs. It looks heavy—it's not empty anymore.

"What have you done?" A man's voice behind her. She stands and faces him, the firelight highlighting the fierceness of ice-blue eyes.

Xavier.

"What have you done? He will find us, and he will kill us."

"Not us. I'm going. I will go and you will no longer be in danger."

"I told you we were safe. He knows nothing of us, of you and me. Of the child. I made a promise, Delia, an oath of fealty—I cannot so easily go back on it."

"You made an oath to the devil." Delia's hand moves to her belt, to a pearl-handled knife—the one Aveline used to stab Henry back in Washington.

Delia pulls it from its sheath. "I'm leaving. I've taken what is mine, nothing else."

Xavier's black curls, coiled loosely against his head, bounce as he slides to the left and pulls a curtain aside, seemingly unfettered by the knife gleaming in Delia's hand. "You have signed her death warrant," he says, his voice low. On a bed, behind the curtain, lies a very young girl, her long black hair mussed with sleep, her tiny body wrapped in rough blankets. She stirs and when her face emerges from the covers, she's the spitting image of her father.

Despite her youth, I'd know Aveline's face anywhere.

"Keep her safe. He won't come for you," Delia says. "It's me he wants, and I cannot wait any longer."

Xavier drops the curtain and makes a move toward Delia, his own hand on the hilt of a blade at his waist.

"Forgive me," she says before he can draw his knife, and then she's out of the cabin, astride the horse, racing through the darkness of an endless forest.

Henry releases my hand, and even though I know I'm safe, it always takes a moment to reorient.

I've seen the end of this scene—Delia on horseback—painted on one of the murals in Lucian's study where his *AVRAKEDAVRA* slept in its glass case.

"From Delia to Alicia to me to you," Henry says, patting

the beads of sweat off my forehead with his paper napkin. "She thought you should know what happened before . . ." He hands me a canteen; I finish it off, looking through the plexiglass at Xavier. Delia broke his heart—she left them, both of them—and then somewhere along the line, they were all captured and Xavier tortured, most definitely worried about the fate of his young daughter who would be lost to him forever.

Aveline Darrow, my sister, has her own ax to grind, but now it's clear that Xavier's is even bigger.

"That vision just complicates everything," I say. "How could Xavier ever forgive Delia enough to conceive another child, and hundreds of years later?"

As if he heard my whisper, Xavier looks at me. Our eyes lock for a beat, and I swear to god he's heard my question. My recent meal turns over in my stomach.

Henry slides his gloves on again and nudges me against his side. "Get some rest. We'll figure it out."

"How?" I ask.

He doesn't respond.

15

When Xavier announces we're entering Barcelona, I scoot across the floor toward the open square in the plex wall, stretching to see what I can through the windshield and front-door windows. Even though it's still dark, the freeway and area bordering looks very much like California—low-rise hills covered in brush and deciduous trees. Traffic has picked up, and though there's still a lot of greenery, the area is dense with office and apartment buildings and semitrucks and power lines and homes and graffiti and life.

And then the city explodes before us. We enter a labyrinth of streets, block after block of balconied apartment buildings and huge glass storefronts and cars and a dedicated bike lane and more mopeds and motorcycles than I have ever seen parked in narrow spots along the wide sidewalks. So many palm trees and what might be eucalyptus and date trees line the streets in front of the buildings.

The sun is coming up over the incredible architecture—places I've only ever seen in pictures on the internet—painting the partly clouded sky in shades of blue and pink and orange. Streetlights flicker off, but apartment buildings still sparkle with their interior lights.

Xavier turns to look at me through the square. "We will be going to the apartments across from the venue at the Port Vell Marina where the circus is. When we stop, we will proceed directly into the building where we can prepare for the day."

A marina—we're going to be near the water. I hope we get a moment to feel the Mediterranean sand in our toes.

Charlene exits a huge roundabout and pulls into a rear lot behind a tall, light-blue concrete building. She puts the van in park, and then she and Xavier exchange polite kisses on each other's cheeks. "See you soon, orphans," she says, pushing a button on the dash that opens the van's sliding door.

Xavier hops out, throws his pack over his shoulder, and gestures us onward. The van drives away as we follow Xavier toward the building. He enters a security code, and then we're inside, to the stairwell, and up four flights. The carpet runner in the hall we land in looks like it's seen better days; every other apartment door leaks a new smell, a different blast from music or a TV up too loud. And it's barely seven in the morning. I can't imagine how loud this place is going to be when everyone's awake.

Xavier stops at the last apartment on the right and unlocks the scuffed black metal door. After ushering us in, he sticks his head out and looks up and then down the hallway before locking three dead bolts. He clicks on a pendant lamp over a short bar that separates a small kitchen from the living room. The main seating area hosts a well-worn plaid couch with two mismatched chairs, a lopsided bookshelf with a bunch of paperbacks shoved into it, windows covered in tired blue drapes, and a coffee table with initials carved into its top. The dingy white-tile floor needs a good scrubbing.

But pulling back the drapes, it's the view that sells this place. Overlooking a marina, and what I assume is our venue, judging by the festive circus colors of the pointed tent roof and the spire flags flapping above long, ornate locked gates. Beyond is a hint of the glistening Mediterranean stretching toward the horizon.

A circus *and* an ocean? How long can we stay?

"Bedrooms down the hall—take the one with two beds." Xavier nods toward a short hallway. He drops his pack and pulls his cell from the thigh pocket of his cargo pants. He then proceeds to crack a window so he can smoke.

"How long will we be staying here?" I ask.

"I don't know yet," Xavier says. "Put your packs down and have a seat." He points at the rickety wooden dining table that looks older than Delia.

Once Xavier has finished his cigarette, he digs into his pack and pulls out a mesh-covered cylinder that looks like a speaker. He turns it on, but no music comes out. Another sound-masking device?

"Charlene is *La Vérité* but she does not know who you are or what you're truly doing here. No one does. Let's keep it that way," Xavier says. "I have made contact with the first Guardian. I am working out the details of our meeting. Once we collect the item we need, we're off to our next stop."

"How long? Until we meet the Guardian?" I ask.

"I will tell you when I have an answer," he says, spinning his silver lighter on the tabletop. "In the meantime, you will be working."

"In what capacity?" Henry asks.

"In whatever capacity Charlene says."

"What about our packs?" I ask. "We can't wear them while we're working. That would look too obvious."

Xavier lights another cigarette and blows the smoke toward a yellowed ceiling. "It is not ideal, but I have a secure trunk in the room where you will be sleeping. Opens to my thumbprint only. Would I prefer you have the items on you at all times? Of course. But that is not practical, or smart. Now, please get ready to work. I have to make a phone call."

Xavier stands and rummages through his pack once again, this time pulling out a satellite phone.

"If that's Croix-Mare, please ask about Baby."

Xavier nods and turns away to dial. Henry wraps an arm around my shoulders and kisses the side of my head as he directs me down the hall. In the room with two lumpy twin beds covered in rough wool blankets, there are dark-green, long-sleeved shirts with the *Circ*'s logo, one for each of us folded on the pillows. We also find Xavier's secure trunk, pull what we need from our packs, and stash them within. We turn away from one another long enough to change our shirts.

"We've not even been gone two days, and already someone has died," I say.

The bed squeaks as Henry sits. "Thierry was doing his job, Gen. He was a good and brave man who served the people and the cause he loved."

The words sound pretty, but they do nothing to relieve the guilt and grief.

"I don't know what I'm going to do if the Etemmu keeps finding me. I don't know what they think it'll achieve to keep torturing me like this."

"Same thing they've always done. Same thing they did to your mother," Henry says, his voice barely above a whisper. "They want to break you down."

"I can't be responsible for more people dying. I can't stop worrying about it getting to *you*."

"Don't find things to worry about, Genevieve. I can't see it—whatever magic is keeping it from me is clearly still in place—but if it happens, we'll fight it. Together."

He clasps my hand in his and kisses the back of my fingers.

Xavier whistles from down the hall.

"That's our cue," I say, a deep breath in to prepare for whatever is coming once we step foot outside this crappy apartment.

"Let's go make friends and influence people," Henry teases, standing and then pulling me to my feet.

"Let's concentrate on staying alive until bedtime."

Henry offers his gloved fist for a bump. "Solid plan."

16

Circ de l'Anell d'Oro is adorable.

The flat-faced entry tent is separated from the wide concrete-brick walkway by a short picket fence and held steady by thick gray guy-wires anchored to the ground. Its canvas is in deep shades of red, purple, yellow, and green, the circus's name huge, painted in gold across the façade. The eggshell-colored awning flags wave good morning in the early breeze. Converted, old-time train cars stretch out three to each side of the main entry, light strings in red, green, and purple hanging from their curved black tar paper roofs. Tall palm trees provide shade, chilly right now but it probably feels awesome when the sun is on full blast. A low, decorative retaining wall mosaicked in rainbow-colored tile provides an inviting entry into a public space that will likely be full of tourists in a few hours.

As we walk through the front gate, people dressed in forest-green shirts with the *Circ de l'Anell d'Oro* logo turn to look at us, almost all waving at Xavier. The main entry opens into a wide tented space with wooden support pillars and dark-red carpet underfoot. More converted train cars, three to each side, offer everything from stuffed animals to boxed meals. Xavier doesn't stop or slow to let us take it all in—I wish I had Baby's phone with me so I could sneak photos for Vi and Ash.

Xavier takes us into the main performance tent. It's an intimate tension-frame tent with gallery-in-the-round seating, again with the string lights extending from the cupola and fanning out over the audience. The single dirt-floor ring is big enough to accommodate a decent number of performers, but my Gertrude would never fit.

God, I miss them so much.

I elbow Henry just before he steps into the ring. "Remember—right foot first. For luck," I remind him.

We follow Xavier toward the rear of the ring, bordered by a detailed wooden set piece that holds the weighted curtains separating performance area from backstage. Xavier holds the curtain aside, and we walk through—I'm surprised at how much space there is to move around back here! Way more than what we had in our two-ring tent, before the three-ring behemoth that Triad Partners brought in.

The circus is shutting down. Everything is falling apart, Vi said in her text. How can I ever fix this?

Xavier turns quickly and looks back and forth between us. "Talk as little as possible."

"*Buenos dias*!" Charlene says, standing with a man probably around Ted's age who looks like he's never heard of sunscreen. But when he smiles, it's wide and friendly. "Excellent. You found your shirts. Diana, you will be with me today"—I'm confused for a beat before remembering I have a new name—"We will be cleaning out the costume trailer because it's a mess. Jack, you're going to be with Damon to work with the grounds crew. We're close to the ocean, and the city, so there's always bird poop to be scrubbed and floors to be swept. Come!"

I turn to Xavier. "Where will you be?"

"I'm always near." And then he's off.

I follow Charlene out into a partial-grass courtyard bordered by more converted train cars. The one marked *VESTUARIO*—inside, I'm not surprised to find it just as messy as she promised. I've cleaned out the costume department at Cinzio many times. Today it's a lot of cleaning out stuff crammed into overhead compartments, sweeping out cobwebs (and hoping they're empty), washing handprints and lipstick marks from counters and cupboard fronts, and organizing costumes. This show employs a lot of acrobats and contortionists, judging by the outfits.

Charlene is not chatty. She's not unfriendly, but she gives me a job and I set to it, hearing Xavier's words in my head to say as little as possible. And working gives me some quiet time where my hands and joints don't burn with electricity, where I can *almost* forget why we're here.

But it also gives me time to think about Thierry, and his family, if he has one, and the loss to Nutesh and Hélène. Because of me. Because of the Etemmu.

And what about Baby? Xavier didn't say anything about him after his call. Does this mean the news is bad?

Once we're done in the costume trailer, we break for

paella and tapas in the courtyard area. Henry and I inhale our food—seriously, some of the best I've ever eaten—but the thing that might make me move to Spain forever: churros dipped in chocolate.

And then we're back at work, repeating the cleaning spree in the makeup department, washing more mirrors and purging drawers, more hands-and-knees scrubbing of the old vinyl floor, more organizing of grease paints and makeup. They use a lot of feathers and glue-on sequins here . . . Delia would've fit right in.

I'm cleaning underneath one of the makeup counters when I hear the commotion outside. I wait for a second, my heart pounding as the voices get closer, and louder. Setting my scrub brush aside, I look out the window just as two men plus Henry carry an obviously injured fourth man into the courtyard, lying him gingerly on top of one of the picnic-style tables. Within a few seconds, blood dribbles onto the white tablecloth that hosted our lunch just a few hours ago.

I run down the three trailer steps, alongside a dozen other people responding to the hollers in Spanish.

"*¡Necesitamos ayuda*! *¡Ayúdanos!* Help!"

Charlene flies out an adjoining trailer, her face a mix of panic and confusion. Henry stands off to the side, eyes wide. All of the men have blood on their boots.

"What happened?" Charlene yells. One of the men, covered in muscles and tattoos and a black beard that reaches his sternum, rattles off whatever has befallen the young man in the *Circ* uniform now motionless and bleeding on the table.

I can help him.

I yank off my cleaning gloves, just as the whiff of burned rubber fills my nose, and step over to the unconscious man. Hands on his head, I feel that the back of his skull has caved in; there's a central hole about an inch and a half across, like he fell from higher up and landed on something pointed—a rock? A guy-wire bolt? I don't feel brain matter yet—a lot of blood making his hair sticky—but two fingers to his throat show he still has a pulse.

I can save him.

"Diana, get back!" Charlene tries to push me aside. I yank away without making eye contact.

"I can help him!" I say, my eyes on the man's as-yet-pink face, the star in my head charging as I get ready to lay my hands against his broken skull.

And then Xavier grips my shoulder and whispers gruffly, close to my ear. "Whatever you're thinking, stop. Step away."

I whirl on him. "And just let him die?" I know it's a risk, but I can't walk away. Not when I can help.

He tries to pull me back, but my bloodstained hands are charged like resuscitation paddles. Henry must see what's about to happen because he rushes over just as I grab Xavier's bare wrist and deliver a jolt that puts him on his knees, teeth gritted.

"Stop!" Henry shouts, grabbing my upper arm so my grip releases. Xavier falls forward onto his hands, gasping. I'll deal with him after I save this man's life.

Charlene barks commands in Spanish, and the bearded guy has another employee's shirt pushed against the back of the injured man's head to try and control the bleeding.

"Please," I say to Charlene, my eyes boring into hers. "I can save him, I swear."

And without waiting for her response, I step next to the table again, slide my hands under his head to cradle it in my palms, and close my eyes, shutting out the yells and questions coming from the people circled around the courtyard.

The sear of white-hot healing energy shoots out of the star in my head, racing down my arms and through my fingers, clenching my jaw with migraine-level pain. It feels stronger than ever before—is this the marriage of the healing ability with the new electricity? I really am a sideshow freak now.

I envision stitching the fragments back together, the skull bone growing to cover the hole, the brain calming itself so it doesn't swell from the trauma, the skin smoothing over, the pain leaving this man's body and melting into the tabletop like a forgotten snow cone.

The longer I go, the weaker I get, but I can feel the hole shrinking; I can *feel* this man's pulse strengthening through the contact between us. When the stink of burned hair wafts upward, I know it's time to stop.

I open my eyes, and the man lying on the table stares back up at me, blinking and confused—but alive.

And then I notice how painfully quiet it has become. A lot of stunned faces looking at me, mouths agape, just as my knees buckle and I stagger to the ground.

Henry is there is an instant, and he shoves a lemon-lime soda into my hand. "Drink," he says, popping the top and holding it against my lips. "Drink."

I swallow a few gulps, grateful as the sugar works through my system and the twinkly lights in my peripheral vision retreat.

"Deep breaths . . . keep drinking," Henry says. "Nice work. You saved him."

I smile, eyes still focused on my feet stretched out in front of me as I wait for the spinny feeling to stop.

But then Xavier is there, and he hoists me to my feet. "That was a very dangerous thing you just did."

I find the strength to pull out of his grip. "I couldn't just let him die." What I don't say: *Too many people are dying around me and I can't do anything to save them. This one, I could.*

I turn to look at the young man, now sitting up on the picnic table rubbing the back of his head, wiping blood from his face and neck onto the shirt the bearded man was using just a few moments ago. A low murmur sweeps through the crowd, but everyone is looking at me.

Charlene steps close, her hands out in front of her, but she stops before making contact. "I should've known. You have your mother's eyes," she says.

She pivots on her heel, and as she does, almost everyone gathered digs under their shirts and pulls out a key hanging from a chain. They all drop to one knee, their heads bowed.

"Welcome to *La Vérité,* Genevieve," Charlene says.

17

Xavier's grip on my arm is painful as he drags me back across the wide busy street toward our apartment building. Henry is behind us, struggling to keep up.

"Let go of me," I growl.

"Not a chance," he says. "And don't even think about zapping me again. Keep those damn gloves on."

Xavier practically chases us up the four flights of stairs—I guess there's no such thing as an elevator here?—and down the hall to the apartment. Once we're inside, he dead-bolts the door and turns the sound mask on again.

"What the *hell* were you thinking? Do you realize what you've done?"

"I saved a man's life. The ambulance wouldn't have arrived in time, he would've bled out there on that table, or worse, his brain would've swollen through the hole and he'd end up with a permanent brain injury and be useless to his family."

Xavier lights a cigarette, pacing between me near the

kitchen bar and the shoddy plaid couch, and slams his silver lighter onto the counter.

"Wonderful! You're a hero! Bravo!"

The fire in my chest flares; I clench and unclench my fists.

"I swear to Hades, if you even think about touching me with those hands again, I will cut them off," he says, rubbing his wrist. It's red—I burned him.

Good.

"Can we just calm down here for a moment? Take a breath to figure out what has happened?" Henry says.

"What has *happened* is she just outed you. Everyone now knows that *Diana* is not Diana at all—a lot of these people knew your mother, or at least they knew *of* her."

"Why is that a bad thing? You saw them—they all dropped to one knee. They were all wearing the keys," I say, pulling my own *vérité* key out from under my shirt.

"It's terrific you're ready to hold hands and sing songs, but the reality is, we don't always know who is on Team Genevieve. The people without *La Vérité* membership—the *Circ* people who have no idea what is going on, other than the fact that they just witnessed a miracle—don't you think those people are tweeting their little hearts out right now? It's only going to take *one* photograph or video of you standing there with that man who should've met his god today. 'Young circus worker miraculously heals coworker with her bare hands.'" He bites out his fake headline. "Did you miss the part about international law enforcement looking for you both? Or about Lucian having allies *all over the world* who would love to get in his good favor by bringing back your heads alongside two of the most precious artifacts ever created in human history? You just made Lucian's job so much easier!"

Xavier grinds out his half-smoked cigarette, and before I can respond, he picks up the glass ashtray and hurls it against the wall, sending shards and ash and cigarette butts everywhere.

He exhales loudly, and then starts laughing. "You're so naive—you think that we're safe here? You think that 'hiding in plain sight' is going to make you invisible? We know Lucian is in Europe. Who do you think was on the safe-house roof yesterday?"

"Wait—what?" I swallow hard. Of course it was Lucian. Who else would it have been?

"Yes, Genevieve. Those were his men. The chatter was put out there to give away our location so that we could get a bead on how close his operation was. It took less than two hours for them to find us."

"You used us as bait?" Henry says.

"Why wouldn't you give us that information?" I yell.

"We needed to know how organized his team is. Seems very. Which means we have to get the hell out of here, considering your faces are probably circling the internet right now."

"Thierry died in that house. *You killed him by setting us up*," I hiss back.

"Thierry knew the risks. He knew the trap had been set. It was just bad luck." Xavier pulls his hands down his face, his scruff like sandpaper. "Get your packs. We're leaving," he growls.

"Where—"

"Not one more fucking question out of your face. You've done enough damage for a lifetime."

Henry slides a hand under my elbow, ever the calming force. "Come on," he says. I follow him down the hall. We take turns in the bathroom—my hands are sticky from that young man's blood. I put my gloves back on right after I healed him; they're stiff, so I wash them too.

When I return to the bedroom, Xavier has been in to unlock the trunk; Henry sits with his pack already on, his head covered in the wool cap despite the warm air, his forest-green *Circ* shirt folded at the end of his bed.

Xavier pokes his head into the room again. "Let's go."

We follow him down to the car park on the first level. The black cargo van from earlier is nowhere to be found. Instead he walks briskly to a well-loved, green-and-white Volkswagen camper van with a magnetic sign on its side advertising what I think might be a coffee shop. Xavier looks around cautiously, and then peels off the sign, not without difficulty. He then tosses it inside, followed by his own pack and another long black bag heavy enough that the van jostles when it lands inside.

"Get in. Packs on the floor next to you. Pull those side curtains closed and stay down."

Then he hot-wires the car. So much for staying above the law.

Once we're in, Henry offers a small smile. "Hope there's no high-speed chase or we're in trouble."

I want to smile back, but I can't.

Xavier says nothing as he winds through Barcelona traffic. He drives and drives, and when the roads sound less congested, and become nauseatingly curvy, I dare to ask where we're going.

"To the rendezvous point. We will camp until the Guardian makes herself available."

The scene at *Circ* plays itself on a loop, Xavier's scolding still fresh in my ears. But I couldn't let that man die. Not when it was *so* easy for me to reach out and fix him. He gets to go home tonight to whatever family he has—they will be hugging him and asking about his day, not planning a funeral.

As angry as Xavier is, I'm glad I did it. I would do it again.

If I'm honest—in a conversation I keep locked in my head—I don't want to let go of that part of myself. I've always been able to fix the people around me. Montague when he tangled with the lion, Violet and Ash when they'd sprain or break something during workouts (as long as their mother didn't know), Baby or my mom whenever something sickened or broke them, even my animals. I love that part of being from this line of wild, magical people. I love helping others, fixing them without outside intervention. It's one of the million reasons I want to become a vet.

But if we destroy the books, I'll lose those abilities to heal with a single touch. What kind of person will I be without my healing hands? How will I find my place in the world that comes after?

I have to be rid of the Etemmu, and I don't want Delia's life—to be on the run forever—but it has occurred to me that

Henry and I could do a lot of good with our gifts, especially with long lives. I could help so many people. . . .

Am I being selfish in wanting to destroy the *AVRAKEDAVRA*? Am I dishonoring my mother's legacy, and the lives of my other extended magical family, if I undo what they've been fighting to protect for millennia?

"You okay?" Henry asks.

"Yeah. Just thinking."

"I always get myself into trouble when I do that." He repositions against the long bench seat at the rear of the narrow van. Henry peels off his gloves, wincing a bit as he does. His palms are blistered, and one has torn open, angry and oozing clear fluid.

"That's from one day?"

He smiles sheepishly. "Some of us aren't as tough as you."

Xavier slows at a stoplight. He's looking at us in the rearview mirror. "Don't heal his hands. He needs to build calluses. No one's going to believe that he's a laborer with soft hands like those, and we still have two cities to survive before we head east."

And by east, he means Iraq. Babylon. The birthplace of the *AVRAKEDAVRA*.

I can't believe this is all happening.

The van moves again, and I anchor myself between the side wall and the dilapidated built-in cupboards. I pull out the medical kit—again. "I can at least clean them and apply ointment so you don't get infected," I say. Henry nods.

"He's right, though. I need to toughen up."

"It's all the years of wearing gloves," I say. "To protect yourself."

Henry nods. "We do what we have to do, I suppose."

Judging by the fact that we're on the run—again—a truer statement has never been uttered.

18

"Saddle up," Xavier says. "We're hiking."

We've stopped down a narrow dirt road in a forest, and the van has been squeezed in among a copse of pine trees whose branches scratch and grab at us as we exit. Xavier pulls an army-green canvas tarp out from his extra bag.

"Some help, please," he says. Henry and I pull the tarp over the van so its white top doesn't stand out in all this greenery.

Then Xavier turns and heads into the bush, telling us nothing, referring only to a digital compass he pulls out of his pocket every so often. We walk until dark, and even for a while after that, climbing deeper into woods.

Even though the sun is long asleep and Spain's February night air is colder than I expected, Henry and I both have slight sheens on our face from the exertion. "Xavier, tell me there's fresh water nearby," I say.

He doesn't respond.

When it feels like I cannot move another step, a tiny

wooden cabin, panels bolted over the windows, appears up ahead. The firepit in front is cold, the small metal stovepipe extending from the roof quiet.

The heavy wooden door looks as if it was shaped out of local trees, but despite its rustic front, the door only opens with Xavier's thumbprint.

"If he dies before this is over, we're going to have to cut off his thumb to get anywhere," I say to Henry.

"I heard that," Xavier says. The door scrapes open, dust dancing like dervishes in the light of his flashlight. We follow him in, waiting while he lights a glass hurricane lamp on a square, rough-wood table in the center. The room takes shape—a small, galley-style kitchen, a cold, black potbellied stove at the cabin's north end, and wooden bunks with tired-looking mattresses lining the walls.

"We camp here tonight. The Guardian will meet us."

"When?" Henry asks.

Xavier drops his pack, claiming a bunk in the far-right corner. "I'll get a fire started," he says, ignoring Henry's question. "Go out and get some wood. We need to boil water and make dinner."

Henry and I drop our packs on bunks on the opposite side of the single-room cabin. I'd sleep under the stars if I could, as far away from Xavier as possible.

Outside, we find a neat stack of dry firewood and each carry an armload inside to get the fire going. Xavier works silently, pulling water out of a plastic water tank attached to the ceiling above an iron faucetless basin anchored to the wall. "This is collected rainwater—there's a rain barrel on the roof. It has to be strained and boiled before we can drink it," he says. "Outhouse in back. Check for snakes before you sit."

Snakes? Awesome.

Once the water is ready, Xavier throws military-issue MREs (meals ready to eat) at us.

"What'd you get?" I ask Henry as he tears his open.

He examines the package front in the dim light. "Spaghetti with meat sauce. You?"

"Cheese tortellini," I say.

The food tastes as disgusting as it looks, or maybe we're just spoiled after the meal at *Circ de l'Anell d'Or*. Doesn't matter. We eat because we've been walking for god knows how many hours and we're starving.

"Wash up and get ready for bed. Lights out in fifteen."

Xavier is out the door, again with his satellite phone, another cigarette at his lips.

"I will never understand what my mother saw in him," I say under my breath.

"He's under a lot of pressure right now," Henry says.

"You are not allowed to defend him. He's a dick."

"He might be, but he's also trying to keep us alive."

I stop digging through my pack and stare at Henry standing at the bed that abuts mine. "Are you saying that you agree with him? That I shouldn't have saved that man's life today?"

Henry sets his gloves down and closes the distance between us. "I know how hard that would've been for you to not help him. After what happened with Thierry."

"So you blame me for Thierry's death too?" I step back before Henry can touch me.

"Genevieve, please. We're tired. Let's not fight. I'm on your side. You know that." When he moves closer to me yet again, I have nowhere left to go—I'm up against the cabin wall. Henry's blistered hands, curled into loose fists, brush under my jaw and he reaches down to kiss me. I let him, but I make sure my thoughts are filled with images of me saving that man's life today, in case Henry gets inside my head with the connection of our lips.

"Let's sleep. Tomorrow we will get the first piece of the key, and then we can move on to the next stop."

"Which is where? He still hasn't told us," I snap back, right as Xavier reenters the cabin.

"Naples, Italy," he says, shoving the wooden door closed and sliding a thick two-by-four into brackets on either side of the doorjamb. It would take a stampeding elephant to break it down. "I hope you don't get seasick."

"We're going by boat?" I ask.

"Naples is about 550 nautical miles from Barcelona. And as I surmised earlier, your face is now making its way around the World Wide Web at lightning speed, thanks to one enterprising, awestruck *Circ* employee with an iPhone. Travel by land is going to be dicey until we are across the Mediterranean. Best to hide in the hold of a fishing vessel and *not heal anyone, no matter how close to death they might be.* Are we clear?"

"Clear as glass," Henry says.

"The Guardian will be here early. Now. I don't want to see your faces again until the sun is up. Please grant me this one kindness." Xavier pulls closed a curtain suspended from a wire stretched from wall to wall. The dust it stirs up makes me sneeze.

The next sound is Xavier's snores. With his every noisy exhale, I again question my mother's sanity when she spent time in this man's presence. She always teased Baby about how he was the perfect partner because he never snored, and here I am, stuck in a fifteen-by-fifteen cabin with a motorboat.

If Xavier lives through this, and Baby doesn't, I truly will be an orphan.

19

"GENEVIEVE . . . GEN . . ." I OPEN MY EYES, SLEEP HEAVY ON MY HEAD AND body like a weighted blanket. "Come here. I want to show you something," Henry whispers.

"Is it morning?"

Henry presses a finger against his lips and shakes his head no. "Slide into your boots."

He helps me put them on. Xavier's privacy drape is still drawn, but I see that the cabin's front door is ajar, the earlier two-by-four barricade resting against the wall. A brisk breeze whistles through the crack between door and frame.

I stand, wobbly for a second. Henry loops his arm through mine and we tiptoe as quietly as is possible in combat boots.

Henry pulls the door behind us, though it's so heavy and noisy, he can't close it tight.

The evening sky is a brilliant blanket of stars—even the Milky Way is visible. It's so beautiful, it doesn't look real.

At the quiet firepit, a rough woolen blanket from our

bunks has been stretched out on the ground; on one of the big rocks that forms the circular firepit rests a familiar rectangle covered in its leather wrapping.

Henry's *AVRAKEDAVRA*.

"What are you doing?"

"Just sit."

I do, and he slides down too, leaning forward to uncover his book. A shiver runs through me as the aged cover is exposed.

"You left it sitting out, unprotected?"

"For a brief moment—and who else is out here?" He laughs once under his breath. He then opens the text and holds his ungloved hand between us. "Trust me," he whispers.

I take his hand, the familiar warmth rushing through. And then sitting next to Henry is Alicia, her glowing form floating above the ground. She moves over the ashy remnants in the firepit and flattens a glowing hand on the *AVRAKEDAVRA*.

"What's she doing?"

"Watch." Henry smiles.

In front of us, like the flicker of a movie, a scene plays out: *The young man I saved earlier walks into an apartment where he's met by a beautiful young woman with a lush ponytail and the widest smile, tears flowing down her face. When they embrace, the chubby baby perched on her hip squeals and pats the man's shoulder. Another little one with bouncing curls and a pink nightie runs barefoot across the tile floor dragging a stuffed cat. She throws her arms around the young man's legs. "Papa! Papa! Papa!" The man and his wife cry and kiss, and then his wife inspects the back of his head, crosses herself religiously, and they kiss again.*

The scene fades out.

"Alicia thought you'd want to see it. To let you know you made the right choice."

"How . . . how did she get that memory?" I ask.

Alicia gestures to the *AVRAKEDAVRA*, and then to Henry. "She's teaching me, Genevieve. She's teaching me to see so much."

"When have you had time?"

"I haven't been sleeping as much as I should," he says, his smile tentative. "It helps that no one else can see her. I can carry on conversations, and no one is aware."

I look at Alicia. "I miss you," I say. "You helped me so much back home."

Her lips move, her hand over her translucent chest.

"She says she loves you as if you were her own."

As my head moves through the initial shock of seeing Alicia, the *AVRAKEDAVRA* out in plain view, and the vision of the young man and his family, I'm overrun with what I should've thought before anything else. I grab Henry's arm with my free hand.

"Can you see Baby? Is he okay? What about the elephants? Please?"

Alicia dims for a moment. She then says something to Henry and nods at the *AVRAKEDAVRA*. "She wants me to show you. Don't worry. It's okay."

And then Henry takes his hand from mine and places both on the ancient text. Alicia shimmers from sight—I can only see her through Henry now—but another image flickers in front of us.

It's Baby. Still asleep. Still in Croix-Mare. But lying on his bed next to him—

"Is that *Delia*?" I ask, incredulous.

"Since we have Alicia, Delia is watching over Baby," Henry says.

I don't care that Henry sees my tears. I'm so happy to know that Baby isn't alone, that Delia is out of the mausoleum, that she's not trapped in that stone box for eternity. I don't know what good she can do to help Baby, but in my heart, I hope he knows she's there with him.

"I wish I could see her again. Here. Now. I wish I could just *talk* to her again."

Henry nods. "I know. I'm sorry."

Seeing my mother and Baby, together, both reassures me and breaks my heart. And yet it also reaffirms what we're doing here. I have to keep fighting—I have to save Baby's life. Delia would fight. So must I.

"And what about the elephants?" I ask, scared to see the truth.

Henry pulls his hands away, murmurs under his breath, and then pauses before placing his hands back on the book. Again an image floats into shape. I hiccup with tears and pure relief to see Gertrude with Ted and Dr. Philips in the field, Houdini running around like the nut he is. Gert has her trunk looped over Ted's shoulder as he feeds her mango and bananas. Though Ted's lips are moving, I can't hear what he's saying to the veterinarian.

"I wanted you to see. I wanted you to know that your family is okay," Henry says.

And before his hands lift from the *AVRAKEDAVRA*, a whisper lands right in the middle of my head, the voice unmistakable: *Use the magic, little bird. Don't be afraid.*

I love you, Mom, I whisper back to her.

With Henry's hands off the book, night again falls into a darkness lit only by the constellations. He closes the text and rewraps it in the thick leather. "It's almost a shame that we have to destroy them."

I freeze mid-swipe of the tears off my cheek.

"Of course, I know it has to be done. But losing our abilities—me losing the connection with my mother—it's just not fair," he says, scooting back onto the blanket. He picks up a stick and digs at a rock embedded in the hard dirt.

I contemplate telling him I had these same thoughts just a few hours ago. But if he sees a chink in my armor, he might work at it until I change my mind—and I can't change my mind.

"If we don't do this, Henry, we will never be truly free. We will be on the run *forever*."

His head bounces in agreement. "I know the consequences. But think for just a moment—when this is over, you will still have Baby—"

"He won't survive if we don't do this."

"He's strong. And when the books are destroyed, the curse will be broken, so he'll recover. You'll have Baby, and the Cinzios, and Violet and your circus family. And Xavier—even if you don't like him—he's still your father." Henry's face is drawn with the weight of his thoughts. "I will lose my mother. Forever. And how do I ever go home? My father is lost to me. And yes, he's a despicable person, but he is still my father. I still love him."

A hard knot forms in my throat. "We have no choice," I say, my words hard.

He looks up at me, his eyes almost glowing. "We *do* have a choice—we just have to make sure it's the right one."

With that, he stands and reverently cradles the *AVRAKEDAVRA* under his arm. When he offers me a hand up, I don't take it. I walk ahead, up the three sagging steps, and directly to my bunk, watching to make sure Henry secures the door as Xavier had it earlier.

When he climbs onto his bunk, he whispers good night. I don't respond.

20

The aroma of fresh coffee replaces the dusty itch in my nose. I take my time pulling on my boots, watching Henry and Xavier at the table—I slept like shit after the show Henry put on around the firepit. He's digging in to another MRE; Xavier is hunched over carving a small piece of wood, the shavings gathering in a heap at his feet.

"Good morning," Henry offers. I nod and then step out to use the very primitive facilities, careful to check for snakes as instructed, about jumping out of my skin when a lizard skitters out from behind the privy. Xavier has set up a bucket for us to wash, and just as I'm drying my hands off on my pants, I hear low voices behind me.

I rush back into the cabin. "Someone's coming."

Xavier pockets his carving and his knife. He checks his sidearm and moves to the window, his body ready for whatever is coming through the trees.

And then his shoulders and face relax, his relief obvious.

"The Guardian. She's here."

Xavier goes out to meet her; I rush to rinse my mouth with toothpaste, throw on a clean shirt, and wet down my wiry hair very much in need of some shampoo.

"Get any sleep?" Henry asks.

"Not much. You?"

"Some. I'm nervous about meeting this Guardian," he admits.

"Me too." But I also know that it's been almost forty-eight hours since the last Etemmu haunting, and if these people were with Lucian, there's a good chance the Etemmu would've made itself known, if the pattern is anything to trust.

Henry stands behind the chair he'd just been sitting in; I move over to join him, careful not to make contact. I don't want him in my head—I don't want him to see the seeds of doubt now growing there in light of our firepit conversation.

The door opens, and Xavier walks in, followed by a small woman with the blackest skin I've ever seen, her head wrapped in a dark-green scarf, her outfit in the same dark green that would help her disappear in a forest as dense as this. She isn't alone; a young man, thin but very tall, is with her, attired in the same camouflage-colored gear.

Xavier scoots the door closed, replacing the two-by-four in its brackets. He then steps around, a polite smile on his face, and gestures toward the table.

"May I introduce Genevieve Flannery," he holds a hand out toward me, "and Henry Dmitri." Henry and I nod and offer quiet hellos. "This is Shamira and her son Joseph."

"It's a pleasure to meet you both," Shamira says, her words heavily accented. "Xavier, tell me you brought some of that excellent Scotch I requested."

Xavier smiles genuinely, a rare sight. "Single malt, but only a hundred years old."

"Only," she says.

"Anything for my best girl."

He offers chairs to Shamira and Joseph, and then quickly retreats to his pack from which he pulls a stout glass bottle. He grabs three short glasses from the "kitchen," wiping them clean with a questionable towel, and then pulls a fifth chair from the wall for himself.

"Sit, please," Shamira says, nodding at Henry and me.

Xavier pours two fingers' width of whiskey and doles out the glasses to our company. Waiting for them to sip and exchange pleasantries about its oaky taste has my heart in my throat.

Finally, Shamira sets her glass aside and flattens her hands on the rough tabletop. "Xavier tells me you are the rightful heirs."

"Yes," we say together.

"You are also Xavier's daughter?" she asks me.

Xavier leans back in his chair, his face hard, eyes downcast. The chair whines under his weight.

"Allegedly, yes," I say, eyes on Shamira. "But the man who is my father lays dying in France. I'll do anything to save him."

"Bamidele. I know and love him." Sitting here with Shamira, a hundred new questions pop into my head.

"How old are you?" I ask.

"Old enough to know it's impolite to ask a woman how old she is," she says, followed by a hearty laugh. My cheeks flush with embarrassment. "No, no, my child, it is okay. It is a good question. The Guardians are very old. Nutesh gave us a great gift, though it is not without sacrifice." And like the *Circ* people yesterday, Shamira pulls a key from under her the scarf wrapped over her head and neck and kisses it. I stare at it, willing it to not turn black like Mathieu's did back in Croix-Mare.

It doesn't. She tucks it away again.

"This day has been a long time coming. Centuries in the making. If Nutesh deems it time for the *AVRAKEDAVRA* to return to the fertile lands of its birth, then I as Guardian will fulfill my sacred duty."

"Thank you for your commitment, Shamira, Joseph," Xavier says, stretching his hand across the table to rest on top of hers. When Shamira smiles, her eyes twinkle as if made of starlight.

"My dear children, if we only had more time, I would love nothing more than to tell you stories of our people, of our past, of the beautiful work we have done to heal this planet. However"—Shamira slides her hand from Xavier's and reaches to the floor to pull up her pack—"time is not on our side."

Shamira nods at Xavier, who then turns to Henry and me. "You must present the texts to the Guardian as proof of your identity."

I'm sweaty with nerves, grateful that the electric burn behind my sternum rests on simmer. I don't want to hurt this beautiful woman.

Henry and I move to our packs. I unzip the secret compartment that holds my *Life* text; even through the leather wrap, it hums when I make contact. Carefully, I pull it free, whispering a silent plea to Alicia and any other nearby benevolent spirits to keep us safe. Henry's eyes are wide as he looks to me, his back to our guests but his text resting in his hands.

We turn together and set the books on the table before Shamira and her son. She looks first at me, and then at Henry, and then nods. I unfold the leather wrap, and as soon as the *Life* text is free of her sheath, my heart flutters and I'm breathless.

"Please lay your hands atop your texts, children," Shamira says.

Tentatively, we follow her instructions. As soon as my hands are on the book, it's like a million strands of light blow through me. I swear I look like I'm on fire. The contact is so intense and stunning, I can't turn my head to see if Henry is experiencing the same thing.

Shamira speaks, reciting what sounds like a prayer. She then reaches toward me, places her hands flat on mine, repeats her chant, and then breaks my connection to the book. I'm winded and mildly nauseated, but I also feel like I could lift this entire cabin over my head.

I watch as she repeats the ritual with Henry, though he seems to be in better control of whatever energy courses through him—probably because he's been spending time with the book and his mother when he was meant to be asleep.

When Shamira is done, she bobs her head at Xavier. He

pours her more whiskey. She swallows it in a single pull and daintily sets the glass back on the table.

"I am satisfied that these heirs have met the requirements set out by the Original Creators, our forefathers of the healing arts. I shall now relinquish the treasure I have been charged with all these long years so that we may bring this journey to a close and move toward the next adventure that awaits all the good people of the *AVRAKEDAVRA*, and of *La Vérité*. The key to good is found in truth," she says.

Joseph and Xavier repeat her, in unison. "The key to good is found in truth."

Shamira then looks to her son, who hoists his own pack onto his legs. From it, he pulls a polished onyx box. He sets it before him, and then slides it toward us.

"Inside you will find the first piece of the temple key. I am relieved it is now your responsibility, and no longer mine. It is finally time for me to go home, and die in peace," Shamira says, suddenly standing and pulling her pack onto her shoulders. Joseph follows suit. "We wish you the safest travels, and the greatest luck. I will look forward to the lifting of my heart that tells me the deed is done. Be well, my children."

Xavier stands and embraces Shamira, offering her the Scotch. "I'll look forward to drinking this when I get to Juba."

"My country waits for you with open arms, Xavier Darrow," Shamira says, pulling him down to kiss his forehead. "Take care of yourself." She cups his cheek, and then turns to follow Joseph.

We stand on the narrow porch and watch as Shamira and Joseph disappear into the trees. "Get your things," Xavier barks, the kinder demeanor of just moments ago vanished like his Guardian friends.

21

We hike out of the woods to another dirt road—I have no clue if this is the same one we came in on, but a different vehicle has been stashed in the brush and covered with a green canvas tarp. Whatever network Xavier has working here, I hope to hell he trusts the people manning the controls.

Because I don't. How do we know there aren't more Mathieus waiting in the wings?

Not like I have much of a choice at this point.

Just before we left the cabin, Xavier opened the black box and showed us the piece Shamira delivered. I braced for another physical reaction at being so close to this piece of *AVRAKEDAVRA* magic, but the piece lay dormant on its velvet bed inside. Oddly shaped, I wasn't sure how this could possibly be a key. It's flat and occupied a third of my palm when held, made of cut, polished gray stone. Upon closer examination, my imagination filled in the missing parts.

I think back to sitting in Baby's truck at the post office in Cannon Beach, seeing the symbol for the first time on the wax seal of my mother's cryptic letter. And then on Lucian's tiepin when I initially believed him when he said it was "an old magician's symbol, from back when magician meant 'healer.' A protection against evils."

Oh, the irony.

It was carved into Udish's festering flesh; it's emblazoned on the front of the *AVRAKEDAVRA* texts; and it's Nutesh's tattoo.

This "key"—a circle overlying an inverted triangle—will undo our gifts and send those closest to us, finally, to their last days.

Xavier tucked the box with the piece into his own pack. "If we get separated, neither of you can have a text and the components of the pieces we're collecting. It's suicide."

I'm glad to not be carrying it. And after my conversation with Henry last night, I'm glad he doesn't have it either.

Xavier backs the car out from where it's been squeezed between the trees. This time, it's an unremarkable blue SUV with faded paint and bald tires. As soon as the locks click open, Henry and I climb in.

"The windows are tinted, but not enough to keep you invisible. Sit with your backs toward the glass so when we're in the city, in traffic, no one can see you."

"Where are we going?" I ask.

"Another marina. Not Port Vell—we can't be anywhere near *Circ de l'Anell*."

"We're getting on a boat?" Henry asks.

"God willing it hasn't sunk yet," Xavier mumbles.

The road back to civilization is long, curvy, and bumpier than I remember. I catch Henry smiling every once in a while, his head bobbing as if in agreement with a conversation only he can hear. Probably because it *is* a conversation only he can hear.

When the city appears through the windshield, her many blocks of humanity stretching east toward her coastline, I'm tempted to roll the window down and hang my head out like a dog. Barcelona is gorgeous. If only we were here like regular people—I want to visit all those famous landmarks you see in the tour books. La Sagrada Familia and Casa Milà and Gaudí's other famous works; if we could walk through Parc Güell or La Boqueria, which is supposed to be one of the most amazing markets anywhere. Or maybe we could hang out on one of the area's famous beaches and I could work on giving my translucent skin some color. Violet did a school project once on Spain, and we used to tease Ted that he should move us overseas so we could hang out with beautiful Spanish men. Well, that was Violet's idea. I mostly just wanted to see someplace that wasn't America.

Be careful what you wish for.

Xavier has a different cell phone from the one at the apartment. It dings with a notification; he picks it up and reads the screen, the car behind us wailing when we don't move on a green light.

He then tosses the phone over the seat to me. "Have a look."

I click through, and Lucian's face fills the screen as my stomach drops. "Henry . . ." He scoots closer to me.

According to the BREAKING NEWS banner along the bottom of the video, Lucian is in France, talking to reporters, in perfect French.

"Can you—"

Henry holds up a hand and cranks the volume. And then Xavier's face fills the screen.

"Oh my god," I say. "They know you're alive. They know we're with you."

I look up at Xavier. His jaw clenches, his knuckles white on the steering wheel.

"Enough," Xavier barks. Henry swipes the screen closed.

"Someone please translate?"

Henry's face is flushed, eyes wide.

"There's a reward," Xavier bites out. "He's moved on from being the concerned father to angry art collector and preserver of history wronged by outsiders. He's doubling down on Bamidele being the mastermind, and they've thrown me into the mix as the ringleader."

"Ringleader of what?"

"A dangerous religious cult. And Bamidele Duncan has abducted you into it. Your family in Oregon is joining forces with Lucian to find you, and Henry, and bring you both home safely."

"This is bad—surveillance cameras are going to pick us up somewhere. If Lucian is spreading your photo like he has ours, it's only a matter of time before someone recognizes us."

"I knew I shouldn't have renewed that passport," Xavier says, rolling down the window to light up.

"You're making jokes?" I say. "You're going to have to shave your head or something. You have to change what you look like so it's not so obvious."

"I'm not shaving my head," Xavier says.

I sink into the seat. It's bad enough that Henry and I could be spotted—even with our appearances changed—but the three of us together and Xavier with his mop of black curls and those *eyes* . . . He could wear a clown wig and his eyes would give him away.

Henry stares out the front window, but I can see the wheels spinning in his head.

I don't know if this will work, but it's worth a try.

I pull my glove off, and then gently, Henry's. He watches me—I lock eyes with him and slide my hand into his, careful of his blisters.

The exchange of his calming energy is immediate, a pleasant contrast to the constant low-level hum coming from me.

Unsure if he'll be able to hear words, I conjure an image of Henry with his hands on Xavier, crawling through his head to get the information we need to find the next two guardians. And then once we have that, I paint the two of us on our own, leaving Xavier behind.

We have to go, without him. It's too dangerous for the three of us. We can do this, I think to Henry.

I'm shocked when he nods yes.

Xavier eventually pulls into an underground garage, and as with every time we abandon a vehicle, he repeats the same instructions: packs on, heads down, follow me. He allows us to leave the wool caps off—given the warmish day, we'll stand out more if we're wearing hats—but thankfully, he pulls a ball cap out of his bag. At least it shadows his piercing eyes a little.

The briny smell of salt water and the sun on my face are welcome, though I'm careful not to make eye contact as we pass street vendors hawking their fresh catch or the buyers bartering over price. It's impossible to know how many people have been watching international news this morning, or how many people care.

But it only takes one person with good recall of faces. One is one too many.

We follow Xavier down the wharf, moving farther away from the more crowded parts of the marina, onto narrower wooden walkways that extend over the water where boats are moored. Whereas the boats we saw first were fishing vessels, this part seems to cater to higher-end toys.

"I thought you said we were taking a fishing boat," I say.

"Plan has changed. Something faster in light of recent developments."

"By recent developments, you mean what Lucian's doing?" I ask.

"Nutesh is monitoring the situation. We adjust accordingly," Xavier says.

We follow him through the maze of the marina; he constantly scans, eyes on everything.

Finally, he turns down one of the walkways between boat slips, slows in front of a long, very sleek, expensive-looking, white-and-black boat with sparkling gold racing stripes. Xavier knocks on the heavily tinted angled window along the side.

"Heyyyyy! Xavier!" A tall, very tan man with an impressive mustache and slicked-back hair opens the thick glass door at the rear of the cabin. He shakes Xavier's hand over the boat's side. "Come aboard, guys!"

He sounds American. I'm weirdly relieved—maybe because I won't need a translator. If I survive this, I'm going to learn every new language I can. I've never felt dumber.

"Welcome aboard the *Beauty Queen*. She's named after my future wife," the guy says, arm outstretched to showcase his boat. His teeth are so white, they can't be real. They match the cotton shorts that reach just above his knee; his legs are just as hairy as his face. "My name is Keller. And no, I'm not related to Helen." He waits for a beat; Henry and I don't respond. "Tough crowd, X. Who are these kids again?"

"Trouble One and Trouble Two," Xavier says, nodding toward the boat. "Let's get going."

We board by stepping onto the teak deck that stretches from the rear of the boat to the glass wall that Keller emerged from. White leather bench seats are built into the boat's uncovered exterior deck. We follow Keller inside. I feel like I should wash my hands before touching anything. More white leather, polished wood floors, brass and teak everything.

Keller points out the cockpit; tinted narrow windows stretch along the sides and front of the boat giving the driver a clear view ahead. He gives us the grand tour—this vessel has three staterooms below, a galley with stainless steel appliances, a sitting area with leather chairs, a flat-screen TV mounted on the wall, and a well-appointed bathroom complete with a shower and flushing toilet.

"There's so much space," I say.

"Looks can be deceiving, right?" he says, winking at me. "It's why the *Beauty Queen* has such a big nose." He holds his hand up and speaks behind it. "Just don't tell her I said that."

He opens a door to our left. "This stateroom is tight, but perfect for kiddos. Which you are. Two bunks—one person to a mattress, if you please. No teen pregnancies on the *Beauty Queen*, thank you very much!" I don't have to look at Henry to know his face is as beet red as mine. "Galley is here, *obviously*," he says, opening the well-stocked fridge. "Everything you might want to nosh on. Per X's instructions, I hit the market first thing."

It bugs me how he calls Xavier "X." I hope it bugs Xavier too.

Keller shows us where the life jackets are stashed and explains a few basic safety procedures about what we should do if the vessel founders.

"The *Queen* moves quick—top speed is about sixty-one miles per hour but we'll be cruising at about fifty, fifty-two, depending on chop. You can sit here in the main sitting area or in your cabin, but if you want to be on the exterior deck, life jackets are required. That way if you fly into the Mediterranean, you can bob like a cork until I can come about and scoop you up."

Sounds . . . terrifying.

"Our range is about 400 miles, give or take, so we'll be making a stop at Porto Torres at the northern tip of Sardinia to fuel up. I gotta run onshore for a pickup, but we won't be there long. Half hour, tops."

"How long will it take us to get there?" I ask.

"To the Bay of Naples? Hmmm, about twelve to fourteen hours, including gas-up. Gonna be a lot of blue. Forecast calls for clear skies but the Mediterranean can be tricky the farther out we get just 'cos of the time of year. Either of you landlubbers get seasick?"

"Is landlubber a real word?" I ask.

Keller smiles and points at me. "This one has a pulse!"

Xavier clears his throat. "Shall we get underway?"

"Sure thing, boss."

I'm not sure if I'm meant to see it, but Xavier handing Keller a very fat envelope tells me that our sun-kissed captain probably isn't doing this job for the joy of philanthropy.

Once Keller is up the stairs and out of earshot, Xavier turns to us. "Stay below deck and away from windows until we're offshore. I'll let you know when you can come out. If you need to puke, do so in the bathroom." He lowers his voice. "As always, packs close. Keller is an old friend, but he's not *La Vérité*. Stay down here until I tell you otherwise." He hurries up the stairs and shuts the main cabin door behind him.

The boat purrs to life. Through the dark, thin side windows, I see Keller hopping onto the dock as he unties, and then he's back on the boat.

"Keller seems nice," Henry says.

"As long as he can steer a boat without crashing into Italy, that's all I care about."

Henry sits on the couch's edge, his bisected eyebrow lifting in question. "We need a plan," he whispers.

"I have to use the bathroom first. Meet me in the stateroom in five minutes." I take my pack with me, even though the bathroom is barely big enough for the both of us. But . . . I want to try to get a cell signal before we get too far away from land. Double-checking the door is locked, I dig through, unwrapping Baby's cell phone from the socks at the bottom. I power on, holding my breath that the signal won't somehow be discovered, but after a whole minute of staring at the narrow wood and brass door, I'm clear—no one pounds on it.

A flood of text messages—all from Violet, their tone progressively more panicked—and the last few texts ask about Xavier.

Hey, Vi. I can't answer all your ?s right now.
Henry & I are safe. Can't wait to see you
again. Tell me something from home.

Gen? OMG! Are you OK? Lucian said you
were kidnapped into a cult?! Is that man
hurting you? We are FREAKING OUT!!!

Not kidnapped. Totally ridiculous.

But maybe they brainwashed you so you
don't know what you're saying?

My brain is still plenty dirty. LOL

LOL . . . That sounds like my Gen. Are you really in Europe? I gotta tell Ash you're OK.

Vi, let's just keep this convo between you and me. Like our tea parties!

But everyone's so worried. When are you coming home? Who's that guy on the news?

He's related to me. It's fine, I swear.

K. Something from home: Houdini squeezed out of their open pen & figured out how to open the kitchen door. He got into the fridge & made a huge mess. Ate so much fruit, he's still pooping.

I laugh into my sleeve. Houdini is the smartest baby elephant ever.

Also Mara Dunn came back from Quebec to help search.

My blood runs cold and I drop the phone onto my backpack like it's a snake, staring at it for a minute before the screen lights up again.

Geni?

GTG, Vi. I love you.

Power off.

Vi still knows Aveline as Mara Dunn. And she's back in Eaglefern, with my family, my animals?

I'm going to be sick.

Bent in half over the compact vanity, I splash cold water on my face, letting the tap run over the heat stampeding through my hands.

Aveline is with my family.

Aveline is near the elephants.

Which means she's not in Europe with Lucian.

Is this part of their plan? If they know I'm worried about what's going on at home, then I won't be focused on the mission ahead?

This is impossible.

"Gen?" Henry says from outside the thin door.

I rewrap the cell phone and bury it in my backpack. Do I tell him that I have it? Do I risk him taking it or worse, telling Xavier? He wouldn't do that, would he? He might, if he thinks I'm endangering our mission. Which I am. That cell phone has to ping off somewhere. Someone will trace it.

I should flush it. Throw it overboard. I plunge my hand into the backpack again—

But it's my only connection to the outside world that isn't controlled by Xavier.

This whole situation is controlled by Xavier. And even if he has Nutesh's trust from working together for nearly five centuries, Xavier has not yet earned mine. Since we've been with him, a man has died, and another nearly did.

I zip my bag closed, take a deep breath, and open the

bathroom door to Henry's worried face. "I thought maybe you got sucked into the toilet," he says.

"If only." I nod toward the stateroom door. "We need to talk."

Our shared cabin is small, but cozy, our beds bunked. I lock the door and then move the plump white bed pillows on the lower bunk and replace them with my pack.

"The look on your face is making me slightly more nervous than usual," Henry says, sitting on the bed. I'm careful not to touch him, but I lean closer so he can hear me. I don't have one of Xavier's sound-masking devices, and I have no clue if this boat is bugged.

"I think staying with Xavier is dangerous," I say, "especially now that his picture is on the news. People were looking for us with Baby, but now, somehow they've figured out that he's not with us so they'll be looking for Xavier. His refusal to change the way he looks—"

"His eyes would give him away anyway," Henry says.

"Exactly."

"I knew the moment we met him back at the safe house that he was Aveline's father."

"Right? So if we noticed it, other people might. He's a target. Which means we are too."

"As if we weren't already," Henry says, adjusting his bent leg on the mattress. "Your idea in the car—how do you propose I get my hands on him, and what happens after?"

"It would be great if we could do it while he sleeps—"

"Guessing he doesn't sleep so heavily to not notice my hands on him, digging through his thoughts."

"You heard him snore last night," I say. Henry smiles. "We need an opportunity. Maybe if I pick a fight with him or rile him up somehow. You move in to separate us."

"You could just throw some extra electricity into a shove and put him on his knees. I could help him up."

"By his bare hands . . ."

"It's plausible. Flimsy, but plausible," he says.

"The point is, we need to see where we're going next. Naples is a big city. And then once we have that information, we need to ditch him. If he's with us, we *will* get caught," I say.

"But how will the Guardians know to trust us without Xavier?"

"I haven't worked out that part yet. I'm still trying to figure out an escape," I say. "*Unless* . . . didn't the boat guy say we have to stop in Sardinia to refuel?" I ask.

Henry's eyes widen. "Genevieve, we don't know how to get from Sardinia to the Bay of Naples."

"That's what GPS is for."

He laughs under his breath. "You crazy circus kids and your unquenchable thirst for adventure."

"It's genetic." A small smile escapes.

"All right, so say we can maneuver our way to Naples without Xavier on board. Then what? How do we find the next Guardian?"

I pause as a plan blooms in my head. "We don't. We're going to let the Guardian find us."

22

Henry and I agree to an idea that will require action sooner than later. If we want to ditch Xavier before Naples, I need to create an opportunity for Henry to get his hands on Xavier's skin and hope it's enough time to find the necessary information.

Our boat's captain wasn't lying when he said the kitchen was stocked. Henry offers me a juicy slice from the huge orange he's peeled. Our stateroom smells amazing.

"Man, we do not get oranges like this at home," I say. Henry smiles and offers me another slice. I notice a slight shake in his hand.

"Don't be nervous," I say. "We'll work it out. Trust me."

He nods. "I do. I trust you." He leans in and kisses my cheek.

"You heard the captain, sir," I tease. "No teenage pregnancy on the *Beauty Queen*."

When the burn begins in my left forearm, I assume it's because I'm overexcited from trying to reassure Henry while mulling over the steps we need to take to achieve our objective. But to have it start in the soft skin above my wrist is new. I rub at my arm, but the burning quickly intensifies into a painful, stinging itch, that feeling after a scrape when you pour water onto the open skin.

"Help me get my jacket off," I say, dropping the fruit onto the plate. "Please!" Henry obliges, just as the pain worsens to a string of relentless beestings, burning and aching all at once.

"What's going on? Genevieve?"

I can't answer him because I don't know what the hell is happening, and it hurts too much.

"Shirt too! Shirt off!" Henry struggles with my tight-fitting sleeves as I fold in half, cradling the painful arm against my stomach.

"Jesus, you're bleeding!"

Nausea buffets through me and my head aches suddenly, burning behind my eyes as if I were preparing to heal someone. Thing is, I can't heal myself, so this uncontrolled energy is going to end up somewhere unintentional.

Before I can get the sleeve pulled all the way up, the pain hits nine out of ten, and I'm on the floor.

"Help me!" I scream.

"Gen, what do I do? What's happening?"

Xavier will kill me for making such a racket. Henry grabs my wrist and fights to hold my arm still; I scream again as he peels the last of my shirt off.

Banging on the door. Henry lets go of me long enough to unlock it.

"What the hell is going on in here? Can you not—" Xavier stops speaking midsentence, his eyes fixed on my forearm. I'm trying so hard not to lose consciousness, but this pain is something else.

"Please—help me. What is going on . . . ?"

An intercom speaker crackles to life on the wall. "Everything okay down there?" Keller says.

Xavier stands and depresses the red reply button. "Diana saw a spider. Everything's under control."

"Big beasties in the Mediterranean, baby. Just throw it overboard. Don't smear bug guts on my carpet!"

"Breathe, Gen," Henry whispers. "Hold still. Let us have a look."

"It hurts, goddammit! What is happening to me?"

"*Keep* your voice down!" Xavier hisses, kneeling beside me, taking hold of my arm. I'm overcome with pain shivers. "What in the hell is this . . . ?"

"God, it hurts . . . it hurts so much."

"Henry, get something for the blood. Who has so much fucking white on a boat?" he grumbles. "And a cold cloth for her forehead. Her eyes keep rolling back, and the last thing we need is her passing out." Xavier's still got a firm hold on my wrist, careful to avoid my charged hands, but I can't keep my eyelids open. The boat has picked up speed in the last hour, and the constant bounce and whoosh worsens my queasiness.

"Genevieve . . . Genevieve, wake up," Xavier says, patting my cheek harder than he needs to.

"I'm still awake, dumb-ass," I slur. The original pain slowly dials back, but I'm winded, like I've been running. Xavier slides a towel under my arm.

"Wring the washcloth out over the wound," he says to Henry. "Genevieve, this is going to sting."

When the water hits whatever is going on, I howl.

I crack my eyes open and watch Xavier's face go rigid. He lifts my arm gently, pointing to where he wants Henry to squeeze more water. I suck in through my teeth.

"Can you stop with the water already?"

"I need to clean it off. So I can read it," Xavier says.

"What?"

Henry's eyes lock with mine, and I struggle to sit upright. He maneuvers around Xavier and helps me.

On the soft pale skin of my left arm, Aveline Darrow has inscribed a message just for me:

Say hello to Daddy for me.

23

Xavier opens the narrow closet and scrounges through the shelves until he finds a dark blanket. He strips the bunk to the waterproof mattress and then spreads out the coarse wool knit to protect Keller's precious boat.

"Get her up on the bed. We have to stop this bleeding," Xavier says. I hear him, and I see them both, but barely.

"She did this to Baby," I say, my voice a whisper. "Xavier, it can kill me. Please, tell me you know how to fix this. She's your daughter too. Tell me you know how to stop her."

Xavier's jaw pulsates, a look I'm getting too used to when he's dealing with me.

Henry presses the back of his fingers against my forehead. "She's burning up."

"Backpack. Antibiotics."

Xavier spins and kneels with my pack in front of him, pulling stuff out until he gets to the medical kit Nutesh and Thierry put together. Panic flashes like a popped light bulb in my head—Baby's phone!

But he pulls out the medical kit and rolled sterile bandages without finding it.

When I brave a look at my arm, blood oozes like lava from the words she's cut into my flesh.

"And I thought *I* had daddy issues," I say. Henry smiles, but he looks terrified.

"Glad to see your sense of humor hasn't been carved out," Xavier says. I think there might even be a hint of a smirk on his dark face, but I don't want to get too excited.

Xavier grabs one of the extra towels and throws it over my chest. I guess seeing his newfound daughter in nothing but her bra is uncomfortable for him. I grew up with a circus. There's no such thing as modesty. He then pulls the injectables with my name written on the packaging and stabs my outer biceps once, then twice.

"Ow."

"Sorry. I'm giving you the injections now," he deadpans.

"Your bedside manner leaves something to be desired." I close my eyes. "How many more years are we going to be on this boat?"

"At least until you're old enough to move out and get a job," Xavier jokes.

"Did Keller give you something other than tobacco to smoke, 'cos all of a sudden you sprouted a personality."

"Don't worry. It's temporary." The warmth from the injected medicines washes through me.

Xavier quietly gives Henry instructions for when he returns above deck: more cool rags, keep pressure on the wounds, watch the fever. "She should be pretty loopy for a bit, but calling Nutesh via sat phone out here is risky." He lowers his voice. "Keller is a good enough guy, but I don't trust him as far as I can throw him."

"That's such a weird thing to say. Would you really be able to pick him up and throw him? Like, seriously? How would that help us?" Mmmm, these painkillers are nice.

"Keep her away from sharp objects and anything magical. I'd like to get to Porto Torres in one piece," Xavier says. I hear the crinkling of paper as he wads up the used medical supplies. I have no idea where he's going to put all that blood-soaked stuff if he wants to keep Keller in the dark. "I'll be back in an hour. Keller likes to talk, so no need to raise suspicion if we can avoid it."

"Keller should shave his mustache . . . I'll bet food gets stuck in all that fuzz . . ." I feel like I'm floating above my body. It's not a terrible feeling, to be honest.

"Don't let her out of this room." Xavier clicks the door closed behind him.

Henry scoots next to my head on the skinny bunk, his hand resting on my shivering shoulder.

I look up at him, trying to stay above the pleasant numbness. "Did you . . . ?"

"I got it. I got what we needed," he says.

And although I have no idea when Henry was able to work his magic via Xavier's skin, I bob my head gratefully and let the rocking of the boat and the chemicals in my veins wash me out to sea.

"Promise you won't leave me, Henry."

"I promise." He kisses my forehead again. "Sleep."

My arm burns so badly. And I smell . . . lavender?

"Mom . . . ?" I don't want to open my eyes. They hurt too much. But I smile. Lavender means Delia is near. "I miss you, Momma."

The lavender gets stronger. Someone is rubbing it into my temples. "That feels nice. Thank you. You always know how to fix stuff."

"Gen . . . it's Henry. And Xavier. Can you open your eyes? You need to drink some water."

It hurts, but my lids part. "Where's my mother? Where is Delia?"

"She's not here right now," Xavier says. "Genevieve, I need you to bear with me for a second and not scream. We have to stop this bleeding. Can you work with me? Can you stay quiet?"

I nod. I don't have any idea what he's talking about. I'm being quiet. I'm being a good girl, aren't I?

And then the stinging begins again, and I of course scream, and Henry's hand clamps over my mouth. I sit up abruptly, dislodging a clump of dried, white star-shaped flowers with straggly roots that I think were tucked into my bra strap.

"*What* in the *hell* are you doing? That hurts!"

"No more painkillers for her," Xavier says. "She doesn't listen to directions stoned or sober."

I look down at my arm, still bleeding way more than it should be. Xavier is squeezing a fresh lemon over my arm.

"Lemon juice is a styptic. Nothing else is working,"

Xavier explains. He hands Henry the lemon. "Keep squeezing. Up and down the wound. Every last drop. I only have two lemons until we reach land."

"I'll bleed to death if this keeps up," I say.

"Your mother was always very dramatic too," he says.

I jab a finger in his face. "Not a word about Delia," I hiss.

Xavier ignores me, picks up the bunch of dried flowers, and rewraps them in what looks like silk. He then tapes them to my sternum with Band-Aids.

"What are you doing?"

"It's edelweiss. It will provide protection against blades," he says. "Like the one she is using to cut you."

"You believe that? A dried plant can stop this?" I say, easing back against the bunk.

Xavier glares at me. "Have you a better idea? I'm doing my best with what I've got. It might help you to say a quick prayer to Gula if you want this all to go away."

I've heard Delia use that name before—a Mesopotamian healing goddess—but my mother wasn't spiritual in a theistic way. She said her plants were the deities she relied upon.

Xavier digs into his black duffel and pulls out a plastic food storage container. From inside, he pulls green feathery stems that almost look like fern. "Yarrow," he says. "Helps with clotting."

"Delia used yarrow," I say.

"This is hers. From her plants in Nutesh's greenhouses. He keeps us all supplied." I've seen Nutesh's greenhouse. It's awesome to think that my mother's plants—and in turn, my mother—was around me the whole time, and I didn't even know it.

I angle my head so I can watch Xavier. Once Henry has

extracted every last drop from the lemon, Xavier quickly moves to set the delicate green fronds along the wound. "The lemon appears to be working," he says, drizzling aloe gel over the yarrow. He then points to a roll of gauze.

"That's the last one," Henry says.

"We're about two hours from Porto Torres," Xavier says. "I'll see if I can get more there."

Henry sits me up and holds a cold canteen against my lips. I don't realize how thirsty I am until I taste the water.

"She's still very warm," Henry says.

"Advil. That's all I've got for now. It's been long enough since she had the narcotic." Xavier reaches into my medical kit and then tosses Henry a small white bottle. "Two capsules should do it." Henry pours out the brick-red tablets into my palm; I swallow them down.

"You know a lot of medical stuff," I say.

"I've had good teachers," Xavier says, almost under his breath. His teachers . . . Nutesh? My mother?

"Does Keller know anything? I'm sorry I keep screaming. It just really hurts."

"Keller is fine. For now."

"That wad of money will keep him quiet, right?" I ask. Xavier lifts an eyebrow at me as he wraps my wounded forearm in gauze to hold the feathery yarrow stems in place.

"You're nosy."

"I'm observant."

He snorts. "This is all I can do until we reach land. Henry will get you something to eat. You have to keep your strength up, and you've lost a lot of blood."

"Nothing a raw steak won't fix," I say. Xavier doesn't smile but again wads up and stuffs away more blood-soaked towels he's probably going to have to pay Keller back for.

"You'll need a fresh shirt once we know the situation is under control. The fewer questions," he says, nodding his chin toward the door, "the better."

Xavier leaves and Henry helps me scooch up against the cabin wall and rest my bandaged forearm on a towel over my thigh.

"Any better?" he asks.

"A bit. The lemon juice still stings." Gingerly, I lift my forearm off the towel, afraid to upset Xavier's handiwork and restart the bloodbath. "Growing up, I used to beg Delia for a sister," I say. "How ironic."

"I don't think anyone would want Aveline as a sister," he says. "I'm really sorry, Gen."

"I don't understand how this is happening. How is she doing it?"

"Xavier thinks she must have something of yours. He said that when someone uses black magic like this—like what's happened to Baby—the person doing it probably has something that belongs to you, and she's using it as part of the ritual."

"I suppose she's had plenty of opportunity to go into my trailer, and Baby's for that matter, and get whatever she needed." I stop before telling Henry about Vi's text—that Aveline is in Oregon.

"The next Guardian," he whispers. "The plan is to meet him in Pompeii, at the ruined city."

I sit up straighter. "Are you serious?"

Henry presses a finger against his pursed lips. "The circus we're supposed to be going to—it looks like it's underground?"

"Leave it to Xavier to find us the weirdest circus ever."

"If we do this," Henry whispers, "we're on our own. We won't have any protection from Xavier or the *La Vérité* people. Are you sure that's wise?"

"Hmm. I dunno. We should ask Thierry what he thinks about that," I say.

Henry looks down at his hands.

"They used us as *bait,* Henry. That's all we are right now. As long as we are with Xavier, people are going to keep dying. It would be better if we could just get the piece and then move on to the next stop."

"So we will be on the run from not only Xavier, but all of my father's followers too? We don't know where we're going, Genevieve—"

"We're going to Naples."

"Yes, but then what?"

"Did you not see the next stop after that?"

"Izmir, in Turkey. But that's all I was able to get," he says. "I agree that continuing on with Xavier is dangerous. I agree that him not sharing his plans with us is dangerous. All of this—dangerous. But we cannot get ourselves to Babylon. We can't get visas to get into the country or hire a car to drive us south from Kurdistan to Babylon. We *need* my grandfather's help. We simply cannot do this on our own," he says.

I don't want to admit that he's right. Of course, he is. Even if we slip out of Xavier's grasp and get what we need from the other two Guardians, there's no way we can get into Iraq on our own.

Head back against the bouncing boat, I stare at the underside of the top bunk, thinking through the pain in my arm, searching for a workable plan.

I sit up, careful to keep the towel over my chest so I don't flash Henry. "Grab my backpack," I say. This could backfire, but it's all I've got right now.

Henry drops my pack onto my bed, and I scavenge through it with my good arm. My hand locked around the wadded socks, I pull them out and hand them to Henry.

"Socks? Does this mean I'm a free elf?"

"I would be a lot happier if we were going to Hogwarts and not the Temple of Doom," I say, watching Henry as he realizes there's a shape in the black cotton bundle. He pulls out the phone and looks at me, worry and confusion all at once.

"It's Baby's. I took it before we left. We can use it for GPS and whatever else we need—it's a secure way for us to get in touch with Nutesh. I had to take it—"

"Genevieve, what have you done?" He drops the phone on the bed and looks over his shoulder toward the still-shut cabin door.

"It was a calculated risk. I keep the phone off. It's not detectable if it's off, right?"

He's shaking his head. "We don't know if this phone has a tracking device in it."

"It's Baby's. I can't imagine he'd have a tracking device in his phone."

"You need to get rid of it. Have you made any calls? Any texts?" We lock eyes. "Oh, dear god, you have."

"Aveline is in Oregon. She's with Violet and Ash and everyone. I had to know the elephants were safe, that my family is safe—"

Henry bounds from the bunk and paces the short distance between the tiny bathroom and end wall. "I can't believe you kept this from me."

"They're my *family*, Henry. I had to know!"

"And what about me? Am I not your family now too? You have put *all* of us in danger with this!"

"It's a phone, not a nuclear weapon," I say.

Henry drops to his knees next to the bed. "At the crappy motel in SeaTac, when Baby dug the tracking device out of my shoulder—I didn't know it was there, Genevieve. I didn't know until Baby made a cut in my skin and dug it out." He jabs a finger in the direction of the phone. "That device, if it's from Nutesh, is absolutely going to have a tracking unit in it. If Baby were to get separated from us, Nutesh would be able to track him. Don't you see why this is dangerous?"

"No one knows I took it."

"Of course they do! Nutesh will know! And if he can track it, so can Lucian. You might as well send up flares."

"Henry, we need a way to communicate with the outside world."

"So we buy a burner phone!" He throws a hand to his head, his fingers looking for the cowlick that is no longer there. He then grabs the phone and claws at its back cover.

"What are you doing?"

"What do you think I'm doing?"

"Please—I need to be able to keep in touch with Violet. Aveline is in Eaglefern, with my animals!" Henry peels the heavy-duty phone case off and pops the back from the phone. He examines its guts, his face turning white as he turns the unit so I can see it.

A blinking red light, no bigger than a grain of rice, sits nice and cozy among the phone's circuitry, right above the battery.

"But the phone is off . . . what's the light coming from?"

Without another word, Henry kneels on my bed and unlatches the handle on the sleek, arrow-shaped window. Before I can protest, he throws the phone out into the Mediterranean, slides the window closed, and climbs off the bed.

He pauses, his face sad. "We will not make it through this if we at least can't be honest with each other."

Henry then turns and leaves, the stateroom door quietly closing behind him.

24

"We're nearing Porto Torres," Henry says, coming in and sitting on the bed. He presses the backs of his fingers against my forehead. "You're still feverish."

"I'm fine. I need a shirt," I say.

Henry digs through his own pack and gives me one of his. "The sleeves should be looser. Might feel better against your arm," he says. It does.

"I'm sorry I got so angry," he says, resting his hand on head. "I'm just scared."

"I'm scared too."

"Promise me—no more secrets."

I scoot closer and nuzzle Henry's cheek with my nose. "No more secrets," I say. He turns his head and kisses me.

"Are you feeling strong enough to commandeer this vessel?" he says.

"Aye-aye, captain. Let's commandeer the shit out of this vessel."

When I move out into the main cabin, Henry is on the couch edge, like a cat about to pounce. We wait as the boat glides into the marina, stops at the fuel station, and then finally quiets in a moorage space, the calm water under us a welcome reprieve from the bounce over the last twelve hours.

The main cabin door opens at the top of the narrow staircase, flooding us with late-afternoon sunshine. Xavier steps halfway down. "We're fueled up. I'm going onshore to see about replenishing our medical supplies." He nods toward my arm. "Everything under control?"

"She's much improved," Henry says.

"Is Keller staying here?" I say, hoping my nerves don't show through my voice.

"He's going in to pick something up. Should only be half hour, hour at most. Stay below deck. When we get back, we're out to sea again."

"How much longer? Until Naples," I ask.

"Six, seven hours. It will be very late when we arrive so as soon as we dock, we're moving."

"X, you comin', man? There's a cold one with my name on it at *le osteria*," Keller interrupts.

"I'll be back shortly," Xavier says, climbing the three short stairs and shutting the door behind him.

We watch through the narrow side windows as they walk down the wooden dock toward the port. Henry offers me a hand up the stairs—I'm definitely feeling the effects of Aveline's dark dealings, but now is not the time for weakness.

As soon as we lose visual of Xavier and Keller, we move upstairs. Henry jumps onto the dock to untie, and then we move into the cockpit.

"How hard can it be? Like a car, right?" I point at the gear shift, the gas gauge, the odometer, more to reassure myself than anything—I don't know what the other gauges mean, but let's hope we won't need to know.

"He took the key fob to start the engine," Henry says.

"I figured he would." I kneel and place a hand over the ignition button, careful to not let out too much electrical charge—last thing we need is for me to fry everything.

The boat purrs to life.

"Man, you are handy to have around," Henry says. He's already standing at the wheel, and when he eases the boat out of the slip and into the water, I realize he's done this before. "We had boats."

"You didn't mention that before," I say, bracing against the front console. "It's a rich-people thing, I'm guessing?"

Henry smirks. "Something like that," he says, one hand on the wheel, his other typing onto the touchscreen GPS embedded in the dash. "Watch behind. Let's hope they're far enough into the port they won't see us."

We slide out of the marina unnoticed. Henry obeys the speed-limit buoys, and when the Mediterranean opens before us, he throws the boat forward and we're back to cruising speed within just a few seconds.

It's way more fun up here than tucked below in the stateroom where you can't see anything. The sapphire-blue water is wide before us, the pristine, late-afternoon sky above its perfect match. "It doesn't even look real," I say.

I settle into the built-in sectional and watch the Mediterranean stretch out endlessly, the boat gliding like a skater on ice. I hope we'll put enough distance between us and Porto Torres before Xavier and Keller discover we're gone. The boat surely has a tracking device on it—hell, even Cece's crappy Toyota had an anti-theft system installed—and this is a multimillion-dollar boat, without doubt.

But I'm less worried about Keller and Xavier tracking us—they know we're going to Naples—and more worried about what Xavier will do if he catches up to us.

Then again, what's he going to do—ground me?

I find a crappy paperback and read aloud to Henry as day turns to night. Who knew Keller was into romance novels? It's a pleasant diversion, and it makes me laugh when Henry blushes over the naughty bits.

The GPS beeps. "We're almost there," Henry says.

"Already?" I jerk to sitting, instantly regretting the sudden movement. I sit up and look out the cockpit windows behind us. "No pursuits. Are we overly lucky here?"

"We need every bit of luck we can score."

"Xavier's gonna be pissed."

Henry chuckles. "I think that's probably a fair estimation of his current emotional state."

I put both feet on the floor, but my head feels thick and my arm hurts like hell. I've sweated through my borrowed shirt. Standing, I brace myself against the furniture. My balance is off, even without the movement of the water.

"I'm going downstairs to grab our stuff," I say.

Henry nods, slowing the boat in accordance with the posted limits as we approach another marina. "As soon as we dock, I'll come down for mine." He quiets, but his worried eyes scan my face. I'm guessing I look as shitty as I feel.

Once in the stateroom, I dig ibuprofen out of my pack. Chug the remaining water in my canteen. A little more deodorant. Move to the tiny bathroom and splash some water on my face, run a wet hand through my short hair, refill my canteen.

I remove Xavier's edelweiss and drop it in the trash because it's just too itchy to deal with. I'll have to take my chances without it.

I'm ready to go, even if my body feels heavy with plague.

In the second cabin, I find Xavier's backpack and the black duffel. I'm not keen on digging through someone else's personal belongings, but I need the first part of the temple key, the one Shamira gave us back in Spain. Where before I thought it would be too risky to have texts *and* the key parts with us, we now don't have much of a choice.

Henry proves to be a capable skipper, pulling the boat into a slip in a small marina in the Bay of Naples. I bring up his pack too, rejoining him in the cockpit just as he turns off the boat and jumps onto the dock to tie us in place. The city at night sparkles with lights from streets and buildings, but apprehension washes over me as I realize we are in yet another foreign place, with absolutely no idea where to go next.

"You ready?" Henry says, his hand extended toward me. "Taxi first." I nod and take his hand, climbing off the boat. My legs feel like I'm still on the water. As we hurry out of the maze of docks before someone stops us, I go over the plan in my head.

Take a taxi to the neighborhood where the next circus is located.

Find a hostel nearby.

When the sun comes up and the shops are busy, we set our stage: a quick slice to Henry's abdomen; he stumbles into the area outside the circus venue where I will be loitering; theatrics will ensue; I will heal him.

People will see.

We need people to see us, just like they did in Spain.

Then we wait and watch to see who our fishing expedition brings us.

Our taxi driver seems quite happy to have a 2:00 a.m. fare to share his narrated tour of the city. He drives north and then east from the marina, pointing out the *Castel Nuovo* as we pass. His broken English/Italian is thick, though, so I'm hardly catching the rest of the landmarks as he takes us deeper into the maze of Naples.

When he turns down a street that hardly seems big

enough for the tiny Fiat we're squeezed into, he hits the brakes hard and points out the passenger's side window. "Here—in *Napoli Sotterranea*—we have our world-famous circus, *Circo della regina*. Circus of the Queen! Named after Queen Margherita. Very popular Italian woman. Fighter for our people," he says. "You want a circus? You must go! Tomorrow. You will looooove it. *Molto bello*."

"We love circuses," I say.

"You need a place to sleep? I know a place—a hotel. *Piacevole*—very nice. Cheap too. My cousin will give you a great price," he says.

Henry is already digging Euros out of his bag. "*Grazie*. We will get out here. *Grazie, grazie*," he says, adding a nice tip.

"Be careful on these streets at night," the driver says. "Not safe for tourists!" He then speeds away.

"I think you offended him," I say.

"I don't want to end up at his cousin's hotel paying out the nose for dirty sheets," he says, looking around us. "Come on. We passed a hostel just down the way. Let's move. You need rest."

With our backpacks secured, Henry wraps his arm around my shoulders and pulls me along to keep up his fast pace. Naples is chaotic. It's very dark, and the cobblestone streets are crazy narrow. Even though it's late, life bubbles around us, especially in the tiny cars and mopeds that scream past and from the skinny balconies that stretch all the way up the structures. Centuries-old brick has been exposed on building facades where modern concrete has fallen away. Walls sullied with weathered posters, patchwork plaster repairs over damaged brick, so much graffiti, tired awnings flapping lazily in the cold wind that whips down the alleys—definitely a different vibe from Barcelona.

When we reach the hostel, I'm about to drop from exhaustion and pain. And my fingers feel swollen and sticky in my glove. I know I'm going to find blood when I pull it off.

Henry ushers us inside, giving the small brass bell on the wooden counter a jingle.

"*Buonasera,*" says a white-haired woman emerging from a velvet curtain behind the check-in desk. "May I help you?"

"Do you have a room?"

She looks at us over the top of her glasses and my breath catches in my throat. Please tell me she doesn't recognize us . . .

"She looks sick. Are you unwell, *mia cara*?"

"I'm fine. We had a bumpy flight."

"Ah, *sì,*" she says. "I do not like *aeroplani*. I will bring you sparkling water. That will help your tummy," she says, moving the mouse to bring her small computer to life. She offers us a room with our own bathroom, and Henry pays her for two nights. We then follow her down a short, dark, tiled hallway, up a flight of stairs, and down another hallway. We wait while she unlocks the door into a cozy room with a set of bunk beds, the space lit by a candle-shaped lamp on a small side table with two chairs. The room overlooks the street, which is actually perfect. The hostel-keeper hands Henry the key and says she will leave water and bread outside the door for me.

"My name is Maria. Do let me know if I can be of help to you. *Benvenuti a Napoli,*" she says as she exits.

Henry draws the curtains over the window and helps me out of my pack, but when he clicks on another small lamp, he sucks in his breath. "Genevieve, your *hand.*"

Sure enough, the blood has soaked through the fabric of my glove. I can feel my heartbeat in the still-open wounds of my arm. My head is heavy and I'm nauseated as he leads me to sit.

"Help me wash it," I say. "I'll just take more antibiotics."

However, when I stand again, it's obvious I'm in big trouble. I can hardly bear my own weight. Henry helps me into the bathroom, onto the cold, white-tile floor. As he pulls off my coat, he gasps. My shirt sleeve is soaked in blood, dried and fresh, and a quick glance at the wood-plank floor behind us reveals I have left a drip path.

I cannot heal myself.

And Aveline knows this.

If this continues, I'll be dead long before Iraq.

"God, I'm so tired."

"Genevieve, we have to get help."

"*No.* Wait—I'm fine. Help me clean and rebandage it. I'll be better in the morning. I need to sleep for a bit."

"You're sleepy because you are *hemorrhaging.* Whatever Aveline is doing, it's going to *kill* you," Henry says. He sounds panicked. "Please—you might need a hospital. A transfusion or something—"

"We *cannot* go to a hospital, Henry. You know that as well as I do. We just have to figure this out."

Henry kneels on the floor next to me. I'm now lying on my side, my left arm stretched out, leaking onto the floor. "Genevieve, please, I can't do this without you. I . . . you are my best friend. You're everything to me," he says, stroking my forehead. "You have to let me get some help."

I close my eyes, and when I open them again, Henry has slid a folded towel under my head and is cutting the bloodied bandage off. He washes the wound by squeezing out a washcloth soaked with warm water, which sets me into yet another vertiginous spin of overwhelming pain. Aveline's carving burns brightly with my blood. Worse, streaks stretch angrily from the sliced, malodorous flesh.

"This is very infected," Henry says. "You could lose your arm, or worse, if we can't stop it."

Henry sits back on his heels. The room is quiet, other than the noise floating up from the street.

"Gen, darling, can you hear me?" I can. He pets my forehead, but I feel like I'm floating above my body. "Genevieve, please—look at me." Henry's voice is tougher than I'm used to. And when I manage to shove my fifty-pound eyelids up all the way, he looks scared. "I am going to help you remember what it feels like to be healthy. Alicia and I will force your body to heal itself. We can fight this—we can fight Aveline—but you need to help me. You need to *concentrate* and show me a time when you were healthy and strong so I don't have to dig through your head. Can you do that?"

Eyes are so tired. Just let me sleep . . .

A strong pat to my cheek jolts me awake again. "Oww."

"Did you hear me? Alicia and I are going to help you.

Please—think of a time when you were physically healthy. When your body was strong. When you were powerful enough to care for Gertrude and Houdini and play the violin and perform on the silks for the adoring crowds and run through fields with Violet. *Remember*, Genevieve. Your life depends on it."

"I miss my elephants . . ." I whisper. The tear burns as it drains from my eye. It feels like the last drop of moisture in my body.

"And we're going to get you good and strong again so we can go home and be with Gert and Houdini and even your humongous house cat. All right? Think, Genevieve. *Think*. Show me how brave you are."

Henry clamps on to my left hand, not pausing even when my blood transfers to his skin. The warmth from his touch swarms through me. I smile. Like standing in the first rays of spring after the longest, coldest winter.

My eyes flicker open. "Alicia . . . hi . . ."

"Remember for us, Genevieve," Henry says again.

It's July. We're in a tiny town in Minnesota, and it's so hot, so humid. The venue where we're performing is on a huge lake. Everyone is deliriously happy about that. The big top is up and the day's rehearsal is over—no performance today—so Baby and Delia and I have Gertrude down at the water's edge. She's pregnant with Houdini, so she's even happier than the humans to be splashing in the cool water. She sucks up the lake and sprays everyone and everything, throwing her trunk back and forth, splashing like a preschooler, flopping onto her side to create waves, and then trumpeting so loudly it echoes off and pings around the towering trees.

She's so boisterous, cabin residents are out on their docks with cameras and binoculars to get a glimpse of the beautiful queen of Africa frolicking in their backyard.

Even Violet and Ash are in the water with us, Vi being unusually brave near the elephant as Baby hoists us on to Gert's back over and over again so we can dive in and then swim around her front to feed her mangoes and banana from the huge bin on the sand.

We cannot stop laughing, even as we handstand and then backflip off Gert's rump. Every few flips, she sucks up more water, lifts her trunk over her head, and douses us. Delia screams with glee when Baby throws her over his shoulder and sprints into the water with her. When they surface, they kiss.

Violet and I pretend to be disgusted and then see who can do the longest handstand before Gertrude knocks us back into the lake.

I feel strong and free and powerful. My balance, my muscles, my acrobatic body, my boundless energy . . . I want to stay here forever with the people I love most in this world.

"Genevieve," Henry says softly.

I take a huge breath in, like I've just broken through the surface of that cold Minnesotan lake, my eyes wet not with lake water but tears.

But the pain . . . it isn't eating me alive and I don't feel like I'm going to puke up my kidneys.

Henry releases my hand so he can scoot close and help me sit up. I look down at my arm—the rivulets of blood have stopped. The carved wounds are still angry, but the streaking is lessened. "Henry . . ." My eyes meet his. His upper lip and forehead are damp with perspiration but his cheeks are pink and his eyes could light up a night sky.

"Did that help?" he says, smiling.

"It worked. You did it."

"*We* did it." He puts a hand behind my head and kisses me hard on the mouth, his forehead pressed against mine when our lips part. "Please, promise me if it gets that bad again, you'll tell me sooner. Genevieve . . . I can't do this without you. I can't do anything without you." He kisses me again.

Once we're sure I'm steady on my feet, Henry cleans up the blood and sets to washing out my shirt in the sink. When he's done and the shirt's shaken out to dry over a towel rack, I gently wash my arm and hands, goose bumps rising on my bare skin. We find a single roll of gauze in his pack, barely enough to cover the wound, so we use it to wrap a maxi pad layered with antibacterial ointment over the carving. It'll have to do until we can get to a pharmacy in the morning.

"You're like a real grown-up," I tease. "You didn't even blush when I suggested this MacGyver-ed solution."

"It's quite clever, actually. Super absorbent. That's what we need right now." He smiles.

As I dry off, my reflection in the oval, gilded mirror looks pale, the dark circles under my eyes more pronounced than they've ever been. Henry places his hands on my bare shoulders, over the straps of my black sports-style bra, sending a frisson of warmth through me.

"I'm so glad you're okay," he says, kissing my shoulder before moving to pull off his own shirt. "I'll take the top bunk."

I grab his hand. "No. Please. We can squeeze in together. I don't want to be alone."

"Do you promise to behave yourself?"

I stretch up and kiss him. "Never."

As I move out of the bathroom, I feel so much stronger—it's amazing, and I'm so grateful and relieved. *Not today, Aveline.*

Henry has brought in the small tray Maria left outside our door—sparkling water and a few delicious-looking round buns. I drink down the water and inhale the sweet bread, glad to have something in my stomach so I can swallow more ibuprofen before sleeping.

Henry scoots against the wall on the bottom bunk, the blanket open and inviting me under. I tuck in, shivering as he stretches the coarse bedclothes up and over my shoulder.

"Do you suppose Xavier has lost his shit yet?" I ask.

Henry wraps his arm around me over the top of the blanket. "I know he has."

"Right. Alicia."

He kisses the back of my head. "Sleep now. We will deal with reality in the morning."

"Henry . . . thank you."

"I can't do this without you," he repeats from earlier, his voice low. "I love you, Genevieve."

My eyes pop open, but I don't move. He's never said that before. To me. Out loud.

No one has ever said that to me unless they were related. Well, except Violet. But she and her dumb brother are practically my siblings, so that's not unexpected. But hearing it from Henry . . . it brings on that warm-and-fuzzy feeling I always swore I'd never succumb to. Boys were Violet's thing. They just seemed like heartache and trouble to me.

Henry doesn't seem like heartache and trouble, though. And his words make me feel like we're more of a team, that when it comes down to it, both of our individual doubts about what we're doing—to burn the books, or not to burn the books—will dissipate and we'll make the right decision. Preserving the books would mean we could live together basically forever, like Nutesh and Hélène or even Delia and Baby, and I won't lie . . . there is romance in that.

But there is no romance in living a life where we are always looking over our shoulders, where no one can be trusted and we are never safe to stay in one place for long. Where the Etemmu is never more than a few putrid breaths away from sending me to the psych ward.

I lie still watching the slight dance of the curtain against the thin windowpane, my heart racing but fuller than ever. When Henry's breathing slows to suggest he's asleep, I'm finally brave enough.

"I love you too, Henry."

And his arm tightens around me.

25

In the morning, Maria leaves us another plate with bread, oranges, two bottles of sparkling water, as well as tourist brochures for the local area—including one for *Circo della regina*.

Upon seeing it on the tray while I'm kneeled in our room's open doorway, I look both ways down the hall, at once nervous that maybe Maria the hostel-keeper is on to us—that she saw a news report or somehow knows who we are, that she knows we're loosely affiliated with the circus people. How odd is it for two teenagers to arrive in the dead of night and pay cash for a room? Is that normal?

But then I see trays waiting outside the other rooms, and the *Circo della regina* pamphlet is on those too. I'm being paranoid. Maria is just doing her job to support local tourism. I hope.

I grab the tray, grateful for her generosity. Henry's in the bathroom, and the sun is slowly transforming the sky from the predawn purple to a soft baby blue. I scoot one of the room's rickety wooden chairs over by the window so I can watch the street. This second-story room is perfect—if I get my face right against the glass, I can just see the venue where *Circo della regina* is held.

I bite into one of Maria's sweet rolls and read the circus brochure, thankfully written in English. I want to know how many people these performances draw so we can time our own performance just right.

"*Circo della regina* takes place in the underground of Naples, *Napoli Sotterranea,* rich in 2,500 years of history dating back to the ancient Greeks. This unique underground realm has been used as aqueducts, reservoirs, and cisterns to provide water to the city for nearly twenty-three centuries. It also holds the Catacombs of San Gennaro, 280 miles of tunnels, the Hypogeum Gardens where vegetable plants thrive without sunlight, and even an old Greco-Roman theatre.

"Nero, heir and successor to the Roman emperor Claudius, was also a poet and actor. When he performed in *Napoli,* he would do so at the Neapolis Theatre. This underground space, carefully renovated with a generous grant from the Ministry of Cultural Heritage and Activities (MiBAC), now serves as the perfect backdrop for our shows.

"*Napoli Sotterranea* draws thousands of tourists a year, and *Circo della regina* is just one small part of the beauty. We look forward to welcoming you into our *Circo della regina* family!"

"Doing a little reconnaissance?" Henry's voice makes me jump. "Ahh, food."

I fold the brochure closed and slide it onto the table.

"Reading—and watching the street. Holding my breath Xavier doesn't come waltzing down the cobblestone."

"We're going to need real food here soon," Henry says. "You need to eat an entire cow to replace the blood you lost last night." The second chair creaks under his weight. "How's the arm?"

"Sore. But better, I think." To be honest, I'm afraid to look. "So—I've been thinking . . ." I let the flimsy curtain drop back over the window.

"Uh-oh, that look on your face means mischief," he says, peeling an orange.

"Naturally." I stand to reach under my bunk's edge and grab my black boots. "And yes, we do need some real food this morning—I'm going to need the strength for our little show."

Henry puts his orange aside and digs into his pack for the four-inch automatic knife stored within. We both have one, except today he'll use his to slice into his own flesh.

"Lift your shirt," I say. He does, and I draw a line with my fingertip where he should slice. "Don't cut deep—and cut over the shirt. We need it to bleed a lot and the blood to soak into the fabric so it looks more dramatic."

"Is this something you did to get out of school?" he asks, his face a bit pale. I lean over him in his chair, cupping his cheeks in my hands.

"Everything will be fine. Trust me." I kiss him.

"I do. I just don't like pain."

"Think of it as taking one for the team."

"We'd be cooler if we had a team name," he says.

"At this rate, Team Carnage seems appropriate."

Henry laughs and offers his fist for a bump. "Team Carnage it is." I meet his fist with my own. "Now, my clever co-conspirator, let us find a stage for our play, shall we?"

Neapolitans are a boisterous, loud group. The *caffetterie*, shops, vendors of everything from produce to purses—it's *busy*. The buildings are coated in graffiti, the streets packed with people and a million mopeds. The air at ground level early in the morning is cold but stinks of exhaust—the tightly packed structures on every single block seem to prevent the sun from reaching us all the way down here.

Henry and I took a huge risk leaving our packs in our room but having them on our bodies seemed even riskier. Besides, if everything goes to plan, we won't be on the street for long. Once we're done with our outdoor display, we'll sneak back to the hostel and plant ourselves in front of the window to watch what comes next.

We find a trattoria a few blocks over that serves the strongest coffee ever and *sfogliatella*, made with layers of crispy, flaky pastry and dusted with powdered sugar. Henry's had it before on prior trips to Italy; I have not, and I tell him maybe we should consider relocating here forever.

"You said that about the churros in Spain," he teases.

"I'm definitely on the wrong continent."

Next, we stop at a tourist-trap shop to buy Henry a long-sleeved white shirt—the three shirts we have left between us are all black, and we need something to showcase his blood—a touristy white sweatshirt for me that says *Italia* across the green, white, and red Italian flag, two burner smartphones, as well as sunglasses to go with our knitted caps. When we catch our passing reflection in a shop window, we agree that we look like low-budget bank robbers planning a heist.

Which is sort of not too far from the truth.

When human and vehicle traffic on *Via dei Tribunali*—the street where our hostel and the gloriously ornate *Napoli Sotterranea* are located—seems to hit a frenzied peak, it's showtime.

We establish a post-event rendezvous spot, an art gallery two blocks southeast, and then we split. I stroll into a *caffè* just off the *Piazza San Gaetano,* across from *Sotterranea,* grateful they have outdoor seating, though I do have to wait a few tense moments for a table to come available.

I order an espresso and thumb through an Italian magazine someone left behind. The pictures are beautiful, which is good since I can't read a single word in the articles.

When it seems the time is right, I text Henry's new burner a single word:

Go.

I try to look casual, like I belong there. The first scream from my right tells me the show has begun.

Henry stumbles out of an alley just down from the *Napoli Sotterranea*, his white shirt drenched in blood under the hand that clutches his abdomen. Chaos erupts on the street as he makes eye contact with me and drops to his knees on the sidewalk across the way.

Powered by pure adrenaline, I jump up from my table and leap past the black barricade poles cemented into the ground to keep people and cars separate on this busy street. I run across to where Henry has collapsed, shoving people out of my way.

I burst through the last few bystanders to see that a shopkeeper already has a phone against his ear; another woman is shoving her coat under Henry's head. I throw my hands in the air.

"*Posso aiutare!* I can help!" I yell, likely butchering the Italian Google Translate taught me an hour ago. I tear off my gloves, the left one still stiff and mildly damp from Henry's earlier efforts to wash clean the blood. "Sir, what's happened? Let me help you."

When another man tries to shove me out of the way to see what's going on, I deliver a quick jolt to his wrist that puts him on his knees, but people are so focused on the blood spilling out of Henry's exposed stomach, they don't notice when the other guy's teeth knock together from the surge of electricity. At least he lets go of me.

"Stand *back*!" I yell. And then I close my eyes, a few breaths in, and I let the nuclear reactor in the back of my head take over and push the electricity aside. My hands on Henry's bleeding belly, I shove all that healing energy into him, my wound singing with renewed pain. He did a good job cutting into himself—almost too good.

When his eyes flutter open, a collective gasp rises from the crowd. I exhale, wishing I'd thought to stuff a bottle of OJ in my pants pocket.

I help him to sitting, asking again if he's okay. "*Sì.* I'm okay. *Grazie mille,*" he says. A bystander hands me tissue to wipe off my hands. I take it and then help Henry stand, glad for the sunglasses that still shield my eyes from the dumbstruck faces surrounding us.

People are stunned silent, and more than a few cellphones record the event.

Perfect.

"*Merci beaucoup, mademoiselle,*" Henry says, his French accent flawless. "You saved my life." His words sound a bit stilted, but I don't think our rapt audience is much interested in any dialogue exchanged between us.

"As long as you're sure you're okay," I say.

He nods. "*C'est bien. Je suis bien.*"

"Okay, well, good luck, then. And be careful." Our eyes lock when we hear sirens in the distance—definitely our cue to get going.

I disappear into the crowd, pushing myself into a fast walk, forcing what little energy I have into my legs the closer the sirens get. I jog down the block and dip into an arched recess in a dank alley where a desperate cat watches under a garbage bin; I pause to tear off the *Italia* sweatshirt, the sleeves damp with Henry's blood, as well as the sunglasses and the black knit cap, throwing everything into the trash. I replace the hat with a muted gray one and then I'm moving again, slower, so I can catch my breath.

Instead of bounding into the art gallery sweaty and shaken, I slow down and rejoin the throngs of tourists on the sidewalks, pausing to buy a few apples from a vendor across the narrow, cobbled street. I watch the surroundings, the art gallery door, looking for evidence that I was followed or that someone maybe saw what happened a few blocks over. My heart feels lodged in my throat, which makes swallowing even small bites from my sweet apple difficult.

When Henry finally emerges from an alley down the way, he's changed his shirt and has his sunglasses and a new knit cap on, a newspaper under his arm. I'm so relieved, I almost collapse.

I finish the apple—I need the sugar—and dodge scooters and crazed tiny cabs, following him into the art gallery at a safe distance. It's a small place but brightly lit, the air a mix of cologne, old building, and paint thinner. Bold, multicolored canvases hang on the snow-white walls next to florals and nudes; sculptures of glass, metal, and reclaimed items on pedestals split the main room in half. Areas not available for viewing are cordoned with red-velvet rope between ancient-looking brass posts.

I watch Henry from across the cavernous space, marking the time; we are to browse for two minutes and then leave, me first, then him. As the clock clicks to that 120th second, I walk out of the gallery, looking back only once to make sure Henry's behind me before I slide my new sunglasses into place. We make our way southeast and then loop around, back to the hostel.

As I pull open the front door, I'm relieved to see Maria is busy talking to other guests—a young couple with their own heavy travel packs still on their shoulders. It feels like the fire of hell is breathing down my neck as I break into a run up the staircase and down the hall to our room.

It's not the fire of hell, though. Just Henry, his face as flushed and his eyes as worried as my own.

When he throws the secondary safety lock, we collapse, him against the door, me on the bottom bunk.

"We did it," I say.

He smiles. "Now let's hope our performance gets rave reviews."

26

WE TAKE TURNS IN THE BATHROOM WASHING OFF THE REST OF THE BLOOD—his, this time—before positioning one of the wooden chairs in front of the window. Maria's hostel has free Wi-Fi; Henry opens up YouTube, and sure enough, we're there. We're on Twitter too—"Miracle Girl Strikes Again"—the video shitty secondary to the low-quality phone. No matter, though. The intended damage has been done.

"Show me again who we're looking for?" I drain the last of my sparkling water. Henry sits on the bottom bunk and reaches for me, flattening his hand over my open palm, making contact, the warmth rushing through me as the Guardian's face appears on the screen in my head: he's a small-statured man with thinning grayish hair and crooked teeth and large, hooded brown eyes topped with thick, unruly eyebrows.

Just as quickly, Henry withdraws, but the visual stays put.

"Those eyebrows should make it easy to spot him." Henry smiles and scoots back.

"Sort of like yours." I nod at him. "We should pencil in that missing slice. It's pretty noticeable."

"We could use a Sharpie."

I push my face against the window again, afraid to miss a single moment of scanning the activity on the street below.

"You should also know that Xavier is in the city," Henry says, his face serious again.

"We knew he'd make it here. Tell your mother thank you, for me," I say, not knowing if Alicia is in the room with us. "Any idea how much time before he finds us?"

Henry closes his eyes for a beat. "No. But if we can't spot the Guardian by sundown, we should move to a different hostel. Just to stay one step ahead."

"Except he'll probably notify the Guardian that we've gone rogue. Maybe the guy won't meet with us without Xavier," I say, biting at my lip. "If only one of us could tell the future instead of the past."

Henry chuckles. "Now, what would be the fun in that?"

We decide to break up our watch into one-hour shifts. If we don't spot the Guardian by dinner, we'll look for another place to hide out and come up with a plan B, likely involving another day of surveillance around this neighborhood. Maybe the Guardian doesn't have access to the internet, so he won't see the bright, shining beacon we've thrown onto the sky of the web.

During my first watch, Henry steals downstairs with more of our dwindling cash stores to talk to Maria about food for the rest of the day, and a request to look through the lost and found for any clothes that might fit us. We concoct a story about how our luggage went missing so until we can get our new traveler's checks, shopping in the fashion capital of the world won't be possible.

The street below is so busy, and the angle of our window makes it frustratingly hard to see the *Sotterranea* very well. My eyes are tired from too little sleep and too much anxiety, and the longer I sit here, the more I worry this plan was stupid from the outset, that I've done nothing but put us in more jeopardy.

Henry returns with a few new-to-us shirts draped over his shoulder, three plastic-wrapped rolls of gauze in his pocket, a tray with a huge bowl of pasta with tomato and fresh basil, a loaf of Italian bread, and more sparkling water. "Any luck yet?" he asks.

"No."

He pushes the door closed with his foot. "I think Maria likes us."

"Oh my god, that smells so good."

After we eat, it's Henry's turn to take watch. My arm aches and when I pull my shirt sleeve up, I'm not surprised to find the sanitary-napkin-bandage soaked through. I grab the gauze Henry brought back, my medical kit, and then close myself in the bathroom to clean the slices in my flesh.

Say hello to Daddy for me.

"You're a psycho, Aveline," I say to the tight space, holding my breath for a beat as I wait to see if the Etemmu will take offense and find me.

Nothing but the drip of the old faucet.

Once the wound is cleaned and the bandage wrapped tight—without any of Xavier's/Delia's yarrow that I really wish I had—I clench my jaw and stab myself in the butt with another of the antibiotic injectables. Which, of course, leads to thoughts of Baby and how he's doing. "Alicia, check on Baby. Please. Tell Henry how he's doing. Tell Baby and Mom I love them," I whisper.

Before I rejoin Henry in the main room, though, there's one more person I need to check in with.

From the thigh pocket of my black cargo pants, I dig out my burner phone, hoping the pay-as-you-go service plan Henry paid for will reach America.

Vi, it's Gen. New phone. Tell me if you get this.

I wait, watching the screen, holding my breath. Google "current time in Eaglefern, OR." They're eight hours behind Naples, Italy, which makes it—

Gen, OMG! Hi! Prove that it's you.

I think for a moment. What would be one thing only Vi and I would know about each other?

Your 1st kiss was with that redheaded kid in
LA & we planned your wedding & decided
you'd name all your kids after the Weasleys.

I smile, staring at the phone as I await her response.

I'd marry him if he showed up again!

LOL . . . hi, sis. I miss you. How's it going?

Miss you too. Cece & Ted & Ash OK?
Elephants and Othello?

Everyone here's OK but worried. Still lots of police. Dad is making us rehearse nonstop & we might be going to another show if Cinzio folds.

The thought of the Cinzio Traveling Players closing down hurts my heart. Ted and Cecelia Cinzio built that show from nothing and have traveled with it for nearly thirty-five years. If it goes under, it will take the livelihoods of dozens of my closest friends with it. And where will Gert and Houdini and Othello end up?

I don't even know how to respond. How can I ever apologize for doing this to my family?

Gen, you there?!

I'm so sad—I hope I can get home before Ted
has to close the show.

My eyes burn; my nose stings. *This is all my fault. If I'd just given Lucian the book . . .*

Dad's adding Mara to our act. She's really great on the trapeze. Will help us get a new gig, maybe even in Europe, if we have more trapezists.

I'm shaking so hard, I can hardly hold the phone. Aveline is still there—but why? Why is she not in Europe with Lucian looking for us?

Gen, you should call Cece.
She's not doing very well.

I'm going to implode from the pain.

Vi, can you tell her in secret that I'm OK & I'll be home as soon as I can & she shouldn't worry?

Which is a lie. She should totally worry. I may not make it home ever.

Henry taps on the door. "Genevieve? You need any help?"

"No, I'm good. One sec," I say, hiding my phone under the hand towel. When I hear the old chair squeak with Henry's weight, I pull the phone back out.

Vi, I gotta run. I'll check back ASAP.
I love you guys.

Love you too. Please be safe.

I power down and tuck it into my thigh pocket before opening the bathroom door.

"How're you doing? See any possibles?" I flop my back-pack onto the lower bunk.

"No one yet."

"Can Alicia not find this guy for us?"

"She deals in memories, not soothsaying," Henry reminds me. "Plus, I already asked. She can't see him. He might be protected by the same spells that kept Lucian blind to you, and the Etemmu blind to me."

"We could live a thousand years and never understand this magic, Henry." I'm half joking but I realize as the words cross my lips that I shouldn't give him an invitation to discuss anything other than destroying the texts. With every passing moment we spend together, I see what a good team we make. If we were to live long lives, what greatness could we accomplish together?

Destroying the texts will take that all away. Will our friendship change if we are no longer magical? Will we become "normal" young people who go our separate ways, to our own lives at different universities, on different trajectories, and realize that long-distance relationships at our age are silly, that we're not mature enough for real love, that there are too many other temptations?

If we destroy these books, will it change *us*, this couple forced together by circumstance and shared terror?

Who are we singularly—and together—without the *AVRAKEDAVRA*? Who is Genevieve without her healing hands? Who is Henry without his facility with memory?

But with the *AVRAKEDAVRA*, our lives are in danger. Forever. There is no "normal" as long as these books are allowed to survive.

If I give Henry that moment to sway me, to try to convince me we can do great things and live in our own bubble on the fringes of reality, then we are no better than the monsters hunting us.

I must stay focused on the mission objective. I will have to take my chances that the nonmagical Genevieve and Henry will still love each other after the books are ash on the Babylonian wind.

"If you're good for a second, I need to reorganize my bag and see what medical stuff we have left. Xavier made a mess of it on the boat."

Henry waves me to it, so I turn from him and dump out my backpack, except the *AVRAKEDAVRA*. I'm glad to find an unexpected gauze roll at the bottom as well as two foil packets of antibacterial ointment. I zip everything into the proper medical kit—I have six doses of antibiotics left before I'll have to use Henry's—and then I swallow two ibuprofen with one of the waters Maria left us. The fever rages on, and it's wearing me out.

Out of the corner of my eye, the top card of Delia's hand-painted deck catches my attention. These cards—my mom was a talented artist, in addition to her magical abilities with plants—she made them during her many inpatient stays when the Etemmu would get to be too much and no one, except Baby and me, knew what was really happening. The cards are one of the few things I have left of her—they are the story of her past. They're beautiful and precious to me.

This top card has a purple iris on a white background (the purple iris is Lucian's sigil), the top third framed by the bloodred banner with golden writing etched into the banner's fabric. There's an identical painting to this one hanging in a detailed mural in Lucian's study at their estate in Eaglefern. I saw it when I went snooping where I shouldn't have been, but where I also discovered Lucian's *AVRAKEDAVRA* resting in its secure glass case.

As I stare at the iris card, the writing in the painting *moves*, like it's trying to reshape itself.

I blink and blink. Maybe the fever is higher than I thought.

No. The gold lettering is vibrating on the card.

"What the . . ." I push my other stuff aside and pick up the stack, untying the leather lace that holds it together. I spread the cards out on the rough green-and-gray wool blanket, placing them in a square. The cards closest to my backpack—to the *AVRAKEDAVRA*—their images are *dancing*.

The delicate vines around the card borders twist softly, circling the card's rectangular borders in an endless loop. The scenes portrayed on the card fronts look animated: Delia on horseback where the horse is actually galloping, the faces of healers and friends, including Alicia, Baby, and who I now recognize as Xavier, castles and estates and dank dungeons and even the Seine River snaking along, birds flying above a ziggurat, trees swaying in a heavy forest . . .

But it's the vines around the edges. They're reshaping themselves—into letters?

A buzzing noise brushes my ear. Unconsciously, I swipe at it, a trained response from constantly whisking away flies that follow the circus like groupies. But then the buzzing gets louder. I look around me, breath short, terrified this is some new manifestation by the Etemmu, but when I move my head closer to my pack, the buzzing intensifies.

The insistent sound is coming from the backpack—from the AVRAKEDAVRA.

"Do you hear that?" Henry asks.

I double-check that our main door is bolted, and then I slide the text out of its compartment. When the book is on the bed next to the cards, the artwork moves in a frenzy, and then the book, all by itself, opens.

"What is going on?" Henry asks, closing the short distance between us.

"Are the images moving for you too?"

Henry nods.

"Thank the gods. I thought I was losing my mind."

"But what *is* it?"

"No idea." The drawings on the left page the book opened itself to are exquisitely detailed. Like looking at a *Gray's Anatomy* (the anatomical illustrations book, not the TV show)—it depicts a wound and then various plants drawn in seed, sprout, and full-grown form. I recognize the yarrow, but I can't read the language written in perfect script throughout.

Across the top of both open pages, words have been written in a golden ink. "Any idea what language that is?" I ask Henry.

He's shaking his head. "It doesn't quite look like Hebrew. Maybe Aramaic?"

On the right-side page, the author has drawn an inverted triangular amulet using a word with eleven characters. With every subsequent line, a character drops off, until the final line contains only a solitary letter. The ten pictures surrounding the inverted triangle show a sick person, a healer, family members caring for the patient, offerings of food and fruit to the ailing. On the tenth drawing, it shows the ill person standing straight and tall with his back to a river and throwing the amulet over his shoulder.

"This amulet—it looks sort of like the inverted triangle and circle symbol. This must be the healing ritual the *AVRAKEDAVRA* was based upon," I say.

"But why are the pictures on the cards moving?" Henry points to them, still animated where they rest on the blanket.

A knock hits the door and I'm not sure who startles harder.

"Hide it!" Henry whisper-yells. He zips to the table and grabs his knife, but as he's tiptoeing toward the door, the spring-loaded blade open and ready for business, an envelope slides under the one-inch gap between door and floor. I drop onto my belly to watch for feet or a shadow on the other side, sure that if a bad guy is here for us, a flimsy wooden hostel door will not keep him or her out, even with both locks thrown.

Henry points anxiously toward the bunk; I right myself and bury the text under the blanket and pillow, scooping the cards into a pile and wrapping them in one of my new lost-and-found shirts before burying the deck in the backpack.

We don't move for at least ten minutes, me on one knee near the bunks, my own knife drawn, electricity coursing hot through my hands, Henry against the wall near the door, ready to strike if someone bursts through.

When it's clear no one is coming in after us, Henry quickly bends and picks up the envelope. He stretches it toward me, silent as the grave. When we hear excited conversation walk past our door, we freeze.

Nothing more than fellow hostel guests.

Henry tries the doorknob—still locked. He nods, and I nod in response, a silent agreement that it's safe to move again. He slides onto the bunk next to me as I hold the business-sized envelope in my hands.

"Put gloves on before you open it," he says. "For safety."

I do and then slide my finger under the sealed edge, holding my breath against what could come flying out at me. Instead of an Etemmu or other nasty surprise, though, it's an entry ticket from *Napoli Sotterranea* for *Circo della regina*.

"One ticket?" I ask, turning it over. Words have been scratched onto the back.

"Pompeii, 3 a.m. *Porta Marina*. I am the Guardian you seek. ~G."

27

However the alleged Guardian found us, it's freaky enough for Henry and me to pack up, write Maria a brief note of thanks, and sneak out a rear entrance, our faces and heads obscured by hats and sunglasses, our hearts beating out of our chests.

Our half-baked plan to draw out the Guardian worked, but we can't risk staying at Maria's one more second. We find accommodation in another hostel a few blocks over and sequester ourselves in our room, studying a map of Pompeii and surrounding areas picked up from a rack of touristy brochures. The note on the *Sotterranea* ticket said *Porta Marina*, which is one of the three entrances into the walled city of Pompeii. Henry finds it on the cartoonish map. Plus, the venue matches the info Henry pulled out of Xavier's head, so at least this part seems true.

But—the grounds at Pompeii aren't open for visitors at three in the morning, which leads us to one of two arguments: 1. The Guardian is legit and has arranged for our meeting to happen in a location where *no one* will be in the dead of night, a smart move; 2. This is a setup and we're walking into an ambush.

I'm not going to admit this to Henry, but I'm definitely doubting my earlier bravado about ditching Xavier.

"It says here that Pompeii is heavily haunted. Maybe the benevolent spirits will keep us safe." Henry winks, sprawled on his bunk. I think he's joking, but the idea of being surrounded by the ghosts of more than two thousand people who died when Vesuvius blew its top kind of creeps me out.

Especially when my sworn enemies are allegedly in control of the souls in the Afterlife.

Though we're wired on enough caffeine and pastry sugar to take down a bull, once we have our plan of action, we try sleeping, both of us tossing and turning until the phone alarm goes off just after midnight. The smart, legal way to get to Pompeii would be to hire a taxi. But we're not necessarily smart, or legal.

So we will be hot-wiring a car instead.

Just another little circus-kid trick I can share with my posh, sheltered Henry.

But finding a car without a bazillion people hanging out nearby proves more difficult than we expected, especially in a part of the city where mopeds and scooters outnumber humans, and citizens stay up way past a North American bedtime to eat, drink, and socialize. We need a vehicle that looks reliable, but not flashy. Considering we're going to abandon it outside the grounds at Pompeii, we don't need to attract any unwanted attention.

We zero in on a suitable candidate but bypass it because the lights of the closest villa are on with people visible through the window. We find another car that might work but the model is too old so when I try to zap the electrical system through the handle to unlock it, I leave only a scorch mark and the door doesn't budge.

Panic prickles through me, but then Henry spots a lone black Fiat up ahead, sitting under a burned-out streetlight.

"Might work," I say. Fate is on our side as the driver's side door is unlocked, and the ignition is push button, like the one on Keller's boat.

Surge of energy through my index finger, and the little sweetie comes alive.

"You're getting the hang of that," Henry says. "Maybe a future in grand larceny for you?"

"This is like cheating. I'm disappointed I didn't get to pull wires from the steering column and show you how to really steal a car."

"There's always tomorrow," he says, smiling as he pops open the paper map across his lap and the dashboard.

With me behind the wheel, Henry navigates with both his phone's GPS and a paper map when the cell signal drops. We weave out of the maze of streets and find the freeway that'll take us southeast toward Pompeii.

"If this Guardian named 'G' is for real and we get the piece, we're going to need to get in touch with Nutesh." I check the car's rearview and side mirrors obsessively, watching the headlights behind and around us for a possible tail. "We've done Spain and Italy. He said Turkey was next. What's the name of the city you plucked out of Xavier's head?"

"Izmir," Henry says. "In the greenhouse, Nutesh said air

transport could be arranged. We will call him, explain the circumstances—"

"Oh, I'm sure Xavier has taken care of that."

"And as yet, we have no idea where Xavier is or when he'll show up again, so the plan is we call Nutesh, arrange a pickup, and we go to Izmir."

"And when we're there, what, do we put on another show like the one we did here?" I ask.

"Why not? It worked, didn't it?"

"Violet will be so jealous that we're YouTube famous without her," I joke, even though I know there's nothing funny about any of this. Call it a coping mechanism because racing along the Italian freeway, it goes without saying that we are way out of our depth.

When we finally reach the neighborhood where the ruins of Pompeii are nestled—thank goodness we left as early as we did because we totally got lost when our phones decided to stop connecting—I'm happy to see the street leading toward our entrance quiet and free of pedestrians. Henry points for me to park alongside a tall stone wall. Full, fragrant trees and bougainvillea sway and rustle over the wall's edge. The ever-present buzz of scooters drifts from the small city behind us, even at this incredibly late hour, but so far, none seem to be interested in the quiet ruins at two thirty in the morning.

The person calling themselves "G" said to be here at three, but now we have a few minutes to squeeze between the buildings and watch to see if we were followed. I follow Henry down the darkened street, marked with the occasional crosswalk and worn white and yellow stripes indicating parking spots, our steps lit with wide-set street lamps and Henry's flashlight. Closed businesses flank the right side of the road—looks like tour guide and souvenir shops as well as maybe a restaurant and a *caffè* separated by decorative metal railings. Knee-height rectangular planters with thriving plants sit along the sidewalk.

The closer we move to the entrance, the quieter it gets, the only sound the occasional breeze stirring the trees and squawking birds either out for a late night or anticipating the sunrise in just a few hours.

Sure enough, the entrance to the ruins rises before us, a proper modern welcome center of white and gray concrete, spiked black fencing, and silver lettering announcing itself: *Scavi di Pompei / Porta Marina.*

A flashlight up ahead, behind a locked gate, flashes once.

We freeze.

It flashes again.

Henry flashes twice in return.

And then the gate opens. We step through, pausing in front of a man who might actually dwarf Baby, dressed in a white button-down and dark-wash jeans under a mid-thigh, black leather duster, his face in need of a shave. "The key to good is found in truth," he says, his English heavily accented. He pulls a key out from under his shirt.

Relief shudders through me. I pull out my own key and

repeat his greeting, kissing the key before replacing it under my layers.

"Where is Xavier?" he asks.

"It's just us. I'm Genevieve; this is Henry."

The man nods and offers a gloved hand to each of us. "Pietro. Come," he says, gesturing behind him. "Gaetano awaits."

We fall into step with Pietro, walking through the modern parts of the site, past a quiet information center and glassed-in ticket booth, and down a few wide, paved steps and toward our first glimpse of the ruins. We hop the closed ticket turnstiles, and Henry clasps my left hand, his firm grip reminding me that my carved forearm, though no longer hemorrhaging, is still a serious problem.

The paved walkway is bordered by railings and well-manicured shrubbery at first, but then the smooth concrete is exchanged for the large-stone roadway of antiquity. The ruins are quiet, and eerily beautiful. Because it's so dark, we're only given brief glimpses of the damaged buildings as we come upon them, uplit by evenly spaced floodlights, the space green with grass as well as palm and other trees. We head up a very steep stone walkway flanked by modern-day metal railings bolted into the stone. Ahead are two arches but Pietro is no tour guide.

The chilled and seemingly endless arched tunnel empties onto a longish stone street bordered by a towering stone and brick wall on the right, delicate pillars encased in metal exoskeletons and gated courtyards and ruins of what might have been homes on the left. A small marker notes our location: "REG VII / INS VII."

Though the road is flanked by sidewalks, we're walking down the center of the stone street. The rocks have been smoothed by centuries of wear, the effects of being buried by volcanic material, and now the millions of tourist feet that plod through on an annual basis. Strategically placed across the road are large flat boulders set about a foot apart—ancient crosswalks, perhaps?—as well as large rocks along the wall that maybe were for resting. It looks weird to see the addition of garbage and recycle bins, but time stops for no man.

Someone should remind Lucian of that.

The brick-and-stone walls, now on both sides, extend to the block's end and the road leads directly to a huge open rectangular space (about the size of a football field) bordered by tall, capital-topped columns. At the western end, we can see the twinkling lights of a city against the shadow of a slumbering Mount Vesuvius. An imposing bronze sculpture of a centaur holding a spear sits on a tall brick pedestal directly ahead of us, and when our Italian guide's flashlight hits it, a shiver runs down my spine. The air here feels heavy.

Pietro speaks barely above a whisper, his voice gravelly. "The Forum. Center of life for Pompeians. Gaetano will be here. One moment."

We stand next to the centaur sculpture and wait. Pietro points as he speaks. "Down there, the Granary. Artifacts and plaster castings of Pompeians who died in Vesuvius. *Molto sacro,*" Pietro says. *Very sacred.*

When Pietro unbuttons his leather coat, my heart skips

a beat at the very large weapon hanging in a hip holster. I guess I shouldn't be surprised by seeing this. Not everyone has Tasers built in to their hands.

Pietro tells Henry to kill his flashlight and then moves around the side of the centaur, hand at his belt. Henry's grip on me tightens.

When instead of a gunshot, we hear a pleasant greeting and the sound of patted backs, Henry and I both exhale with relief. Pietro reappears at the front of the sculpture pedestal, waving us forward. "Come," he says. "Gaetano is here."

We step out from the centaur's shadow and are greeted by the man from Henry's memory. He smiles politely, but his lips quiver with the effort. I'm guessing he's as nervous as we are.

"I am Gaetano. It is a pleasure to meet you both," he says. "You had a clever, and dangerous, way of making contact with me. I expected it to be Xavier to make the arrangements."

"Change of plans," I say. "Thank you for meeting with us."

"Xavier is an old friend. Should I be concerned for his welfare?" Gaetano asks. I can't tell if the tremor in his voice is from age, or fear.

"We were separated en route to Naples," Henry says. "Our mission is one of urgency, as you likely are aware."

Gaetano nods, but his watery eyes don't look convinced. He then gestures toward the western end of the Forum, and then turns to move toward it, his steps shuffling. He's not nearly as fierce or determined-looking as Shamira and Joseph were.

"A podium sits down there adequate for our needs," Gaetano explains.

The gravel underfoot is the sole sound as we move toward the squared-off pile of bricks. Some of the columns along the Forum's sides are still topped with what looks like might have been part of a roof structure; when the flashlight is aimed at the marble tops, carved letters appear.

Sure enough, as we approach the western end, a brick podium/pedestal construction surfaces out of the darkness.

Gaetano stops before it and turns to me. "I knew your mother," he says. Just like Shamira did. Unlike Shamira, however, he doesn't offer condolences or pat my hand. When he pulls out the key under the neckline of his button-down shirt, he doesn't kiss it or whisper a prayer or tuck it away again.

I watch the key closely, praying it doesn't turn black before my very eyes. My unease is not soothed when I note that Henry is taking his gloves off, slowly, one at a time, his eyes wide and alert.

The hair on the back of my neck stands on end; the fire behind my sternum blazes.

Gaetano then turns to Henry and me. "You must present your texts to prove your identity." I stare at Henry for a moment, wishing I could speak directly into his brain—*This doesn't feel right*—but I can't risk touching him or conjuring any images. We don't have time.

"Do you have the key piece?" I ask.

"Of course," Gaetano says. He nods at Pietro, who then pulls a square jewelry-style box out of his pocket. Pietro opens the hinged box, and inside is another polished, gray-stone piece of the temple key.

Henry and I pull off our backpacks. As soon as my hands make contact with the text, the vibration begins, even through my gloves, only this time it feels sharp and almost painful. Not like before.

Gaetano motions to the podium and pats the surface gently.

"Please place your texts here and lay a hand atop," he says, his voice wavering.

As we did with Shamira, Henry and I follow Gaetano's instructions. I pull off my right-hand glove. Like it did when I was first sealed to it, as my skin touches the book's surface, energy blows through me, rattling my teeth and initiating an instant searing headache.

Gaetano begins speaking, extends a gnarled hand first on top of mine and then on Henry's. The exchange between me and the book slows, but whereas before I felt strong and invincible after the prior ritual, I now feel depleted and anxious.

As the last words cross Gaetano's lips, the key hanging from his neck turns deathly black.

And bright light floods the area around us.

Gaetano is shaking, his hands clasped in front of his face in prayer formation, his head bobbing and tears flowing down his cheeks. "*Mi dispiace molto!* I'm so sorry! *Ti prego, perdonami!*" His *La Vérité* key shimmers in its own cloud of black vapor. Pietro is already lying flat on the ground, his arms outstretched. Gaetano is near wailing at this point, alternately raising his hands into the air and clasping them in front of his face.

"It's an ambush," I say quietly, as if commenting on the weather.

An ambush made worse when a third man emerges from the black night.

Gaetano attempts to speak, but only a pained squeak emerges.

"*Benvenuto*," Xavier says. "Welcome to Pompeii." He steps forward, arms outstretched. Three other men emerge from under the glare of the blinding lights.

Xavier stops in front of me, lips pursed in amusement.

"You're a fucking *traitor*." I spit on his boot.

His eyes flash in warning as he withdraws the weapon at his hip. "This is my associate, Enzo," he says, gesturing toward the grinning Italian now next to him, his own weapon drawn. Enzo looks like a movie star—clean-cut brown hair, no hint of stubble, large brown eyes, perfect white teeth that gleam in a terrifying smile. He and his associates are dressed like they're going to an exclusive nightclub—shimmery button-down shirts with coordinating ties, dark slacks, expensive-looking shoes, suit coats.

Except Enzo's tie is held in place with a shining silver pin: the inverted triangle overlying the circle.

He catches me looking at it.

"That's right. You know what this means, don't you?" Enzo purrs, reaching to pull the knitted hat from my head. "And she does look so much like her mother, even without those fiery, flowing locks. I heard she did." He brushes a finger under my chin and tosses my hat away; I flinch from his touch just as Henry moves to step in front of me. The man laughs at him. "Your girlfriend is beautiful. You are a lucky man, Henry Dmitri. Your father sends his regards."

"Enough," Xavier barks. "Get what we came for before the morning guards show up." He stares hard at me, then down at my hands, then back up to my eyes, nodding ever so slightly.

What the hell is going on?

"You heard the man," Enzo says, signaling with one finger at the books. The two goons with him move toward us; one hits Gaetano upside the head to stop his wailing. He crumples to the ground next to Pietro. I don't know who's more the coward—a hired muscle beating up an old man, or the old man's bodyguard stretched out like a dead starfish.

I'm clenching and stretching my fingers, but Enzo sees my movement. "Ah, *no, no, no,* my young friend, Miss Aveline warned me. You put both of those gloves back on, or I will make you watch while I kill everyone else here first, starting with lover boy. Do you understand what I am saying?" Enzo raises his gun arm at Henry. A chilling click as the safety releases. I stare daggers at Enzo and tighten my fists against the rage burning inside me. A breeze wafts past carrying the smell of singed skin and fabric.

Enzo's lackeys shove the *AVRAKEDAVRA* texts and both key pieces in a large, leather satchel.

"Please don't do this," I say, trying to mask the frustrated horror coursing through me. We can't lose these books here tonight. We can't have suffered so much for it to be over so soon.

Henry, standing close enough that I can hear his rapid,

scared breaths, grabs my wrist, the bare skin just above where my glove ends and my sleeve starts. Alicia appears next to him.

"Genevieve, give me your energy," he says under his breath. "Help me."

And then Henry drops to his knees and slams his other hand flat onto the ground in front of him, immediately conjuring a horrifying scene of the earth shaking, the sky blackening, the air choked with hot ash. Smoldering debris rains from the sky, settling alight everything it touches. The Forum is as it was nearly two thousand years ago, the colonnade supporting a roof over our heads, and the space is filled with panicking people running and screaming and shoving one another to escape. Carts are overturned; produce and bread is mashed underfoot. Amphorae holding wine and oils smash to bits, their aroma spicing the smoky air.

Children separated from parents howl and shriek; horses rear and bolt and goats bleat, stampeding over whatever gets in their way. The air is so thick and hot, every inhale burns like I will never breathe again. People drop around us, choking and foaming at the mouth, eyes wide with the terror that they're being asphyxiated by the tantrum of an angry mountain just miles from where we stand.

It's having the same effect on Enzo and his men, all of them spinning in confusion, grabbing at their throats, coughing, spitting, gagging on the sooty air, dropping to their knees, eyes bulging and neck veins protruding as they struggle for one clean breath.

Enzo relinquishes his hold on the leather satchel containing the *AVRAKEDAVRA* texts.

Xavier is on his knees, bent in half, choking and coughing, but his fingers are wrapped around the grip of his handgun.

"Genevieeeeeve, everything you have!" Henry yells. I'm frozen in place but I look down at him, light blowing out of his eyes like frigid blue spotlights, and I see Alicia with her arms outspread, her ghostly form glowing, lit from the inside. I close my eyes and force the inferno burning inside me down through my arm and into Henry's hand. I know by the agonizing holler that he feels everything I'm giving him, a long, painful sound that manifests in the worsening of the ash plume choking the men around us.

Just when I think my lungs can't possibly bear another airless second, Henry lets go and the vision dissipates.

No one else is left standing.

Enzo's men are still and coiled in the fetal position, their eyes fixed open, their foamy lips purple and faces blue. Enzo is on his back, coughing and sputtering, his formerly pristine complexion splattered with streaks from tiny broken blood vessels, his irises floating in the blood that has flooded the whites of his eyes. Xavier, still huddled over, drops his gun but then draws a formidable knife from his boot.

"Henry!" I scream as Xavier stumbles toward him. But my father doesn't slice into Henry's flesh. He bends down and buries the blade in Enzo's neck.

Holy shit. He didn't kill Henry. He killed Enzo.

What the hell is happening? Is he going to take the books for himself now?

Unsteady, Xavier stands and stabs both of the other men in the heart, even though they look plenty dead to me. He then drops his knife, coughing and wheezing in air that is once again free of sulfuric contaminants.

Henry collapses onto his side, his face sweaty and red and his breaths short like he's just sprinted a race.

I turn and vomit onto the sacred ground. I spit and cough, and then kneel next to Henry. "I didn't know you could do that."

His eyes closed, he hacks his lungs clear. "I didn't either." He rolls flat onto his back, a dusty arm over his forehead, smearing dirt into the moisture on his skin.

Xavier crouches at Henry's feet. He tucks his right hand inside his jacket, wincing with the motion. When he pulls his hand out, it's slick with blood.

"Where is that coming from?" I ask, pushing to my feet.

Xavier pulls his jacket back. I grab Pietro's discarded flashlight and click it on—Xavier's dark-blue shirt is soaked with blood.

"What—"

"Enzo's gun. He fired just as Henry conjured the scene." When he looks at me, I see fear. "Help me up."

"I can fix this. Just lie down for a minute," I say, even though I don't know where I'll find the resources to heal him after what we just went through.

"In a minute." Xavier stumbles to Gaetano, miraculously still alive, and helps him into a sitting position against his own damaged body. Pietro lies unmoving nearby. Between raspy breaths, Gaetano tries to talk, his efforts impeded by his sobs.

Henry pushes himself upright. Gaetano clasps Xavier's hand in both of his.

"What's he saying?" Henry asks solemnly.

"He doesn't want me to leave him here alone. Enzo killed his family. He wants to join them." Xavier looks straight at me, his eyes sad, but anger sparks behind it. He unzips a narrow, hidden pocket on his jacket just below collarbone level. From it, he extracts a capsule. "One of you give him a canteen." Xavier cups Gaetano's hand in his own, dropping the capsule within.

I pull out my canteen and give it to Xavier. "What is that?"

"Aconite."

I grab his wrist. "That's poison."

Xavier yanks free and looks directly into my eyes. "He has nothing left, Genevieve. It's what he wants."

Henry moves in behind me, and together we kneel and place our hands on Gaetano's leg, thanking him for his sacrifice. I don't know if he understands us, but the smile through his tears makes me think he does. He stretches toward me, something in his hand—into my open palm, he drops his *La Vérité* key. "You are beautiful and good, like your mother before you," he says.

"Thank you, Gaetano."

"Get the texts," Xavier says. "I'll meet you by the centaur. The sun will be rising soon."

"We'll wait here. With you," Henry says. I nod in agreement and tuck Gaetano's key—restored to its usual aged silver—into my pocket.

With the rate at which he's losing blood, Xavier won't live to see the sunrise if I don't get my hands on him.

And I have some big questions that require his heart to still be beating.

28

Henry grabs Xavier's black duffel. We then each take one of his arms over our shoulders and stumble down the Forum toward the centaur. My left hand feels sticky through my glove; I look down and am not surprised to see blood dripping onto the dusty ground.

"It would be great if this would heal. I'm out of gloves."

"Can you help Xavier if you're bleeding yourself?"

"We'll make do. Just get us to the sculpture."

Henry coughs again. "Is this what you feel like after you heal someone?"

"Weak and breathless and legs made of Jell-O?"

"I'm not a fan."

We reach the sculpture and help Xavier slide down the ancient brick to the rocky ground. "I need to see the damage," I say, ripping off my gloves and carefully lifting his shirt. It looks like the bullet went right through, but there's no way to tell if any organs were hit. It's a messy wound.

"Hurry up. We made too much noise," he snaps.

"Or I could leave you here to bleed to death." I wipe my hands off—his blood, and mine—on a shirt Henry's handed me. "How do I know you're really one of us?"

"Because Enzo is dead, and you aren't," Xavier says, glaring up at me. I lean back on my heels. "Is there a problem?"

"You show up in the dead of night with the minions of our sworn enemy in a clear ambush and point a gun at Henry's head, so forgive me for being a little confused about where your loyalties lie."

Xavier winces, the wound obviously hurting him. "Maybe we should back up and you can explain why you stole a speedboat and left me with its crazed owner in the middle of the Mediterranean."

"Genevieve, we need to make a decision here—heal him, or let's just go," Henry says.

"Yes, Genevieve, heal me, or leave."

Henry hands me his canteen and I use the water to pour over the wound, to get a better visual of what I'm dealing with. Xavier sucks in against the pain.

"Big baby," I say.

He smiles as I nudge in closer, hands at the ready. I'm not gentle about it. I hope the energy I'm shoving into his body hurts like hell.

I don't have much left in the tank, but when Xavier's teeth grind together and he grimaces, I know he's feeling every surge of healing energy—and maybe a little electricity thrown in for good measure.

I get him to the point where he can walk on his own, and

Henry helps him to his feet. My heartbeat pounds through the carving on my left arm, sending fresh waves of nausea.

Henry lifts me up under my armpits and hands me the bloodied shirt from earlier. "Wrap this around your wounds until we can get some more gauze." He helps me strip out of my coat, and I'm instantly chilled by the midwinter air.

"What is aconite?" he asks close to my head as he wraps the shirt and then ties it with the sleeves.

"Monkshood. It's a plant," I say, my voice solemn. "Deadly plant."

"Where would Xavier get that?"

I look over at Xavier as he walks in a tight circle, stretching his newly repaired side slightly as he lights a cigarette. "Probably from Nutesh's greenhouse. From my mother."

"How can we be responsible for so much death, Gen?" Henry asks, his eyes sad.

"It's not our fault, Henry. We just have to fix what Nutesh and the rest of them have screwed up so we can keep countless more alive. Lucian gets the books; Lucian turns back time; us and all this is *poof*."

He nods.

Xavier stuffs the *AVRAKEDAVRA* texts and key pieces, one each, into our respective packs. He checks the inside of Enzo's leather satchel, and then throws it aside. "That bag has a tracker in it. We need to move," Xavier barks.

We're all beyond the point of exhaustion, but there are dead men cooling on the ground at the other end of the Forum, and Xavier's right—we made way too much noise.

We manage a lumbering jog out of the Forum, down the main road, and through the *Porta Marina*. Xavier stops suddenly, arm outstretched as he flattens us against the wall. Flashing blue lights bounce off the tourist-trap shops at the far end of the street.

Polizia.

Xavier's eyes scan frantically, looking for a space between the buildings across from us.

"Can we go back inside? Exit through one of the other gates?" I whisper.

"The gates won't be safe now, if they think someone is on the grounds," Xavier says. "Follow me. Stay close." He takes off as quietly as he can across the street to the farthest end of the last building, a sleeping restaurant. It's a tight squeeze between a concrete retaining wall and the building's exterior, especially with our hefty backpacks, our steps made noisier by dried leaves underfoot.

We come out the other end; the area behind the businesses is fenced, the other side a thicket of spiky bushes. "Climb it," Xavier says, pointing to the black metal fencing. "Quickly!"

Henry is up and over, landing noisily in the scratchy branches and bushes on the other side. I follow, though I'm clumsier than usual thanks to my left arm and utter exhaustion. Xavier tosses that ever-present black duffel over at us, and then we're through the bushes and off down a narrow two-lane street flanked by tall, skinny stucco-and-tile houses on one side.

New sirens whine loudly behind us.

More *polizia*.

Dear god, I hope Xavier has a car nearby. The black Fiat we came here in is back where the police are, and we can't exactly jog to the airport.

Up ahead is a dark blue, older-model four-door Volkswagen hatchback parked along the street. Xavier stops beside it, looks inside and then around us, and with the butt of his knife, he breaks the driver's side window, unlocks the doors, and hisses at us to climb in.

"Can you start it so I don't have to deal with wires?" he asks me, stretching to look at the street behind us. I lean over from the passenger's seat and send two fingers' worth of electricity through the silver metal ignition. The car turns on.

Xavier tears down the street and curses under his breath, taking a corner too fast. I shimmy out of my backpack and glance at the dash—and see why he's cursing. The fuel light on the dashboard is lit up. "No gas?" I ask breathlessly. The chilled evening air whips through the glassless driver window, filling the interior with the hum of road and diesel engine noise.

Xavier's jaw grinds as he meets Henry's eyes in the rearview. "In my bag—find the satellite phone." Henry looks and then passes it forward; Xavier fumbles with the keypad, only one hand and one eye on the road.

"Maybe you can drive and have one of us dial?" I hold out my open palm, hoping he doesn't slam us into the back of a parked car.

"Down!" he yells as police whiz past. Finally he gives me the phone. "Saved dial number two." I figure out how to dial what he's asked for and then hand it back. He speaks in French to the person on the other end.

I turn and look at Henry, raising my brows in question.

"Nutesh. Xavier is telling him we're en route to the airport," he translates.

"It would be a lot easier if he'd do that in English," I say.

"It would be a lot easier if you spoke more than one language," Xavier says, hanging up and tossing the phone back to Henry.

"What are we going to do about the gas?"

"Pray," he responds, reaching into his pocket for his cigarettes.

"How do I know you called Nutesh?" I ask.

"Call him yourself," Xavier says, blowing a long plume out his nostrils. He doesn't offer anything further, which is just as well—the roar of air through the missing window makes conversation difficult.

I settle back against the seat, backpack at my feet, head against the headrest, my hand wrapped around Gaetano's key in my pocket. I sniff against the emotion, and Henry scoots close behind me, whispering in my ear. I swipe at a tear before he can see it. "You all right?"

I nod. He won't be able to hear me if I were to talk anyway.

Why was Xavier with Enzo? How do I know he's not driving us into another ambush? What is our plan to escape if we do indeed end up in another trap? Why did Enzo have to kill poor Gaetano's family?

I'm so sorry, Gaetano. I'm so sorry you had to suffer for these books. I hope you find your family, wherever you are now. Thank you for your sacrifice.

I don't know how I will ever wrap my head around the horrors we just witnessed or be forgiven for the scene we were a part of that left four dead men lying on the graves of thousands more.

29

For the record, praying for a gas tank on *E* to continue pushing your vehicle forward is a stupid plan.

The Volkswagen sputters to a stop on an off-ramp minutes into our escape. Xavier wrestles it to the side of the road, but finding a new car that isn't alarmed or locked behind a garden gate proves an unsettling challenge. This neighborhood is a lot nicer than the last one. Big houses and not very many cars on the street. The ones that are blink with alarms, and I don't know how quickly I could disable it before we attracted attention.

After another fifteen minutes of scurrying through the streets, we come upon a small all-night market. Xavier sidles up alongside the building and points at a vacant car parked against the aging brick wall.

"A taxi?" I whisper. "Isn't that a little obvious?"

"It's unlocked, and no alarm," he says, pausing for a second as he stares at my hands.

"Climb in. Close the door quietly," he says to Henry. Again, I take the front seat.

The spark wakes the engine, and this time, the tank isn't on empty. A stroke of luck!

Xavier heads back to the freeway, and within twenty minutes, we are wrapping around an airport—the sign reads *Aeroporto Internazionale di Napoli*—and moving toward the private hangars. And just as before in Seattle, a needle-nosed jet sits in a steel building separate from the main terminal, waiting for us, stairs extended, the cockpit and exterior lights on with evidence of pilots on board, and heavily armed guards around the perimeter.

Henry pulls the last of our euros out of his pack and wedges the bills under the headrest on my seat. "Bad enough we stole his livelihood. We should repay him for the favor," he says.

Xavier snorts and climbs out, throwing his duffel over his shoulder. The bright hangar light accentuates the sickly pall of his skin. It's a wonder he's still standing up.

"Are you coming?" he asks, pausing to look back at Henry and me.

"I don't trust you. How do we know you're not double-crossing us? How do we know these aren't Enzo's men, or that Lucian didn't set this whole thing up?"

Xavier drops his bag hard onto the ground and bends at the waist, his hands on his knees for a count of three before he pops back up. "I do what I have to do to keep these books safe, Genevieve. I'm getting on that plane. If you two think you can find your way to the next Guardian on your own, have at it." He digs into his duffel, and I tense, not sure if he's going for another weapon or—

He throws a banded wad of money at us.

"I need a drink," he says, hoisting the bag over his shoulder and then climbing aboard the jet.

Henry picks up the money but then turns to me. "Come on. What choice do we have?"

"We could choose not to *trust* him."

"He saved us back there."

"He *ambushed* us back there."

"You heard him. He does whatever he has to do to keep the books safe," Henry says. He offers an outstretched hand. "Let's just go."

He's replaced his gloves, so I take hold. "If we die, at least we'll be together," I murmur as we climb the stairs.

Unlike in Seattle, there is no Nutesh to welcome us or Montague to tend our wounds. Just strange faces, all of them serious and scary-looking as the plane is sealed and creeps forward to wait its turn for takeoff.

One of the bearded sentries from the hangar locks his weapon in a huge metal chest, un-Velcros his body armor, and then removes his dark cap and glasses.

"Lucas?"

He turns and smiles, but it's sad. And then I notice the black band around his upper arm. I look at the other soldiers on board. They're all wearing arm bands.

For Thierry.

"Bonjour, mes amis," he says.

"It's good to see you again," Henry says, extending his

hand. Lucas meets it. His eyes are bloodshot and his mouth drawn at the corners, visible even under the heavy beard. "We are so sorry about Thierry." I'm grateful that Henry speaks—I can't make it past the lump in my throat. And my guilt over Thierry's death is very, very fresh.

"*Merci*. He was a good man." Lucas nods.

The cabin lights click on as the plane's nose angles upward. Through the ovoid windows, the sun peeks over the horizon, pinking the early-morning sky. Once we level out, Lucas moves to the small galley kitchen and brings Henry and me bottles of water and takeout-sized boxes. "Hélène wanted to make sure you ate," he says. "It's cold—it was in the refrigerator—but it will fill your belly."

"We're happy for anything, especially if Hélène made it," Henry says, his smile made even brighter by the dirt smudged on his face.

Xavier emerges from the cockpit. He grabs one of the meals and slumps into a seat across from us. "When you get done there, clean up. There's a washroom in the rear cabin." He nods toward it.

"How are you feeling?" I point at his abdomen.

"It's fine."

"You don't look fine," I say, setting my lunch onto the small table between us. "Why were you there, Xavier? What the hell was all that about?"

He glares at me. "I'm tired. If you're not going to use the facilities, I will." He scoops up his boxed food and heads toward the back of the plane, slamming the lightweight door behind him.

Henry stabs at his pasta. "Maybe leave him alone for a few minutes."

"Excuse me?" I swivel in my chair to face him straight on.

"We've been through a lot tonight. Perhaps give him a few minutes to take a breath. He just saw his friend die."

"Which friend was that, Henry? Enzo, or Gaetano? Which side is he *on*? And how can you be so calm about this?"

Henry slides his fork into his lunch and then sets the box down next to mine. "Give me your hand."

"What? No. Not safe to hold my hand when I'm pissed off."

"So take a deep breath and stop being pissed off. You should see something."

I stare at him for a beat before I realize what he's saying. I should see something—a memory. "What, so you're going to just explain away what he did back there? How he showed up with Enzo and his thugs? Did you see the gun Enzo pointed at your head, Henry? All the magic in the world wouldn't have put your skull back together again if he'd fired." I don't realize I'm crying—again—still?—until the first hot tear slides down my cheek. I'm freaking out—the adrenaline is wearing off and the reality of what we just survived is making me shaky and crazy.

"But he didn't fire—at least not at me—and we're here and we're safe, for now, and Xavier is not going to do anything to hurt us. Give him a chance to be your father."

I laugh angrily through the tears spilling down my face. "That man" —I jab a finger toward the closed door, my teeth gritted—"is *not* my father. My father lies in a coma back in France, or did you forget that already?" I don't know why I'm being mean to Henry.

I just need to be mean to someone. At home, when I'd get mad at someone or something, I'd grab my violin and play for the elephants or hide in my bunk with the privacy curtain drawn and binge-watch Netflix or go into the nearest field or woods and scream my guts out.

But those moments all seem so stupid now. Stupid, but simple. Being angry because I'd been scolded for doing something dumb or Ash had ignored me for some pretty girl in the crowd or someone didn't save me any brownies.

The real anger happened when Ted and Cece would call the police and they'd put a psych hold on Delia—again—or when the assholes at the hospital wouldn't let me see her. But at least I had Baby with me. I don't have Baby with me now. Just some unkempt, snarling, chain-smoking Frenchman of questionable loyalty with whom I allegedly share DNA.

"Geni, please . . ." Henry's hand lies open on the armrest between our seats. I look down at my own hands, sticky and gross, my nails torn and cuticles bloodstained, but I take a deep breath and push the electricity aside as I slide my palm across his. My eyes closed, the warmth I've come to expect from Henry's touch washes through me. I love the way it feels . . . if only it didn't come with the uneasy side effect that he can see basically everything stored in my head.

The images start right away. *It's Enzo, alive, in a café, hunched over his phone, steam swirling toward his stubbled chin from an espresso. He's handsome, especially when he's not sneering at us from behind a handgun. He laughs at something on the screen and turns to show a guy at another table who I recognize from the Forum. Enzo then turns and finishes his espresso, only lifting his eyes from the phone's screen when another man, bearded and dark-skinned, approaches.*

They greet one another in French, and Enzo gestures for the man to sit in the chair opposite him, making small talk that is nothing more than buzzing in my head. The new man declines an order for coffee from a cute blond waitress, and in English, he says to Enzo, "Show me the targets."

"A man of action. You always were." Enzo closes whatever was making him laugh and scrolls to something new. When he turns the phone for the man to see, it's photos of Henry, and me—what looks like Henry's school photo, Henry and his father Lucian, then my circus promo shot, me with Baby and Delia. And then shots of Henry and me together: screen captures from the circus in Barcelona, us on the street in Naples, and then as we're walking out of the art gallery after our staged, on-street healing.

My chest aches with the panic in my heart.

"They have two texts, and whatever this thing is that has them running all over Europe."

"Do we know what it is?" the man asks.

Enzo shakes his head. "Dagan says it has something to do with the books. But you know how close-lipped he is. This is a big job. If we get what he wants, we're set for life."

The man looks unimpressed. "Your plan?"

"We found the guy they're supposed to be meeting. After some . . . persuasive negotiation, he politely revealed they will be meeting at Pompeii. Tonight, around three," Enzo says. "Ah, look at us—just like old times. I've missed you, mon ami.*" His coarse laugh suggests he needs to cut back on the smoking.*

The conversation then turns into the buzzing again, and

I'm about to pull my hand free because I have no idea how this is relevant to the betrayal Xavier demonstrated tonight. But Henry holds fast, and as the conversation between Enzo and *son ami* wraps up, the man stands.

And in the mirror that runs the entire length of the café, the face I see is not the bearded stranger who was just sitting at the table, the face Enzo was chatting with so amiably—it's Xavier.

Henry finally lets go.

"What . . . how . . . ?" I ask, winded from the exchange. Henry hands me a water bottle.

"I don't know. We need to ask him. But I'm guessing it's the same brand of *AVRAKEDAVRA* magic that has helped Aveline mask herself."

We were told that Aveline is a master of disguise. And all this time I just thought it meant she was good with makeup and wigs.

"But how? He's not an heir or descendant. How do we know if who we're seeing is really the person we can trust?"

Xavier appears over the back of the plane seat, his face still pale but cleaner now. "You can't trust anyone."

"And that includes you?"

He sits across from me, leaning forward, elbows on his knees. "I'm probably the *only* person you can trust. In *any* of this."

"Don't flatter yourself," I say.

"I'm not. The only people who can see through the bullshit magic I was using are *AVRAKEDAVRA* descendants. Like you and your boyfriend here. So even if I wanted to 'conjure' a new face, you wouldn't be able to see it. You'd only see me."

"Lucky us," I say under my breath.

"What is even more pressing, however, is why *voux deux imbéciles* thought leaving me behind in Sardinia was a smart idea," Xavier says.

"Well, for one, your face is all over the news, alongside ours. I told you to change your appearance, and you refused."

"A conundrum I have just now explained that I don't need to shave off my hair to change the way the outside world sees me," he says.

"It's your eyes we were concerned about," Henry offers. "They are strikingly different from most. We didn't know you had this . . . ability . . . so we were worried that people would notice, and then realize it was us."

"Fair enough," Xavier says. "Any other reasons?"

I lock eyes with him. "I don't trust you."

"We've established that."

"And you haven't let us make any decisions or have any say in any of the plans—and yet *we* are the ones doing all the dirty work."

Xavier's head bobs. I'm already strategizing my reply for his smart-ass comeback—

"You're right. We're asking you to undertake this terrible, perilous mission, and neither of you has been invited to participate in the plans. *C'est vrai.*"

I did not expect him to say this.

"So how about, from here forward, we agree to transparency? Plans will be made among the three of us. This will maybe cement your trust in me a little better, and it will keep me from being abandoned in the middle of the Mediterranean with a guy who can't stop talking about *les seins*."

Henry chuckles.

"What? What's funny?"

"You should learn a second language, *ma fille*," Xavier says. "So—do we have an accord?"

"Fine. But we want to know everything. No more secrets."

"Agreed," Xavier says.

That was easier than it should've been. And I still don't trust him.

"Sooo, if you're done in the washroom," Henry says, throwing a thumb over his shoulder in the direction of the sleeping quarters.

"Help yourself," Xavier says. "Are you going to finish that?" He points at Henry's food.

"No, please, it's yours." Henry excuses himself, but when he nods once at me before exiting, I know what he's doing. He wants me to make peace with Xavier.

With my father.

"There are, like, a half dozen other packed lunches in the fridge."

"Maybe . . . but I like fettuccine," Xavier says, shoving the food into his mouth. I've never seen anyone eat so greedily—except maybe Othello. But he's a lion, so he can eat however he wants.

I stare out the window at the wispy clouds under us bathing in early morning sun, my jaw and fists clenched in annoyance as Xavier slurps his pasta and scrapes at the side of the cardboard container, and then gets up, grabs another lunch—his third?—and dives in. This one is crispy. I want to shove my fist through his forehead.

"I'm sorry I wasn't there for you. For your mother," he says through a mouthful of Caesar salad.

"Really? We're going to do this now?"

"I'm sure you have questions. I know I would if my father appeared out of nowhere."

"Baby is my dad."

Xavier looks up at me, his eyes, and voice, softening. "I know that. And you're lucky. He's a good man."

"Which is why I'm doing all this. If we destroy the books, the black magic he's suffering under back in France"—I point at my own wounded arm—"will disappear and he'll recover."

"Is that what Nutesh told you?"

I pause. "Is that not the truth?"

"I'm sure it is. But the one thing this life has taught me—question everything."

"I need him to be well again," I say, my voice straining. "I really miss my mom. I can't lose Baby too."

Xavier shoves another huge bite into his mouth, nodding his head as he chews. "Your mother was something else," he says. "I loved her. She was the last person I ever loved."

"That's really sad, Xavier."

He plunks his salad box on the table and wipes his face clean. "I think it's great that you and Henry are finally doing what these other idiots didn't have the strength to."

"Meaning?"

"Meaning Nutesh should've handled this years ago. There's no reason for this to have gone on as long as it has. He tells himself he's doing good, that he's 'protecting humanity.' How many dead in the last few days, Genevieve?"

I sit back against my seat. Thierry. Gaetano. Enzo and his thugs. *Five dead.*

"Now multiply that by two thousand years."

Jesus. "But . . . the books have also saved people. I saved that man in Barcelona."

"*Oui*, you did. But maybe it was his time to go. Maybe your intervention wasn't necessary or needed."

"If you really believe all this, why are you still here? Why are you still working for him?"

"I was near death when Dagan was finished with me. Nutesh brought me back. That engenders a certain allegiance, I suppose." He pauses. "*Se batter jusqu'à mort.* Fight until dead." He finishes a bottle of water without taking a breath. "Which is how you came to be."

"How does this have anything to do with me?"

"Aveline is very powerful. Even more so than Dagan—Lucian—but he won't admit that to himself. He will, before this is over, I promise you." Xavier pats his pocket but then seems to remember we're on a plane, so he can't smoke. "After Delia chose her family's book over Aveline and me, it wasn't long before Dagan came to collect. Delia left that night with the physical obsession that brings us to today." Xavier flicks the lid of his silver lighter, open, closed, open, closed.

"Torture is Dagan's preferred entertainment, but I couldn't tell him what I didn't know. And I knew he'd found Delia. I heard her screams in that dungeon, but I couldn't get to her. I couldn't save anyone, not even myself." Xavier shudders slightly, his face stoic but his eyes pained. "She must've hidden the text by then. Nothing he did to her—or to me—would loosen her lips."

The echoes of Xavier's agony ricochet in my head: the vision that Alicia showed me, of my mother when Nutesh rescued her, when he recited the prayer over their conjoined hands while she writhed in Baby's huge arms, the spell that made Baby her living talisman.

How Nutesh left the prison with only Delia. No Xavier, no Aveline.

"Dagan must've sensed Aveline's potential, like a vampire smells blood in a mortal's veins. I knew she was powerful, even as a small child, before I lost her. Dagan took her and raised her. She became someone—something—else under his tutelage. But her talents surpassed his centuries ago. It's all he can do to keep her under his thumb.

"When Delia and I learned she was alive, we knew she was too far gone. Far too dangerous. We couldn't let her be the heir to this book. Nutesh felt that because Aveline had grown so strong, we needed to counterbalance her with a child of the same bloodline." Xavier runs a hand through his mop of curls. He looks so tired. "My first daughter has a lot of issues. It's not been easy for her."

I lift my throbbing, carved arm in the air. "Do not try to make me feel sorry for her."

"I'm not. I wouldn't do that."

"So, you're saying I was conceived out of necessity."

"Don't be so dramatic," he says. "It's not like you weren't

loved or that you were raised in a lab. You meant everything to Delia. And she was with Bamidele, heart and soul. Your conception was very clinical. We all knew what we were doing. We all knew that we had no other choice."

"You could've destroyed the books."

"*Oui*, but only willing heirs can do that. Lucian would never give up his text. So you can see how this problem loops around itself, like a snake eating its own tail."

My heart sinks a little. I was born not because my mother wanted another child, but because she needed someone other than Aveline to carry on our family's legacy.

Our family's curse.

And everyone—except me—has known the truth my entire life.

"And you never wanted to know me?" Our eyes hold for a minute before he leans sideways and pulls out his wallet.

He shoves aside the lunch containers and lays out five small photos—me when I was a baby, me with Gertrude when I was about six, and three school photos, the last one my senior-year picture with me wearing my cap and gown and standing next to Gert. Even though we were schooled via tutors due to our travel schedule, we still had school photos every year.

"You could've called. You could've shown up."

"And what?" His voice echoes off the tight space and catches the attention of the guys up front. "And what? Hey, kid, I'm your dad, let's go get a burger and talk about boys?"

He's right. It would've just made things more difficult.

"This is a dangerous life, Genevieve. The last thing you needed was to lose both parents."

"And yet . . . Baby lies in a coma."

"Baby knew what he was getting into. And like I said, he's a good man—he's done stuff I couldn't. Maybe it's because he's half my age so his heart isn't a stone in his chest, I don't know." Xavier sighs and leans back hard in his seat. "I'll do whatever I can to make sure he survives this."

We examine one another for a quiet moment, and then I nod. "Thank you."

"You're welcome," he says, the hint of smile frosted with sadness and regret.

Henry reappears, and Xavier scoops up the photos of me, tucking them back into his wallet, as if the preceding life-altering conversation was only about the plane's fancy seats.

"You should clean up. You look terrible," Xavier says, quickly standing and disappearing into the front to talk to his comrades.

"Everything all right?" Henry asks. My eyes burn.

"I need a minute." I push past Henry.

I lock myself in the tiny bathroom and sit on the closed toilet lid, my head in my hands. I don't have to look in the mirror to confirm Xavier's rudeness about how I look—it's been a long night. My left arm burns under the bandaging that likely needs changing after the mess at Pompeii. I don't even want to check yet.

God, I just want to go home. I want to click my ruby-slippered heels together three times and *go home*.

Home. Violet. *My cell phone.*

I move so my body is against the door, sliding onto my butt. The burner phone is still in my thigh pocket, as yet undiscovered, so I pull it out and power it on.

The screen loads with message after message after message from Vi.

Gen! Where are you? Have you been on YouTube?

Gen, we SAW you. Did you heal a guy in Spain? I thought this was a secret! Millions of hits on this vid. CALL ME.

OMG, GEN, Cece & Ted are losing it. I heard Ted tell my dad they want to hire a private investigator because they don't think the police are doing enough.

ANOTHER VIDEO? Is that Henry? DID HE GET STABBED? OMG OMG OMG, Gen, please text or call.

I'm so worried about you. I don't understand what's happening.

The last text: *Please just text & tell me you're safe. Come home so we can have a tea party. I love you.* And attached to this text is a photo—my darling Violet, holding one of the tiny teacups from my tea set I left behind for her to look after. But she's not alone in the photo—it's Vi, and Aveline.

"Genevieve? You okay in there?" Henry.

"I'm fine. Be right out."

"Gen . . ."

I listen—he's not walking away. Growling, I power off and shove the phone back into my pocket, and then stand and throw the door open. "What's so important you couldn't give me—"

Xavier is standing behind Henry, and the expression on both of their faces . . .

"What? Is it Baby?"

Henry's eyes are rimmed red and damp, like a tear is there but hasn't quite fallen. Xavier's brow is furrowed so hard, it might break his face in half. Henry's lips part but no sound comes out.

"Guys . . ."

Instead of speaking, Henry closes and locks the stateroom door. He grabs his pack and from it, pulls out the *AVRAKEDAVRA*.

"What is going on?"

No one will answer me. Henry opens the book and, like he did around the campfire pit in the Spanish woods, he places one hand on the text, offering me the other. I step closer and take it; Alicia appears in the stateroom next to us, floating over the fitted duvet of the queen-sized bed.

The images form above the *AVRAKEDAVRA*, their only soundtrack the whir of the plane's ventilation system.

It's Ash. He's climbing into the Jónás family's RV—the vehicle bounces a little under his weight. His mouth moves—there's no sound—but I can read well enough on his lips. "Vi?" He grabs a handful of the trail mix their mother Katia always leaves in a bowl out on the counter. His lips move again as he picks up the remote and clicks off the TV, probably chastising his twin for leaving the volume up too loud. Again.

He walks down the narrow hallway toward the sleeping quarters, but ahead, he sees a foot. Violet's tiny foot, in pink socks, of course, and it's on the floor, just sticking outside the doorway of Katia and Aleks Jónás's bedroom.

"Vi?" Ash's face contorts with confusion, and then panic. As he shoves the door open, difficult because something is behind it, the true horror unfolds.

I try to pull free from Henry, but he won't let go.

Violet is on the floor, her long blond ponytail around her head like a halo, her honey-brown eyes fixed and staring at nothing, her complexion an unnatural blue, lips purple, vomit still caked on her mouth and cheek. Ash drops and puts his head to her chest, immediately starting compressions and screaming for help, screaming so loud, I can hear him in my head despite the absence of sound in Henry's vision. He scoops his twin sister from the floor and carries her through the RV, her limp feet and legs knocking over my tea set sitting on the coffee table as Ash maneuvers her through the tight space. He kicks open the front door and howls into the open air . . .

Henry finally releases my hand and collapses against the foot of the bed, his hands wrapped around the back of his head.

"He revived her, right? He saved her? She's alive?"

Henry looks up at me just as that tear finally does escape. "I'm so sorry, Genevieve. I am so, so sorry."

"No. *No*. Come on . . . not Violet. She is an *innocent*. She did nothing!" I say.

My best friend. My sister. My Violet.

"What happened? Did she—did she kill herself? Was she sick? Was there a gas leak or something?"

No one answers me.

That night in the big top, when Lucian and Aveline threatened me over Delia's text: "My darling sister, I suppose how fast you look will be in direct correlation to how quickly the people in your family tree start to fall," Aveline said.

"*You did this*! Your daughter did this! She murdered my best friend!" I slam my hands into Xavier's chest so hard, he loses his footing, wincing as he stumbles backward into the wall of closets.

"Genevieve, please, I had nothing to do with this—"

"You could have *stopped* her! You could have killed her when you had the chance! Violet was *innocent*. She didn't deserve to die!" And then I melt onto the plush carpet, sobbing and screaming because my Violet is gone.

Henry wraps his arms around me and rocks me on the floor. Xavier runs a hand over his face and through his hair and he paces back and forth a few times before walking out of the stateroom. He may be used to so much death—maybe he hasn't loved anyone since Delia—but I still love. I love Delia, I love Baby, I love my elephants and Othello, I love the Cinzios and Ash and Violet.

I love Henry.

And one by one, Lucian—and Aveline—are ticking them off their list.

Xavier returns a moment later holding paper cups and a silver flask. He pours an inch of amber fluid into each cup. I'm crying so hard, I can hardly hold onto mine. And beating him to a bloody pulp isn't going to bring Violet back to me.

Xavier recaps his flask and lifts his cup before him.

Henry raises his cup. "To Thierry. To Gaetano. To Violet." His voice cracks on Vi's name.

"The key to good is found in truth," Xavier says, an edge in his voice. "Some bullshit truth it is." He finishes his drink in one long swallow, crumpling the cup in his hand. "Six hours until we're on the ground. Clean up that arm and try to rest." He walks toward the door and turns to me. "Genevieve, I am so sorry. For all of this."

As the stateroom door clicks closed behind him, the words my mother used to say to me when I messed up and had to make amends float across my lips. "Sometimes sorry isn't good enough."

30

I peel off the layers and wash my bloody, infected arm the best I can, which isn't much because I am slowly losing the will to give a shit. About anything. I cry until I throw up, Xavier's whiskey burning a second time as it comes out my nose. I'm feverish again—still—but my nose and sinuses are so swollen from crying, I feel like I have the worst head cold ever.

My forehead balanced on my uninjured arm across the toilet seat, I could be anywhere right now. The ride is smoother than an RV or a truck or even a train, lulling me into a sense of safety that I know, in my heart, could fall away at any second.

Violet is dead.

The other half of my childhood is dead.

What's the point of any of this? Let's just give Lucian and Aveline these fucking books and be done with it. When he goes back to save his precious ancient family, it won't hurt because we will have not existed anyway.

But then flashes of my life pop into my head: my circus

family. The people on this plane and at the Croix-Mare compound. The Guardians and members of *La Vérité* who have kept my mother's secrets for all these years. The future I had planned for myself.

Henry.

Is it enough to fight for?

I pull up to the sink, rinse my putrid mouth, and grab for the travel-sized mouthwash in the decorative silver basket mounted to the wall. I don't dare look in the mirror. I already know I look like I'm two steps from my own early grave. I can feel it. Hollowed cheeks and purple eyes and bruises and smears of blood, not all mine.

But I force myself to look, because I'm still alive, and Violet's dead. It's my family's fault. All these magical people, and there's nothing I can do to bring Vi back.

The reflection confirms what I've known all along. I'm not a superhero, and I'm not made of sterner stuff.

I am Genevieve, and Violet is my sister not by blood, but by choice.

And Ash. God, what is he going through? How is he coping?

I have to call him. I have to find a quiet moment to reassure him he's not alone, that I will do whatever I can to honor Violet's life.

When I open the bathroom door, Henry is alongside the queen bed, folding clothes he's pulling from a blue bag.

"Hélène sent fresh supplies." He points at my arm. "Do you need help?"

I shake my head no and sit on the end of the bed. "When Delia would come back from a long hospital stay, she would randomly drop tidbits of her experience, not all good. Her therapist, Dr. DeGrasse—he would tell her that she had a tendency to compartmentalize, to put painful things in boxes in her head to avoid dealing with them." Henry sits too and wraps his arms around me. "Do you think that's a bad way to handle stuff?"

He kisses the side of my head. "I think you need to do whatever it is that will help you get through this."

I turn and meet his tired eyes. "What about you? How are you getting through every day?"

"You. If I can just stay focused on keeping you safe, then I don't have time to think about my father and what he's done. What he's doing."

"Does that work?"

He gives me a small smile. "Mostly. For now."

"You'll have to deal with this eventually," I say.

He takes a deep breath, his whole body moving with the effort, his arms loosening their hold on me. "Is it weird that I'm really angry? Lucian kept all these secrets, and yet somehow, I still love him, Genevieve. He's my father." Henry takes another slow breath. "But how could he do this? How could he have turned his back on me? On so many good people?"

Henry drops his arms altogether, rubbing his palms along the tops of his thighs. "I am his child. He murdered my mother, and yet I still want to believe there is good in him somewhere. Does that make me crazy?"

I shake my head. "It makes you decent. You want to believe the best in people, to give them the benefit of the doubt."

He kneels on the floor in front of me, his hands encasing mine. "I have had every advantage in this life. Food, shelter, warmth, the best education, global travel. And yet . . . I feel this *hole.*" He flattens a hand over his chest. "It's this emptiness. Even with my newfound connection with my mother . . . it's not enough. The hole aches, like something is missing."

He again perches on the bed beside me and digs into the inside pocket of his jacket. From it, he pulls out his small notebook and pen—he never goes *anywhere* without something to draw on—flips it open, tears out one page, and then another.

He hands me the first one. It's a cartoonish drawing of himself, his face sad and tired, shoulders slumped, a flame-shaped, cookie-cutter hole in his chest that goes all the way through.

After a moment, he hands me the second drawing. It's himself again, but I'm in this one, my long hair replaced by the current curly, dark fuzz. In the drawing, I'm looking at him, my eyes bright, and he's looking at me. Christopher Marlowe, the floppy, stuffed blue elephant Henry brought me at the hospital after the Etemmu attack on movie night, hangs clutched in my left hand.

I smile. "I wish I could've brought him with us. For luck," I say.

But it's the object in my outstretched right hand. Between us, I'm cupping a flame in my palm. The flame is shaped exactly like the hole in Henry's chest.

"I know it's dumb," he says, looking between the drawing and my face, his own expression expectant and nervous. "You're a flame. People are drawn to you—"

"For better and for worse," I interject.

"It's been the better for me. I just want you to know . . . you fill that hole in my chest. You're a flame. And when I'm near you, I feel warmer and stronger. I feel invincible, and I would do anything to protect that feeling. I would do anything to protect you, to protect what we have together. Our friendship, and whatever else may come later." He moves to tug at the cowlick that is long gone.

"That hole, the only time it doesn't hurt is when I'm with you. You give me something no one else ever has. And no matter what happens in the next day, the next week, the next month, I want to thank you for being my friend. For being the person going through this with me."

He leans forward so our foreheads are touching. "I'm so sorry about Vi."

"Thank you, Henry."

Henry sets the drawings aside and closes the space between us. He kisses me, hard, his hand against my head, his other arm pulling me closer. He whispers against my mouth, "I love you. We can do this. Together."

He kisses me gently but deeply, and I melt into him.

When he pulls his lips from mine, he holds me against him, rubbing my back as the last of my tears soak into his shirt.

I decide in that moment that I'm okay with compartmentalizing. Because the only way I can get through the next ten days, the next ten *minutes*, is to take my darling Violet into a beautiful pink room in my head filled with everything that makes her the happiest. *"I have to get through this first, Violet. I'm going to make it right."*

31

I SWALLOW MORE ANTI-INFLAMMATORIES TO TRY TO BRING DOWN THE fever. My eyes are swollen, and my face is blotchy and puffy, but no one mentions it. We're all pushed to extremes right now. Xavier, being Xavier, fights me trying to look at his gut, but I persuade him to lie down for five whole minutes so I can shove some more healing into his gunshot wound. Whatever ammunition Enzo was using, it was nasty and left a wide field of damage—Xavier could use another round when my strength recovers.

When we're as reassembled as we can be, Xavier asks Henry and me to take seats in the cluster closest to the rear stateroom. Lucas hands him a tablet, and then makes himself scarce.

Xavier's voice is low, even though we're allegedly among people who we can trust. "So—you want to be a part of the planning, now is your chance."

Henry and I look at one another. "Meaning . . . ?" I ask.

"What you did in Naples was reckless," he says, "but it

worked. So, I am interested to hear how you think we should approach the Guardian in Izmir."

"Any background information, for context?" Henry asks.

Xavier nods and starts talking, flipping through the screens, each swipe filled with maps and detailed intel about the situation on the ground in Turkey. "Word travels fast through the *La Vérité* network, and Gaetano's death will be major news on all sides. However, Turkey is Dmitri country and therefore isn't like any other we've been to. Dagan spent hundreds of years living in this part of the world—before he moved into Europe in the 1100s." Wrapping my head around this kind of history is nuts, filling me with that unhinged feeling from that day in the field behind the big top when Baby confirmed the truths presented in the academic journal *ANTIQUITY*, in the article by Dr. Andreas Schuyler.

No one lives for thousands of years.

"The talents you and your mother have—your mother's ability to see and talk to Alicia and Udish—everything stems from this book. Your mother's line, her family, have been custodians of this book since the days of Babylon—Mesopotamia—around a thousand years before Jesus."

Xavier's voice floats back in front of my memories. "*La Vérité* is much diminished here—and naturally, local loyalty to Lucian is strong."

"That's because they don't know the truth about who he is," I say.

"They know he's invested a lot of money in infrastructure and business and philanthropy in Turkey and surrounding areas for a long time. Where do you think those pictures of him smiling outside of newly built children's hospitals come from? They may not understand or know anything about the *AVRAKEDAVRA*, but they think they know the man. They love him here. And they know he's been wronged. Combine that with the viral video of you healing that guy in Barcelona, and then Naples—they will be looking for you," Xavier says. "Not to mention the press attention Dagan has secured, and his influence over local law enforcement."

"So basically, we're sitting ducks the second we show our faces in the city," Henry says.

"Maybe," Xavier says.

"Or . . . maybe not." I lean forward, thoughts churning.

"Gen, the final Guardian will be very nervous once he hears about Gaetano," Henry says.

"The first meeting with Shamira and Joseph in the woods went fine. Yeah, we were ambushed in Pompeii, but that had everything to do with Lucian finding the Guardian before we did. I'm pretty sure the only reason we aren't dead is because you were there to intercede." I nod at Xavier. "If we had a way of knowing if Lucian and Aveline have gotten to the last Guardian yet—"

"If they had, he'd have ghosted," Xavier says.

"And is he still in contact with you?"

"So far." Xavier spins the satellite phone on the coffee table.

"Okay, so instead of a plan where we put ourselves out somewhere isolated in the dead of night, we do the opposite. Weren't we supposed to work at a circus?" I ask.

"That was a component of Nutesh's original plan."

"But Nutesh isn't *here,* and we are. We're the ones doing the footwork."

"*Oui,* but after what happened in Barcelona, he's not going to want to move forward with the original plan."

"Which was what?" Henry asks. He flips a coin across his knuckles, back and forth from index to pinkie finger and back again, like magic.

"*Tanrilar Sirk*—'Circus of the Gods'—a huge traveling circus that sets itself up in Izmir at this time of year. The handoff for the final piece of the key was supposed to happen there. But Nutesh doesn't want to do that, and I doubt the Guardian will want to either. Too risky."

"Crowds are never riskier than isolation," I say. "Delia's favorite expression— *the greatest thing about a circus is a person's ability to hide in plain sight.* Meeting after-hours in the dark didn't go so great. But, meeting at the circus could totally work in our favor."

Xavier angles forward on his elbows, so I keep talking.

"What if, instead of sneaking into the city and hoping Lucian's people don't find us before we can arrange some supersecret place to meet, we convince the Guardian that the circus *is* the best place to make the exchange. We can put the word out to the *La Vérité* network that we'll be there—and we want to meet the members and offer whatever assistance we can."

Xavier is already shaking his head. "That is counterintuitive."

"Of course it is! And that's why it might work. We've already gone viral. We're all over the news. People think we're the bad guys, but if we can *show* them that we are the victims, maybe they'll help us."

"*La Vérité* members in Turkey won't trust Henry. He's a Dmitri," Xavier says. Henry nods once, but the look on his face makes me feel bad for him. He's not his father, not in any way. "Okay, so if it's too dangerous for both of us to be involved, I'll do it—line 'em up. I'm the one who can heal people. I'm Delia's daughter. And these people were loyal to Delia, right?"

Xavier steeples his fingers under his nose, his eyes distant as he considers my idea.

"No way can this be done in an open venue," Xavier says. "There's a bounty for your heads, and the books, and lots of Dmitri loyalists who would be all too glad to collect it."

"Like I said, then—me only. Hang on—"

I hurry into the stateroom, digging into my discarded pants for the key I took from Gaetano. Then I dig in my pack and grab Mathieu's. Both keys have returned to their normal state, no residual of their traitorous metamorphosis.

Returning to my seat, I lay the keys flat across my palm. "When things went south with Gaetano, his key *changed*—the same thing happened at Croix-Mare." I look behind to see if any of the soldiers are within earshot. "One of Nutesh's guards—Mathieu—freaked out. This was his key."

"Nutesh told me. A mole."

"I saw both keys turn a vaporous black as it hung around their necks when things were going to hell. That's how I know when someone is disloyal. We can *use* that, Xavier. I can tell you who shouldn't be in the room or the tent or whatever. If we only invite *La Vérité* members—and the Guardian—they will have to present their keys. Then I can tell who is who. The Guardian can line up with the rest of the members, and no one will know who he is.

"And because it's a circus, there'll be loads of locals out for a nice family afternoon. It's just a crowd of regular people—but also a lot of regular people who could become collateral damage if things were to go sideways. I'm guessing Lucian doesn't want civilians getting hurt, or worse, because of some absurdly dangerous action he's taking to get the books, especially if everyone here is so loyal to him."

Now Henry is shaking his head. "Way too dangerous. We could be kidnapped. We could have every member of *La Vérité* in the world there, and it wouldn't stop Lucian, or Aveline, from bringing in armed assailants and carrying us and the texts out."

"But they won't. Not if civilians are there. And it's why we absolutely cannot have the books out in the open. We're going to have to prove ourselves to the Guardian without the books. The only way to do that is to *show* him our skills just by touching him. I'm serious—set us up in one of the sideshow tents, put all these soldiers undercover so we can fight back if we need to. Then put the word out to *La Vérité*, and then the Guardian lines up with everyone else. No one knows who he is or that he's any different from the rest."

Xavier pushes a hand through his curls and stops midway, hand resting on the top of his head, his ice-blue eyes looking at me but not really. "This could work."

"No." Henry slams his coin on the table.

"Henry, come on! Why not? Do you have a better plan?" I ask.

"What if we used decoys?" Xavier suggests.

"People have seen our faces on the videos and on the news," Henry says.

"The photos on the news are from before you changed your appearance," Xavier says. "And the video quality from Barcelona and Naples was not high-def—we could find reasonable stand-ins for both of you, I think."

"Can't you use some of your face-changing hocus-pocus on other people?" I ask Xavier.

"Works only on me. I am but a mere mortal, remember. Not like you two freaks." He winks at me.

"So—that's our plan, then, yeah?"

Henry looks pissed. But unless he has a better suggestion, this seems like a reasonable option.

"I will speak with Nutesh," Xavier says.

Henry gets up without saying another word, goes into the stateroom, and closes the door behind him.

I must've dozed off in my seat. When my bladder wakes me a few hours later, I've been covered with a blanket. The stateroom door is still closed—guessing Henry fell asleep in there. Alone.

I toss the blanket onto the empty seat next to me. I'm faint and sweaty with fatigue and infection and the antibiotics are doing a number on my stomach. My hands and elbows ache with unspent energy—I haven't zapped anyone in a while. Too bad Xavier and I are getting along at the moment.

I stand and walk the few feet to the stateroom, pushing my ear against the door. I crack it open, and sure enough, Henry is zonked out on the bed, his sleeping face peaceful, and less pale. A quick look behind me—everyone else is either resting or reading as the jet silently slices through the bright daylight toward Izmir.

I pat my pant leg, touching the secret hiding in my pocket.

I could call Ash.

I tiptoe through and into the bathroom and stuff a towel along the bottom of the closed door—there's no fan or faucet to mask any noise I might make with a call—I hope the towel is enough soundproofing. I think it's still predawn in Oregon, but I'm hoping that a ringing phone will be answered.

My breath is shallow as I dial.

It's ringing. And ringing. And ringing.

On the fifth ring, just before the call slides into voicemail, he picks up.

"Hullo . . . ?"

"Ash?"

"Who is this?" His voice is raspy. Tired. "Who is this?"

"Ash, it's me. It's Genevieve." Silence. I hear his breathing pick up. "I just heard about Violet . . ." Emotion cracks my voice in half. "My god, I am so, so sorry. I can't stop worrying about you—I called as soon as I was able—"

"What the fuck do you want?"

"I—I just wanted to talk to you."

"Why? Why bother?"

"I'm so worried about you, Ash. If there's anything I can do—Violet was my sister too—"

"She wasn't your sister. She wasn't your *twin*. Where the hell are you? Where have you been? Do you even know what you've done to Ted and Cece?"

"I . . . I can't tell you. But it's not what the news is saying, I *swear*, Ash. Please don't listen to the bullshit they're feeding you. *Please* believe me."

"Then why can't you tell me where you are? You're with Henry? Is Baby dead? Did he plan this whole thing? What is going *on*, Genevieve?"

Another fissure cracks open in my heart. "I can't tell you right now, Ash, but I'm so worried about you—"

"God, Mara Dunn was right. You *poisoned* her to get back at me because I didn't want you. You're a psychopath, Genevieve, just like your mother. Lose my number."

"Wait—what are you talking about? It's *me*! You're my brother—I love you—"

"Shut your witchy, lying mouth. We are not family. The pain you have caused—I don't even know why I'm talking to you."

"No! Ash, wait!" But he doesn't hear me. He's hung up. Just as the bathroom door flies open and slams into the wall, Xavier's face an inferno I might not survive.

32

Xavier yells and paces, waking everyone on the plane, waving my burner phone around in his fist. But I hear nothing he says. Only Ash's words, cutting through me like a hot knife through butter . . .

God, Mara Dunn was right. You poisoned her to get back at me because I didn't want you. You're a psychopath, Genevieve, just like your mother.

Mara Dunn. He still knows her as Mara Dunn, not as who she really is—Aveline Darrow—the puppet master manipulating the strings of her own reality show.

And what does he mean, I poisoned her? I poisoned who? Mara?

I'd ask if this could get any worse, but I know the answer to that: it can always get worse.

Xavier breaks the burner phone open and takes out the battery before tossing the whole thing into his bag. He then slams his hands against my seat, one on each side of my head. "What were you *thinking*? You have put us *all* in grave jeopardy. If we manage to land this plane without interference from Dagan, it will be a miracle. Whatever gods you believe in, Genevieve Flannery, *start praying*."

He forcefully rights himself and gives Henry a dirty look as Henry hands over his burner too. Xavier then stomps down the aisle toward the cockpit. When I turn and watch him go, Lucas and the other soldiers give me a hard stare and then turn away.

Awesome.

"Henry, I'm sorry—I shouldn't have called him, but—"

"No. You're right. You shouldn't have called him," he says. The disappointment is clear in his eyes. I follow him back into the stateroom. Silently, we tidy up and repack our travel backpacks with the new stuff from Hélène.

I sit on the side of the bed, tying my boot. "You should've heard how Ash talked to me," I say. "He thinks this is all my fault. Mara Dunn—Aveline—she's gotten to him. He said something about poison, but I don't know if he meant it literally or like I've poisoned everyone against me by my actions."

Henry stands in front of me, his pack over one shoulder, a fresh pair of gloves on his hands. "He just lost his twin sister. His emotions are volatile right now, and he doesn't understand what's really going on." His words don't sound very convincing. Probably because no one in their right mind would believe this story. Not the truth of it, anyway.

My ears hurt as we begin our descent, and the captain's commanding voice over the intercom requests we take our seats. Henry pulls me up from the bed.

In the main cabin, everyone settles into their respective spots, except Xavier who doesn't return to join us at the rear cluster. He can be as mad at me as he needs to be. I didn't mean to cause any harm—but I had to call Ash. Even if the result has gouged another wound in my heart.

Out the plane window, I can just make out the approaching city over the jet's wing. It looks beautiful—vast blue water, a densely packed metropolis of red roofs clustered along the shoreline, roads like carvings from this height. Groves of green, rounded trees are interspersed with cultivated fields and huge swaths of brown earth.

The descent is subtle but quick, and soon the tires are screeching on the concrete under us, the outbuildings of Çi li Air Base zooming past. Lucas and the other soldiers are on their feet, body armor again in place, guns unpacked from the secured cases. When Henry reaches over and grabs my hand, I realize how hard I'm shaking. He's pale again, eyes wide, but he nods in reassurance. "You are the flame," he whispers. I give him a small smile, relieved that he might not be as mad at me as Xavier is.

The plane slows, curves around the runway's end, and taxis toward yet another private hangar. Outside the building we're approaching sit three large black SUVs with heavily tinted windows. I hear the safeties unlocking on the frightening weapons Lucas and his cohorts hold. Xavier is behind them, his own firearm again holstered on his belt.

The plane eases to a stop, a handful of ground crew in high-vis vests scurrying about under the aircraft to secure it in place. A soldier in front of Lucas holds a huge, riot-style shield; Lucas throws his weapon into his shoulder, ready in attack stance. I look worriedly to Henry, and then Xavier, and then grab on to Henry's hand.

The side of the plane opens. Stairs down. The shield moves forward, close steps, as Lucas and his second move in sync. The front soldier yells out of the plane's door to the ground. "Are we clear to disembark?"

"Clear to disembark, sir!" the cry comes back. The shield is dropped slightly as the first soldier inspects the stairs and surrounding area through the bulletproof viewer in the shield, his handgun drawn at his side, finger resting on the trigger guard. He takes one full step out, and then another, and then the three soldiers, thankfully, relax.

I'm still holding my breath.

Xavier motions for us to move. "Do not stop. Go to the car you're directed to."

We near-jog down the center aisle, to the plane's open door, my first inhale of Turkey filled with jet fuel and car exhaust. "Down. Go," Xavier says behind us, his weapon pointed at the ground. The doors of the SUVs are open and waiting. The soldiers stand at attention, joining their comrades already at the ready in and around the hangar.

Step. Step. Step. I look up from watching where I'm going, and freeze.

I can't even scream.

Xavier slams into me. "Move! Do not stop!" Henry's hand stretches between us and I yank away, slipping as I try to back up the staircase.

"Wrong way! Go! Down!" Xavier yells again.

But I can't.

Because standing right next to the open door of the SUV is Aveline Darrow.

And the smile on her face is all I can see, my screams overriding the whining whirr of the jet's cooling engines.

33

I'm kicking and still screaming as Xavier throws me over his shoulder and hurls me into the back of the SUV. Once I'm in the car, Xavier wraps himself around my upper body, but this can't be happening.

"Genevieve, what the hell is wrong?" Xavier wrestles against me there on the middle bench seat, my legs thrashing and kicking the back of the front seats as I try to get away before Aveline can climb into our car and take what she came for.

"Let me go! She's here! What are you doing? Heeeeelp!" I scream. When I slam my elbow into Xavier's still-sore gut, he grunts and squeezes even tighter.

"*Stop*! No one is here. You are safe. You are safe," he says against my head, over and over again, the same way Baby would do when Delia was in the midst of an Etemmu attack.

Only there is no Etemmu, no spiders, no stench.

Only Aveline.

The front door to the SUV opens, and I open my mouth for a renewed scream when the black-haired female climbs in. She turns around to look at us, her eyes wide, mouth set in a firm line, ponytail draping over her shoulder.

"Is she all right?"

I can't catch my breath.

It's not Aveline Darrow.

Xavier loosens his grip and Henry scoots in, looping his arm through mine, his voice against my ear. "You're okay . . . you're safe." I'm afraid to blink, my eyes burning, as I look at Henry, and then back at the woman in the front seat.

"You . . . it was Aveline . . . she was here," I say, breathless. "I . . . I saw her. You—"

"Genevieve, Henry, this is Sevda. She is our handler here in Izmir." The woman named Sevda nods courteously from her position in the front seat, but she stares hard at Xavier before turning to Lucas behind the wheel.

"Move," she says. Lucas throws the vehicle into drive and tears forward. Of the three black SUVs, one moves into position in front of us, the third behind, but I can't stop staring at Sevda.

"I saw her. Henry, I saw her. She's here. Aveline is here." My throat burns from screaming. He lets go of me long enough to fasten my lap belt, but then wraps his arm around me once again.

"She's not here. We're safe," he repeats. I don't fight against him, and once I'm convinced that Aveline Darrow isn't sitting in the front seat of our truck, I will apologize to Xavier for hurting him.

Until then, however, I once again miss the passing landscape of a new country because I cannot, and will not, tear my eyes from the back of that woman's head.

If Xavier was worried about us not sticking out like a sore thumb, he didn't plan our transportation very well. Three black SUVs with heavily tinted windows screaming through the city? Uh, yeah. We're attracting attention.

Sevda points out landmarks as we travel along the Aegean Coast into the heart of the port city formerly known as Smyrna. She explains how Turkey has been occupied for the last 8500 years, the Greeks here from 2000 BCE until 1920; how much of the city's Old Town was destroyed in a massive blaze during their War of Independence after the first World War, how it's a shame we don't have more time to visit the Roman ruins at Ephesus an hour south of here or the "architectural triumphs" of the Byzantines and Ottomans in Istanbul.

The few glances I steal out the window shows block after block of buildings, apartment and otherwise, a ton of ferries and a few cruise ships, and the Turkish flag—red with the white crescent moon and singular star. Flags *everywhere*.

But then our view changes as we take a hard left. "Any attempts at tailing us will be confused about which vehicle to follow," Sevda explains. A few blocks into the concrete jungle, a sharp right takes us into a downward-spiraling garage.

"We're here," she announces. "Prepare to exit the vehicle."

The Suburban squeals to a stop near a door marked Stairs. Everyone offloads quickly, and Henry keeps his gloved hand wrapped loosely around my upper arm. Probably worried I'm going to freak out again. In the muted parking garage light, it's not too far-fetched to see why I might have thought she was Aveline.

But when she turns to quickly throw an order at Lucas, I'm startled by a new revelation: she looks like Lucian. Same nose, same hazel eyes, though hers are more almond-shaped.

I shudder. Fever, fatigue, anxiety, stress—too much. My brain is messing with me.

"Come," she says, and we're in a stairwell, following Sevda up two flights, Xavier and one of the soldiers at our back. We exit into a wide hallway, the floors marble, the walls eggshell and decorated with photographs of what I assume are Turkish landmarks. This place is way nicer than the apartment in Barcelona.

Sevda stops in front of a black door but instead of a key, she uses her thumbprint and a PIN code to grant us entry. We pile inside, the door closing behind us with a comfortingly heavy lock. Floor-to-ceiling windows are covered in opaque sheers, our view of office buildings across the way.

"No one can see in. Rest easy," Sevda says, unfastening the Velcro that secures her Kevlar vest across her chest. "Let's have tea. We have much to discuss." As if summoned by the word *tea*, a tiny woman with black-and-gray hair pulled into a tight bun appears from another room off the stainless steel and marble kitchen.

"This is Sofi," Sevda introduces. "She will help make your brief stay with us more comfortable. Her English is rudimentary at best, but she is eager to please. And an excellent cook." Sevda smiles at the diminutive woman, who then bobs her head at us and smooths the white apron over her plain black dress. She then turns to ready the tea service.

Xavier points to a corner where we can put our packs and then makes himself comfortable on the huge red leather sectional that takes up most of the bright living room. He pulls out his silver lighter and tobacco kit to roll a fresh cigarette.

"That shit will kill you. Why do you persist?" Sevda scolds, her accent making the word *shit* sound glamorous. She carries over a tray with six tea glasses and a bowl of sugar cubes with silver tongs and sets it on the round glass coffee table at the room's center. Within just a moment, Sofi follows with a silver teapot, and then disappears, her steps soundless on the gray shag area rug and marble floor.

"We don't have time to get acquainted, so I will get directly to our plan." Sevda pours tea and Lucas passes out the steaming glasses, offering sugar and teaspoons. The quick look of longing he gives Sevda when he takes each glass, and the way her eyes soften when she looks back at him—yeah, they're a thing.

Sevda is seated on the very edge of the couch as if she's ready to spring into action. "I am a member of *La Vérité,* as Xavier probably told you. I am a handler for the network, trained in jujitsu and hand-to-hand combat. I spent fifteen years training with the Turkish military, including special and covert operations, before going undercover with *La Vérité* full-time. My history before that prepared me for this life, and I am good at my job." She looks at me. "Delia was a dear friend of mine, and the world is colder without her here." She then pulls an antique silver key out from under the neck of her fitted black shirt, kisses it, and bows her head.

"Thank you, Sevda," I say.

"Xavier told me about Pompeii. I am so sorry you had to be a part of such a terrible ordeal." She picks up her tea and sips it. This woman, whose hands are lethal weapons, looks dainty and dancer-like as she cradles the cup. "Xavier also tells me you have a unique idea for our meeting with the final Guardian."

Xavier nods at me. I set my own tea down and sit up straighter. "We do."

"So, let's hear it."

I explain our new strategy to Sevda the way I did to Xavier, and a reluctant Henry, on the plane. She nods a few times, looks to Xavier now and again, refills her tea. By the time I'm done explaining—and Xavier and Sevda have discussed potential issues—we have finished the first pot and Sofi has brought another.

"I do not love the idea of making you visible to the network, but there is definitely some value in letting *La Vérité* members meet you. So many of them loved your mother," Sevda says. "But I agree that Henry should not be made front and center. We can arrange for you to heal a few people discreetly, and of course, Henry will need to be present for Mazhar, the Guardian, but the less ceremony, the better. The more we blend in, the better. And you're right—Dagan wouldn't do anything that could be traced back to him. If he were to hurt civilians, there would be swift retribution in the local networks."

I sit back against the cushions, relieved to have presented my plan and not been laughed at or reprimanded that it's dumb because I'm only a kid so what do I know.

In fact, maybe the warm feeling in my chest, for once, isn't electricity but a little pride—like, maybe I *can* do something that will save Baby and avenge those who have been taken from me and also help my mother's *La Vérité* friends, all at the same time.

If I—if we—can finish what our parents and grandparents started, maybe there's hope. Maybe I am making the right decision to destroy the books, even if it means losing our gifts.

"Xavier and I will set to work at once making the arrangements," Sevda says, putting her cup down for a final time. "For the sake of time and safety for everyone, I propose one additional change: I will serve as proxy to verify your possession and identities, which will in turn serve as confirmation for Mazhar that you are indeed the true heirs, that he is justified in turning over the piece you seek."

Henry and I look to Xavier. He trusts her, but showing anyone who is not a Guardian the books . . .

"Is that wise?" Henry asks.

"It would preclude the need for Genevieve to reveal anything about herself other than a polite hello to her mother's companions. This would also support use of decoys to conceal your true selves," Sevda says. "You say you can tell when a *La Vérité* member is untrue or serving a malicious intent?"

"Yes. Because of their key . . . it turns black and sooty, like vapor."

"So, if we're at the venue and Genevieve sees a blackened key, my validation to Mazhar that you are who you say you are will be doubly proved. We can make the exchange and slip right out the side."

Sevda pats her key where it rests over her shirt. Not gonna lie—I've watched it over the last hour while we've talked.

"How do we prove our identities to you?" I ask.

"The same way you would for the Guardian." Henry and I look at one another. He still looks doubtful but remains quiet. "If we are in agreement, then let us proceed." Sevda stands and nods at Xavier.

"Bring your packs," he says to Henry and me. We stand and retrieve them, and then in a line—Xavier, Henry, and myself—follow Sevda down the hall into yet another room, secured by another thumb reader, the room windowless with expensive-looking wood-paneled walls and a massive circular Persian rug in the center. Sevda locks the door behind us.

Xavier nods first at Henry and then me, signaling for us to extract the *AVRAKEDAVRA* texts from their compartments.

"Please place the books on the rug in front of you and kneel," Sevda instructs, kneeling herself. We place our books, and then Henry takes my hand; together we fold ourselves onto the floor. As happened with Shamira and then poor Gaetano, Sevda instructs us to place our ungloved hands onto the texts. As soon as we make contact, the energy exchange is intense and hot, though minus the painful bite that it had at the Forum in Pompeii.

I hope that's a good sign.

Sevda places one hand each on mine and Henry's and recites a prayer or incantation, in what might be Aramaic.

Within two minutes, the ritual is over, Sevda's olive skin flushed and sweaty from the effort.

"I am confident you are the sealed heirs to the *AVRAKEDAVRA*. Thank you for your service," she says, bowing her head to us. My heart thuds against my breastbone, the burn of electricity begging for release, the wounds scored into my left arm screaming with renewed pain. I blink rapidly and hope the faintness passes quickly.

She lets go of my hand, but maintains her hold on Henry's, inspecting his face, reaching a finger to touch his bisected eyebrow, his closely shorn head. "I never had the opportunity to meet your mother," she says to him. "But I know her story. I am all too familiar with the pain she lived through, torn between her love for father and duty, and for a dangerous man. Romantic love is blinding, and deadly—but so too is blind loyalty based on a shared blood. One only has to look through the history books for confirmation of that," she says. She leans back on her ankles but does not release Henry's hand.

I glance at Xavier, now rigid with the tension that fills the room, with the alarm fixed on Henry's face.

"Do not fear me, Henry Dmitri. I am your friend, and alongside these fine people, I am your true ally," she says, finally letting go of him. She's shaking—her whole body, just slightly, like she's nervous. "I know your personal hell, your mother murdered, your own life dimmed in the shadow of your father's indifference, your experiences darkened by the pain of learning Dagan's true nature."

Sevda then pulls her sleeve back, revealing a faded but

still definitive tattoo—the inverted triangle overlying the circle. "I know, because before you, I was in line to be the heir."

What is she saying . . . ?

She looks at me, her words hard. "I have felt the consuming pain of a murderous loss of family, of identity, of country at the hands of those who seek to undo our righteous path, at the hands of your *sister*." I am instantly defensive—it's as if Sevda is saying Aveline Darrow's evil is somehow my fault. Xavier steps closer beside me, his hands on his hips.

But then Sevda focuses again on Henry, her eyes softening. She flattens a shaking hand over her heart, her voice thick with emotion. "Brother, your birth changed the course of my life, and for that, I am eternally grateful," she says. "My true name is Sevda Vadat Hakalar Dmitri. Our father thought me dead alongside my mother, killed by the hand of his witch more than a century ago. Imagine his surprise when he learned I survived," she says. "I stand before you today to pledge my allegiance and loyalty. Dagan has been chasing me for seventy years—I too have a magical gift, one that allows me special accommodations in the art of concealment. And yet, I suspect our cat-and-mouse will soon come to its bitter end, one way or another."

She pauses for a moment, wringing her hands in front of her. "I've been waiting for so many years for this." She wipes her flushed cheeks. "I feel like the weight of the world has been lifted off my shoulders. I have a brother! And he's so handsome and brave and wonderful!"

She leans in and hugs Henry tightly, and when she lets go, her smile is equal parts genuine and secretive before it melts back to something angrier, her eyes darkening with vengeance.

"But together, we will put Dagan's unholy campaign to rest, once and for all, and send Aveline the Witch back to the hell from whence she escaped."

34

THE ROOM IS DEADLY SILENT. EVEN XAVIER'S EYES ARE WIDE WITH SHOCK.

And Sevda's key is again tucked under her shirt. *Shit. I should not have revealed that I could see a member's duplicity so easily.*

The uncertainty of what will come next—if Sevda will murder us all and take the books, or if she's true to her word—lies like a fog around us. But then Sevda wipes her tears from her cheeks and pulls Henry to standing so she can embrace him again, and the tension in Xavier's body melts. Henry hugs her back, but tentatively, his creased brow expressing his confusion clearer than any words could.

"You must rest. Xavier and I have much to do—*La Vérité* can be activated with a few hours' notice, so let us get busy with that, shall we? Sofi will have food for us, and then we will prepare for our visit to *Tanrilar Sirk*. It really is beautiful, I will admit—if possible, we should arrive early to take in the sights. As yet, you are still children, and children need to smile too." Sevda unlocks the door and pulls it open.

Xavier steps closer and lowers his voice. "You look like you're about to blow something up."

"Probably because I am." I need to get rid of the electrical energy in my hands without an audience, and without catching anything on fire.

Sevda shows us to another room, this one comfortably appointed with twin beds and a huge bathroom, yet more marble and glass. I can't imagine how much time Sofi spends cleaning all the shiny surfaces in this apartment. "You can freshen up and rest here," she says, quietly moving down the hall and back into the main living area.

Xavier steps into the bedroom with Henry and me.

"What the hell was that?" I whisper.

He's shaking his head, looking at the floor. "I . . . I honestly do not know."

"How long have you known this woman? How could you not know she was a Dmitri?" I want to be sensitive to Henry in the aftermath of such shocking news—I know exactly how it feels to learn about a mystery sibling—but this is a major red flag that *Xavier*, of all people, didn't know Sevda's lineage.

We are sitting ducks, locked in an apartment in a foreign city of Dagan loyalists by a woman alleging a familial tie to Henry who may or may not be preparing to kill us and steal our books to give to Dagan.

Xavier pushes his fingers into his eyes.

I turn to Henry. "Did Alicia not show you this? How the hell can you *both* not know?"

No one has an answer.

Henry sits on the bed, his head in his hands, staring at the floor.

A waft of burned fabric floats up from my clenched hands. Upon opening them, I've singed holes in my gloves.

"I need to phone Nutesh," Xavier says quietly.

"Ya think?"

"Do *not* move your eyes from those bags," he says. "If you must nap or piss, take turns."

"What about Lucas?" I ask. "They seem very friendly with one another, he and Sevda—Xavier, are we cornered here? Have we been double-crossed?" Xavier wasn't at the compound in Croix-Mare when Mathieu held a gun to the back of Henry's head. Mathieu who smiled and ate dinner with us and pretended we were allies.

"If she were dangerous, Alicia would've shown me," Henry says.

"But how could she? You heard Sevda—she has gifts in the art of concealment. Why has Alicia shown you nothing about her at all? Is she here, Henry? Can you talk to her? Why am I the only one freaking the fuck out about this?"

Xavier closes the space between us. "You are not the only one," he hisses, "but cooler heads prevail. Nothing can be set in motion without that third piece of the key, not to mention they don't have Nutesh's *AVRAKEDAVRA*—if their plan is to take the books, they're certainly not going to make a move until after we meet with Mazhar. He won't relinquish that piece to anyone but you."

"Unless she meets with Mazhar claiming she is serving as our proxy and collects the piece!" I say.

"No. He wouldn't do that. He won't release anything until he sees me. Until he sees you."

"Or unless she murders him and takes what she wants. Maybe we're just the bait to draw him out," I whisper fiercely. "Xavier, I want to believe you—I really do—but this is not the wrench I was expecting at this stage in the game. We made it through Pompeii, but what if our luck is running out? Can we survive another ambush?"

I'm trying not to panic, but the fact that we are not running out of this place right this second, guns drawn, is absolutely nuts.

"Genevieve," Henry says, nodding at my hands. They are fully smoking now. And they burn like they're on fire. Probably because they are.

"Help her before she burns us to the ground," Xavier says to Henry. "Do not leave this room. Do you understand?"

Henry stands and cups a hand under my elbow. He and Xavier exchange nods, and then we're moving into the bathroom, Xavier rushing from the room to make the call that will, I hope, shed some light on what the hell is happening.

The bathroom is wall-to-wall mirrors, above the long counter that houses double sinks and on the wall behind us. Our joint reflections go on for infinity, the light from narrow windows just below the wall-to-ceiling intersection bouncing on and on in the glass forever.

Henry throws open the faucet and eases my hands under the cold water.

"Gahhhhh . . . oh my god, this hurts . . . ," I growl, trying to catch my breath, eyes clenched closed against the smell of burning fabric and skin. "Grab the medical kit. I'm going to need sterile tweezers and gauze and some aloe." The water flowing from the sleek silver faucet stings like a bitch but at least it helps loosen some of the glove material seared into the tender skin of my palms.

Henry returns quickly with medical supplies, leaning against the counter with a fresh pair of tweezers in hand. "What can I do?" he asks.

Our eyes meet in the mirror. "I don't even know, Henry. As if the carved-up arm weren't enough to deal with." I peel as much of the gloves off as I can with my blistering fingertips, biting my lip so I don't yell, and then take the tweezers from him. "I've got this. You need a moment. Maybe a breath of fresh air, if that's even possible in this place."

"I have a sister. A *half* sister," he says. I turn the faucet off; the ventilation fan in the ceiling whirrs quietly.

"You do. Weird way to find out," I say. "Alicia gave you no clue? No indication?"

He shakes his head.

"You can ask her about it though, right?"

"Yes." He unwraps some gauze pads and gives them to me, one at a time.

"Sevda said she's gifted with concealment. What, like she can make herself invisible?"

"If she's from Belshunu's line—from the *Death* text line—concealment might be a useful skill," Henry says. "She must know how to keep herself hidden, to warp the truth so no one ever learns what it is."

I swallow hard. "That's exactly what I'm worried about, Henry."

He nods. "I'm going to see about that fresh air." He kisses my temple and walks out, closing the door behind him.

I manage to pluck off the rest of the glove fabric, teeth clenched as it takes skin with it, disgusted that this so-called "gift" continues to cause me so much damage. I won't be sad to be rid of it.

But "concealment"—I need to know what that means specific to Sevda. Xavier can change his outward appearance. Is she the same? No—her magic has to be stronger, if she's truly of Lucian's blood. If it is, how can we ever know if she is who she says she is, especially after I swore she was Aveline when we disembarked?

Or did Aveline just project herself through my eyes onto Sevda?

God, I'm so tired. I don't know what I believe anymore. I just want this to all be over.

I dab at the raw open skin, and then coat the new wounds with Hélène's fortified aloe. The fragrant smell is at once overridden, its tickle in my nose sending an instant tremor through me. I close my eyes and hold my breath against it.

If I can't smell it, it's not here.

Etemmu.

"You're not real. You're not real. You're not real," I chant, the smell growing stronger. I don't dare open my eyes. I can't bear to see the howling black horror, the legion of spiders, reflected in so many mirrors. My *Life* text is in the other room; I can't fight the Etemmu without the book's help.

"'*Once upon a time, there lived a young girl with hair like the sun's fire, feet like the wind, and hands that enchanted even the lowliest sufferer.'"*

The line from my mother's story.

"You're not real. You're not real," I say again, stronger this time, willing it to be true.

"Ohhhh, but I am," the voice hisses as a hand grabs the back of my hair, forcing my eyes open. Staring back at me in the prism of mirrors is Aveline Darrow, but not just one face—a thousand malevolent grins, her ice-blue eyes alight with the pain she's about to inflict. "I warned you what would happen to your family if you crossed me." She moves closer, her lips almost touching my ear.

"I'll bet you didn't know that our brilliant mother was also a clever murderess in her day? She was once renowned for her cultivation of the most potent castor bean plants." I struggle against her grip but instantly regret it. An explosion of pain blasts through me, dropping me to my knees, my chin impacting the marble counter on my way down, causing me to bite through my tongue.

And then I'm flat on my back, oppressive weight on top of me, her hands tight around my neck, choking off the putrid air that surrounds us. "Nothing says tea party like French cookies and ricin. The police will find your prints all over that tea set . . . if I don't finish the job myself, I know a dashing trapezist back in Oregon who would love to wrap his strong fingers around your pretty. Little. Neck."

I gurgle on blood from my lacerated tongue through a barrage of muffled screams—soon made louder by the excruciating physical pain at the cellular level as Aveline's ability to command a body's internal workings tears me apart.

"Violet begged for death at the end, just like you will."

And then through the front of my shirt, Aveline drags her pearl-handled blade, carving into my flesh like she's trying to reach my heart. I try to struggle against her, but she's so much stronger than I am and her abilities mean I'm not in control of my body.

I can't be the hero of my own story when I am outgunned at every turn.

As I feel consciousness drifting away, the bathroom door splinters open and at once the weight is lifted, leaving me choking on blood and spit. I gasp, desperate for one clean breath. Xavier throws Aveline against the wall, her body smashing the mirror behind as she slumps to the floor; just as quickly, Sevda is there, a knife at Aveline's neck.

But it's not Aveline at all.

It's Sofi, the housekeeper, her crumpled figure smiling like she's just won the lottery, blood from the top of her head spilling down her face, staining her teeth and lips. She coughs and then spits onto the floor. "Dagan is coming for you all. And you, you duplicitous monster," she reaches up and digs her claws into Sevda's arm, "Aveline Darrow will see you dead before this is over, and the rightful heir will take her place—"

Her words are cut off with one fast slice of Sevda's blade. Sofi's grimace fades, the fierce taunting in her eyes frozen forever. As she flops over and her life essence cascades like water over a dam onto the pristine floor, Sevda falls back onto her butt, reaching for one of the snow-white towels hanging on the warming rack above her. She wipes Sofi's blood from the steel, as if cleaning a knife after slicing into her dinner, and then slides it back into its sheath under her black pant leg.

I'm shaking so hard, my teeth chatter in my skull.

There isn't enough therapy in the world to erase this madness.

Sofi is dead. Sevda killed her. In front of me.

Every time I think things can't get any worse, they always do.

"Get her cleaned up," Sevda says to Xavier and Henry as she stands and wipes Sofi's blood from her hands. "We need to do something with the body." She exhales, her own body and face rigid, and stomps out of the room.

35

If Xavier and Sevda don't stop yelling at one another, Dagan's entire loyalist army will find us and storm the building before we can throw towels down to soak up Sofi's blood.

Henry does what he can to help, starting with a crash course in first aid. My tongue is too swollen to swallow pills at the moment, so painkillers in the muscle it is. Aveline—or Sofi—inflicted a tremendous amount of damage in a very short time. On top of the charred hands of my own doing, the initial fall and impact with the marble counter broke my right front tooth, basically in half, and I bit nasty holes in my tongue—so much for solid food for the next week. My muscles hurt like I've done a ten-hour workout on the silks *and* been trampled by Gertrude. The bleeding has renewed, oozing through the ongoing infection in my left arm from Aveline's earlier handiwork. And the new carving in my chest . . .

Well, that is a pretty sight indeed.

Over my sternum, carved into the flesh just below the collarbone and into sensitive breast tissue, I now have an inverted triangle overlying the circle—just like the wound that festered and killed my fifth-great-grandfather Udish, when he died in Delia's arms that day in the field outside the medieval settlement.

Aveline's vicious words echo in my ears as I sit on the bed, letting Henry do what he can, per my instructions, to treat this latest assault. It hurts like hell—all of it, on every level—but I'm too tired to cry.

Violet begged for death at the end, just like you will.

She's probably not wrong.

I probably will beg for death.

But not until I take her with me.

"It would be quite convenient if you could heal yourself," Henry says, trying out a sympathetic smile as he packs antibiotic ointment into the curves and lines opened in my skin. I don't even have the energy to be embarrassed that I'm sitting here in my bra and yet another pair of blood-covered cargo pants in front of Henry. "That pain medicine helping at all?"

"Hardly. Did Hélène not send anything stronger?"

"No . . . I'm guessing they're worried about us not being on our toes."

"I was awake and perfectly unmedicated and yet it did nothing to prevent Aveline from getting to me," I say. "Doesn't Xavier have a flask lying around here?"

Henry looks at me pitifully as I suck in against a painful swipe of cotton swab. "Sorry. Almost done." I walk him through taping sterile gauze over my new wounds.

"I thought Xavier's carving was working," Henry says.

"His what?"

"Remember the carving he was doing at the cabin in Spain?" I pause, thinking back. "He told me it was a figurine of Aveline. After we ditched him, he burned it with her hair and an herb. Thyme, I think he said. Apparently, it's a Mesopotamian ritual effective against witchcraft."

"He did that?"

"It's supposed to keep you safe from the Etemmu. And from Aveline."

"It didn't work."

Henry crumples up the medical wrappers and sits next to me, barely touching me with his shoulder. "He did it because he wants to help. We need you, Genevieve. And even if you don't believe it, he loves you."

"Where did he get Aveline's hair?"

"I didn't ask," Henry whispers. "But it's probably safe to assume he's had it with him for a while."

I revisit the vision of Xavier confronting my mother in that quaint cabin, of a tiny Aveline curled in her blankets. Before all this deception and treachery ruined their lives.

"You should thank him," Henry says.

I lock eyes with Henry, my throbbing jaw painfully clenched against words I don't want to fall out of my mouth. But they do. "Thank him? It's almost as if you didn't just bandage me up. Again."

"Gen—"

"Do we have any clean shirts left?"

Henry nods. I don't want to talk anymore. I especially don't want to talk about how *grateful* I should be that my biological father carved a tiny piece of wood to try and stave off yet another attack from *his* daughter.

Henry finds me a shirt and helps me slide into it. He sits again. "I don't think we should do this meeting with the *La Vérité* members. After this?" He points at my new injuries. "It's too dangerous."

I turn to face him. Every movement is a poke with a hell-fire-red branding iron. "Seriously? Henry, is there something you know that you're not telling us? Hey, Alicia, are you here? Do you have intel about tomorrow? Did you know Aveline was coming for me?" My voice sounds weird as it bounces off the walls and hits me with the full force of my anger.

"Genevieve, that's not how it works. You know that . . ."

"Right. Memories only. No fortune-telling. I get it," I say, easing back onto the bed. "This plan will work. This plan *has* to work. I don't want to talk about it anymore."

Sevda and Lucas interrupt us, announcing their entry with little more than a knock. They walk through to the bathroom—Lucas has what I think might be a body bag under his arm—and Sevda carries a bucket with bleach and industrial-strength paper towels. The smell of cigarette wafts down the hall after them—guessing Xavier isn't going to help with the cleaning party.

Henry tries to get me to look away, but I can't. Together they hoist Sofi's body into the bag, zip her up, and then wrap her in a secondary black tarp that Lucas duct tapes into place. I can't imagine where they're going to put her now—that is so clearly a body.

Lucas scoops it up like it weighs no more than a pillow. "I'll be right back to help with this," he says to Sevda and then exits.

I stand and walk across the room, pausing just outside the bathroom's open doorway. "What will you do with her?"

"Better not to ask."

I watch Sevda, not bothering an offer to help because even if I wanted to, I can't. I'm in so much pain, just walking over here has winded me. Sevda looks up from where she's crouched on the floor, sopping up human blood and mirror shards. "Please. Go rest. Don't watch me do this. You've seen enough." She urges me backward without touching me, closing the bathroom door between us.

"Genevieve, come now. Rest while we can." Henry's hands are gentle on my upper arms. I don't resist. I'm too tired to resist.

I'm too tired to do anything.

My eyes fly open when weight depresses the mattress.

"Just me," Xavier says. A small bedside lamp is the sole light in the room. The fabric against my cheek is rough—not like a pillowcase. I push up and look at it, unsettled to see that someone has placed a towel under my face, and it's bloody. "When you fell asleep, your mouth bled a bit. I thought that would be more comfortable for you."

"I'm so groggy."

"I gave you something a little heavier than ibuprofen. You needed the rest while we are in a secure environment."

This environment doesn't feel very secure.

My tongue is killing me, but it's less swollen than before. "How long was I out?"

"About six hours. We have food, if you think you can eat." Xavier helps me sit up and hands me a glass of water.

"Only if you can put it in a blender."

"Open your mouth?" I do. "Tongue?" I stick it out. Xavier looks at it, gently lifts my lip to inspect my broken tooth, and then nods. He stands and walks to the medical kit, grabs two pills, and brings them back to me. "The pain meds will be wearing off. We have to keep the swelling down."

"How is she doing this? How is she getting to me?"

Xavier scrubs a hand over his face. "I don't know."

"Henry said you carved an effigy. That you tried to burn it, with her hair, to protect me."

Xavier's head bobs.

"Thank you," I say.

"A Mesopotamian *Maqlû* ritual. I'm sorry it didn't work." Tentatively he reaches up and flattens his palm against my cheek. "You look so much like your mom, sometimes it takes my breath away." His ice-blue eyes glisten. "I want to help you, Genevieve. Please let me help you. I'm sorry I wasn't able to be your father"—he swallows hard—"but I want to be your friend. I want to do what I can to make this right. You said it earlier, that all these adults are asking you to fix their mistakes—but you are so strong. You are so much like Delia." He stops talking and wipes at his eyes, looking away for a beat like he's embarrassed for me to see him showing real emotion. "Goddammit, I didn't realize how much I missed her until I saw you."

And then the tears are openly flowing down his face, and I feel so terrible for being mean to him, I push the blanket aside and wrap my arms around him. When he wraps his arms around me right back, I don't freeze or pull away.

I just let my father cry against me for as long as he needs.

Xavier mentioned that Sevda and Lucas threw out every piece of food Sofi may have touched—just in case—so tonight's offerings are pretty basic. I can't chew anything, so Sevda whips together a smoothie with banana, almond powder, and pomegranate juice. It tastes good, though the cold is uncomfortable against my broken tooth.

When we're all sitting again, Sevda passes around a plate of flaky pastries while Lucas pours fragrant Turkish coffee.

"During your rest, Xavier and I arranged for reinforcements to provide additional security tomorrow. Per our prior plans, everything will go forward—we will have a small, private gathering of *La Vérité* members on the site of *Tanrilar Sirk*—many of the performers are our people, so our numbers are not few. People are very excited to meet you," she says. "At that time, Mazhar will join us. Once we have acquired the final piece that we need, I will accompany you into Iraq."

I look at her, and then Xavier, the storm clouds returning to his face.

"I don't think that's a good idea." I set my smoothie down.

"Which part?"

"The part where you come with us into Iraq."

"It's not open for debate."

"And why is that?"

Sevda wipes her fingers on a white cloth napkin. "I'm sorry, Genevieve, but have I not proven myself to you yet? Have I not proven my loyalty?"

"I can't help but be a little concerned that you might be a magnet for our troubles. I've been around you not even a whole day, and already I've had two run-ins with Aveline Darrow. Convince me that's a coincidence."

Sevda pulls her shoulders back. "It has nothing to do with me."

"Then why did I think you were *her* at the airport? Why did she attack me in *your* bathroom?"

"I told you, it's this place. It's Turkey. Aveline is finding her way into your head through whatever route she can. I can't protect you from what I can't see, but I know Dagan, and I know he won't kill you yet, not until he has what he wants."

"And how convenient that once we meet Mazhar, we will have what Dagan wants, all in one place at the same time."

Sevda shakes her head, her face annoyed, and glances briefly at Xavier. "We will not have the third text. Dagan wouldn't waste his energies on an ambush at *Tanrilar Sirk* unless he knew the third text was in our possession. A smart man would wait until Iraq when all the players and all the parts are present."

"And this is your educated guess?" I say. "Based on what?"

"Based on years of tracking Dagan's decisions and movements," she says. "I believe it's best to know thy enemy."

I laugh. "How ironic."

"If you truly believe that I am working with my father and his witch"—she stands and pulls a knife from her boot. She walks around to my side of the dining table and offers me the blade, hilt first—"finish me now."

"Tempting," I hiss.

Xavier clears his throat and glares at Sevda; she replaces her blade. "I saved you in that bathroom," she says.

"No. My *father* saved me. Slicing an old woman's throat does not make you a hero."

"Are you two done?" Xavier says, impatient.

He then crosses his arms and nods at Sevda. She resumes her seat and picks up her baklava, finishing it in one bite. She pushes her plate away and leans forward on her crossed arms. "If I were working against you, you'd already be dead. I would have the books and the pieces I need, and I'd be en route to redeem myself in my father's eyes," she says. "But he is my father by blood only. *He murdered my mother too.* It's a sick club we have going here," she circles a finger among Henry and herself and me, "but we are fighting the same enemy. And I will endeavor to prove my loyalty to you until such time that we are on the sands of Babylon and I spill my own blood alongside yours in the Undoing."

I squint at her, then Xavier.

"More spilling of blood?" I say, tone flippant. "Hell, what's a few more red blood cells between friends?"

"In order to complete the ritual, the safeguards dictate that the key to the temple is not enough. The blood of heirs from each family must be present," Sevda says. "With the three of us, we now have representatives of each family. You from Udish," she says to me, "Henry from Nutesh, and me from Belshunu's line."

She locks eyes with me. "Surely you know you were created to stand in Aveline's way . . ." She steals a sideways glance at Xavier; he looks pissed. "Just as Henry was created to stand in mine."

"Have we not suffered enough already? Now you're going to throw us on an altar and bleed us?" I yell.

"It's a mere slice to the hand. A few drops more. No one is going to bleed you, Genevieve," Sevda says. "Xavier, this one is so theatrical." She flicks a finger in my direction.

"What new revelations are yet to come?" Henry asks under his breath. "I am representative of two families. Is that not enough? Is any of this ever going to be enough?" His voice is hard.

The ensuing silence is broken when Xavier's satellite phone rings. He answers and then excuses himself to talk out of earshot near the sheer-covered windows. I watch him, counting the heartbeats in my swollen mouth. They could be discussing anything, and by the way Xavier's face darkens, whatever words are being exchanged can't be good. He looks over at me before turning his back to the whole table, shielding his conversation from the rest of us.

Henry takes my hand, but I hold my breath, hoping that it's a gesture of affection only and not him preparing to show me some terrible new vision of a recent event his mother has shared with him. I'm grateful he has his usual soft leather gloves in place.

Xavier hangs up and rejoins us. "If we're done here, I'd like to go over the Iraq plans with Genevieve and Henry."

"Was that Nutesh? Is Baby all right?" I ask.

"No change. He's stable," Xavier says.

"But he's not better."

Xavier shakes his head. "And yet he's not worse either."

Okay, I will concede that. If Baby's heart is still beating, then I still have a purpose.

"Come. Much to cover before sleep, and tomorrow is a big day for us all," Xavier says. Henry thanks Sevda and Lucas for the meal, and then we follow Xavier down the hall, back into our room. Sevda has cracked a rectangular window open but because this is an apartment building, the four inches of open space doesn't allow a lot of fresh outside air in. I try not to think about why the room smells of bleach. I try not to think about Sofi's life spilling out all over the marble floor, about if she had children or grandchildren who will miss her.

"Close the door," Xavier says. Henry does. It's a minor comfort when the flimsy lock clicks over, but I'll take it. "Sit." The room has a small, highly polished wooden table with four colorful, modern art–style wheeled chairs. Henry pulls one out for me, and then sits himself, scooting closer so he can drape his arm over the oval back of my seat.

Xavier pulls out his tablet and sets it up, followed by that sound-masking device he's so fond of.

"Paranoid much?" I ask.

"Aren't you?"

He flips the tablet on and navigates to a new screen—more maps. "If tomorrow goes to plan, we will have a nice, quiet meet and greet. We'll get the piece from Mazhar, and then slip out. We are so close to the end game," Xavier says. When he flips to the next screen, my stomach squeezes.

Iraq.

"Nutesh has arranged with an airfield in Sulaymaniyah, widely regarded as the capital of Kurdistan, in northern Iraq. The air base is controlled by the Peshmerga, Kurdish guerilla fighters—they're friendly to Nutesh. And they have an appreciation for the help Americans offered in recent ongoing conflicts, which is in your favor." He nods at me and Henry. "This area has been rebuilt, very pro-Western—and friendly to our cause—so I don't expect to run into trouble there." He swipes to another screen. "Babylon, however, could be a different scenario altogether."

"Thierry mentioned we might be staying at the university in Babil?" My heart twinges when I think of Thierry.

"Doubtful now. We thought we'd be able to secure overland transport into Baghdad and then stage at the university, but after Pompeii, Nutesh doesn't want to take chances with us out in the open for any longer than necessary. For now, it looks like we will helicopter in to the site direct from Sulaymaniyah. Nutesh is negotiating with a private contractor right now, an old friend of mine."

I close my eyes against a new swarm of dizziness. I demanded earlier that Xavier allow Henry and me to be a part of the planning process, but given we still have no idea how tomorrow is going to go, I'm quietly grateful Xavier has taken the reins on Iraq.

Because it's *Iraq*.

This isn't even real life anymore.

Xavier lets the screen time out as he leans back in his chair. "I am probably not wrong in guessing that everything you know about this part of the Middle East has been fed to you by the Western media. I've been there many times, to both Sunni- and Shia-controlled regions, and I can say with confidence that in peacetime, the country is vibrant and culturally exquisite. That is not to say that dangers don't lurk around every corner, especially with ISIS still active in the area and continued instability between the Kurds and Iraqis. But most people of Sulaymaniyah and Erbil and Baghdad are warm and friendly, the food is good, and the smiles are genuine. It is where your people come from," Xavier says, leaning forward, elbows resting on his knees. "You are not soldiers; you are not entering to occupy their lands or impose your will on the proud people who have inhabited this geography for thousands of years. You will be welcomed as guests, not shunned as invaders."

"Until they figure out why we're there," I say.

"Which will not happen. That is why you have the new passports. As far as anyone outside the network is concerned, you are university students from Canada and the UK on an expedition with me to study the ruins as part of a preservation project in conjunction with ongoing efforts of the Iraqi government."

I don't mean to laugh. "Us? No one is going to believe we're working with their government."

Xavier pats the pocket of his jacket, his nervous habit when he means to pull out his cigarettes. Instead he extracts yet another fat envelope, thumbing the flap open to expose the contents.

Money. A lot of American money.

"They will believe whatever we tell them, Genevieve," he says quietly.

My throat feels dry again. I grab one of the three bottled waters sitting on the table center and drink.

"What will happen in Babylon? Once we get there, to the Euphrates," Henry asks. The million-dollar question I don't want an answer to. I close my eyes for a moment, breathing slowly through my nose.

"We will put this all to rest, once and for all," Xavier says, offering no further detail. "I know this part will be frightening." He flattens his hand over his heart. "I swear to you, I will do everything in my power to help you accomplish this mission. Do not let your fear root you to the ground. Have faith that the strength you need will come when it is summoned, and I along with it." Xavier stares long and hard at me, and then at Henry, his face soft yet determined. He then grabs his own water and leans back in his chair, the hard set of his jaw returning to its resting state.

He drinks nearly the whole bottle in one pull. "Now—bed. You get a whole night of rest before we're on the move again. Make use of it." He closes the tablet and grabs his backpack. "I'll be close by. If you need anything." He nods, unlocks the door, and leaves.

The room is quiet, except for the outside sounds of nighttime busyness sneaking through the opened window.

Henry stands and situates himself on one of the twin beds.

"I thanked Xavier for the effigy," I say. Henry smiles slightly.

"And?"

"And I just wanted you to know that I am making an attempt at not being a jerk."

"I never said you were being a jerk."

"Except it feels like we're at odds over all of this. You don't want us to go tomorrow—"

"Because it's dangerous."

"And earlier on the plane, we were talking and you got up without saying a word and shut the door basically in my face," I say. Henry crosses his arms over his chest. "And then when I called Ash, you sided with Xavier."

"Firstly, I didn't have anything further to offer when you and Xavier were constructing the big plan for tomorrow. Again, I still think it's far too great a risk—"

"So make a different suggestion!"

"I don't have one. Which is why I didn't chime in. And with regard to Ash, you put us all at risk. I understand why you did it, but it was selfish."

"How is that any more selfish than you having all these private conversations with Alicia? Don't you think we all see you? I know who you're talking to but everyone else thinks you're *nuts*, Henry."

"My conversations with my mother don't put anyone in danger," he says.

"Don't they? Because I think they do. You and your mom are getting so close, how do I know you won't decide at the last minute that you don't want to go through with the Undoing? How do I know that you won't decide that losing her is too much, that you want to keep your book?"

"Are you being serious right now, Genevieve? You know that isn't going to happen—"

"No, I *don't* know that."

"What, you're a hundred percent certain that what we're doing is the right course of action?" he says, moving to the edge of the bed.

There is no other choice for us. "Baby is in a coma and the only way to save him is to break the magic that has cursed him. I was almost murdered in the bathroom tonight by a possessed woman. When Sofi attacked me? Aveline confessed—she told me everything she did that killed Violet. She murdered my best friend, and she's making it look like *I* did it. Violet is *dead,* and there's not a fucking thing I can *do* about it."

Henry jumps up from the bed and charges toward me. "We are doing *everything* we can. And just because I don't have a huge plan to throw at you and Xavier or Sevda even doesn't mean I'm not thinking. It doesn't mean I'm not trying to strategize and come up with solutions too. I don't know how else to show you my commitment, that I'm on board."

He spins around and grabs both of our backpacks. From his, he pulls out his *AVRAKEDAVRA*. Without asking me, he yanks mine free too, digging through my stuff until he finds my mother's painted playing cards. He sets the books a few feet apart and in between spreads out the cards.

"What are you doing?"

"Lock the door," he says without looking up.

I do, and then move back to the bedside, facing opposite him.

"Look." He points at the cards. Just like in Naples, the script on the playing cards is going crazy, moving and vibrating and spinning around the edge of the paintings.

"Put your hands on your book. Both of them." I look up at Henry, not sure where he's going with this. "Trust me."

Bent at the waist, I do as he instructs, placing both of my hands on the *Life* text; Henry does the same with *Memory*. The energy is warm and soothing this time, but it's not the energy transfer that grabs my attention—it's the cards.

The movement along the script is forming letters.

"What is that?" I whisper.

Henry, his hands still on his text, meets my eyes. "It's the incantation for the Undoing. It's our backup plan."

"But . . . I thought only Nutesh knew it."

"Well, now we do too," Henry says.

36

It's a pain to get the letters to hold still long enough for us to transcribe the incantation. The whole thing is mostly in French, which Henry translates—my mother, always thinking ahead. We put our books and the cards away and shake on it that we're not going to tell anyone else about this, including Xavier.

We take turns in the bathroom, but when I come out, Henry's pushed our twin beds together. He's sitting on the bed closest to the bathroom door. "You need help with anything?"

I shake my head no. "How did you know about the prayer?" I ask, and immediately recognize the look on his face.

"She offers memories she thinks might help us. That's all," he says.

I nod. "And she showed you this?"

"She showed me your mother painting the cards. Which means Delia wanted you to see it. The memories have to be shared willingly."

"Or taken unwillingly."

"Yes . . . or that. But if Alicia and Delia think we need this, it's important."

"It would be a lot easier if either or both of them could do something about Aveline."

"I know. I wish that too," he says, his voice barely above a whisper. "Can we be friends again?" He stands, and I fold myself against him.

"We're never not friends, Henry. There's just a lot going on and I think we're both trying to get through it without losing our minds."

"I'm so sorry about Vi. I'm sorry I got angry about you phoning Ash," he says against the top of my head.

"Thank you." I bite back a sob. "We have to focus on the next few days. If we can get through this, we can get through anything. When—if—we get home again, then I'll fall into a million pieces."

"And I'll be right there to tape you back together."

"Literally," I say, pulling my shirt out from my sternum and looking at my bandages.

Henry reaches down and kisses me, his ungloved hands clutching my shoulders and nestling me against him. The images he sends into my head through the contact with his lips show me how worried he was when I was so sick from the infection in Aveline's carving on the boat and later in Naples, how worried he was earlier when he stood by helplessly and watched Xavier save me from Sofi's Aveline-driven attack.

"I would give anything to be able to do more," he says. "To heal you myself."

"But you did, remember? You and Alicia saved me back in Naples."

"I love you, Genevieve." But before I can say another word, he scoops me up and carries me over to the twin bed pushed next to his. He climbs in alongside, in the same bed, promising to keep his gloves on but his arms around me. "No one is getting to us tonight."

He kisses my forehead, and I nuzzle in against his chest, grateful for this one perfect moment in a sea of so much awful.

In light of Sofi's performance yesterday afternoon, we're moving to a different apartment this morning, across from *Tanrilar Sirk*, so we can do a little reconnaissance before we step foot onto the circus grounds. Even though that plan is a new development no one consulted Henry nor I about, it's smart, and necessary.

I have enough time to cradle a cup of strong coffee near the floor-to-ceiling windows in the living room while watching the dawning sun paint the sky in hues of pink and orange. It reminds me of Southern California—the skies aren't the deeper blue of the Pacific Northwest but rather like someone took a wide brush and whitewashed the atmosphere.

Xavier helps me tend my wounds, followed by a quick check of the broken front tooth to make sure it's still embedded in the gum. Not like he could do anything about it here anyway. Xavier is many things, but I don't think dentistry is among his special skills.

Then our packs are on and we're moving. I'm not sad when the apartment door clicks closed behind us.

The air in the parking garage reeks of exhaust, but even under that, you can smell we're near water. And it's cold. For a city that is reportedly sunny 80 percent of the year, the chill is a subtle reminder that it is only February.

How is that possible . . . it feels like a million years ago, and not just six weeks, that my mother fell from her lyra and took her final breath in my hands there in the circus dirt. And yet, it feels like only yesterday.

We're back in the hefty SUV from before, flanked by our escort cars, and just as we pull out of the underground garage, Sevda informs us that this vehicle is virtually impenetrable. Bulletproof glass, reinforced side panels, the works.

Surreal we even need this.

The *AVRAKEDAVRA* texts, still in our backpacks, have been locked inside a lead-lined case in the very back, accessible only via thumbprint—Xavier's or Sevda's, but I insisted they add Henry's and mine, in case something goes wrong—and a code dialed into the digital pad. "They would have to blow up the whole car to get to the box, and even then, good luck cutting into it."

I want to believe her, but I also know that if a thief wants something badly enough, they'll find a way to take it.

The streets are busier than I expected—people and cars and horns everywhere—but just because my life has been turned on its ear doesn't mean the rest of the world doesn't still have jobs and bosses and bills to pay.

As we approach a stoplight, a woman at the corner looks up from her phone and stares at my darkly tinted window, as if she can see right through it.

My heart thuds.

Aveline.

The light turns green and we're moving again. She watches me as the car screams down the street.

A few blocks down, we're stopped again. Whose idea was it for us to be holed up in the city? We're vulnerable stopping at all these lights. I don't want to look out my window again—my mouth is so dry from fear, it's making my injured tongue throb—but I feel eyes on me.

I look.

A crowd stands waiting for their light to change; many are looking at the car in front of us, ours, the one behind us. We're about as inconspicuous as a fireworks display.

But there she is again. Except it's not just one Aveline—it's two, then three, then four and so on, until every woman in that block of humanity is staring at me through the dark glass.

I'm panting with terror.

"Gen?" Henry asks.

"She's here. She's everywhere. Aveline. She's in my head. I see her in every face," I say, stuffing the butts of my hands into my eyes so I don't have to look out the window. My stomach aches. I'm so thankful when the light turns green, to get me away from the unbearable pressure of all those eyes, like a lead blanket on my back pushing me to the ground.

"Eyes forward. Don't let her in," Xavier says from my other side.

Easy for him to say.

Sevda is quiet, bent over a black padded case opened in her lap. She turns in her seat, her hand cupped and extended toward Henry. "Earpieces. Everyone gets one." He takes the tiny, flesh-colored device with the clear coil running from its end. He fits it in his ear and then she hands him a small square black box to clip to his belt. "It's a transmitter outfitted with a mic and GPS. That way we can hear you and find you should we get separated."

She proceeds to give me one too. Seems Xavier's and Lucas's are already in place, except theirs have mics wrapped around their wrists, like watches. We're screaming down a six-lane highway, three lanes in each direction separated by a pretty green space, along Izmir's iconic waterfront. What I would give to be one of the people walking along the promenade or leaving the port on a ferry, destined for a day out that doesn't involve risking my life.

We turn inland again, and Sevda explains that the circus is set up in a sprawling municipal park built over land that once was home to a huge number of Greek citizens before a raging fire chased them to the sea. We'll be staging in an apartment just across the way until we receive word from Mazhar that he's in the city. There too we will meet our decoys—they've managed to find people who look enough like Henry and me after all. The decoys will wear American-style clothing while Henry and I will be outfitted with Kevlar vests under impact-resistant jackets.

"The fabric is made with spider silk," Sevda explains. "No one gets stabbed on my watch."

A chill washes through me. I don't want to get stabbed on *anyone's* watch.

Certainly enough, through the wide windshield, the first glimpses of *Tanrilar Sirk* come into view. It's a massive big top with three spires, much bigger than I'd anticipated for how it was described earlier as just as traveling circus.

Nostalgia flickers in my chest. God, I miss home. I love the circus, so much a part of my whole life, the excitement of seeing the big top, the promise of delicious food and death-defying acts and side-splitting hilarity just inside the tent.

My eyes sting with the memory. It makes me forget this hellscape for a few welcome seconds.

The main big top is flanked by at least half a dozen smaller tents. Sevda explains these house the menagerie, side acts, and vendors who offer everything from temporary tattoos to palmistry. "One beautiful thing about Izmir is the tolerance for differing beliefs—though most Turks are Muslim, they live in peace alongside followers of Judaism and Christianity, and have for millennia. It is why so many followers of *La Vérité* make it their home."

"And why so many of Dagan's loyalists do as well," Xavier says.

Sevda nods in agreement, and then points out the window as the car slows. "We will have our gathering in one of those smaller tents. If we wait until the circus grounds open for visitors, no one will be the wiser."

Our convoy slows and turns into the underground of a tall building across the way from the circus grounds. Sevda adjusts in her seat to face us fully. "We will exit here. Fifth floor. Follow closely. Stop to talk to no one." Lucas brakes hard in front of the elevator bank, and we pile out, waiting only for Xavier to unlock the lead case and retrieve our packs with the texts and two key pieces.

This latest apartment isn't nearly as fancy, and it's not empty. Sevda introduces us to two new faces: the couple who will act as our stand-ins. I eye them warily—I have no way to tell if they might be loyal to Lucian based on outward appearance.

They look enough like us from a distance that people will probably buy it, but that's only if they're going off the photos they've seen on the news of us with our shorn, darkened hair. The girl, named Doria, is pale like I am—and at least the eye colors match.

As do the *La Vérité* keys each of them pulls free upon introducing themselves. I watch; as they recite my mother's line, the keys don't turn black. Then again, they're just standing here. Does the key only reflect the evil within when the wearer moves against us or appears before us with malicious intent? And how do I know they're real keys or that they keys actually belong to them?

Xavier's voice whispers in my ear. "Don't worry. We are among friends. I can smell the electricity coming off your hands."

My fists unclench, my shoulders dropping from their perch near my ears. The energy dissipates in a puff of ozone.

"The next few hours will be a wait. These windows aren't coated so people can see you if you're looking out onto the street. Stay behind the curtains and leave the surveillance to us," Sevda says.

Xavier and Sevda position themselves at the window, again covered by a set of sheers that just mask their faces from the outside, sharing a pair of binoculars and exchanging tips on the best approach, the best way to exit, what we do if something goes sideways.

Over the next few hours, while one watches, the other gives Doria and Jakub, our stand-ins, a few simple answers for questions *La Vérité* members might ask. "Mostly they will just want a blessing from you," Sevda says. "'The key to good is found in truth' is enough. You may wish them well or tell them you will pray for their good health. Less is more."

"Especially since your accents are different from Genevieve and Henry," Xavier points out.

"I've been practicing my American accent all night," Jakub teases. "Hey, who likes baseball and Katy Perry and look at my new Nikes!" Good for a laugh, except he sounds like a guy from New Jersey who maybe got hit upside the head with a brick one too many times.

And Henry's accent is decidedly British.

"Like Sevda said, less is more." Xavier pulls out his cigarettes. When Sevda gives him a dirty look, he stuffs them back into his pocket, grumbling before replacing the binocs at his eyes.

The hours crawl by, but they're thankfully uneventful. Plus it's kinda fun to talk to Doria and Jakub about their lives in Turkey. It's nice to be still and safe for a minute.

Especially when Xavier announces it's time to go, the main room takes on a raw, frenetic energy that puts everyone on edge. Sevda pulls us into a back room where she and Lucas outfit us with the promised tactical vests and black, impact-proof coats. My head and neck are wrapped in an olive-green scarf, and Henry is given sunglasses. He's near indistinguishable from Lucas and his cohorts.

Doria and Jakub are dressed casually in jeans and plaid shirts and jackets, given backpacks that look just like ours. Our actual packs are locked in the lead case again, and then we're off.

Henry grabs my hand where we're standing next to the SUV in the parking garage. "You're shaking like a leaf."

"Aren't you?"

"Let's move," Xavier announces. Our lineup is predetermined—Lucas and another soldier in front, Doria and Jakub in the middle, and then Xavier, myself, Henry, and Sevda in a line along the back. We walk out of the parking garage via the driveway where we entered, and then it's down the block, around to the front of the building, and across the wide boulevard that separates the apartments and the grand park where *Tanrilar Sirk* is set up.

Men, women, and children excitedly move down the sidewalks along the expansive green lawns and into the heart of the park toward the big top. Henry nudges me with his elbow and speaks under his breath, just loud enough for me to hear. "If we survive this, I promise I will try Shakespeare again," he says, his lips quivering with a nervous smile.

"Well, in that case . . . you will learn to love *Hamlet*. Trust me."

"I do. Implicitly." He winks.

"Eyes front, lover boy," Xavier scolds.

The approach to *Tanrilar Sirk* brings about such a whirl of emotions. It's a beautiful tent in reds and golds, the tallest of the three spires topped unsurprisingly with a massive Turkish flag flapping proudly in the coastal air. The excitement of the crowds making their way toward the entrance gates is palpable. Vendors around the edge offer everything from skewers of fresh grilled meats to ornate ribbon-style candy twisted hot onto bamboo sticks that will cool into lollipops. My stomach growls. Music pours through speakers mounted at the tent corners; families take photos and videos of small children dancing and posing with the clowns who roam the grounds.

Food and happiness and smiling people everywhere.

Like I've said before, circus is the great equalizer.

Rather than follow the circusgoers toward the main ticket gate, however, Lucas and his partner lead us around the edge of the big top. How I wish I were here as a tourist, to visit the menagerie and watch the acrobats, and not as an heir to a book that has the power to erase all of this with a single uttered spell and a few drops of blood.

Sevda presses a finger against her ear, speaking softly into the mic at her wrist. I'm trying not to look at faces, especially those belonging to women. But with Sevda's quiet utterances into her sleeve, I notice eyes in the crowd among us, eyes attached to bodies that change course and start moving in our direction. Men and women in plainclothes, scarves around necks and heads and purses draped over shoulders. Only upon closer inspection do I notice the lumps of concealed sidearms under a long coat or the bulge in a fashionable boot that extends up a leg.

My chest aches with the effort of not freaking out, and my hands sing with renewed electric pain. "Xavier," I whisper.

Sevda's voice crackles in our ears. "They are with us. *La Vérité*. All is well. Stay focused."

We approach the back of one of the long side tents. Though I don't at first see the split in the canvas, Lucas reaches out, pulls it aside, and ushers us in. It's about the size of our mess tent back home—it will easily hold a hundred people or more. It has a doorway at its northern front side, blocked by a sapphire-blue velvet rope and two men dressed like Lucas, standing guard and looking a little too obvious.

As soon as we're inside, Doria and Jakub are placed on sturdy wooden chairs with thick upholstered seats on a small dais along the middle of the southern wall—like some sort of royalty. It looks like *La Vérité* members will then be allowed in via the front, once the velvet rope is moved, to pay their respects. The tent interior otherwise is laid with thick carpet, stacks of ornate pillows in rich earthy colors, as well as a long table along the northern wall with shining silver teapots, small glasses, and an endless buffet of pastries, dates, and tiny oranges. Incense sits heavy in the air.

Henry and I stand along the eastern wall, watching. With

a few quick exchanges via the earpieces, the velvet rope is unhooked, and people enter—all of them pausing just inside to pull their keys free and show them to Lucas.

"Genevieve, keep your eyes on the keys," Xavier says.

One by one, people move to the dais and say hello to the fake Genevieve, the fake Henry.

"Do we have a twenty on Mazhar?" Xavier asks.

Sevda pulls her phone out, scrolls through, and tucks it away again. She presses a finger against her earpiece. "He's here. Making his way toward us."

I watch the keys but also the faces of the people greeting Doria and Jakub, relieved when none of these strangers takes on Aveline's visage. Many of the guests are dressed in their circus finery—they're performers—but still others who enter are limping or holding a sick child or their own skin looks pallid with illness. They stop in front of Doria and she only utters a few words and pats their hand or arm but doesn't *do* anything to help them—because she can't.

"This is wrong," I say.

"Stay where you are," Sevda warns.

I turn to Xavier. "I have to help these people. Look at them—they feel cheated. They came here for help, not a pat on the wrist."

"Genevieve . . ."

I don't care what Sevda is hissing at me through my earpiece—my mother would be disgusted if she saw all these sick people and we did nothing to help.

In one swift move, I yank off my green scarf and push through the small crowd that has gathered in the center of the tent. Before anyone can grab me, I'm on the dais—Doria's eyes about pop out of her head. The woman standing at the front of the line is holding a baby with a terrible burn on its face.

"What happened?" I ask. The woman speaks; I look to Doria to translate.

"She said the child pulled a pot of boiling oil off the stove. The doctors don't think she will live."

"How old is she? The little girl?"

Doria asks the woman, who looks between me and my stand-in. In fact, a lot of people in the line are noticing that they're seeing double. "Two."

"I can help you," I say. Xavier growls in my ear to stand down, but I pluck the earpiece free and let it dangle from my collar.

I can't help anyone if I can't concentrate.

"Doria, I need you to go get me something to drink—tea is fine but add a lot of sugar to it. Can you hurry?" Her eyes widen with confusion. "It's okay. Everything's okay, I promise." She nods and stands. I turn to Jakub and speak quietly next to his ear. "You should stay up here with me. If I start to fall or faint, please help Doria give me the tea. I need sugar between healings."

As my translator goes to fetch tea, I indicate to the woman what I need her to do with her baby. She obliges, lying the child on a huge pillow along the dais front. The murmur in the tent has quieted, and I know all eyes are on me.

This is probably the stupidest thing I have ever done.

I slide off my gloves and close my eyes, pulling from

that white-hot star in the back of my head. My hands on the child, I heal the burns, the underlying tissue, the damage to her left eye blinded by the oil, the marbled skin on the top of her head.

You could hear a pin drop.

And then the mother is wailing as the restored child sits up on her own and starts crying when she sees all the people staring at her. The baby is scared, but she's very much alive, and her mother can't stop kissing the back of my hands and thanking me.

A cheer erupts in the tent, followed by a pause as everyone kneels, their keys out, heads bowed. The woman speaks, and Doria translates: "Thank you, Beloved Delia, for giving the world this great gift." I feel like my heart is going to burst out of my chest—these people loved my mother too. And I had no idea she had so many friends in so many places.

In that moment, looking at this beautiful group of people in every size, color, and shape, my swelling pride for the important work my mother did is rivaled only by one other emotion: guilt. Who am I to undo this magic? Who am I to deny these people the hope that they can live free of pain, to go forth and do good for others, for this world?

Am I making the wrong choice?

The woman strokes my arm one last time before clutching her daughter and stepping off the dais. Quiet and orderly, the line reforms. The *La Vérité* members shake my hand, touch my face, touch the top of my head—a few even crouch and touch my feet—and so many have quick anecdotes about my mother that Doria thankfully translates.

By this point, it's clear I've disobeyed orders, so Xavier has stepped in to provide sugared tea, allowing me to help those who present with injuries and illness. Due to a lack of time and personal energy, I can't fix the really complex stuff, like cancer, but my efforts will buy the sufferers a little time.

As I wait for the next of my mother's followers to step toward the dais, Xavier tucks my earpiece back into place. "Don't remove it again," he says. "After the woman in the red coat, we're leaving. We have what we need."

I stare at him. *The piece?* He nods.

I wish I could help every single one of these people, but I'm sweaty and shaky. My wounds are on fire under the layers of gauze, and stars of exhaustion twinkle in my peripheral vision. I almost cry when I see one of the soldiers has returned with a cold Coke.

An announcer's voice takes over the speakers that blare through the grounds, and judging by the uptick in the live music coming from the main tent, the show must be starting. Sevda steps to the front of the tent and again, I can't understand what she's saying, but the grateful smiles on the faces around us tell me we're among friends.

Jakub moves off the dais, making room for Henry and Xavier to help me from my seat. I don't realize how depleted I am until I try to stand.

"You should not have done that," Xavier says. "I cannot carry you out of here. It will give us away."

"I just need a second."

We move to the eastern side of the tent again. Henry

hands me a napkin with dates and baklava. "Eat. You're white as a ghost."

"I feel like a ghost." I chew as fast as my sore mouth with allow, my back to the crowd so I can replenish my energy and not faint in front of everyone.

Midbite, I freeze as the fetor of decay floats past. There's a small yelp behind us, followed by a scream. I spin just as Jakub falls face first onto the ground, convulsing, his face purpling and foam forming around his lips. Chaos erupts in the tent, but before we can escape, something brushes my cheek and leaves a stinging laceration behind. The stench is so strong now, those urgent calories I just consumed surge upward in my throat.

Xavier and Lucas move into position on each side of me, and my feet are hardly touching the ground as we tear through the back of the tent, Henry right behind, Sevda and a line of other soldiers forming a barricade around us as we move south across the park. I turn my head to see Doria running to catch up with us, and then she freezes and falls, overcome with the same convulsions that took Jakub down moments ago.

"Help her!"

"Keep running!" Xavier screams. "Do not stop!"

Just before I turn away, a woman staring at Doria's seizing form is overcome. She looks up at me, stunned, and then collapses.

"*Go*! *Go*! *Go*!" Sevda yells.

Judging by the screams and toppling bodies all around us now, whoever is in control of this terrible magic is targeting anything that moves. There's nothing to hide behind—how can a person hide from what they cannot see? A panicked clot of scattering circusgoers on the grass ahead of us is making it impossible to run any faster.

There are no words to describe the horror of watching helplessly as people are picked off, collapsing into seizure, some screaming, some silent, all of them wearing grimaces of torment as their bodies betray them.

I know what this is.

Sevda tumbles and falls in front of us, her body jerking uncontrollably, the whites of her fixed-open eyes filling with blood as her jaw clenches to the point of cracking.

"Nooooooo!" Lucas hollers. He lets go of me and races back to pick her up, throwing her over his shoulder, a feat made near impossible because of her thrashing body. Xavier shoves me behind him; another soldier steps in to take Lucas's place, but a woman in front of us falls. I don't adjust course fast enough and I trip over her body, landing awkwardly on my infected left arm. I feel the bones give, followed by the blinding flash of pain that steals my breath.

Henry jerks me back to my feet. "Cars ahead! *Run*!"

My left arm tucked tight against my midsection, we skip-hop through the hysterical crowd, jumping over bodies, some motionless, some in the grips of gruesome convulsions. Ahead are two of the three black SUVs screaming toward us down the street from where they were staging, horns blaring, lights flashing. The first SUV screeches to a halt. We run awkwardly toward it, bent in half in a vain attempt to not get hit by whatever invisible assailant is responsible for so much pain.

Another soldier falls.

And then Xavier, stiff as a board as he hits the ground face-first, his body convulsing wildly, an unearthly howl sneaking out between clenched teeth. Just like with Sevda, I watch as blood fills the whites of his eyes.

A sinister voice in my head: *"I will take him from you, just as he was taken from me. I will take them all."*

"Get out of my heaaaaad!" I scream, and then Henry's by my side as we scramble to get Xavier off the ground.

Lucas yanks open the door and tosses a still-jerking Sevda into the SUV's third row. Henry and I struggle to get Xavier's writhing form into the car—the driver leans over the front seat and tugs Xavier's shoulders so we can clamber in after him.

Out of our original party who went into the tent, we're all that's left.

Doors barely closed, the driver burns the tires against the cold asphalt, flips a U-turn, and tears out of the area, away from the horror of people being knocked down like ducks in a carnival shooting gallery.

"Genevieve, please, help her," Lucas begs between gasps from the back seat, but I'm exhausted to the absolute limits. Sevda's deafening screams echo off the car's interior, lessening the farther away we get. Henry and I are squeezed on the floor between the front and second row of seats as Xavier's seizing form slowly relaxes.

"What was that? What just *happened*?" Henry asks, raw fear wrinkling his forehead.

"Aveline . . . it was Aveline," I say, defeated. I warned Nutesh—I warned him what she can do. I had no idea she could do it to so many people, at the same time, with such deadly effect. And why attack innocents? I thought they said Lucian wouldn't risk something like that.

There isn't much help I can offer Sevda, or Xavier, while we're racing through the streets of Izmir, unsure if we're being pursued or if we'll be run off the road at any moment. We've lost our escort SUVs somewhere in the maze of streets; emergency vehicles scream past and around us heading toward the circus grounds.

Instead, I rub a soothing hand over Xavier's unconscious brow, whispering that everything will be okay, that we'll get help soon. "Please stay with me. Don't let her win," I whisper.

"Genevieve, *please*." Lucas grabs the back of the second row of seats.

"I can't do anything until we stop. Just keep her calm. Tell her she'll be okay." My voice is barely audible. My heart pulses in my left arm instead of my chest and my eyes struggle to stay open. "My arm . . .I can't help her yet."

Lucas's quiet comforts helps Sevda to finally settle. My ears ring in the absence of her cries. But it's short-lived as Sevda comes around, a renewed panic in her voice.

"I can't see. *I can't see*!"

"Sevda, honey, you're safe. It's me. It's Lucas. Everything's okay. We got out."

"I can't see!" she wails again. She struggles against him, hands flailing to orient herself. The grisly damage in her eyes, the blown capillaries in her face, and bruising around her jaw—so much injury in so little time. And I don't know if I can fix that, not if it was Aveline's handiwork.

"What's going on? Why can't she see?"

I don't have any answers for Lucas, or Sevda, right now.

I flop hard against the door and lean closer to the seat so my forehead touches Xavier's. "Stay with me . . . stay with me . . . don't let go . . . we have so much more to talk about," I whisper to him.

"Xavier? Where is Xavier?"

"He's here. He's still out," I say quietly, brushing a curl off his forehead. But as if he knows we're talking about him, his eyes pop open, the ice-blue irises a macabre contrast against so much blood in what should be white. He coughs once, and then he's coughing so hard, he can't catch his breath.

"Henry, we have to sit him up." Henry moves to adjust Xavier to sitting, but it's no use. The coughs have taken over. His eyes bug out, strained with exertion as he coughs to the point of near vomiting. I grab my discarded headscarf from earlier and shove it against his mouth. He takes it, but when he pulls it away, it's soaked with blood.

Xavier begs for air between coughs. "The last piece . . . to the key?" I look at Henry, his eyes as wide as mine. "Sevda?"

"She's alive."

"The key?" he asks again, his chest spasming with bloodied coughs.

Lucas looks around him, around Sevda, on the floor of their row. The color drains out of his face as he shakes his head no. "We must've lost it when we were hit."

"Fuck," Xavier mutters, dropping his head into his hands.

I stifle a sob into my sleeve—we were so close. And Aveline got in the way, just like she promised she would.

Xavier's coughs start again, breaking the stunned silence in the SUV. "Xavier—" His face strains with exertion as coughed-up blood coats his lips.

And then his eyes roll back in his head.

37

"DRIVER, *HURRY*!" I SCREAM. I'VE POSITIONED MYSELF UNDER XAVIER'S torso to keep him on his side so he won't choke to death on his own blood, but he's in and out of consciousness, and now the bluing of his face and wheeze in his throat tells me he can't breathe. I've heard the same wheeze and gurgle in the crew members Delia treated for asthma or terrible colds.

"Henry, help me!" Painfully, I slide out from under Xavier. We lie him across the bench seat, pulling at his jacket. Henry un-Velcros the body armor over Xavier's chest, slides me a pair of scissors from the medical kit, and holds taut the fabric so I can slice up the front of Xavier's shirt with my still-functioning right hand.

"Oh no . . ." I balance myself on my bent legs against the front seats. Xavier's formerly olive skin is a patchwork of dark purple and red, mottled and angry. He looks like he's been trampled by horses.

"Is that blood? Under his skin?" Henry asks quietly. I nod.

"She tore him apart. Henry . . . I can't . . . I'm not strong enough."

"Genevieve, put your hands over his heart," Henry says sternly. "Just keep his heart beating until we can get on the plane." Moving my left arm almost does me in, but I need both hands for this job, fracture or no.

The sun is near setting, but as we scream into Çiğli Air Base, the plane is waiting for us. We screech to a halt in front of the hangar and Nutesh emerges from the metal building—I swear to everything holy, it's like seeing an angel descend from above.

Surrounded by his ever-present security—and my Montague!—they throw open our doors. Lucas is out with Sevda in his arms, yelling at the soldiers to help with Xavier.

"If I move my hands, he dies. It was Aveline . . . I warned Nutesh . . ."

Montague nods curtly and barks commands at two of the guards. They ease Xavier across the seat as Montague supports his head; Henry holds Xavier's legs together so he doesn't slide off the seat.

"Geneviève, keep your hands in place, if you're able," Nutesh says. I don't feel like I can, but I also know that the intense waves of nausea buffeting through me are an indication of how severe the damage is.

I cannot let go.

Henry exits the other side, runs around the SUV, and with a supportive arm around my waist, he helps me walk without tripping alongside Xavier's body as we climb the jet's stairs. We rush Xavier into the rear cabin, onto the huge bed. Nutesh throws more orders at his soldiers; the side of the plane is sealed as he strips away his black jacket and rolls his sleeves, preparing to undertake the healing I'm unable to accomplish on my own.

"Geneviève, I can see you are hurt yourself, but if you could keep focused on his heart while I repair the damage inside, we might save him yet. Everyone else, buckle up!" he commands.

I slide onto my knees next to the bed, right arm stretched so that my hand is firm over Xavier's still-beating heart. Nutesh braces himself against the rear wall as the aircraft picks up momentum. He rubs his hands together and closes his eyes, placing his splayed fingers over the horrific bruising in Xavier's chest. Xavier jerks under the influence, but I can feel the healing energy coursing through him, the increase in his heartbeat under my own beat-up hand, the calming breaths Nutesh pushes through him and, by default, into me, offering a small respite from the pain in my infected and broken left arm.

Nutesh moves through Xavier's upper body, front and back, the terrible purpling dissipating under his hands. So much damage in so little time . . . My face burns with the memory of all those innocent people falling.

"I don't understand," I whisper. "Why would she do this?"

"Focus on Xavier," Nutesh says.

"His chest is so bad. I didn't know until we took off his vest. He doesn't complain."

"Because he's seen so much worse."

"We didn't get the third piece, Nutesh."

He nods, as if he is not surprised, and concentrates on his work.

The plane banks hard, making it that much more difficult to stay focused on what I'm doing.

"Genevieve . . ." Xavier's voice is so soft. I look up at his face, consumed with relief that he's looking back at me, his face pinking up. "Thank you." He reaches to take my hand from his chest. *"Thank you."*

Nutesh sits on the bed next to Xavier, outstretched arm against the headboard for balance, his face flushed, forehead sweaty. "Welcome back, *Monsieur Darrow*."

I can't cry. Not yet. If one tear escapes, they all will.

"How many made it out?" Xavier asks.

"You, Henry, Lucas, me, Sevda . . . she can't see, but she's alive."

"We are going to fix everyone," Nutesh says, standing as the plane levels out. "And then we are going to discuss how to open a temple without a key."

38

Nutesh heals me first after Xavier—yet even after he knits my left arm back together, the infected carving remains, and perhaps might even be worse. The new laceration on my face—from the Etemmu—it won't heal either, but Nutesh is able to at least suture it closed and stop the bleeding. He scolds me gently that the healing I did at *Tanrilar Sirk* drew from my body's reserves. "Your mother would be proud of you, but sometimes you just have to say no, Geneviève."

Nutesh wasn't there, though. He didn't see that warped, scarred baby made whole again.

Delia would be proud of that, I'm sure.

Xavier insists that he's well enough to sit in the main cabin, freeing up space to help Sevda. She's in rough shape. I try to offer assistance, but Nutesh calls for Henry, who then drags me to a seat and hands me a cup of Hélène's restorative tea. I do manage to help Montague prepare a healing wrap soaked with some of Delia's herbal concoctions they've brought along before Henry coaxes me back to a seat.

He sits next to me but leans close and kisses my undamaged cheek. "You were incredible today."

I smile and nod at him—I can't talk. The adrenaline is wearing off, and the faces of the dead are floating through my head.

Doria. Jakub. *La Vérité* soldiers. Countless other civilians just out for a day at the circus.

I almost lost Xavier too.

"Thank you, Henry," I squeak. My mended tongue won't leave the rough edge of my broken tooth alone. Nutesh wasn't able to fix it.

"Is that . . ." Henry touches a finger to his own cheek, questioning the slice on mine.

"The Etemmu. In the tent, right as everything fell apart." And just like that, I'm consumed with sobs, the loud, hiccupping, embarrassing kind.

Henry scoops me onto his lap, rocking and shushing against my head as I cry about our dead friends, about missing home, about Violet and the horrible things Ash said, about how much I miss my elephants and that big fluffy house cat, about how scared I am that we won't make it out of this alive.

"I'm trying so hard to be brave and strong, like my mother would want. But I just want to go home. Please, please tell me we can go home soon, that everything will be okay, Henry. Promise me," I say into his shoulder.

"I promise, Genevieve. I promise." Tears track down Henry's face too. I don't even care that he can't promise me we'll live through this. It has to be enough just to hear him say it, to give me a moment where we're not heirs or warriors or the last two children in a long line of magical people.

For a single moment, I'm just a seventeen-year-old girl who misses her pets and her family and is in love with a really great guy. That's it.

Xavier sits across the aisle from us, and when I meet his ice-blue gaze, the look on his face isn't one of caution or disapproval—it's one of gratitude.

I'm plugged into the plane's audio system—Nutesh thought I'd calm better with classical music in my ears. It sort of works. But a low chatter behind me interrupts my half-assed attempts at meditation.

I slide my headphones off one ear. Seems they're trying to keep their conversation quiet—Henry's out across from me, reclined as far as the plane's seats allow. He looks so young when he's asleep. Sevda must still be in the stateroom; I don't see her or Lucas.

I kneel on my seat toward the conversation. The lights in the main cabin have been dimmed, other than a soft electric-blue glow coming from the cluster of seats where Xavier and Nutesh are huddled. They're the ones speaking, except it's in French so again I'm unable to understand what they're saying.

Until a single word passes between them: *Violet.*

"What did you say?" Nutesh and Xavier look toward me. "Did you say something about Violet?" Neither responds.

And then I see the tablet on the table between them—an American news channel streaming, and Violet's face on the screen.

"What—" I throw my headphones aside and rush over, crouching on the floor in front of the table, the tablet in my hands so I can read the scroll at the bottom. I fumble for the volume button but Xavier takes the tablet from me and closes it.

"No! What is that? That was my Violet on the screen. What's going on?"

"Geneviève, please sit down for a moment." Nutesh offers his hand. I take it and slide into the seat opposite him. "First, I want you to know that we've gotten word to Ted and Cecelia Cinzio that you are safe. They're angry and skeptical, but relieved that the news reports, and Lucian, have painted a false picture of your current situation."

"Okay—but why is Vi on the news? Is this about Aveline killing her? Is Aveline a suspect? She goes by the name Mara Dunn at the circus—"

"I am so very sorry about your friend's death. According to the American news reports, it seems it is still under investigation," Nutesh says. My heart bangs against my chest. I hear Aveline's words in the bathroom at the apartment in Izmir: *Nothing says tea party like French cookies and ricin. The police will find your prints all over that tea set.*

I'm already shaking my head, the burn behind my chest igniting, hands clenching, unclenching, the fresh skin threatening to tear itself apart once again.

"It was *Aveline*. She *told* me in the attack at the apartment—she *told* me! When I called Ash, he screamed at me for poisoning her. I didn't know who he meant until Aveline attacked me. She did it, Nutesh, not me! Violet was my *best friend—"*

"Geneviève, of course it wasn't you, but you must control your hands. They are sparking, and we are on an aircraft thirty thousand feet in the air," Nutesh says, his voice calm but firm. "It will take some time to untangle what Aveline has done. She laid a trap for you. The tea set has been identified as yours. When I spoke to Ted Cinzio, he said that Violet's parents and brother have sworn statements that the two of you often played with the tea set as children, that you left it for Violet before you disappeared—that you were jealous of the new girl in the circus, Mara Dunn, so you took it out on the Jónás family by coating the tea set with the poison. Under warrant, they stripped the trailer you shared with your mother and found castor beans and evidence of plant components that can be used to manufacture ricin—"

"Delia had plants and seeds in there that could kill an army of men, but that doesn't mean we were using them for bad. We only helped people. She *helped* people!"

"Of course she did. And this will get sorted out. But with that said, we're not taking you back to the United States until the legalities can be handled and we can prove your innocence."

"But I want to go home! You said that once this is all over, I can go home."

"And you can eventually. But not until you are absolved of any wrongdoing."

"I *have* to go back, Nutesh. The elephants—what if she hurts them too?" I'm so tired of crying.

"Your animals are safe."

"How do you know for sure? Look what she did to Violet!"

"Your circus vet, Dr. Philips, is caring for them. And he works for me," Nutesh says. I'd say I'm shocked that Philips is one of Nutesh's people, but not much is shocking anymore. Not even the news that I'm a suspect in Violet's death.

"Further, the circus is still under the purview of the Triad Partners Group. Any harm to those animals would reflect very poorly on Lucian Dmitri, and despite everything, he is still a vain man who seeks to protect his public reputation. The animals will be protected."

"That's what Sevda said about Izmir, about a public spectacle, and yet they were *destroying* people. God, it's the perfect setup." I laugh bitterly. "The Airstream was there for Aveline to do whatever she needed. It's so easy for her to frame me because we left it all there for her."

"We will let the lawyers do their jobs," Nutesh says.

"Not to mention that Delia's psychiatric history will be paraded around for the whole world to see. Of course I'm guilty! I'm the daughter of a crazy woman, didn't you hear?"

Nutesh opens a bottle of water and soaks a blue surgical towel; he then gives it to me and nods at my hands. The cool, wet fabric sizzles but tempers the burn.

"It is important to note that where we're going, they watch the news too. It will be crucial, for both of you," Nutesh says, looking between Henry and me—I don't even know when he joined our little party—"that you maintain your identity story once we arrive: you are university students from

Canada and the UK respectively, on an expedition with me to study the ruins of Babylon as part of a preservation project in conjunction with ongoing efforts of the Iraqi government." He repeats the earlier false directive. "This story will apply to *everyone* you meet. We have absolutely no way of knowing who we can trust here, other than the contacts who have had direct interaction with me. Not even the *La Vérité* keys can be trusted. As you saw in Izmir, with the housekeeper—we cannot risk this again."

"Aveline will find me. A new geography and made-up identities won't protect me, or anyone else."

Nutesh looks tired—for the first time since I've met him, he actually looks like this shit is wearing him down. "It seems that the closer we get to Babylon, the stronger you are. All of you. It is why you were able to heal so many people without collapsing."

"And it's why Aveline could take down so many people at one time. She's still coming for me. You know that, right?"

Nutesh's expression is grim as the overhead speaker bings to life. The captain announces that we're thirty minutes from our destination. Nutesh stands and straightens his black cargo pants.

"Geneviève, let us focus on the mission still to come. We will see this matter resolved so you can go home again," he says, patting my shoulder before disappearing into the stateroom.

Home.

I don't even know where that is anymore.

39

Before we land in Sulaymaniyah—or Sulay for short—Nutesh reviews a few things about Iraqi Kurdistan. Despite the fact that this land is all *technically* Iraq according to the maps, Kurds call it the Kurdistan Region, and they don't like to be associated with their southern Arab cousins. The country's history is rich in violence, the lands soaked with the blood of millions of men, women, and children after centuries of political, civil, and international conflict. While started under different pretenses (and not sanctioned by the United Nations), the Iraq War of 2003 brought an end to Saddam Hussein's brutal regime, which had systematically murdered hundreds of thousands of Kurds since the 1980s.

But it's just one horrifying piece in a huge puzzle of carnage. The land along the Euphrates where the mystical *AVRAKEDAVRA* temple sits shares space with one of Saddam's former palaces, as well as the 2,600-year-old black basalt Lion of Babylon, a statue that dates back to Nebuchadnezzar II and perhaps even farther back to the Hittites.

A lot of history has happened here. The United States is basically an embryo in comparison.

"I could spend a year lecturing you on the history of Ancient Mesopotamia to modern day, and it would take a hundred years more. My people—our people—have suffered greatly," Nutesh says, his face melancholy for a beat. He clears his throat and stands tall. "Practical advice, however: You must keep your passports on you at all times. Checkpoints are common, so learn your identities. My contact will present you with visas as soon as we arrive—they are offered in the names on your passports, good for fifteen days in Kurdistan.

"However, when we travel across the border into Iraq proper, it will be by air rather than by land. While Kurdish lands are relatively safe, there is still tension with Baghdad to the south, and the Islamic State of Iraq and the Levant, or ISIL, is still present in the country—we cannot leave any options open for kidnap or violence against us."

Oh my god, this is really happening. We are really in the Middle East.

"As we cannot secure papers for you and stay off the radar, we will fly south covertly with the help of a private contractor. Former British Armed Forces man running a private, for-profit operation here," he explains. "Xavier and I trust him—he knows we're here on *La Vérité* business—but for everyone else, the façade must stand. No one can know your true identities. Do you understand?" Henry and I look to one another, and then nod at Nutesh.

"Geneviève, you will not be required to cover your hair in Sulay, only in Babylon, but modesty at all times. No bare shoulders, legs, or chest. No excessive skin, which should be reasonable as temperatures this time of year are moderate. The two of you shall not engage in any public displays of affection—not even holding hands—and do not talk to anyone unless you absolutely must. It's best that they not hear your accents—your skin color will be enough to announce you're foreigners.

"From the air base, we will proceed to the secure compound where we're staying tonight. Our hosts are *La Vérité*, but their house staff is not. They have been told we are guests of the Kurdish Regional Government, the KRG. Our entire team will be based at the home of my friend and *La Vérité* member, Şivan Malkandi. He is an Iraqi Kurd who works for the KRG, so his influence here is great," Nutesh explains. "However, Şivan's elevated position also puts him at risk for helping us, which is why secrecy and discretion are imperative.

"Once we have arrived at his compound, we will eat and show our gratitude for the hospitality of the household. We will rest tonight, as it has been a trying day, and Sevda's eyes will require additional, albeit discreet, treatment. First thing in the morning, we will review our mission plan so everyone is clear as to what their role is. Do you have any questions?"

Yes. Yes, I have a million questions, but the FASTEN SEAT BELT sign is on. We're about to land.

As we descend into the city, the scant light from the moon shows sprawling hills, not unlike those found in California's San Joaquin Valley, but these are covered in a soft layer of white, like powdered sugar. "It snows here? I thought this was a desert!" I ask, surprised.

"It is February," Nutesh says. "You should see it during the day. A rare beauty! And in the spring, before the oppressive heat sets in, the hillsides explode with green."

The city itself is snug in the valley of these hilly ranges. Blinking lights on construction cranes suggest that Sulay is open for business; cars move like ants below on paved streets illuminated by wide-set streetlamps. The city is awash in electric light, although occasional dark patches make it look like someone forgot to flip the switch, a black lake in the middle of it all.

"Rolling blackouts," Nutesh says. "Their power grid lacks the oomph to keep the entire city on at once." That doesn't sound creepy at all. "Otherwise you will see that Sulay is very modern. Restaurants, coffee shops, public parks, the Grand Bazaar. Azadi Park even has a small lake and Ferris wheel! They have recovered well in the post-Saddam years. The soldiers you will see at the airport—they are Peshmerga, the Kurdish army. Friendlies. We're safe here, as long as we don't draw attention to ourselves."

"That means *no* heroics, Genevieve," Xavier says, hiking an eyebrow. "I mean it."

Once our tires meet pavement, the same routine happens as has on prior landings: soldiers, then Montague, then Xavier line up at the plane's door before it opens. Once it's unsealed, the area has to be cleared. We're then rushed down the stairs and into black Range Rovers. Faster, less bulky cars, but also smaller, which means we're not all in the same vehicle. I don't love this.

Xavier and Nutesh ride with Henry and me; Montague

is with the still-ailing Sevda in a second Rover. The other two carry half of the security detail from the plane; apparently, Lucas, along with the remaining guards and our pilots, will stay at the air base—a decision Sevda is *really* not happy about—to ensure the jet isn't tampered with.

That's both reassuring and unnerving at the same time—someone might tamper with our *plane*?

The trip through Sulaymaniyah with a line of four black, fast-moving vehicles doesn't seem to attract the attention it did in Izmir. At a stoplight in the city center, I'm so relieved when none of the citizens on the sidewalk or street stare into my soul through the darkly tinted glass. No Avelines here—at least not yet.

As we turn off from the busy commercial area, we're suddenly in a quiet residential neighborhood with huge houses tucked behind high walls—Nutesh tells us that Kurdistan is undergoing a sort of renaissance. The architecture of some of these homes rivals what I've seen in our daydream drives through Beverly Hills.

The convoy slows in front of one of these ginormous homes, a heavy steel gate sliding open to grant us entry. The front walkway is made of decorative interlocking bricks, lined with palm trees uplit by floodlights planted into beds of river rock and tall, decorative grasses that sway in the evening breeze. The house itself is all rounded edges and glass and concrete and lights, better suited to a movie star than politician.

Before our doors are even opened, a stout, dark-haired man with a well-trimmed black goatee, dressed in a white button-down and loose gray pants comes down the walk, his arms spread wide. "Nutesh! My brother! *Hun be xér hatî ye!* Welcome, welcome!"

Nutesh steps out and embraces the man. As usual, I can't understand what they're saying, but they seem genuinely happy to see one another, and I'm glad for it. Nutesh then signals for the rest of us to unload; Henry and I slide into our backpacks before exiting the vehicle.

"Şivan, thank you for granting us accommodation at your incredible estate. These are the members of our security and research team," he says, gesturing to Xavier and Montague, and then a sweep of his arm toward Sevda (in sunglasses) and the others. "And these bright faces belong to my eager students, Gemma O'Connor of the University of British Columbia, and William Fraser of the University of Edinburgh. We are all very excited to be here with you. Thank you for your hospitality. *Spas dikem.*" Nutesh bows at the waist.

"So wonderful to meet you all! You must be tired from your journey. Come! Inside there is refreshment." He leans closer to Nutesh, "And maybe some of that excellent French wine, *oui*?"

"*Absolument, mon ami,*" Nutesh says, leading our party up the walkway alongside Şivan. The two seem like old friends, which, given the way things have gone for "friends" lately makes me more than a little nervous. And the fact that we're playing the game from the very first moment—god, I hope I don't forget my new Canadian identity. What if he asks me about British Columbia? I've never even been there!

The inside of Şivan's home is just as elegant as the outside. Rich rugs and paintings that would make even the art-savvy Lucian Dagan Dmitri envious. Honey-colored woods and lighting accents everywhere. Massive glass-and-marble kitchen. Through an expansive glass wall, a pool shimmers in the darkness, lit from the blue depths with underwater bulbs.

Şivan introduces us to his head maid, a young woman called Gona, and we follow her down a long, wide hallway to a suite of rooms where we'll be staying. Of course, Henry and the men are given separate quarters from Sevda and myself, which again spikes my anxiety as I consider how being apart from Nutesh may open the door for Aveline to crawl into my head.

Once our gear is put away, Gona leads us into the dining room where Nutesh and Şivan have already cracked open the wine. We're seated, minus Montague and Sevda—he's helping her with a "migraine"—and a string of nameless house staff bring in dish after dish of fragrant local foods to the long wooden table that looks like it came from the heart of a California Redwood.

"*Noshî can be!* Bon appetit!" Şivan says.

Thankfully, Nutesh handles the pleasant conversation and steers most of it back to Şivan so Henry and I can avoid the shaky creative license that might come from him asking questions about our university programs. Nutesh mentions that we'll be cataloguing major markers and mostly taking photos for survey, including river water and soil samples. Şivan knows the truth about why we're here, but his staff, including Gona, are always standing nearby.

I'm grateful these men don't take unnecessary risks in conversation that could otherwise expose us.

When we've eaten our fill, Şivan excuses us to freshen up, and then invites whomever is interested to the rooftop patio for a "night cap." Though I'm underage, I'm not going to say no if I'm offered a glass of the Kurdish wine Şivan raves about, made locally by a former Peshmerga soldier who "risks everything because he loves fine wine, and he loves this country."

But the drink is strong, and after a few sips, I can hardly hold my head up. I lie down on my corner of the cushioned, U-shaped patio couch, warmed by the flames of the open firepit and the conversation of my traveling companions.

For a few moments, peace.

The predawn house is quiet as I sneak into the kitchen for juice. My tongue is like cotton and I have a headache. The kitchen staff are already busy. When one offers me coffee, I take it, even though it's dark as motor oil.

"Go to the roof," she says. "Beautiful sunrise."

"Thank you. I will." I gesture with my cup.

Upstairs, I'm not surprised to find Xavier crashed out on a chaise—or Henry perched on the patio couch, sketchbook open, pencil in hand.

"He's serenading you?" I ask, referencing Xavier's loud snores.

"It's like a symphony," Henry teases. "They have coffee?"

"Yeah. You can have mine." I give him my cup. "Did you sleep?"

"I did. You?"

"Some. Sevda talks in her sleep."

Henry pats the seat next to him, and as I sit, he leans over and kisses my forehead. "Must be careful. No PDA allowed," he says.

"Seriously, this place is not at all what I expected."

"Because we're north. And we're used to the stuff we see on the news." He shivers, so I grab the blanket off the back of the couch and wrap it around us both. "Feeling rebellious, are you?"

"If we hear someone coming, you can slide a respectable distance away."

"Your virtue and good name are foremost in my mind," he says, bowing his head.

"You know, I could burn a line in this other eyebrow so they'd match," I tease.

"Let's save your flaming hands for more practical purposes."

"Like burning some books?" Henry nods. "I can't believe we're going to burn books on purpose," I say. Henry's body language seems a bit depressed. "Hey . . . you okay?"

"Mm-hmm. It's just a lot to take in. You know, new day, new shocking revelations," he says. "How are your injuries?"

"I'm all right. Aveline's carvings won't heal. Tires me out. And this broken tooth is super annoying."

"It looks cute. Gives you character."

"What, like a peg leg gives a pirate character?"

"A broken tooth is hardly a peg leg." He smiles.

"Not until I try eating corn on the cob, at least," I say. "Nutesh's medicine helped. He's good at what he does."

"It will be a shame that he will lose that, once this is over."

"I've thought about it too. Even in the midst of all this death and terribleness, it felt so good to help all those people yesterday."

"You were amazing. That little baby . . ."

"I know! And when she started crying because she was scared?"

"Truly unbelievable. You saved her. Untreated, that injury would have ruined her future, if she'd even been able to survive it," Henry says. "I don't think you understand the impact your gift truly makes on the lives of others."

"I do. I saw it. It felt so warm to help all those people who loved my mother." Henry rests a hand on my knee. "I wish we could find a way to keep all this without having to deal with Lucian and Aveline and everyone who want us dead."

"And therein lies the dilemma."

I look toward the sunrise. "Nutesh said the choice is ours, but really it's not. You know that, yeah?"

"We've talked about this, Genevieve. Except . . . a lifetime of sunsets and sunrises with you? That might be worth fighting for." He kisses the side of my head. "Then again, the last few days have been so overwhelming—my brain is still playing catch-up."

"You mean Sevda," I say.

"Partly." His head bounces in confirmation. "I have a *sister*. Well, a half sister."

"And she seems to be a good guy. I mean, compared to my newly discovered bad-guy sibling."

"She's quite freaked out about her eyes," he says.

"Nutesh will fix her. Sometimes things just take a little bit longer. Aveline did a lot of damage very quickly."

Henry is quiet, watching the slowly lightening sky.

"There's something else, though . . .," I say.

"My mother has been *flooding* me with memories. Like it was when I was a kid, only times a thousand. Every time I fall asleep, I wake up with a new database of stories I didn't have just hours before." He lowers his voice and leans closer. "And the text—if it's anywhere near me, even in my backpack, I can see *so much*. I don't even need Alicia's help anymore, to be honest. And they're not necessarily memories she's been given—they're from *everywhere*. It's weird."

"You heard Nutesh—the closer we get to Babylon, the stronger we are. What are you seeing?"

He laughs under his breath. "God, everything. Alicia showed me more about her relationship with my grandfather. She seemed a bit of a rebel, like someone else I know."

"Umm, running off and having an affair with my father's mortal enemy, an affair that resulted in a child? Yeah, I'm not that brave," I say. "But the world got a Henry out of the deal, so it was an okay choice."

"Okay?" He laughs. "You do flatter me, Miss Gemma O'Connor from Canada."

"We're a kind people, we Canadians."

"But wait—Lucian is your mother's mortal enemy, and you and I . . ." Henry waggles his eyebrows.

"Are we having an affair?"

"As long as my wife doesn't find out, we should be fine."

"Those teen brides are vicious. Tell her to show mercy," I say.

"I'll put in a good word." His smile is radiant, even in the low light. "It is fascinating, though, to see the memories of Alicia, alive and vibrant and full of love—and the visions of her with my father, when he looked at her like the world was made just for her to live in it. As much as she butted heads with her own father, she wanted to believe that Lucian was capable of good. For a while, she thought she had won him over. But then he found out who she was, who her family was . . .

"My grandfather tried to warn her. He knew she was playing with fire, fighting a battle she could never win. He was right. She paid for it with her life." He looks down again, his smile laced with sadness. "I've seen a lot of Lucian's life—how he worked to accomplish good things for centuries, how much of the bad has been done not by him directly but under the guidance of Aveline Darrow. There is a distinct line in his history: before Aveline, and after. I know that makes it sound like I'm defending him—and I'm not. He has done some truly horrible things."

Like, killed Delia.

"But I've seen more moments of him with Alicia. He did love her. It was Aveline who convinced Lucian that my mother couldn't be allowed to live, that there could be no more heirs in Nutesh's line, not if they wanted to get hold of his text. God, he's just so blinded by this bloody book."

"Which is why *we* are here."

"I know." Henry swallows hard and looks down at his clasped hands. "That vision I showed you back in Washington, after we met Dr. Schuyler, of my mother dying in the hospital right after I was born? I was supposed to die that day too. Lucian stopped it."

"He protected you," I say quietly.

"He did. And he has for eighteen years. It's why I didn't know who Mara—Aveline—was when she showed up at your circus."

I wrap both of my hands around Henry's. "And I *hope* that once we get to Babylon and put this to rest, Lucian will come back to you. I *hope* that whatever hold these books have had on him, that it dissolves and he sees what he has standing in front of him."

Henry leans into me, nodding. "I *hope* you're right."

I let go of his hands and instead wrap my arms around him, speaking close to his ear. "Your father has been chasing ghosts for two millennia. He has forsaken real, here-right-now love in pursuit of a family that he can never have again. How can a person still want something that should have faded from memory so long ago, especially when he has *you*? And now even Sevda? He has two children here—children who could love him and bring him years of happiness, if he would just let them."

"I think he will see that, before the end. I really do, Genevieve," Henry says. "Somehow, he must see through the glamour that Aveline Darrow has cast over his aspirations. And

I really think that's what it is. The memories of him being a good man, and then doing something terrible—she's always in the terrible ones. She's managed to get into your head lately . . . what's to say she hasn't been in his for all these years?"

All I know is I will never get my mother back, and Lucian had a great deal to do with that.

"If that's the case, I can't even fault him for being weak," he says. "You're one of the strongest people I know—and Aveline still gets to you."

"I don't know, Henry. I don't have an answer for that."

"Somehow he must see truth again," Henry says.

The key to good is found in truth.

"Henry, remember . . ." I turn his chin with my finger so he's looking at me. "Whatever happens, *I will be your family*. If things go south at Babylon, I will be your family until the bitter end. All of us will." He looks into my eyes—really looks—and then kisses me, his lips soft and tasting of strong coffee.

"Don't let Gona see you doing that," Xavier says from across the deck, rolling on to his other side.

Henry smiles and pushes his forehead against mine. "I love you, Genevieve."

I flatten my hand against the side of his face, the hint of light stubble against my palm. He'll need to shave—his beard is growing in blond.

"I love you too, Henry. Let me be your family." The muezzin's haunting call cuts through the air, beckoning the devout to prayer.

When I kiss Henry one last time before the sun cracks the horizon, I hope we are prayer enough for each other.

40

"Our voices are protected in here, but video surveillance is nearly guaranteed," Nutesh says, turning on Xavier's sound-masking device. We're in a huge common room near the sleeping quarters, minus any of our host's house staff. "And I understand that you both appreciate having a voice in our plans." Nutesh lays eyes on me and then his grandson. "If you have anything to add, please do speak freely."

Xavier and Nutesh, tablets in hand, tag-team with the plan to get us into Babylon. "Aerial surveillance from a month ago shows a small airfield with what looks like two parked military helicopters directly north of the Babylon ruins. This is land currently controlled by the Iraqi military, so we can't get clearance to land there, but our contractor—his name is James—will drop us slightly northwest, on a privately owned palm farm. Babil Governorate is a major date palm producer, and James has a connection with a farmer here—his helicopter is not unusual on the farmer's land. He often transports goods for them back and forth from Baghdad and elsewhere, so we won't raise suspicion." Nutesh tightens our view with the swipe of his fingertips.

"We land here." Xavier takes over, pointing to a brown expanse just to the right of the deep green of the snaking Euphrates River. "And then you can see this irrigation pond, attached to a canal system that moves east toward a well-traveled road. We will go west, right to the river's edge. You will be supplied with equipment to take soil and water samples—to look legitimate, just in case—plus we'll need a bit of Euphrates water for the Undoing. Nutesh will cover your 'archaeological mandate' more specifically in a few minutes.

"From here, we are going to loop around the side of this pond, and back into the treed area. There is concertina wire still left in place—the Americans and Polish had set up bases here in '03 and '04, and they didn't clean up after themselves. We have no way of knowing what the locals have moved or how recently they've moved it; our intel shifts often, depending on who we ask. Very frustrating, as you might imagine." Xavier swipes the screen again. "Here—this grouping of uniform rectangular structures—we will be avoiding that. Tents. Military, probably Iraqi." He then drags a finger over toward a copse of green. "Drought has wreaked havoc on this country but last year showed above-average rainfall in many parts. This benefits us—full bushes and palm trees mean better coverage."

Xavier then pans out a bit, showing a huge structure sitting on a massive mound of earth, a long driveway spiraling from bottom to top. "This is Saddam's former palace—we have no business there, and security is heavy—we definitely don't have the visas or clearance to go near it. From the sky, it looks deserted, but the Babil government has control over this area now. Definitely not deserted.

"The actual ruins of Babylon have been reopened to local tourism, specifically the replica Ishtar Gate." He points at its location on the aerial view. "Opens every day at 8:00 a.m. and doesn't close until nearly midnight, which means there will be at least a few workers there early to prep for the day. Local tourists flock here"—he points to what's called the Processional Way—"and here," explaining that the dark blob on the screen is site of the ancient Lion of Babylon. "Lots of locals means we have to get in, do our job, and get out. If we are stopped or questioned, we have a forged permit, but again, no visas. So, our secondary plan will be initiated." Xavier reaches into the case he pulled his tablet from and extracts another envelope of money. "Nutesh or I will handle it."

Nutesh takes over again. "Here is the site we will be moving to, east of the ruins of Nebuchadnezzar II's palace. We will be going into the Temple of Ninmakh—the oldest temple in Babylon, named after a Babylonian goddess, often called the mother of all gods. I ask you to tread lightly—we are literally walking on history. This area has not been well excavated—cuneiform tablets, pottery, other pieces of ancient lives can still be found in the dirt. Securing this area has been a real challenge for the Antiquities folks.

"But here is where we run into our first problem," Nutesh says. "This temple is a re-creation. Saddam Hussein rebuilt it over the ruins of the old—and it is on the grounds where we performed the ritual that secured the magic to the

AVRAKEDAVRA texts nearly 2,400 years ago, when this whole area was still a bustling city."

Every time I hear how old these books are, I want to laugh—it sounds so *ridiculous*.

But so is mending a broken bone or electrocuting another person with my bare hands.

Xavier stands and leans on the top of his brown leather chair. "The Ninmakh is constructed so that we will have privacy from the outside—it's a long rectangle with very high walls. It's our plan to call up the *AVRAKEDAVRA* temple on this spot so we can perform the Undoing ritual here."

"Buuuut, we don't have the third part of the temple key," I remind him.

"That's correct," Nutesh says. "We don't have it *yet*."

"Don't tell me you're sending us somewhere new to try and get it."

"No." The tablet screen times out and goes black. "Those who have the third piece of the key will be coming to us."

The room is deadly quiet.

"I'm sorry, what did he just say?" Sevda asks from the couch, moving the herbal compress over her still-troublesome eyes aside.

"You think they're going to show up with that third piece? It's basically just a race to the finish?" I ask, mouth dry.

Nutesh nods. "Our efforts to buy a little time have worked—that's why we have had today to plan and rest. We made reservations on commercial flights under your real names departing Izmir, going to Şırnak in southeastern Turkey. They're certainly watching what we're doing, so now that we've given them something to chase, it has bought us a few hours. Dagan's law-enforcing lackeys will think you're landing in Şırnak where we will inevitably rent a car and drive south into Iraq—very few border crossings there, and we'd have to go through Ibrahim Khalil crossing to get visas into Kurdistan—so they will be watching for you there too."

"You're a regular James Bond, Nutesh."

"It is very basic tradecraft—more red herring than anything—but it will buy us hours when every minute counts. However, you all must be aware that where there is cheese, there will be mice," Nutesh says. "Dagan knows the general area where his father's text was born. It won't take them long to find us. He also is no fool. He knows I would never put you, and those books, on a commercial airline. But how foolish would he feel if we actually *were* there and he let us slip through his fingers?"

"So—your plan is to wait for them to arrive at the temple and then strong-arm them into handing over that third piece of the key?" Henry asks, his tone laced with the frustration I feel too.

"We have three heirs, all with unique abilities. I think Dagan will realize he is outnumbered."

Henry's already shaking his head. "That was Aveline's doing back in Turkey—all those people she injured or killed. She's been taunting and torturing Genevieve—and Baby—this whole time. The only reason the Etemmu hasn't been able to hurt Genevieve is because you both have been here to help block it. If they have the third piece—and who else would even know about it—there is no way they're just going to hand it over, even if you ask politely," Henry says. "If Aveline Darrow truly does have it, the only way you're going to get it is to kill her first."

Nutesh and Xavier look at one another, their eyes darkening. They then look at the rest of us.

Oh my god. They're going to kill her.

I laugh. Loudly. "You're delusional. You won't get near her before she has you on the ground, begging for a quick death. Xavier? Have you forgotten already?"

"She is just one descendant; you are three. Xavier has told me what you accomplished in Pompeii with just the two of you working together," Nutesh says, pointing a finger between Henry and me. "There is power in a triad."

Triad Partners Group—Dagan's company. Three sides to the inverted triangle. Three founding fathers of the *AVRAKEDAVRA*. Three texts.

Three descendants with three murdered mothers.

I wonder if this is the part where the narrator tells us to get our affairs in order.

The remainder of the morning and into the afternoon includes a briefing on archaeological stuff, the script for what we're meant to say to Iraqi officials if we're intercepted, followed by more tending to medical issues—the infections in my carved left arm and chest just will not let up—as well as Sevda's fuzzy eyes, which I hope are restored soon because she's being a real pain in the ass about our efforts to help her. Xavier seems to be back to baseline, though even if he weren't, he wouldn't admit it.

Everyone is on edge, even Nutesh who seems to never get rattled about anything.

After a late lunch, I find Nutesh sitting outside on the polished-stone pool deck in the pleasantly cool afternoon, a hazy sun overhead. "Please. Sit." Nutesh cradles a small cup of dark coffee.

He smiles. "Geneviève, now that we have a moment—what you did in Izmir, for all those people . . ."

"I know. Stupid."

He chuckles. "Not to the people you helped. Was it risky? *Oui*. But it was beautiful. Your life with Delia taught you compassion. It lacks in so much of the world these days." He sips his coffee. "Who am I kidding, though, *ma chère*. Compassion has been in short supply for millennia. It is what gave rise to the *AVRAKEDAVRA*." He straightens in his red rattan cushioned chair.

"I wasn't strong enough to help Baby. Will he recover, after this is done?"

"Once the magic Aveline has used is gone, her poison should leave him. He is a strong man."

"That's my Horatio," I say under my breath.

Nutesh's eyes are distant over the huge manicured lawn that stretches away from the pool deck to a distant stone fence. "It amazes me that Şivan is able to keep this grass so green, given the water shortages this area is prone to."

"It's like this in Los Angeles. Million-dollar homes have the greenest lawns while the rest of the Valley is brown with water restrictions."

He smiles. "I haven't been to Los Angeles in many years. Are there still orange groves in the city?"

I laugh. "Ahh, no. Only out in the rural areas now. The city is all people and cars, as far as the eye can see."

"Maybe I will take Hélène there for a trip when we get home. Take in the sights in America, once it is safe for us to travel again. We've seen everything there is to see in Europe a thousand times over. Watched the whole continent grow up." His expression is full of a lifetime I could not imagine in my wildest dreams.

"Thank you. For your help. With everything."

He pats the back of my hand where it rests on the arm of my chair. "*Vous êtes ma famille.* You are family."

I lean closer, so as not to be overheard. "If we're successful tomorrow—will it be hard for you to say goodbye to the books? To this life and your healing gifts?"

"Certainly it will be sad to see the books burn. We worked very hard on those, my brothers and me. But I've committed what I need up here," he taps his temple, "and I will transcribe it again before my death. The rest is more a matter of antiquity—I've become a skilled physician, far outpacing the information in those ancient pages," he says.

"My Hélène and I have been blessed with more good years than any two people deserve. We have lived through the ceaseless pain of losing Alicia, and we are looking forward to the undeniable joy of watching our grandson become a man. I have spent the whole of my life studying the human condition, in all its many forms, and I'm confident I can continue to help people until my time is over. Which," he laughs sadly, "is going to be sooner rather than later. But, it will be nice to not have to pay taxes anymore."

I smile.

"I know it must've been hard for Henry to grow up without his mom . . . you've lived such a long life, did you only have one child? Is that too forward to ask—" I regret the question the moment it crosses my lips.

Nutesh pauses. "We had two other children, many, many years ago, before the *AVRAKEDAVRA* was as potent as it is now. But life back then was dangerous. We didn't have things like antibiotics. No one knew what a germ was. When tiny bodies were racked with fever, you did what you could, and you prayed." He runs a finger along the edge of his cup. "Saying goodbye to your children, when it is their bodies being lowered into the dirt, is something no parent should ever have to experience."

Lucian spoke of the same thing, that last night in the big top back in Oregon. It's why we're here today, on the run. His parents, his wife—his children—died too young. He never recovered from the loss of that family.

"Nutesh, I'm so sorry."

"It is where the *AVRAKEDAVRA* came from. When I got tired of praying to gods that weren't listening, I, along with my closest companions, so close we were like brothers—we decided to do something about it. Belshunu's mother was a gifted healer, the true source of our magic. She taught us. And we learned."

"You've saved a lot of people in your time, Nutesh."

He looks at me, his amber-brown eyes damp with tears.

"It has been a hard life, but a good one." Nutesh again reaches over and lays his strong, broad hand flat on the back of mine. "Even without these books, you and Henry are the future now. The *AVRAKEDAVRA* served its purpose. It will now live on through you, but only the best parts of it. The tyranny will end. No more running, no more destruction, no more heartbreak."

"How do you know we will survive tomorrow?"

"I don't."

I slump back into my chair.

Nutesh smiles wistfully. "I know in my heart, like I know my own name, that when a person is faced with impossible odds, she can surprise even the biggest doubter." He reaches up and gently pulls on the chain that holds Delia's key under my shirt, holding it reverently against his palm. "I saw your mother face monsters, and win. She was ferocious, made of fire and love." His eyes are baleful. "I am confident that you will rise to the occasion tomorrow, that you will fight as hard as you can to save your people—Baby, your circus family, your elephants, Henry . . ."

My cheeks blaze.

"I am no fortune-teller, Geneviève, but I have lived enough lives to know when two pure hearts have found one another. It is a good match." I smile, my embarrassment over discussing my love life *involving his grandson* obvious from the space station. "But make a career, a life, independent of Henry. Hélène has been by my side since we were youngsters, but she always had an independent soul, even when it was culturally dangerous for a woman to have an opinion. She could tell you stories," Nutesh says, laughing heartily.

"I would love to hear them."

"When we land in Croix-Mare, you can ask her yourself. Just make sure she bakes something delicious first. She is a talker!" He sets his coffee down. "Henry cares deeply for you too, Geneviève. He will grow to be a good man." Nutesh sits up straighter, closer to me. "But I see confusion in his eyes. He is scared—he has lost so much in his short life, his mother to murder, his father to madness, and once the books are undone, he will have to endure losing Hélène and me. Losing his connection to Alicia is a formidable choice for him to have to face." Nutesh sighs heavily. "But I see how he looks at you. I see how he watches you, how he looks ready to lay down his life for you at any second. You have been a true friend to him, something I fear he has never had. But you have also had a life full of adventure and heartache that has made you stronger than Henry. As hard as this is, for both of you, Henry will be inspired by your strength. And he will prove his mettle to us all, when it truly counts."

Nutesh then picks up my hand and kisses the back of it. "Now. You—rest. We have a big day still to come, and Şivan will be expecting us for dinner in a few hours."

"Yes, sir." I stand but then lean over his chair and give him a hug. He seems surprised, but then embraces me back.

"Geneviève, you make your mother proud with every breath."

I thank him again and turn before he can see the tears welling in my eyes, my hand clutched around Delia's lucky key.

I hope I make her proud tomorrow.

41

ŞIVAN AND NUTESH RETIRE TO THE STUDY. SEVDA SLEPT THROUGH THE sumptuous dinner served by Şivan's house staff after Nutesh's intensive work on her eyes this afternoon. She can now make out shapes but can't see our faces clearly until she is right up close. Nutesh has promised he'll bring her back to France where proper specialists can be consulted, if things don't improve.

Because if everything goes to plan, in less than a day's time, Nutesh will lose his ability to heal anyone.

As will I.

Xavier pulls Henry and me into the common room, clicking the door closed behind us. The sound-masking device sits on the round table at the room's center.

"Just wanted to have a final sit-down about tomorrow," he says. "We're leaving here at 0400. Babylon is approximately 220 miles by air—we'll be flying low in a retired military helicopter, outfitted with infrared jammers and quieting modifications to keep sound to a minimum. In case you're worried about that."

Me? I'm worried about everything.

"Long sleeves, of course. Mosquitoes and sand flies are prevalent in this area."

Oh my god, I hadn't even thought about local bugs. "Tell me there are no spiders here."

"There are no spiders here," Xavier says.

"Really?"

"No. There are tons of spiders here. And scorpions. Most of them big, almost all venomous. And biting black desert ants. So just stay on your feet and don't disturb any nests, and you should be fine."

I shiver.

Xavier moves to his huge duffel, unzipped on one of the couches, from which he pulls two black-handled sheathed knives. "You will of course have the packs on you. I also want you to strap these into your boots."

"We have no idea how to use a knife," I say.

"Stab for the soft parts," Xavier says, a half smirk on his face.

"Very funny," I say.

"Knives can be used for more than stabbing. You never know when it might come in handy. Plus"—he pulls one of the six-inch blades out of its protective cover—"the ass end of these opens up. Inside are special matches and a small vial of fraxinella oil. Fraxinella burns quick and hot, its oil super volatile. In hot weather, it's said the flower will ignite while still on the plant. It's thought to have been the burning bush in the Christian Bible.

"You'd do well to keep that oil off your hands, given your proclivity toward flame," Xavier warns. He then sheathes the blade and hands one each to Henry and me. "Only you two will have the matches and oil."

"Not Sevda?"

Xavier shakes his head no. "From her, we need a few drops of blood. That's likely going to be the extent of her help."

Xavier moves to a window, cracks it, and lights up a cigarette. Good thing Nutesh healed all his parts yesterday so he can set to blackening his lungs again. "You will sleep in your travel gear. Even your boots. Backpacks next to the beds. Once Şivan and his nosy house staff retire, we want you both, and Sevda, in here. I get that they have gender-based rules in this country, but I don't have time for keeping up appearances. We're up and out at 0350, back to the air base where we came in. Should land in Babylon around 0545."

"What about the Undoing itself?" Henry asks. "What will be required of us?"

"A little blood, the Euphrates water, and Nutesh has an Undoing prayer."

Henry and I exchange a quiet look. Nutesh isn't the only one with the prayer.

"But the temple key?" I ask.

"Nutesh is of the mind that the presence of three direct descendants of each Original Creators' line should be key enough to call forward the ancestors to the place where the book's magic was sealed, in support of the Undoing."

"If we didn't really *need* this key intact, then why send us on a chase after it?" Henry worries the surface of a coin between his fingers.

"Without the key, there's no guarantee the Undoing will work. The ancestors may oppose it without the key and the ritual won't work. So technically, we really *do* need the third piece, and if we were to somehow acquire it on site—"

"You mean, if Aveline and Lucian show up with it," I say.

"Yes, but we don't even know if they have it." Smoke billows out of Xavier's nostrils. My biological father is a dragon. "It could be still lying in that park in Izmir, forgotten."

"Doubtful," Henry mutters.

"It would be best if we had it—the ritual would definitely be guaranteed. But don't count out Sevda's contribution here. She was a true surprise, even to Nutesh. Her blood will make certain all three lines are represented equally."

"She's *blind*—how are we even going to get her down there?" I ask.

"She's not blind. Cut her some slack," Xavier says. "And her gift is in concealment. She's quite good at it."

"Can't she just conceal us tomorrow and then we can get in and out without anyone seeing us?" I rub at my aching arm. All this talk about Aveline must be pissing it off.

"She says her gifts lie in keeping herself hidden from the world, but not a helicopter full of people." Xavier pauses and looks between Henry and me. "Nutesh assures me that the actual Undoing ritual is simple enough. Once we confirm the books are destroyed, we're back on the helicopter and then to the air base where we fly home."

"Home—to France, you mean," I say.

"Back to Rouen, then to Croix-Mare. We'll all need some R and R by then," Xavier says.

"And what about a contingency plan?"

Xavier douses his cigarette in the dregs of a coffee cup. "Me. I am the contingency plan."

"Which means . . ."

"Which means I am not going into the temple with you."

"Wait—why not?" I don't like this. At all.

"I will be on the roof."

Henry and I look at one another, and then back to Xavier.

"I have an extensive combat-based background. Military training. Sharpshooting."

"You're going to *shoot* them if they try to interrupt us?" I can't keep the panic from my voice. "This is Henry's *father* we're talking about, Xavier. Aveline is your *daughter*."

"Aveline has not been my daughter for a very long time." Xavier's jaw pulses. "If it comes down to a choice between your lives or Lucian's, your lives or Aveline's," his voice lowers, "the decision has been made."

Henry drops his coin onto the tabletop and pushes it away.

"Lucian has lived for two millennia. Aveline, five centuries. Most of that time has been spent causing tremendous damage. Do you think I want to look through that scope and put a bullet in my *child*?" Xavier's voice is tight. "Of course not. But you're my daughter too, and *you* are not lost to me. I have a chance to be in your life, to show you I'm worthy of at least your friendship." Xavier turns to Henry. "And I love your grandfather like my own father. I would do anything to protect him, and you. I mourned Alicia's death—her murder—just as we all did."

Henry nods. "I trust that if Nutesh is behind this plan, all other alternatives have been considered."

My mind swirls with everything he's said.

"I need some fresh air." I stand.

"An hour on the roof, and then lights out. Stay together."

"Of course, sir." Henry pauses to tuck his knife into his boot before scooping up his sketchbook. We peek around the corner before entering the hallway to make sure Gona or other staff aren't waiting in the hall to offer help, or to look scandalized by the impropriety of me being in the men's quarters.

Henry opens the glass door that leads up the stairs to the rooftop patio. Montague and his security guys are already up here, sipping canned beers, but when they see Henry and me, conspiratorial smiles are exchanged.

"We'll give you two *l' intimité* ," Montague says, winking at Henry, before they file down the stairway.

Henry leads me to our spot from last night in front of the crackling fire. We're quiet, watching the flames dance, both of us lost in our own thoughts. I don't want to talk about tomorrow, about the possibility that Xavier might have to shoot Lucian or Aveline. About the possibility that this could all end very badly—with our deaths, or with Lucian getting what he's been chasing after for centuries.

About how we'll lose our abilities, and he'll likely never

see his mother's ghost or hear her memories again. About how I'll no longer be able to fix the people I love.

Everything will be fine. Everything will be fine. Everything will be fine.

"Thank you for handling Şivan's archaeology questions at dinner," I say, wrapping myself around Henry's left arm, my head resting on his solid shoulder. "I seriously thought I was going to pass out if he asked me about my favorite world heritage site or whatever."

"You could always say the Hanging Gardens of Babylon," Henry says. He kisses the top of my head, sending shivers through me.

"Dude, I didn't even know they existed until a month ago, so yeah . . . no." I point toward the closed sketchbook tucked under Henry's right thigh. "Can I look at your sketches? Or . . . is that really private?"

Not even the low light can hide Henry's blush. He pulls the sketchbook from under his leg and hands it over.

The first few pages are comics—a lot of self-deprecating bits, Henry drawn with a too-big forehead, the bisected eyebrow, and that unruly curl that is trying to grow back. "Your nose does *not* look like that. Seriously? Have you looked in a mirror? I'd kill for your nose." I turn the page. He's sketched cartoonish versions of me—back at the circus, me with a flame cupped in my hand, like the one he gave me the other day, me with Gert and Houdini, and even of Othello being clever, making jokes about how he'd like to eat Mara Dunn. "I always figured he was thinking that too."

"I doubt she'd taste any good," Henry says.

"Rotten to the core."

On the next page, Henry's style takes a marked turn. Not cartoony, but breathtaking proper still lifes. He's drawn our journey so far . . . the fields outside Paris, the cabin in the Spanish woods, the Mediterranean and approaching docks as we pulled into Porto Torres in Sardinia, and even some from Naples—the bay, the boats, the beautiful buildings and crowded streets.

"Henry . . ."

He's drawn me saving that man at *Circ de l'Anell d'Or*, the exterior of *Napoli Sotterranea* where the *Circo della regina* performs, the faces of the Guardians and *La Vérité* people who've helped us so far, the food we've eaten . . .

The carnage at Pompeii. The beautiful exteriors of *Tanrilar Sirk*.

"I needed a record," he says. "In case we don't make it through this."

"When did you do these?"

"I've not been sleeping much."

"These are phenomenal, Henry."

"It kept my father off my back about not being musical. He wanted me to play the piano, like he does," he says. I think of the piano room at their estate in Oregon. "Once he saw I could draw, he refocused his efforts on art tutors instead of music teachers."

"Money well spent," I say.

More pages follow of scenes I don't understand.

"Those are from new memories. I told you Alicia has been flooding me lately. Plus the memories from the text itself . . . I wanted to draw some of them, just in case. I don't know if they'll disappear when she does."

Page after page of memories, none of which make any sense, naturally.

One page in particular catches my attention. It seems like a compilation of thoughts, of scenes taken out of someone's head. But—"Is this Ash? And Vi?" I swallow hard. "Is that Aveline?"

I follow the separate images around the page. Scenes of my circus siblings with Aveline, who they only know as Mara Dunn, new aerialist with the Cinzio Traveling Players, laughing, in the big top with Mara on the trapeze, hanging out in Mara's trailer, her wine fridge.

And then another of the wine fridge, opened, filled with wine bottles on their sides.

And then the wine bottles removed, and my tea set at the back of the fridge.

Sitting next to a small round capped jar.

"Henry . . ." My heart races.

"Ricin. What she used on Violet."

"But they searched. Nutesh said they searched the trailers."

"He said they searched *your* trailer. They did not search Aveline's trailer. They had no reason to—and no legal right."

"This . . . this is huge, Henry. This could clear my name."

"I know."

"We have to tell your grandfather! This means I could go home to Gertrude and Houdini. We could go home, Henry!"

"I told him, Gen. I showed him the drawings, explained what I saw. He will pass it along, but I don't think the police are apt to believe visions or secondhand memories passed on through possession of a magical text."

The wheels in my head burn alongside the heat singing through my arms and hands. "We need to bring Aveline home alive, Henry. We can't kill her tomorrow. We need her fingerprints—we need her DNA—to prove my innocence."

"But you heard them earlier. If Aveline shows up at the ruins, like we're all expecting she will, we have to do whatever is required to finish this. And it's not like we can handcuff her and drag her back to America."

I'd like to do more than that . . .

"You have to trust that the lawyers will seek out search warrants and go through proper channels."

"What if her trailer is gone, though? If Aveline were smart, her living quarters would've been moved out long ago."

Henry shakes his head. "I don't know, Genevieve. This is just what Alicia gave me." He points at his sketchbook. "Keep turning."

I return my attention to his drawings, my breath catching when I flip the page.

"You're quite peaceful when you sleep," he says.

"You make me look beautiful."

He quirks his sliced eyebrow. "You *are* beautiful."

"Thank you . . . for this. For everything."

Henry takes the sketchbook from my lap. The flames in the firepit dance in the corner of his eyes, the occasional pop sounding from the burning wood. He looks around us. "You do realize we're completely alone for the first time in forever?"

"I do."

"And tomorrow morning, we could both die." He kisses me. I wrap my hands around the back of his head and neck, pulling him closer.

"We can't die tomorrow," I say, a little breathless already. "You promised me back in France that if we live through this, you'd kiss me like this every day until we're old and withered."

"*When* we live through this, I'm going to do a lot more than kiss you," he growls, "though it will be so nice to not feel like licking the end of a battery every time we touch."

I laugh against his mouth. "And it'll be nice to not worry about you climbing into my head and looking at all the dumb things I've ever done."

"Oh, I already know all of those." He plants small kisses on my lips and cheeks and neck, but then stops and pushes away. His eyes widen and he looks directly at me, grabbing my wrist. Alicia appears next to him, glowing like a new star.

Without a word, Henry jumps up from his seat, breaking the connection, and moves to the glass half wall that surrounds the patio.

"Henry?"

He drops to all fours and signals for me to follow him. "What are you doing?" Instead of talking, we crawl forward toward the glassed edge that overlooks the front of the house.

On the street, a black vehicle pulls up, joining two others already idling there. A small figure—a woman—sneaks toward the closed gate.

"Is that Gona?" I whisper. "Who is she letting in?"

Xavier flies onto the patio from downstairs. "Get up! *Move*! *Now*!" he whisper-yells.

We jump up and sprint down the stairs after Xavier.

It's only when our packs are on our backs and our convoy of humans is following Xavier, Montague, and Nutesh through neighboring yards that I realize we left Henry's sketchbook on the patio.

For anyone to find.

42

I DON'T KNOW HOW FAR WE RUN OR HOW MANY CONFUSED YELLS FOLLOW us as we scale small walls and fences and bushes of private yards. No one in our party says anything until we're blocks away from Şivan's house, sliding through a stand of palm trees along an alley and filing into the backyard of a much humbler home.

We're greeted at the rear by the wide, friendly eyes of a woman in a long purple dress, her black hair piled on her head in a loose bun, and her husband standing with a rifle at his side just inside the door.

A spike of relief hits me when I see an antique silver key hanging from around her neck.

La Vérité.

"Come in, come in." She rushes us inside and then closes the heavy wooden door behind us. We pile into a spacious living room, our boots silenced by the multicolored rugs that cover most of the room. A long sectional stretches along two walls. The room is dark, save for a few lit candles.

The front door is outfitted with four dead bolts, the front windows sealed tight with shutters through which only scant light from an outside porch lamp can sneak in through gauzy curtains.

"Please sit. You are welcome here. I am Malalai. My husband is Khan. Please do not hesitate to ask if you need anything," she says. I'm more than surprised when her accent is heavily Australian, especially when she turns to Khan and speaks in Arabic.

"What happened back there?" I finally ask, waiting for someone to give us an explanation.

"Get some sleep, Geneviève," Nutesh says, his voice firm. I look at Henry for backup—he shakes his head subtly. Even a glance at Sevda, to see if she's as freaked out as I am, but she's got her head in her hands, rubbing at her red, swollen eyes as Xavier helps her out of her travel pack.

Malalai hands me a light wool blanket. "The washroom is down the hall. If you need food or water, please ask. You must stay low. Curious neighbors," she says, smiling.

Nine people in this one room—Sevda lies down along one side of the couch. Montague is propped against the front door; everyone else tries to make space for each other to rest sitting up, taking turns thanking Khan for the tea he passes around. Nutesh disappears down the narrow hallway, the satellite phone against his ear.

Xavier sits propped against the end of the sectional. I slide out of my pack and set it next to me, positioning so I can talk to him without disturbing everyone else.

"What happened? We saw Gona moving toward the gate, and then you were there."

"You answered your own question. The house staff."

"I thought she had shifty eyes . . . I'm surprised she didn't poison our food."

"I don't think she had a choice. Şivan has a lot of enemies. They probably threatened her family. Don't judge her too harshly." He flips his silver lighter around and around.

"What now?"

"The plan goes forward. Nutesh is changing our pickup spot. We can't go back to the air base right now. Too dangerous. There's a field not far from here—it's dicey because we don't have clearance for him to land in the city, but that's all we've got."

"And then Babylon?"

"And then Babylon." He pats my bent knee. "Close your eyes for a few minutes. You need the rest. I can smell the electricity coming off you."

I cradle my stinging hands in my lap, playing the tape of Nutesh's voice in my head, reminding me to breathe through it. When Henry slides down beside me and wraps his gloved hand around mine, I close my eyes in the hope that when I open them, we'll all still be breathing.

I'm trying to tie my boots but my ass and legs are asleep from being propped against the couch for four hours. The room smells like sweaty bodies and rebreathed air. Sevda is sitting up, blinking rapidly as Nutesh flashes a pen light across her eyes.

When I see that the bathroom is free, I stumble down the hall to take my turn. My stomach is in knots. I splash water on my face, make use of my travel toothbrush, run cold water over my reddened hands. A closer look in the mirror shows that my red roots are poking through my scalp, like little flames at the base of my otherwise dyed-brown curls.

A reminder that I'm still me under all this.

I open the door and almost bump into Xavier as he pulls the satellite phone from his ear. "James is moving into Kurdish airspace. We're about to go. Keep your eyes on everything," he says. "No gloves, in case we need those hands."

The burning buzz I'm getting so used to prickles under my skin. *Only a few more hours, and it will be gone . . .*

I startle Xavier, and myself, by wrapping him in a sudden hug. It takes a second, but then he hugs me back, hard. We stand together for a handful of breaths before he lets go. "For luck," I say. When he smiles, he doesn't try to hide the shimmer in his eyes.

"For luck," he says quietly.

Our tough-guy faces back in place, I follow Xavier down the hall. Montague is looking out through the curtain over the small window in the closed front door, lined up with another of the security guys, followed by Nutesh and Sevda. I'm stuffed in between her and Henry, and the final two security officers behind us. No one has weapons drawn—that would be way too obvious for any onlookers—but hands are poised near belts, just in case.

"They're here," Montague announces, turning to nod at the tail of people behind him. "Quietly, but quickly. Three cars this time. Four to a car. Do not stop for any reason." Montague then counts down from three on his hand as Khan and Malalai wish us "all the luck in the world."

Then the door opens, and we're out, quietly, in single file, into our cars that sit with headlights off. No one says a word as we pull away from the house. I recognize our driver from the other day, relieved that he's one of Nutesh's guys from the plane.

The field where we're expected to meet James is close by. Turns out it's a treeless dirt soccer pitch, the nearest houses far enough away that the spinning rotors won't spit debris into anyone's yard.

Our driver pushes against a button in the collar around his neck. "Copy that," he says. "Air transport two minutes out. Be ready to move."

I don't know how much readier we can be. Seat belts are off, backpacks are on, knives are stuffed in boots.

Then even over the Range Rover's purring engine, we can hear the unmistakable *whomp-whomp-whomp* of a helicopter. "Thirty seconds," our driver says.

Like a shadow, the chopper moves toward us, dark gray and bigger than I expected—top blades and then a rear rotor, five windows stretched down its side. As it drops down, the landing gear descends from its underside; the extreme wind from the spinning blades sends dirt and dead plants into spiraling devils.

"And you're out," the driver says. Montague helps Henry

and me from the car with our packs. The cars ahead and behind us empty as well, and we're all running hunched as the side of the helicopter opens, another new face welcoming us aboard.

The whole loading process takes less than a minute before we're lifting up, up, and away, the now-vacated Range Rovers screaming down the street, headlights off, to disappear into the very early Sulaymaniyah morning.

We buckle into seats bolted to the sidewalls so we're facing one another. Noise-canceling tactical headsets are pulled off our seat backs so we can hear our pilot's instructions and speak to one another.

"Welcome aboard the *Lady Tigris*, a retired AgustaWestland AW101 Merlin, used quite heroically in the liberation of the Iraqi people," the British male voice says. "I'm James, your captain and cruise director *extraordinaire*. Should you be in need of refreshment, we are happy to offer a selection of bottled waters, probably still warm because the onboard icebox is a fickle bugger and doesn't like Iraq very much and would very much prefer to spend its retirement in a pub on the coast of Cornwall, not that I blame it." Small smiles are shared around the helicopter's interior.

"We hope you find your ninety-minute journey with us into the heart of ancient Babylon a pleasant one. If you have any complaints, comment cards are stashed under your seat. Please fill it out and then stuff it in your bonnet. *Merci beaucoup*."

Once we're underway, Nutesh goes to the front, presumably to speak with—and pay—James. The aircraft looks so much bigger up close, and even though we have the heavy tactical headsets on to deaden the sound, the floor vibrates under our feet and into our seated legs.

Xavier's voice crackles in our ears as he gathers our attention. He spends the next thirty minutes reviewing our approach and asking for questions. Once he's satisfied we all know where we're going once we land, he and the other security guards unbuckle and start putting their gear together.

Xavier unzips the black duffel bag he's had with us the whole time, tosses another pack at one of the security guys, and then proceeds to extract metal pieces and set them on the floor between his legs. I watch in mounting fear as Xavier builds a huge, scary-looking rifle, uncapping the lens end of the scope bolted to the top. I've seen a few guns in my life—the one in Baby's trailer safe, the always-empty revolver Ted keeps in the work trailer in case the work crew gets too rowdy around whiskey-fueled campfires, and then the weapons Xavier and the others have had during this grand adventure.

But outside of a movie theater, I have never seen a gun that big. The rounds he's plugging into it are easily the length of my pinkie finger.

"Don't look. It's better to not think about it," Henry says, squeezing my knee.

I turn to look out the rounded-edge windows. It feels like we're barely flying high enough to avoid rooftops. The houses under us look suburban, though not much greenery. We pass over a spiral-eight shape—a freeway on-ramp system, busy with bouncing headlights despite the crazy early hour—and then the city slowly fades as the brown expanse of rural space takes over, broken up now and again by developed blocks of housing or other bigger buildings.

Once we're out of the city, James takes us a little higher. Because it's still dark, it's tough to see much of the ground below, other than the dark snakes of paved roads decorated with slow-moving headlights and color variations in the patchwork landscape. Some of the lighter areas look like they've been recently scraped with a giant rake; the darker, greener areas lush with vegetation are obviously closer to the water source that coils and twists south underneath us.

We climb higher yet again, and James, in our ears, explains we're over Baghdad so everyone should hold their breath.

I don't know if he's kidding.

"Less than thirty minutes to landing," he says, his tone a bit more serious.

The backpack Xavier threw at the security officer—it had a uniform in it. In the time I've been staring out the window, the officer has changed from the black combat gear we're all wearing into the blue camo of the Iraqi police service, complete with the red, white, and black flag of Iraq patch sewn above the left chest pocket, a nametag in Arabic over the right.

Clever. And also dangerous. But at least we'll look like we belong there.

I bend over, messing with my boot. "The knife is rubbing just above my ankle bone."

"Mine as well. Not used to jogging with a weapon shoved in my shoe," Henry says. "Pity, that. I feel like a superhero."

"I'm clueless with a knife, unless it's to carve a stick for s'mores."

Henry smiles. "Lucian went through a phase when he wanted me to be able to defend myself. He told me that children of wealthy parents were often targets for kidnapping plots. Scared me to death. Probably why I never rebelled very hard. I didn't want to end up tied to a chair in someone's basement."

"Except for sneaking out and providing expensive wine for all your rich friends' parties, you mean," I say, waggling an eyebrow.

Xavier looks up at us from building his rifle, his smirk almost eerie given the greenish light inside the helicopter's gut. "You do realize we can hear everything you're saying?" He taps the tactical headset covering his ear.

"I was just about to profess my undying love and tell Henry I can't wait to carry his many babies, so this is just so much better you can all hear me," I say back to him. Andrew and the other guys chuckle and look at Xavier.

"Smart-ass." He nods at his security brothers. "Kids these days. We should eat them while their bones are still soft."

Xavier finishes his task and then stands and gives Henry and me bulletproof vests and earpieces so we can hear what's going on once we're outside.

"Every precaution," he says, and then climbs back into his seat. He turns to Sevda next to him and taps his ear. She removes her headset, and he whispers close to her head. Whatever he's said to her, none of us can hear.

Henry sees me watching them and squeezes my hand. "We're going to be okay."

I nod and push my chin up so no one sees the sudden panicked tears.

Henry kisses the back of my hand, and then we help each other into our vests, making double sure everything is Velcroed correctly. The thirty minutes evaporates, and James is in our ear again, warning us we're a minute out. Xavier, Montague, and the security guys, earphones in and mic collars in place, are poised on the edge of their seats. Xavier will be going without a mic, which seems dangerous, but they said they didn't want any crackles or feedback to give away his position. Nutesh emerges from the front of the aircraft, his Kevlar vest strapped around his torso. He pats his own pack and winks at Henry and me before pulling it on.

The third text.

We have all three *AVRAKEDAVRA* books with us now, in one unsecured place. This hadn't even dawned on me at Şivan's.

Take the treasure . . . Follow the river to where the bones of kings lie.

I'm here, Mom. I have the treasure. If you're out there watching over this, please help us today.

The two front guards will wear night-vision headsets to be sure we don't run off course on our way to the river—the sun isn't due to rise until 0645, and we're just shy of 0540 right now. Right on schedule.

"When we touch down, Xavier is running ahead to get in

position. You two are out and running straight south. Follow me," Montague advises. "One of you on each side. Got it?"

Henry and I nod and pull our headsets off, stuffing the earpieces into place. Our fingers interlaced, I can already feel my bare palms warming against the fabric of his gloves.

"Thank you for choosing the *Lady Tigris* for your expeditionary needs. We look forward to a full champagne brunch service as soon as you finish kicking some tyrannical ass," James teases.

Xavier turns to me. "I've got your back. Always."

I nod and mouth a *thank-you.*

As we descend vertically, the door latch is thrown. Xavier holds up a countdown hand again as James lowers us all the way onto the ground, the helicopter barely bouncing with touchdown.

Three.

Two.

One.

Run.

43

As planned, Xavier is off and running to his predetermined perch where he and his rifle can watch over us from above once we're in the temple. Two guys are ahead of us—Team A—leading the way; Henry and I run on each side of Montague, packs tight against our backs, the leather sheath of my boot blade rubbing against the already tender skin. Andrew in the Iraqi police uniform, Nutesh, and another soldier helping Sevda—Team B—are behind us. The field we landed in is clay-like underfoot, a challenge to get traction in, but now we're running on harder, drier soil. Small clumps of vegetation grow at the bases of the huge palm trees, and birds squawk at us overhead—we've disturbed their predawn slumber. A house sits about a football-field length away, but only a few lights are on. Maybe it belongs to the farmer who owns this land?

We scale a waist-height wall of mud brick and stone at the edge of the property, and then we're out in the open, with no trees or grassy cover whatsoever. The Euphrates announces herself with the unmistakable algae-tinged scent where water meets soil. We cut sharply across the sandy brown field, diving through another stand of palms to find the river's edge.

It takes my breath away to see it in person.

The water murmurs past thick and black in the darkness. The security guys set up a small perimeter around us; Nutesh unzips the front pockets of our packs and hands us our collection kits. Holding up the three clear vials I have to fill, the water is a brownish-green in the spill of my small flashlight.

First objective accomplished.

Montague and the guards communicate with hand signals as the barks of at least two dogs breaks through the river's whispers. There's a house up ahead, and lights have just gone on. We need to move again.

For university students on an archaeological mission, we sure look suspicious.

The original plan had us running along the Euphrates's edge but we're turning back east, in the direction we came. I can't ask; I can only trust they know what they're doing, and follow. The irrigation canal we saw on the satellite imagery comes into view up ahead. Our two leaders run as close to it as they can—it's protected by a tall cyclone fence topped with coiled wire—but they tell us to run faster. The barking dogs aren't letting up.

We loop south around the side of the wider irrigation pond, and then we're cutting east again, thankfully into a stand of more trees and tall weedy grasses and shrubbery. It's to our benefit that this is all going down near the water, where things actually grow; if we were farther from the Euphrates, in any of those areas we just flew over, we'd be screwed. All brown, no trees. Like the desert outside Vegas. Might as well be Mars.

We stop in another clump of palms and what I think might be eucalyptus and poplar to evaluate where we are and listen to see if those dogs are chasing us, along with their humans.

It's quiet, and no flashlight beams bounce across the landscape toward us.

The relief is obvious in everyone's faces.

"Up ahead—Lion of Babylon, the ass-end of the Processional Way. We're almost there," Montague says. "Move east, right down the side of the Processional walls, as quiet as we can. Ninmakh is directly ahead. Any questions?"

I look to Henry, then around us, and back to Montague and Nutesh. "Wait—where's Sevda?"

Montague turns sharply, looks toward Andrew and the others who are securing our back end, about ten feet behind us. "Do we have a twenty on Sevda?" He talks into his mic collar.

Heads shake. "How could we have lost her already?" I ask, trying not to panic. "Did she fall?"

And then I feel a hand on my arm, and the sand next to me moves with a boot print. It's not that she's invisible, because out of the corner of my eye, I can make out her shape.

It's more like she's . . . shimmering.

"Oh my god," I whisper. "Damn, now *that* is a cool trick."

"Maybe we really are X-Men," Henry says.

"Are you sure you can't cover all of us with this?" I ask her.

"Not strong enough," she says, her voice like a whisper on a breeze.

"Cancel. We found her," Montague says, looking in the direction of where she seems to be standing. *"Ingéniuex.* Stay close. Your eyes aren't perfect yet, *non*?"

A disembodied thumbs-up shimmers in and out of focus.

Montague presses his mic again. "Andrew, can you get a visual on Xavier?"

Andrew puts his binoculars to his eyes. "Negative. Still too far out at this angle."

And then we're moving again. The walls of the Processional Way on our right are *huge*, the brick so uniform and perfect, it has to be the reconstructed sections. Another copse of trees sits to our left; flanking those is a series of long beige tents, several of which bear long canvas signs announcing them as property of the State Board of Antiquities and Heritage, Iraq, bold KEEP OUT signs in English and Arabic.

You don't have to ask me twice.

Gravel, or maybe broken bricks, crunch underfoot—and then the grand Temple of Ninmakh rises before us.

It's a hell of a lot bigger in real life.

As we move toward it, the rebuilt Ishtar Gate appears at our right, the paved entrance surrounded by trimmed bushes and trees, the area still quiet of workers or tourists. The Gate's blue brick is so brilliant, and the yellow and white of the animal reliefs on its front nearly glow in the waning dark.

We're nearly at the Temple's front when Montague stops us, arm outstretched.

"Hold," he says, dropping to a crouched position against

a shoulder-height pile, what was probably part of an actual structure at one point but now is just a melting stack of ancient mud bricks. Like so much of these ruins, it seems.

We follow what he does. He listens to someone in his ear and then whispers into his mic to Andrew. "We still can't get eyes on Xavier?"

"Negative."

The Team A guys crouch and pull bolt cutters from one another's packs.

Something scurries from under us, and I have to throw my hand over my mouth to not scream.

"Probably a mouse. Just a mouse," Henry says. *And you're probably lying.*

When the first waft of that deathly stench washes under my nose, I instinctively grab Henry's arm, eyes wide as I look at him.

"Gen?"

I sniff again. And again. Scan the ground for arachnid movement.

Nothing. At least nothing supernatural.

Nutesh is here. The Etemmu can't get you.

I can feel the vibration of the *AVRAKEDAVRA* against my back, through the layers of fabric in my pack, my coat, the bulletproof vest.

It knows. It's almost home.

"Never mind. I'm fine. Let's go."

Andrew stands with his head just above our hiding spot, scanning the still-dark area. "Scaffold visible. Rooftop rendezvous spot visible. Can't get a visual on X from here." He pauses and moves over a bit, adjusting his angle. "Something's not right."

Henry and I look at one another; he looks as scared as I feel.

"We have to move. Sun's going to be up in fifty minutes," Nutesh says.

"Team A, be ready to cut us inside. Once we enter the temple, A and B will establish the perimeter. Nutesh and heirs will move into position to commence operation. Are we clear?"

"Copy that," echoes in our ears.

Montague gives the signal for us to stand and move, following Team A toward the structure. Instead of entering through the massive arched front, we're going in a side arched entryway—apparently it's a more direct route into the temple's heart.

As we approach, Team A has their bolt cutters at the ready—except the gate is already open. Montague flattens us against the exterior temple walls.

"Did Xavier cut us in?" Montague whispers.

"No cutters," Andrew answers. "Not that I know of."

"*Merde*," Montague mutters. "Be ready." Quietly, sidearms are drawn and safeties are unlatched.

I don't know if I will ever breathe again.

Team A goes ahead.

We hear it before Henry and I can see around Montague's form in front of us.

"Hands up! Hands where I can see them! Don't move!"

Followed by the screams of Team A's two members as

they drop to their knees, weapons forgotten, writhing in pain as blood vessels break and muscle fibers tear.

"Jesus," is the only thing Montague says as we emerge from the arched entryway to be greeted by not only Aveline Darrow wreaking her havoc on our team members, but Lucian standing proudly behind three metal fold-up chairs, to which are attached three humans, still alive:

Hélène Delacroix.

Lucas.

And Ash.

44

"WELCOME TO THE TEMPLE OF NINMAKH," LUCIAN DAGAN DMITRI SAYS. "As this is a holy place, I must ask you to lower your weapons."

I'm afraid to move, but a quick scan around us explains why Xavier isn't on the scaffold, or the roof.

He's slumped in the corner, unconscious and bleeding, hands and feet bound. His scoped rifle sits in the far corner at the opposite end of the temple.

"All of this time and expense and mayhem, Nutesh, not to mention the cost in lives lost," Lucian says, moving behind Hélène. When he puts his hands on her shoulders, she sits up proud and defiant, despite her disheveled appearance, a bleeding cut above her right eye.

My chest ignites like a reactor.

"She was like a mother to me when I was young," Lucian says. "I won't hurt her."

"Speak for yourself," Aveline snarls.

It's unnerving to see Lucian in combat-style clothing—I'm so used to seeing him in a suit. His tiepin that started this whole mystery—the inverted triangle overlying the circle—is affixed to the flap over his left breast pocket.

He looks as dangerous as ever.

Aveline has made quick business of the Team A guys, now behind us on the dirty stone-tile floor, unmoving. She kicks away weapons and drops Andrew and Montague to their knees, roping their hands behind their backs and then shoving them against the wall.

"An Iraqi police uniform? Nutesh, you really went all out here. I'm impressed," she says, standing in front of Andrew. Nutesh remains fixed next to me.

Aveline then steps behind Hélène, Lucas, and Ash and stretches her arm in front of her, fingers splayed, before squeezing her hand into a tight fist.

Which drops Henry and me to our knees. My left arm and the carving in my chest explode in pain, as if the cuts were freshly made. It only takes a few seconds for the blood to seep through my shirt, hot against the weight of the body armor, and make my breaths ragged.

"And here I thought I was going to have to cut you up again for the binding ritual, *sister*," she says. "You've made this so much easier for me. *Merci*."

"Aveline, enough!" Nutesh bellows.

"Yes, please, stop showboating," Lucian scolds. He and Aveline lock eyes, a hard glare between them—a fracture in their veneer?—before she unclenches her fist, releasing the stranglehold on my lungs.

"We're going to make this as simple as possible. I'm sure you all have better places to be. I know I do," Aveline says. "*S'il vous plait, mes amis*, the books. One at a time. Bring them forward, put them here on the brick edge of this very handy firepit." She unzips the left breast pocket in her dark green, waist-length jacket. "What? Do you like my outfit?" She spins once. "I've been saving it for today, just for Iraq. Perfect for playing soldier girl, don't you think?" Her laugh echoes around the enclosed temple walls, and what felt so spacious on aerial photos suddenly feels like a coffin. "You know, I was not old enough to see this place in its heyday, but I can imagine it was magnificent. What about you, Hélène? Was it beautiful when you were here, young and in love with your darling *Nutesh*?"

Hélène turns her head slightly toward Aveline, without making eye contact, and spits.

Aveline laughs at her. "I guess that's a *non*?"

She slows behind Lucas in the middle, blindfolded but frozen as she rests her hands on his chair. "One incentive for each of you, although—I am sad to see that Sevda isn't here. I thought she'd want to save her lover. What has happened to her?"

"You should know after what you did in Turkey," Henry growls.

"Did she fall? I was worried about that. Oh well, Lucas, you will have to rely on the kindness of these folks to not leave you behind."

Henry and I exchange a quick glance. Sevda obviously isn't dead, but we don't know where she is—and neither does Aveline or Lucian.

Aveline reaches into her pack and pulls out Henry's sketchbook.

The one we left on the rooftop patio at Şivan's.

"Henry, I must say, these are really lovely. I especially like the ones of me with my dear circus friends. Who knew you were so talented *and* clever? And wow, you guys have had some *adventures* lately." Aveline then steps in behind Ash, also blindfolded, and holds the open book in front of him. "Ash, my sweet, look at how cute we are—oh wait, you can't. Silly me!"

She tosses the sketchbook away; it skitters across the sandy floor and hits the crumbling bricks at the base of the far wall. She then places both hands on Ash's shoulders. Under the cloth over his eyes, his left cheek mottled and bruised, his white, short-sleeved shirt soaked in dried blood. He's definitely in the worst shape of the three. Aveline runs a pointed finger over Ash's tattoo; he groans under her touch, the skin immediately red and angry. "Ash, my beautiful boy, guess who is here to rescue you? Too bad she wasn't there for poor *Violette*."

"I'm going to kill you," I hiss through clenched teeth.

"Not sitting on your knees like that, you won't," Aveline mocks. She reaches into her unzipped jacket pocket and pulls out the third piece of the temple key. "I think this is what you were looking for back in Izmir, is it not? Man, you guys did not plan for contingencies at all. I didn't get the final toll from that circus, but it was a lot. Shame on you. And now, this," she purrs, pulling the blindfold off Ash's face.

He hollers in agony, his bound body wracked with shudders.

I yelp, a mixture of horror and pain and the consuming need to discharge the energy running through me. Henry reaches to help me up, but Aveline moves like lightning, behind me, hand gripping my short hair, yanking my head back so I have to look at what she's done.

"What's a trapezist with only one eye?" she whispers in my ear. Ash sobs, slobber and blood dripping off his chin.

"Ash, I'm so sorry . . . Ash . . . please, it's Geni. I'm so sorry," I say through strangled cries.

I move my right arm backward, trying to find Aveline's leg, but she knocks me forward. "You'd be wise to keep those hands away from me, *ma soeur chérie*." And then her knee is in my back and she's pulling off my pack and tying my wrists together. I howl, the pain in my left arm and chest blurring my vision. She yanks me up on my feet, dragging me over to the firepit at the far end of the temple, behind Hélène, Lucas, and Ash, and knocks me down to my throbbing knees again.

"If anyone moves to help her, I will stop her heart. Are we clear?" No one says anything. She unzips my pack and pulls out the *Life* text, holding it reverently in front of her. "All of this carnage, all of these *years*—if our darling mother had just given me what was mine in the first place, so much trouble could have been avoided. *Mon dieu*, what a stupid, selfish, willful woman she was." Aveline kisses the front of the book and sets it on the brickwork before digging through my pack again. "Ah-ha! Piece number two!" She sets the key piece onto the front of the *Life* text. I can feel its pull, even with three feet separating us.

Aveline then turns toward everyone else. Lucian stands next to Hélène with his arms crossed, his face displeased, as if he's not enjoying my sister's theatrics.

"Nutesh, if you would please present the text in your possession? No funny business. Just bring it over, set it down, and step away. I will get enough blood from your grandson to cover for you."

Nutesh, without taking his eyes off his beloved wife, slides his pack from his shoulders. He pulls the *Death* text out of its protective pocket. I watch Lucian as this happens, his eyes like Othello's when I move closer with his food bin.

Nutesh carries the book in front of him, murmuring words of comfort to Ash as he passes my friend. "It will be over soon, son," he says. He then sets the text on the firepit edge, gives me a solid nod of his head, and moves back to his prior position.

"Okay, young Henry, you're up."

"Father, please." Henry looks at Lucian, ignoring Aveline's directive. "You won. We'll give you everything you want—please, just let them go. You don't need them anymore. You will have the texts, you can perform your ritual and go back to your own time—just let everyone free so we can spend our last moments together."

I need him to keep talking. Maybe they won't notice the smell of the rope burning behind my back.

Lucian stares at his son, his eyes softening for a moment. "Henry, your text. Please."

"Do you really think Aveline is going to let you have the books? Dad . . . I'm begging you."

I've never heard Henry call Lucian *Dad*.

Don't look back. Don't look at me.

A thin line of smoke coils from my conjoined hands. The rope loosens . . .

Aveline lifts an arm toward Henry, as if she's about to work her pain on him, but Lucian shoots her an evil glare and shakes his head. Henry locks eyes with me, a tear running down his face, and slides out of his backpack.

"I tried to be a good son," he says, unzipping the book's compartment. "I really did. I tried to learn from you. I looked up to you, Father." He pulls the book out. "I can see now that was a mistake."

Snap.

The rope burns through.

My hands are free and fully charged.

The *Memory* book tucked in his arm, as if he were carrying an algebra text, Henry moves quickly and sets the book on the firepit edge, next to its siblings.

Aveline steps in and with more care than I'd expect, she places the other key pieces onto the corresponding books. But then the wickedness returns to her eyes as she holds a knife under Henry's chin.

"Your hand, if you please." She yanks off his glove. "Just a few drops, you beautiful, potent boy. An heir of two families. I should keep you for myself. You will be wasted on my sister." She flashes me a nasty look before slicing a gash into Henry's palm and drizzling his blood over both the *Memory* and *Death* texts.

"You're up next, sis," she says to me.

"Come and get it," I growl. Immediately the fire in my carved arm intensifies.

Aveline leans down and whispers in my ear. "Once this is over and the books are mine, I will kill Henry's daddy and then carve your Ash into pieces, and you will watch." She grabs onto my left arm. "Aww, look at you, clever girl. Burned through your rope. *Tsk-tsk*."

She yanks my arm unnecessarily hard, her thumb digging into the festering wounds, but I can't fight against her, the pain too much as it rips through me. My clenched teeth grind, and Aveline laughs that she doesn't have to cut me again because my arm is already bleeding enough for a lifetime of rituals.

She jerks me forward and squeezes, my blood sullying the leather cover of the *Life* text.

This is it. She has everything she needs.

She shoves me backward next to Henry, and turns away from us.

He looks down at me. I smile at him drunkenly, my consciousness hanging on by a gossamer thread.

"Are you up for a game of cards?" I say. He replies with a sly smile of his own, removes his remaining glove, and flattens his hand lovingly against my bare neck. But it's not affection he's giving me—it's the incantation from Delia's playing cards, shoved right into the front of my head, a reminder of what we can do before anyone else gets in the way.

Sevda shimmers into form and takes my left hand just as Henry crouches, grabs my other outstretched hand, and slams his bloodied palm onto the ground.

Around us explodes into a tempest of sound, memory, and people.

So many people.

Henry and Sevda and I hold on to one another as hard

as we can. I throw all the electricity I have through both of them; Sevda shimmers our bodies so we aren't wholly visible; Henry conjures the past around us, like a film on fast forward with the volume at ten. The temple walls disappear and we're surrounded by the lush greenery that once gave the Fertile Crescent its name, the endless humanity moving produce and animals in and out of the massive city walls, children screaming, soldiers marching past Nebuchadnezzar II's palace, carts pulled by beasts of burden, donkeys braying, birds screeching overhead.

And slowly, the crowd around us begins to build. Ghosts—tens, then hundreds, then as far as the eye can see.

But a gathering in front of us, a middle-aged man and a younger version of himself, a woman with crinkles around the corners of her eyes and gray strands in her long, black wavy hair, a collection of children, including a handsome young boy of about four—Lucian's carbon copy—and a tiny baby with a shock of brown curls on her head, wrapped in a woven cloth in the arms of a stunningly beautiful woman standing nearer to the front—it's this that pulls Lucian from behind us.

He sinks to his knees, hands outstretched. Through the raging memory storm swirling around us, his voice is clear as a bell in our ears: "Tammuz . . . Ningal . . ." he says, reaching toward his dead children. "I've missed you so . . ." His whole body shakes with emotion. He stands, reaches for the oldest man standing there. "Belshunu. Father." Though his hands go through their bodies, like mist, he still tries to touch them. Belshunu speaks to his son, but we can't hear it.

And just as quickly, the happy scene begins to crumble as blistering pain rockets through me, into Henry, into Sevda—our connection means I can feel what Aveline is throwing at us times three. Their agony is mine, and our voices, our screams, meld into one as we work to hang onto the blur of memories that will give someone outside of us a moment to act, to disable Aveline so we can let go and complete the Undoing.

Lucian, however, is transfixed, communing with his dead family, smiling when they smile, promising he will see them again soon. As if in slow motion, he turns to look at us, his truest smile and tear-soaked face the only thing I can see in my tunnel vision. My throat is on fire from screaming and straining against Aveline's assault, but I must hold on.

I cannot let go. I cannot give up.

There are three of us—three true heirs—and only one of her.

A slight tilt of my head proves that she's slowly figuring this out, her clawed hands red and angry, her face contorted and near purple from her efforts, teeth bared in a banshee's screech. Our shimmer falters and we are fully visible again; Henry wobbles next to me, nearly breaking contact. The memory tempest flickers—he's running out of steam.

"Henrrryyyyyy!" I scream. "Hold ooooon!"

And then the light clicks on in Aveline's eyes. Henry is running this show.

If she can stop him, she can stop the storm.

She latches onto his right forearm with both her hands, her focus drawn specifically to him, though the torrent that buffets through Henry's whole body transmits down the line, through me, into Sevda. She drops like a stone, and stars pop in my peripheral vision like Fourth of July sparklers.

Hang on, Genevieve.

I open my eyes, painfully. "Mom . . ." She stands in front of me, just like she did in the mausoleum back in Portland, still in her circus regalia from the night she died, her hair a halo of fire. Alicia is with her, glowing like the heart of a star.

"Hang on, my beautiful little bird."

"Help us. Help us, Mom, *please*."

"You are my brave, fierce girl. *Finish this*. You are the only one who can."

"I love you, Momma. I love you so much," I say, sobbing.

"I love you too. Put to rest what I could not. I will always be near, even if you can't see me. I promise. You are my *Vérité*, Genevieve. Finish this and go home. Take care of our family. Take care of Baby and Henry and Xavier and Ash and all of them. They will need you, as you will need them."

"I can't . . . I can't go on without you."

"You've already proven that you can. I will love you forever." My mom's energy then blows through me, pushing me to fight harder.

I have to take care of our family.

My free arm moves as if through setting concrete, but I lift it high enough to flatten my hand atop the *Life* text, its energy surging through me but doing little to counter the horrors Aveline never seems to run out of.

Aveline's screams ricochet off the Ninmakh walls—she knows what I'm doing.

Through my mother's ethereal glow, Lucian stands and looks at Henry. When his eyes soften and his palm flattens against his heart, I realize he's seen Alicia too.

He then turns back to his ghostly family, his hand outstretched as they reach for him. He smiles, sadness and resolve etched in his sharp features, but also—clarity, eyes wide, blinking fast, like he's seeing a sunrise for the first time.

And I know this is the end.

"Hennnnrrryyyyyyy!" My voice bounces off the inside of my head.

Lucian reaches into his black boot. In three long strides across the temple floor, he's behind his son.

The silver of his drawn blade shines against the flicker of the sun in the bright memoryscape still playing around us, as if on a 360-degree movie screen.

And then Aveline's mouth goes wide and her hands release Henry's arm, stopping the stream of torture as she slides to the ground, the light disappearing from her ice-blue eyes.

Lucian's killed her. Not Henry, but Aveline.

"Son . . . let go," Lucian says. "It's over. Let go." His voice is slow, as if speaking underwater.

"Genevieve, I love you forever. Take care of our family," Delia says again.

Just as Henry falls onto his side, unconscious.

45

I'M FLAT ON MY BACK, BARELY ABLE TO FIND THE ENERGY TO BREATHE LET alone sit up and see what's left of the family around me.

Eyes open. We're still in the temple. Has it only been a few seconds? Were they not able to transport me back to France blissfully asleep so this nightmare can finally be over?

"Henry?"

"Here, Gen. I'm okay." He's trying to sit up. Everywhere around us, blood.

My hands are completely trashed—ruptured blisters, layers of peeling skin. I'm missing more than half my fingernails.

I muscle myself upright and spin toward the firepit. The books aren't burning. I didn't finish the incantation.

And Nutesh is standing before them, his expression distant, his smile one I've not seen on him before.

Something's not right.

Xavier's earlier words echo in my head. *You can't trust anyone.*

No, no, no, we did not come all this way for Nutesh to take control of all three books.

"Xavier . . ." Behind me, Andrew is awake and moving toward my father, still bloodied and unconscious in the corner.

I stand and stumble toward Nutesh. "So much good in these books, young *Geneviève*. We could do so much good with them." Slowly, I turn my head to Henry and signal for help.

"You have already done so much good, Nutesh." Despite the rawness of my palms and fingers, I wrap my hand around his. "Go to Hélène. She needs you."

"Hélène . . ." Nutesh speaks as if in a trance, his head turning slowly toward his wife where she sits pained and exhausted on her chair.

Sevda shimmers into full view beside me and crumples just as Henry steps in next to his grandfather.

"Let us finish this, Nutesh," I whisper. "Let us finish it before Lucian does." Nutesh stares at me, tears cleaning tracks in the dirt on his face. He nods, looks to Henry, and then shuffles across the temple toward Hélène.

Upon saying his name, Lucian's anguished sobs become louder. I'm shocked to see him crouched against the opposite wall, his head in his hands, his shoulders shaking.

Montague has freed Lucas and is slicing through the zip ties on Ash's wrists, but he's slumped over in his chair. I want to go to him, to heal him while I still have the ability, but I can't.

I cannot risk another second of Lucian, or Nutesh, near all three of these books, at the source of their original magic.

"I have to finish the prayer."

The keys are in place, the blood and Euphrates water have been spilled, and the three heirs are present.

I reach out my hands, one each to Sevda and Henry. We circle the firepit, and I recite the incantation again, with Henry's help. My voice is as loud as I can make it. I just hope it's loud enough for the books to hear me, for the magic to realize it's time to go home:

"Come forward, ašipu, bow your head before Mother
Gula, Lady of Life, daughter of Anu,
Restore the health of the deadly sick and bestow long
life
In the great healing temple of E-gal-Makh.
Bring forth your magic to Babylon,
In the walls of Ninmakh
We take this magic from your breast, belet balati,
Lady of Health,
She Who Makes the Broken Whole Again,
Speak our blessing,
Rid us of our blindness,
We are bound unto you,
Forever until the Undoing."

The words hang in the air like ghosts. We move the books into the bottom of the firepit. Henry takes his knife from his boot, pops open the butt end, pulls out the matches, and drizzles the fragrant fraxinella oil over the texts.

And then Lucian is beside us, his hand outstretched, his reddened face and glassy eyes saying what his mouth does not. Henry gingerly places a match into his father's palm.

"The key to good is found in truth," Lucian says.

He then looks around at all of us, stopping for a long beat on Henry, his eyes clearer than I've ever seen them, his features softer. It looks like the weight of the world has been shed from his shoulders.

"I'm so sorry, my son. I'm sorry to have been so blinded by my sorrow, by Aveline's ambitions," he says.

With a single strike against the rough surface of the fire-pit brick, the match lights.

He throws it onto the books, and as promised, they burn hot and fast.

One minute of blue flame erases 2,400 years of history.

"It is done," Lucian says, voice husky and tired. "It is done."

As the last licks of flame reach toward the heavens, a coldness washes through me, like a window has been thrown open on a stormy January morning. I flex and contract my battle-damaged hands in front of me.

It's leaving. The magic is leaving.

Henry meets my eyes, his face pale. He feels it too.

He stumbles over and kisses me hard on the mouth. When there are no images pushed into my head, and he doesn't recoil from staticky pain, he pulls back, eyes widening. "It's really over," he says. "We did it."

We melt into each other's broken bodies, emotion spilling down our faces, and for a brief moment, we are the only people in the world.

We separate, his sliced hand cradled across his front. I can't fix him anymore—but that's okay. Everything will be okay.

"Oh my god, Xavier . . ." I stumble-jog across the temple—Andrew has Xavier's damaged body propped against knees, the bindings around his ankles and wrists cut free. His ice-blue eyes are only half-open, and the blood . . .

I lock eyes with Andrew, fear rising in my throat. He shakes his head.

"Xavier, hey, come on—*Dad*—wake up. Look at me," I say. "*Look* at me!"

Xavier's lids flutter, and he smiles, his teeth and lips stained red. "Is it over?"

"It's over. We can go home now. Let's go home and be a family. All right? Wake *up* and let's get the hell out of here."

"Hmmm . . . I need a cigarette."

"Okay, let's get on the helicopter and I will get you one. Yeah? Andrew and I are gonna help you up. You ready?"

His eyes close again.

"*Xavier.*" A tear tracks down his face as he smiles at me again. I take his hand. "I've got your back—just like you had mine. We're gonna be a family now, remember? You said we could. You promised."

"Henry is your family. Take care of him. I love you, Genevieve," he says. "I'm tired now. Just give me a second."

I squeeze his hand, and he squeezes it back, but then his grip loosens and his half smile fades and his eyes stay closed.

"Andrew . . . ?" I look up at him; he pushes two fingers against the pulse point on Xavier's neck, and shakes his head again.

I lean forward and kiss Xavier. "I love you too, Dad. Delia is waiting for you." And then I lay my head on his chest, listening for the heartbeat that is no longer there, because I want him to know he's not alone, that his family was there for him as the greedy Iraqi soil drank in his blood. "Look after Mom for me," I sob, laughing through my tears. "Loan her a shirt so she can get out of that silly costume."

The inside of the temple is quiet. "*Ma chère*, we must depart," Montague says, his hand on my shoulder. They've given me a few minutes, but the sun is rising.

"We can't leave him here," I say.

"Of course not." Montague flattens his palm against my cheek. "We will take him home."

I nod, and Henry helps me up. He uses his glove to wipe the tears spilling down my face. "I've got you now," he whispers.

"Wait." I move in a diagonal across the temple, to the far wall, and pick up Henry's sketchbook in my singed, stinging, bloody fingers.

A record of everything we've lived through.

There are a few pages yet to be added.

"Now we can go," I say, clutching the book against my chest.

46

"MIND IF I SIT?"

Ash only indicates he's heard me with a slight shrug.

"How're you feeling?" I ask.

"Like I wish every conversation here didn't start with that question."

"Right . . . sorry." I lean back in my chair, my pressure-glove-wrapped hands cradled in my lap. The morning air is brisk, but spring is imminent. You can smell it on the breeze, in the soft rain that drips from the patio cover edge into the bright green grass. Tulips and daffodils are pushing through the soil, and the trees that were bare when I arrived at Croix-Mare back in February have exploded with their spring finery.

The corner of Ash's blue wool blanket has slid off his shoulder; I want to move it for him, to cover him up, to keep him safe.

I sit still. He's been avoiding me for weeks; I don't want to blow a chance to actually talk to him now.

"How long will you have to wear those?" He looks at my curled fingers. The black patch over his missing left eye makes him look older . . . or maybe that's just because of recent events. I know I feel about a hundred years old.

"Nutesh says a few more months. Until the grafts are healed." The skin on my fingers and palms was so burned off after Babylon, Nutesh had to harvest skin from my thighs to repair my hands. "I'm down to eighteen hours a day, though, so that's improvement."

Water *drip-drip-drips* into a flowerpot Hélène has yet to fill with new seeds.

"Vi would've love it here. All this space to flip and run," Ash says, a sad smile on his lips.

My throat aches. "And so many trees to climb."

"She did love climbing trees. The higher, the better."

"At least until she got stuck and you had to go up after her."

Ash shakes his head. "Nah, she never really got stuck. She just knew that if she begged long enough, we'd go up after her. She didn't like being alone." Ash fixes the blanket himself. "I guess that's what happens when you share your whole life with someone else—from the very beginning, all the way to the end."

He wipes his cheek and turns his head away. He hates it when anyone sees him cry, especially me.

"Ash . . ."

"Don't. I don't want to hear it." He sniffs loudly and clears his throat. "Why didn't you tell us? Why didn't you trust us?" He shifts in his chair to finally look at me, the blanket slumping off his shoulders and into his lap. "Why didn't you *warn* us, Genevieve? She would still be here if you'd warned us."

"I couldn't. I didn't know how—"

"We knew you and your mother had 'stuff.' Things we couldn't understand. You know my mother didn't trust you." He laughs on an exhaled breath. "I guess I should've listened to her."

"You know I had no control over any of it. I was *born* that way. I couldn't change it, any more than you can change that you were born with brown hair. I've lost people too, Ash." I swallow hard, trying to dislodge the lump. "Don't you think if I could go back and undo all of this, if I could *choose* to not have been a part of all this insanity, that I would? If I could've saved Delia and Violet and countless others who've died—"

"But you *could* have saved Violet. All you had to do was *tell us the truth*!" His anger bounces off the walls of the patio space and echoes across the grassy field.

"And say what, Ash? You never would've believed the truth!"

"Then you should've found a way to *make* me believe you, Genevieve."

"I did what I thought was right." I stand and move in front of him, blocking his view of the grounds. "I did what I thought was right because I wanted to save *all* of us."

Ash looks up at me, his jaw set. "Well, you failed. You didn't save all of us, did you?"

His comment knocks the wind out of me. He's right. I didn't save all of us.

The newly built stone mausoleum underneath the tree at the crest of the hill, next to the greenhouse, is proof of that.

Tears slide down my cheeks, but what's the point? Tears are powerless to do anything to fix this, to fix *us*. When I look up, Henry is on the other side of the wide door, his hand flattened against the glass.

There's nothing else I can say that will make this right, so I sit again, defeated, heartbroken that after all that work and energy and terror, I can't save the friendship that has been as important to me as a limb for my entire life.

I dig in my pocket for tissue to wipe my dripping nose. "You're going home?"

"Not a lot more that can be done here," he says. "My parents found a pain specialist in Seattle who specializes in traumatic injuries. Who'da thought having an eye carved out of your skull could cause so much trouble?" He laughs, but it's not because anything is funny.

"There will never be enough years for me to make this up to you, Ash."

"You're right." He looks at me, his face hard, his eye red-rimmed. "It's probably best that when my parents get here, you make yourself scarce. They're not quite ready to kiss and make up."

"Right. I know."

He tosses his blanket over the arm of the rattan chair and moves to stand, still a bit unsteady on his feet.

"Can I—"

He shakes his head and glares at me, shoulders back. "I loved you, you know. You were our sister too." His lip quivers, and then he strides past me, in through the door, his form darkening through the glass as the house swallows him up.

Henry waits for a moment, and then joins me on the patio, scooting Ash's vacated chair closer. He hands me more tissue.

"He's never going to forgive me," I say.

"Give it time." Henry's hand is gentle on my shoulder.

"You didn't see the way he looked at me."

"We did what we had to do. You had no way of stopping what happened to Violet. That was so far out of your control—"

"But was it? I should've told them, Henry. I should've told them about her!" I push his hand away and sit back.

"They never would've believed you. No one would've believed any of this. No one outside this world could have possibly understood or predicted what was going to happen. We did what we could, Genevieve. And we saved everyone else in the process. You do realize that, don't you?"

I nod and bury my face in the tissue. I thought I'd done all my crying in the six weeks since we've been home. Apparently not.

Henry wraps his arms around me, rubbing my back, whispering softly that we're going to be okay. "Baby is asking for you," Henry says.

I nod. Even with the books destroyed and Aveline's terrible black magic gone, Baby's recovery has been dicey. I have permanent scarring on my left arm and chest and a fake front tooth, forever reminders of what my sister did to me.

But Baby's alive, and recovering, and I have never been more grateful for anything in my whole life.

Henry opens the door for us, the *whoosh* of warm inside air filled with the scents that have become home. I follow him down the main hall, stopping in my room briefly to grab my book. Baby likes it when I read aloud—the lingering effects of his illness cause headaches when he tries to read himself.

Graduated from the medical suite, Baby is in his own room again, the IV in his arm the last stage on his road to health. I'm pleased to find him sitting upright in bed. Color has returned to his lips and cheeks, and he's wearing human clothes rather than a flimsy hospital-style gown. His room smells like a florist shop—Hélène has filled it with bouquets sewn from Delia's seeds.

"Hey, *a leannan,*" Baby says.

"Hey yourself." I perch on the edge of his king-sized bed. "You're looking good." I grab his paw of a hand in both of mine. "Can I get you anything?"

"Whiskey, neat."

"Ha ha."

"You asked." He smiles, the sparkle back in his deep brown eyes. He needs a shave, and his hair is longer than I've ever seen it, a few sprouts of gray at his temples. When the magic drained from me in Babylon, it drained from all of us. Baby, and Nutesh and Hélène, will age normally now. It's good we're rid of this curse, but it also makes me too sad to think about.

"You been crying again?"

"Ash . . ."

"Ah." He knows. "Give it time."

"That's what Henry said." I kiss Baby's fist. "He's going home."

"Nutesh told me. Katia and Aleks are in Rouen."

"Ash said I shouldn't talk to them."

"Probably best. For now." Baby nods to a coffee cup–sized tub on the nightstand. "Hélène made fresh aloe and shea butter moisturizer for our scars. Henry, you can help her later—use it on her hands?"

"Yes, absolutely," he says. "I'm going to grab a coffee. Excuse me."

As the door closes after Henry, Baby motions for me to move. "Let's go for a walk."

"Now? Shouldn't you rest?"

"I need some air," he says. He points at his IV—I crank down the flow dial on the tube to stop the fluid so he can pull the needle out of the port on his arm. I then help him into a coat. "Bring a blanket. And your book."

He's definitely grown stronger with Nutesh's heroic, real-world medical interventions over these many weeks, but his clothes are loose on him, which freaks me out a little. "Nothing a few good meals won't fix," he teases.

I grab a golf-sized umbrella and we exit through the patio where I was just sitting with Ash, along the walkway toward the greenhouses, and up to the crest of the hill where the massive oak stands alone, watching over the acres of lush green fields. It's slow-going, but every step forward is just that—a step closer to home.

He stops in front of the tiny stone building. The wrought iron gate is always unlocked, and the roof was constructed with two massive skylights to make sure plenty of natural light warms the interior space. It's not dreary and terrible like the mausoleum where I found the *Life* text—it's beautiful and welcoming and warm.

The small pediment over the door is carved with "*Vérité*" in huge letters; just underneath, a second line: "The key to good is found in truth."

The front, sides, and back of the structure have been wound with wire, like clotheslines wrapping the building, from which hang keys.

More antique keys than I have ever seen, some etched with *La Vérité*, others not. Either way, the sentiment is clear.

It's almost impossible to walk inside—it's filled to the absolute limits with flower-filled vases, potted plants, stuffed animals, religious figurines, drawings, bottles of wine and liquor . . . countless tokens of appreciation and gratitude.

Once word got out to the *La Vérité* network that Xavier had died, there was no end to the tsunami of gifts.

I've visited every day over the last few weeks since it was finished, and even before when the workers were cementing stones into place, so I could talk to the plaques on the wall that represent my fallen family. I brought my own tokens to leave on the shelf under Delia's plaque—my tiny elephant figurine duo that Hélène found in my discarded clothing from when we first arrived at Croix-Mare, after the nightmarish attack in Washington State. Under Xavier's, I've left his silver lighter he always had with him. Figured he might need it.

"He was a good man," Baby says, his hand heavy on my shoulder. "I'm sorry you didn't get to know him under different—better—circumstances."

"Me too."

We stay in the stone house for a while, paying respects to our fallen friends—Alicia, Thierry, Violet, even Gaetano, and other names belonging to people who fought long before me. I read cards and tokens, sometimes aloud to Baby, sometimes to myself when I can't talk past the lump in my throat. When Baby's energy begins to wane, I help him outside to the path, but he stops me.

"Let's sit a while." He takes the blanket draped over my arm and spreads it over the verdant lawn.

"It's raining."

"You have an umbrella, don't you?"

"If you get sick, Nutesh will kill me," I say.

"I'm alive. I want to feel like it." He sits and pats the blanket next to him. "You brought a book?"

I nod and pull it from my waistband. Baby props the huge, open umbrella against the oak tree's trunk, creating a canopy for us, and then lies back, closing his eyes, breathing deeply of the fresh, spring air. "What are we reading today?"

"*Fellowship of the Ring*."

"Now you're just being ironic," he says. "Read to me, then. But skip the scary parts. They give me nightmares."

A smile stretches across his face.

47

"Genevieve . . . hey." Henry waves his hand in front of me. I pull my headphones off, pausing the film on my laptop screen. "The captain is asking us to buckle in."

You don't have to ask me twice.

I've been waiting for this plane to land for what seems like a million years.

As I fold closed my computer and stuff my headphones into my bag, Henry pulls the blanket from my legs and folds it. Over the weeks of recovery at Croix-Mare, I'd often tease him about how good he is with tidying up. To which he replied, "At least one of us is." In my defense, it took a solid month before I could even move my fingers again. Poor Hélène spent so much time helping me bathe, she now knows which moles on my back I should keep an eye on as I get older.

Henry helps me tie my boots. My fine motor skills still aren't great. At night, when the pain is the worst, Henry strokes my hair and tells me stories of my mother's life—his store of memories did not go away—to help me fall asleep. It's during these moments that I find myself wishing Nutesh still had his healing gifts, that he could've fixed me—fixed Baby and Ash and even Sevda—so much faster.

But that's the trade-off, right?

Our gifts for a future. Not having to look over my shoulder anymore. Not worrying if I will be assaulted by a demonic swarm with an acid touch and a cloak of spiders. Not having to worry about reinventing my still-young self when all the people I love die of old age. Not having to worry about going to prison for the murder of my best friend.

Turns out, even with the insider tips from Henry's sketchbook cache of drawn memories, Aveline did clean out her wine fridge. But there was enough ricin residue in the trailer—and a string of unsolved deaths back in Quebec—that provided the necessary evidence to clear my name.

And despite efforts to make Ash understand, I've still lost him over it.

Like Henry and Baby say, give it time. Maybe someday he'll forgive me.

And we're alive. The scars left behind, those are forever. The healing, both hearts and wounds, will take as long as it takes. At least that's what Nutesh says, especially when he sits with Lucian, a quiet shell of his former self who spends most of his days either playing his piano, lost in his own thoughts, or wrapped in a wool blanket on the wooden patio of one of the guesthouses on the Croix-Mare estate. When he's lucid, he promises his son better days ahead, but Lucian has his own healing to do.

In the plane's main cabin, Baby sits in his usual window seat, his phone in hand, earbuds in place—heaven help us, he's discovered audiobooks.

"You hungry?" he asks, popping out his earbuds. "We had sandwiches."

"Nah. I'm good."

"Did you moisturize the grafts this morning?"

"Yes, Dad." I wiggle my stiff fingers in front of me. "Still not quite ready to sign that hand-modeling contract." And I haven't even considered touching a violin. Soon. Not yet.

Henry and I take our seats. There's plenty of space on this trip—now that we don't need to travel with security. Montague is staying behind to help Nutesh with some business around the estate, and there's no way Lucas would leave Sevda's side—he teases he's her seeing-eye dog. And the ring that appeared on her left hand a few weeks ago would indicate that she approves of him in that role indefinitely.

My stomach feels funny with the drop in altitude. But out the window, the sprawling green landscape below doesn't feel scary or menacing.

I can hardly wait for this plane to unseal and let me out.

A car waits for us at the hangar. It's nice to disembark like a normal person—no riot shields, no guns, no fear.

Our driver smiles as she closes our doors and then slides in behind the wheel. "Did you have a pleasant flight?" she asks.

"Yes, thank you," Baby answers.

"Well, you've landed at a perfect time—everything's still green and it's not too hot. Not like it'll be in August."

I don't want to make small talk. I just want her to drive.

I wrap my delicate gloved fingers around my mother's key that still hangs from my neck as we leave the airport and merge onto the busy freeway that will take us to our destination. I haven't been on an American freeway for a while. Feels too fast. Folks are a little slower in France.

Twenty minutes later, we take our off-ramp and head west. "Almost there," the driver says, as if the GPS lady hadn't already announced that fact.

The low rolling hills zooming past are alive with their spring coats, their view impeded only by the staccato placement of fences that mark off individual properties.

Our driver slows, her right turn signal on as she pulls off the highway and eases up the gravel driveway, rolling her window down to press the intercom before the huge white gates. The warm outside air flows into the air-conditioned car, along with the fresh scent of long grasses and wildflowers, and of hay.

Henry drapes his arm over my shoulders, his smile contagious. "Almost there, my Genevieve."

The voice on the other side welcomes and buzzes us through, the gate ambling open to grant us entry to the rolling fields, bordered by wooden ranch fencing, the green split in half by the narrow asphalt ribbon we're driving up. Once we crest the hill, three massive red barns come into view, people in matching uniforms of red shirts and beige zookeeper pants and utility gloves doing the many jobs that come with running a place of this stature.

The driver barely has the car stopped when my door is open and I'm running.

Because I can hear her. And she knows I'm here.

Gertrude always was so good at telling time. If they told her I was on a plane to come see her in her new California home, well, then I'd better get inside before she tears the place apart.

When Baby and Henry catch up, I'm already in with my babies, and Gertrude is trumpeting and snorting, her trunk smothering me; Houdini—he's gotten so big!—sniffs and snorts and throws his hay and buffets into me, fighting for space to give me all the slobbery kisses.

"He's been waiting a long time to do that." Dr. Philips approaches the wide-open enclosure—much like their space back in Eaglefern but instead of the scary jail-like bars, the "fence" is plastic-coated steel cabling stretched between wide-set steel posts. He and Baby exchange a solid handshake, followed by a manly hug. Philips then shakes Henry's hand before climbing through the fencing.

I throw myself into his arms, already sobbing. "Thank you, thank you, *thank you*," I say. He hugs me back, and then a look around shows that Henry and Baby are getting in on the tears, though Baby clears his throat and squeezes his fingers into his eyes, reaching down to pet Houdini who stretches his trunk to grab at Baby's wrist.

"What?" he says, lifting an eyebrow at me.

"They've settled in so well," Philips says, wiping the corner of his eye with a gloved fingertip. "Ted and Cece come every day to see them, so that's helped. They've taken a place just up the road."

"Yeah, we're gonna stay with them," I say, dabbing at my nose with the offered handkerchief. "They came to France, after everything . . . to make sure we were okay."

Dr. Philips nods. "Once we got Triad to loosen the legal noose, we moved Gert and the baby the next day. She's used to traveling, so it was a smooth transition. Othello took a few more days, but he's getting a little cranky in his old age," the veterinarian says, smiling.

"I can relate to that," Baby jokes, tapping the pair of reading glasses hanging over the edge of his shirt.

"The people here—they're fantastic. We couldn't have gotten any luckier," Philips says. "And Nutesh's generosity will keep this place going for a decade or more, or at least until you graduate vet school and can take over, yeah?" The vet winks at me.

Gertrude about knocks me over with her trunk, stretching toward Baby. "Get in here, you," I say to him. "She wants some love."

Baby steps through the fencing and wraps his arms around Gert. Then the waterworks he's been trying so hard to stave off really let loose.

And then it's quiet for a few moments, just our emotional sniffs and the grunts and growls and bass rumbling of two happy elephants as we hug and kiss and scratch and feed Houdini from bins of mango and apple so he doesn't tear our arms off. Even Henry comes into the enclosure, an addition Houdini is all too happy to welcome, especially when Henry kicks the giant soccer ball. Houdini's trumpets of approval echo off the high ceiling as he chases after it.

And then the sound barrier is broken by the bellow of a lion just down the way.

"Yeah, he's been waiting for you too," Dr. Philips says.

I kiss Gert's trunk and promise her I'll be right back. "I gotta go say hi to your brother."

Dr. Philips walks with me and explains that the back wall of Othello's space opens into an expansive outer enclosure complete with splash pool and lots of enrichment. "They really have a great big-cat team here. And his new handlers have taken quite the shine to this old boy," he says.

Sure enough, Othello sits panting at his bars. "How could you not love this sweetie? Look at him," I say, kneeling so Othello and I are eye to eye, my hands pressed flat against the bars.

My old lion then chuffs and sniffs and licks, and then he's up on his hind legs, his massive front paws on the bars as he reaches through for me. "They say an elephant never forgets—I think you're part elephant too, you beautiful boy. Did you miss me? I missed you so much," I say, my arms in the bars, my damaged hands scrubbing his thick mane and ears. "You're such a handsome man, aren't you, Othello? I love you, I love you, yes, I love you too," I coo as he rubs his face against the bars, getting as close to me as he can.

We hug and nuzzle, and he drops to all fours again, pacing back and forth before stopping to lick my hands pressed against his enclosure. He paces—I know what he wants.

It's time to run.

I walk down to the far end of the bars, and then sprint back and forth, him easily keeping up on the opposite side.

We run until I'm sweaty and out of breath and he plops down against the bars, panting and asking for a belly scratch.

"I'll go get his lunch, and you some water, yeah?" Dr. Philips says, walking back into the heart of the barn.

I sit on the floor, leaning against the steel, rubbing Othello's chest and chin until he drifts off, more tears spilling down my face.

"After all we've been through, I couldn't have asked for a more perfect ending to this story," I say to my dozing house cat.

Henry's voice startles me. "It really isn't the end though, is it?"

I look up at him, the blue-green of his eyes brilliant and bright. He kneels and leans over to kiss a tear off my cheek. "It rather feels like a beginning to me." He pulls me into him, both of us on our knees as he kisses me.

And when he does, he's just Henry, and I'm just Genevieve.

When our uncovered skin touches now, the only memories transmitted, the only electricity shared, is that which we create together in the moment.

I tug at his curly cowlick that is growing in nicely, his hair back to its natural blond state.

"I thought shaving it off would make it go away," he says.

"What? No way! It's part of who you are," I tease.

"Like the fire that grows out of your scalp? I keep telling you . . . you are the flame."

I hold my hands out in front of me. "Less so now, it seems."

"Never." He takes my pressure-gloved hand and gently flattens it over his heart. "You will never diminish, magic or no."

"Tell me you love me," I say.

"I love you, Genevieve Jehanne Flannery." He kisses the end of my nose.

"I knew it."

Henry's laugh pulls Othello's head up, but he flops back down, still asleep. "Come on, then. We should go outside with Gert and Houdini. They're asking for you." Henry puts a hand under my elbow.

"Absolutely." I wrap my arms around his neck and touch my lips to his. "I've got all the time in the world."

*** *LA FIN* ***

Acknowledgments

Thank you to friends, readers, and my writing, editorial, and agency team for all the support with both *Sleight* and *Scheme*. It's been a long, arduous labor of love.

Thanks to Nicole Frail and the team at Sky Pony for bringing the book to American readers—and to editor (and friend) Alison Weiss for acquiring these stories in the first place.

Thank you to artist Sarah J. Coleman (@inkymole) for your insanely detailed artistry for the American covers of *Sleight* and *Scheme*. You are the mightiest of talents—I'm so glad this project made us friends! Thanks as well to Laura Klynstra at HarperCollins Canada for the elegant, evocative covers for *Sleight* and *The Undoing*. I wish I could forward you both all the positive comments I hear about these covers.

Special thanks to Suzanne Sutherland and Jennifer Lambert at HarperCollins Canada for believing in these books for soooo long—words feel pitifully shallow when trying to convey the depths of my gratitude. Thank you times infinity.

To Victoria Doherty-Munro at Writers House, thank you for keeping the faith and helping with my books over all these years.

A shout-out to the team at Prószynski i S-ka and the awesome readers in Poland who post the coolest photos on Instagram of *Prawda i Iluzja* (*Sleight*). That cover—swoon! How I wish I spoke ALL the languages ...

Thank you to Catherine McKenzie who knows WAY more about writing books than I do. Fall 2018 at the Surrey International Writers Conference, we were chatting over drinks—correction: I was whining, and she was listening—about how hard this rewrite was going to be. After a few patient moments, Catherine looked right at me and said, "Use the magic." Her three simple words were transformative. Like its own magical spell, straight out of the *AVRAKEDAVRA*. It worked. Thank you.

Thank you to my darling Jane Omelaniec, for offering your unconditional friendship and quiet refuge at the cabin so I could work through the many drafts of both books.

Thanks to the Best Book Club Ever, women who have become sisters to me: Alisa Clarke (thank you for the Kurdish help!), Eryn Dixon, Danyelle Drexler, Jacqueline Ewonus, Deanna Mackenzie, Kay Massey, Gail Mawhinney, Gill McCulloch, Shanie Rhodes, Michelle Rothery, Tammy Savinkoff, Yvonne Solway, and Liane Triff.

To author and artist Sarah Glidden for her book, *Rolling Blackouts: Dispatches from Turkey, Syria, and Iraq*, which was a huge piece of my research puzzle. It's tough to get accurate, on-the-ground information from this area—I cannot recommend Sarah's book enough for anyone interested in the complex history of modern-day Mesopotamia.

As well, thanks to the writers, researchers, and globe-trotters at Lonely Planet for the terrific work you do on your travel guides. I'd love to say I went to all these exotic locales to research this book—alas, the guidebooks provided the invisible stamps in my passport.

Thank you to the folks who put dash cams in their cars and GoPros on their bodies and drive/walk around faraway places I'll never get to visit so that my details were spot on. Pompeii really looks beautiful in 4K video.

Thank you to Genevieve, Delia, Baby, Henry, Lucian, Alicia, Aveline, Nutesh, Xavier, Violet, Ash, Ted and Cece Cinzio, Montague the Mauled, Gertrude and Houdini, the world's most lovable man-eating house cat Othello, and the rest of my cast for showing up when I needed you to do the heavy lifting.

And most especially, thank you to my darling family—Gary, Yaunna, Brennan, Kendon, Nuit, and Rosie Cotton. Thank the gods your patience knows no bounds.